Praise for **How I**

'As twisted as a mountain road, Bl... ...ng and unputdownable debut will keep you glued to your seat'

Alex Marwood

'Utterly gripping – brilliant debut!'

Clare Mackintosh, author of *I Let You Go*

'A thrill' *Shropshire Star*

'It's unsettling, unforgettable and you won't want to put it down' *Essentials*

By Jenny Blackhurst and available from Headline

How I Lost You
Before I Let You In
The Foster Child

THE
FOSTER
CHILD

JENNY BLACKHURST

HEADLINE

Copyright © 2017 Jenny Blackhurst

The right of Jenny Blackhurst to be identified as the Author of
the Work has been asserted by her in accordance with the
Copyright, Designs and Patents Act 1988.

First published in paperback in 2017 by
HEADLINE PUBLISHING GROUP

1

Apart from any use permitted under UK copyright law, this publication may
only be reproduced, stored, or transmitted, in any form, or by any means,
with prior permission in writing of the publishers or, in the case of reprographic
production, in accordance with the terms of licences issued by the Copyright
Licensing Agency.

All characters in this publication are fictitious and any resemblance
to real persons, living or dead, is purely coincidental.

Cataloguing in Publication Data is available from the British Library

ISBN 978 1 4722 3529 9

Typeset in Meridien by Palimpsest Book Production Ltd,
Falkirk, Stirlingshire

Printed and bound in Great Britain by
Clays Ltd, St Ives plc

MIX
Paper from
responsible sources
FSC® C104740

Headline's policy is to use papers that are natural, renewable and recyclable
products and made from wood grown in sustainable forests. The logging and
manufacturing processes are expected to conform to the environmental
regulations of the country of origin.

HEADLINE PUBLISHING GROUP
An Hachette UK Company
Carmelite House
50 Victoria Embankment
London EC4Y 0DZ

www.headline.co.uk
www.hachette.co.uk

To Mum and Dad. I couldn't ask for more.

Prologue

'Imogen? Is that you?' The voice on the other end of the phone is breathless, frantic and instantly recognisable.

'Sarah, calm down,' I instruct. 'What is it?'

'It's Ellie.' I hear Sarah Jefferson's voice tremble. 'She left school at lunchtime. I don't know where she is.'

I sigh. Repeat after me, I tell myself. Not your circus, not your monkeys.

'I'm not Ellie's case worker any more, Sarah. I was removed. Her truancy isn't really my remit any longer.'

'You don't understand.' Sarah's voice is urgent now. 'It's not Ellie I'm worried about. It's Lily.'

My hand automatically flies to my stomach before I remember that the baby is no longer there.

'What about Lily, Sarah?'

Sarah lets out a noise somewhere between a sob and a wail. 'She's missing. Ellie has taken the baby.'

1

Ellie

Ellie lies on the bed that isn't hers, in the room that belongs to no one, listening to someone else's family watching TV downstairs. Her thumb grinds against the sharp flint of the cigarette lighter in her hand. Orange flames spring up, then disappear as she lets go.

Flick, flame.

Flick, flame.

Flick, flame.

She runs her fingertips through the top of the flame, surprised to find that it doesn't hurt. She tries again, letting her fingers linger a little longer. It feels hot this time, but it still doesn't hurt. She pushes her finger into the blue of the flame and holds it there until pain sears through it, but it doesn't feel bad. It feels glorious. Is this how her family felt? This pain, this release? She does it again, this time holding the flame under the heel of her hand, keeping it steady, waiting for the pain. When it comes, it's more intense, and she lets go of the flint in shock. Her heart races, but she does it again . . . flick, flame.

Just as the smell of burning flesh licks at her nostrils, the bedroom door opens. Her foster sister, Mary, stands in the doorway. Her eyes widen and her mouth drops open like a cartoon cat when she sees what Ellie is doing.

'Ellie! What the hell are you playing at?' Mary grabs her hand roughly and pulls it away from the flame. 'Are you crazy? You'll hurt yourself.'

All of a sudden her hand burns white-hot with pain and she looks down to see pus-filled blisters forming on her skin.

'I . . . I don't know what I was doing. I was just playing. It didn't even hurt.' She looks down at her palm with mild interest. 'It does now.'

Mary places her own hand gently on Ellie's arm.

'Come on, I'll get you sorted out. Put some cream on it, wrap it in a bandage, and we'll tell Mum you cut yourself helping me with lunch.'

Ellie stares at the blistered flesh, pictures it spreading up her arm, covering her shoulders and neck.

Mary shakes her head as though she can't believe what she's seeing. 'I'll keep an eye on it for you and change your bandages every day, and if it looks like it's getting worse, we might have to make up a new story.' She looks at Ellie kindly. 'Why would you want to do this to yourself, Ellie? Do you think your mum would be happy if she saw you hurting yourself?'

'But my mum can't see anything, can she? My mum is dead.'

Ellie's insides feel as though they're full of pulsating green slime, like when an orange rots from the inside out, the peel still intact and the flesh toxic. She isn't like Mary, she isn't like anyone here. Some of them can tell – she sees it in people's eyes when they spot her out in the street; they cross the road, hold their children's hands a bit tighter without really knowing why. Ellie knows why, though. She knows what they can see inside her.

'But she's watching you, you know that, don't you?' Mary

pushes. 'In heaven your mum is watching everything you do. And she wants you to be happy, and she wants you to look after yourself, and she wants you to grow old and have a family of your own. That's what she'd have wanted if she was here, and that's what she would still want now. You have to try and fit in, Ellie. I know it's difficult, I know we're not your family, but you really need to try.'

'And what if I don't want to try? What if I don't care about being part of your family?'

'I know how hard this must be for you. I've seen a lot of children come and go in this house, a lot of angry children who have never known love. But you're different. You know what it's like to be loved and you know what it's like to live in a home full of compassion and warmth. It might not feel like it now, but one day you will have that again. What you have to remember is that none of this is your fault. You mustn't blame yourself, Ellie, whatever anyone else tells you.'

Ellie nods, but she knows inside that Mary is wrong. She may be older, and she may think she knows everything, but she doesn't – she doesn't know Ellie at all. No one does.

2

Imogen

A canopy of trees lines the road into the town of Gaunt, dappling the tarmac with sunlight where it breaks through the leaves, making me squint. It feels as though we're driving through a tunnel of beauty to the last destination we will ever reach. The end of the road.

Thomas Wolfe said you can't go home again, and maybe I should have remembered that before pressing send on my CV and setting in motion the chain of events that is leading me back to my home town after fifteen years. Maybe I should have known better.

Gaunt stretches out ahead of us as bleak and uninviting as its name suggests, hollowed out and emaciated. The place brings to mind a hall of mirrors, every angle skewed and off centre so that it doesn't matter which perspective you look at it from, something always feels wrong. Grey-fronted houses sit abandoned and desolate. Population: dwindling.

To outsiders, Gaunt could have been great once upon a time; the odd glimpse of a stately home or a striking sculpture hints that someone at some time had plans for this strange place – plans that were abandoned a long time ago. Even as a child I felt fascination and revulsion for my town in equal measure. The same magnetic pull that lured the builders and property developers and the same uneasy, inexplicable air of dread and foreboding that drove them away telling tales of unusable land and untenable planning rules . . . because who wants to admit that they abandoned a development opportunity because of a feeling, sometimes losing tens of thousands in the process?

It's a feeling I've almost forgotten. I've spent so long wrapped safely in the mundane haze of the city, actively forgetting my life here, that I can hardly bring to mind any parts of my former existence, even when I screw my eyes shut and the effort of remembering gives me a headache.

Despite the dazzling sunlight, a bitter chill hangs in the air. A fresh day for a fresh start, Dan said this morning. A good omen, a sign we were doing the right thing.

'I don't believe in signs and omens.' I smiled. My face must have betrayed me though, because my husband put a hand gently on my elbow and said, 'It's going to be great. Like a holiday in the country. We'll both have time and space to breathe.' He didn't mention what he was really thinking about – a family – and for that I was grateful.

'Holiday? I didn't think writers got a holiday. And I certainly don't. I start a new job in four days.'

'You know what I mean. A holiday from all of this.' He gestured to the window, at the street heaving with people moving smartly past one another without looking up from their smartphones, a man in a multi-coloured patchwork cape handing out empty envelopes that I knew from experience contained 'good vibes', and drivers slamming the heels of their hands onto their horns if the speed of the car in front dropped below thirty-five miles an hour. 'From people. And pressure. The daily grind. Just what we need after the crap you've been through.' The crap I've been through. Like what happened in London can just be dismissed as bad luck.

The first houses come into view, the barn conversions and new-builds that sprung up when the building trade found its feet again and were nothing more than fields when I last saw this part of the country. It looks like someone wanted to give Gaunt a second chance. Dan nudges me and points.

'See those? When we sell your mum's house, we could buy something like that. Or build one.'

I grin. 'What do you know about building houses? Apart from in your imaginary worlds. It's not quite as easy as just writing them into existence.'

'Spoken like someone who has never tried to describe a castle in the desert from the point of view of an Orc.' Dan pretends to look stung, then grins back at me. 'Okay, maybe we stick to buying for now. Something open-plan. And big.'

'With a swimming pool and our initials embedded in a marble floor in the entrance hall,' I laugh. 'I'm not sure how much you think old Nanny Tandy's house is worth. Not enough for my mother to ever bother selling it, anyway.' The word 'mother' pulls at my insides. *She's gone, Imogen.*

There is no swirling grey mist enveloping the approach to the town, no wizened old woman holding out a gnarled arthritic finger and warning us to go no further, no jet-black raven perched on the sign that pronounces *Welcome to Gaunt* muttering, 'Nevermore,' and yet I feel icy fingers of dread grasp my lungs, leaving me momentarily struggling for breath. The sign, weathered and rotting – letters so faded that welcome is the furthest feeling from your mind – seems to blacken in front of my eyes, like a spawn of mould is spreading over it as I watch. The turning to my mother's house is just metres to the left. My chest tightens and the road ahead swims in and out of focus. I reach out a hand and grasp at Dan's arm.

'Don't go down there.'

My voice comes out in a barely recognisable rasp. Dan

glances sideways at me, concern shadowing his face, and he slows the car to a crawl.

'Is everything okay, Im? Shall I pull over?'

I glance at the sign, still unwelcoming but clear now of black mould, and feel the colour return to my cheeks as they burn in embarrassment. What was I thinking?

Gaunt sits beyond, watching, waiting.

'No, I'm fine,' I lie. 'It's just that I thought maybe we could go to the high street for a takeaway before we get there. What if the electricity isn't on yet?'

Dan gives a small nod, but the crease in his brow doesn't disappear. He's always worrying about me these days.

'Good idea,' he agrees, looking over his shoulder and indicating right. 'I should have suggested it. Although we should have done a shop, I doubt the cuisine in your town is going to be varied and plentiful.'

'It's not my . . .' I start, then shrug. At least the pounding in my chest has begun to subside. 'There's a fish and chip shop . . . at least there used to be.'

Dan misses the turn to the house and carries on straight ahead to the main street less than a mile away from the house. I remember walking the long, thin lanes with Pammy, convincing the older boys to buy us alcohol if we shared it with them, trying to get a Saturday job at the shop and not having a hope in hell against girls like Michelle Hoffman or Theresa Johnson. I wonder what those girls are doing now; hope meanly that they still have their corner-shop jobs.

'I love that we'll have the best of both worlds,' Dan says, breaking the reflective silence that has filled the car. 'Beautiful quiet countryside and a decent enough high street just up the road. I can still nip out in the morning for fresh coffee and bread . . .'

'Still?' I laugh at the image of my husband in a frilly white pinny picking up fresh bread from the bakery. 'When did

9

you ever do that? I've got to admit, I thought having a house husband would be a lot more like having a housekeeper than an overgrown teenager watching Netflix and eating all the good treats.'

'There's no need for that. I'm not a house husband, I'm an artist.'

'Well, Mr Best-seller, while I'm knocking out all these children you're after, fresh bread and coffee in the morning is the least you can do.'

Dan beams and I instantly regret being so flippant. I have to remember that every remark like that just reignites the fire in Dan to start a family as soon as possible. He doesn't know how the word 'baby' makes my stomach cramp. I turn my head to stare out of the window, hoping that will signal the end of the conversation.

For a Saturday afternoon the high street resembles the early hours of the morning in London. I look up through the windscreen, my attention drawn to a couple of young girls facing one another on the pavement. One has long dark hair that hangs over her face, obscuring it from view. She looks as though she is frozen to the spot while the other, a pretty blonde girl dressed far older than she looks like she should be, leans in close to her. Maybe they are playing some kind of game, although something about the scene strikes me as odd. I'm about to point it out to Dan as we drive past when the blonde girl takes a couple of steps backwards towards the road.

'Watch out,' I warn. 'She looks un—'

My words turn to a scream and I screw my eyes closed as the girl tumbles into the road in front of us. I hear the screeching of the brakes and a dull thud.

3

Ellie

The day has dragged on for what feels like longer than the entire summer holidays had lasted. Even though school started again six weeks ago, they are only now being dragged to the shop to get Mary some new blouses, her foster sister had seemed to grow boobs overnight, and no doubt Ellie will get her old baggy, greying hand-me-downs.

Sarah has been dithering over prices for what seems like hours. She has one of her famous lists and her budget and she's unwilling to waver from either one, even though the poor young sales assistant has tried telling her countless times that they are the only stockists in town, and she won't find anything cheaper if they travel to any of the bigger towns.

Ellie is kicking her toes against one of the stands, Mary shooting her the occasional sympathetic glance, when *she* walks in. Naomi Harper. As if this day could get any worse. Naomi's mother greets Sarah like an old friend, even though Ellie has never so much as seen them share a hello before. They indulge in a chorus of 'Fancy seeing you here's and 'How have you been's. Naomi's mum gives her daughter a fond look and proclaims that Naomi has positively shot up in the last few weeks. What she doesn't know, Ellie thinks, is that it doesn't matter how long the skirts she buys are, her precious offspring will be rolling the waistband over as soon as she leaves the house. Mary, who is four years older than them and only barely knows who Naomi Harper even is, shoots a questioning glance at Ellie, but she just shrugs indifferently.

'God, I didn't think I'd have to see your ugly face at the weekend as well as all week,' Naomi hisses with the malice of a girl much older than twelve. Ellie pictures an arrow shooting from over her shoulder and puncturing Naomi's left eye, sees the pus and blood oozing from the ruined socket and says nothing.

'Don't you ever speak?' Naomi scowls at Ellie's lack of reaction. She has the distinct air of a young child poking at a wasps' nest with a stick, getting increasingly frustrated when nothing flies out. 'Come on, Smelly Ellie, say something.'

Ellie feels her fists clenching, her knuckles turning white. She mustn't let herself get angry, but it's so hard when heat is rising in her cheeks and her heart is thumping faster in her chest. She looks to Mary but as much as she focuses, she can't make her foster sister turn around and punch Naomi in the face. Instead she wills Sarah to announce that this place is far too cheap for their tastes, longs to see the smirk wiped from the faces of the awful girl and her vile mother. But neither of these things happens.

What happens is that Naomi Harper, quick as a flash and without warning, flings out a hand and knocks a row of plimsolls off the shelf next to Ellie, shooting back out of the way before anyone notices.

'Ellie!' Sarah exclaims, dashing over to sort out the mess, her face a deep shade of scarlet. 'What did you do that for?'

There is no point in her objecting, Sarah isn't even listening anyway, and Naomi and her mother are exchanging glances as though Naomi is saying 'Didn't I tell you so?' Only Mary is looking suspiciously between Ellie and her schoolmate.

'May I wait outside?' Ellie asks. She knows what happens when she loses her temper. As much as she hates Naomi at this second, she knows that the only way to keep control of the situation is to remove herself from it.

'I'll come with you,' Mary offers, but Sarah shakes her head. 'You need to try on the shirt, Mary. Ellie is old enough to wait outside by herself for five minutes.'

She *is* old enough, and were everything to finish there, it would all have been fine. If only Naomi had stayed inside.

But just minutes later she is standing next to Ellie, uttering her poisonous bile again.

'Everyone at school wants to know why you're so weird, do you know that?'

'Go away, Naomi,' Ellie warns.

'But *I* know,' Naomi says, ignoring her. She steps back, presumably because she knows that what she's about to say is not so much poking the wasps' nest as cracking it open, peeling it apart with both hands and peering inside. 'Do you want to know what I know?'

'No,' Ellie replies. Her heart sits uncomfortably in her chest, and her upper arms begin to tingle. She knows something is about to happen and she is powerless to stop it. All she can do is watch, a casual bystander in the scene that unfolds. 'Shut up.'

'Did you just say shut up to me?' Naomi looks incredulous. She has no idea. Not yet.

'Just stop it. Go back inside,' Ellie warns, and all the time she can feel the anger gathering inside her, a little ball of wool in reverse, getting bigger and bigger, harder and harder.

'Do you think you scare me? Do I look scared?'

Ellie stares at her, her dark eyes hardening with rage. *You should be, Naomi Harper. You should be.*

13

'Go away. You need to get away. Go away,' Ellie mutters. 'Before you get hurt.'

'What are you doing?' Naomi asks, and although her voice is still arrogant, still with the air of someone who expects to be answered, now it is tinged with something else; laced with uncertainty, even fear perhaps. 'God, you are so weird.' She takes a step forward, reaches out to shove Ellie on the shoulder.

'Go. Away,' Ellie commands, louder this time and Naomi's hand falls short of touching her. Ellie's fists clench by her sides and she squeezes her eyes closed. *Hold your temper. Hold your temper.*

'What are you doing?' Naomi asks, taking a step backwards. 'What are you muttering? Stop it. Stop that!' She takes another step back, stumbling now as her foot lands awkwardly.

Ellie's words come louder now, her eyes still tightly closed, her lips repeating the phrase over and over . . . 'Get away, get away, get away . . .'

Naomi barely feels her heel connect with the edge of the kerb, but her heart registers the sickening moment that her balance betrays her, her arms helicopting as she sails through the air towards the oncoming traffic. And although a horn is blaring behind her, brakes are screeching and people are screaming, all Naomi Harper can hear is those repeated words:

'Get away, get away, get away . . .'

4

Imogen

The car throws me forward violently and I pull my hands from my eyes, dreading the sight of the schoolgirl's crumpled body on the road in front of me. Instead I see her sitting up looking dazed, and the car Dan has hit in the attempt to avoid her embedded in our front bumper. I practically hurl myself through the door to the girl's side and as I kneel down next to her, two women come flying out of a nearby shop, trailed closely by a teenage girl. The first woman's shriek cuts through the air like a hot knife through butter.

'Naomi!' She throws herself down on the road, clutching the dazed girl to her chest. 'Get an ambulance! What happened, baby?'

Naomi, who was frozen in shock, now looks back and forth between the car and the young girl on the pavement, fear and confusion shining in her eyes.

'She fell in front of our . . .' I start to explain, desperate to absolve us of any blame, but the woman isn't even looking at me.

'Did she do this?' She pokes a finger at the young girl left standing on the pavement, and Naomi nods. The woman gets to her feet and rounds on the girl, fury etched on her face. 'What did you do to her?'

The other woman and the teenager both move in front of the younger girl protectively, and the woman – her mother? – speaks in urgent tones.

'Ellie, what happened? What did you do to Naomi?'

Ellie remains silent, still staring at Naomi. Is that look anger? Or fear?

'You could have killed her!' Naomi's mother shrieks. 'She tried to kill her!'

'Now wait a second,' I interrupt, putting out a hand to try and calm the situation before it gets out of control. Who is this woman to start screaming at a shocked young girl? 'I know you're concerned about your daughter, but there's no need to start shouting accusations.'

'Sorry, who are you?' Naomi's mother glares at me, and I know instantly that I cannot stand this woman.

'I'm apparently the only person who saw what actually happened. This girl – Ellie, is it?' I turn to look at Ellie, who still hasn't spoken a word. Her mother nods. 'Ellie wasn't anywhere near Naomi when she fell. I think you need to just calm down.'

'Calm down? Do you have children?' Naomi's mother doesn't wait for me to reply. 'Because if you did, you'd know how it would feel if one of them was pushed into oncoming traffic.'

'She wasn't—'

'What's going on?' Dan appears at my side and puts a protective hand on my shoulder. 'Is she okay? Are *you* okay?' His face is white with shock as he looks at Naomi. She's on her feet now at the side of the road.

I fold my arms protectively across my chest. Keep your cool, Imogen. Don't lose it. He worries enough as it is.

'We didn't hit her, Dan, she's fine.' I keep my voice low and quiet, trying to project calmness. 'And so am I. Are *you* okay? Are you hurt? I think someone is calling an ambulance. Should we get the police? We don't want to be accused of leaving the scene.' I shut up abruptly when I realise I'm babbling, my own shock setting in. For a minute I'd really thought we had hit her. I thought we had killed her.

Dan pulls me in for a hug and I relish the firm comfort of his chest. 'I've already called them,' he says. 'And checked on the person in the other car. Everybody looks fine – except the cars. Bloody insurance is going to go through the roof.'

'Everybody is not fine,' Naomi's mother snaps, obviously determined not to let her anger go. 'My daughter . . .'

Her words die in the air as a paramedic unit and a police car pull up alongside us. 'Oh, thank goodness, finally.'

'We had a report that a young girl had been knocked over,' the paramedic says, his eyes flicking between the girls. 'We advised that no one should be moved.'

'The car didn't actually hit her,' I offer at the same time as Dan says, 'She was already on her feet.'

The police officer looks at Dan. 'You were driving?' Dan nods. The officer pulls out a pen and pad. 'Fine, can you tell me what happened?'

'What happened?' Naomi's mother rounds on the officer. 'I'll tell you what happened. *She*,' she jabs a finger at the young girl, whose face is still a blank mask, 'she tried to kill my daughter! She pushed her—'

'Just a minute,' I interject, feeling my face flood with angry red colour. 'Ellie was nowhere near her when she fell. We saw them; they were just standing there, at least a foot apart, and Naomi stepped back and stumbled into the road.'

'She's right.' The teenager standing by the shaking young girl speaks up. 'I saw it from inside, Mum. Ellie didn't touch her.' She steps closer to Ellie and puts an arm around her, and Ellie nuzzles into her shoulder.

'Was that what you saw?' The police officer looks at Dan.

'I'm pretty sure.' He looks at me, as though for confirmation. 'Yes, I mean it was pretty quick, but I definitely didn't see anyone push anyone else.'

Naomi's mother looks incensed at his words. 'Are you saying my daughter just fell into the road? She's twelve years old; she has no problem staying upright. Tell them, Naomi, tell them what you told me.'

'I . . .' Naomi looks as though she is trapped in headlights. 'I . . . she . . . I fell,' she finishes weakly. At her words, her mother resembles someone who has been slapped sharply in the face. I'm ashamed of the surge of triumph I feel as flourishes of colour appear in her cheeks.

'You said . . .'

'I was wrong. It was an accident, okay?' Was that a flicker of fear on her face? If it was, no one but me seems to notice.

'Well.' Her mother lets out a puff of air. 'I can see nothing is going to be done here. Come on, Naomi.' She takes her daughter's arm, but the paramedic puts out a hand to stop her.

'Sorry, but now we're here, we need to check your daughter over.'

'But you heard her, she just fell! The car didn't even touch her!'

'Better to be safe.' His face creases in apology. 'I wouldn't be doing my job if I didn't.'

'And I need to take statements from everyone here,' the police officer informs us. 'Shouldn't take long – assuming, of course, that you don't want to pursue an attempted-murder charge?'

I momentarily enjoy the way Naomi's mother's face colours again. Serves her right. 'No, it doesn't sound as though that will be necessary.'

Looking at the two girls, it's hard to decide what really

went on between them. Ellie hasn't tried to defend herself during the entire exchange – probably petrified by Naomi's overbearing mother. I look at her properly for the first time. Her face is drained of colour and her eyes are blank, but that's hardly surprising given the fact that she has just been verbally attacked by a grown woman. I try to catch her eye, to offer a look of comfort, but she won't even look in my direction.

'Can we wait in the car?' I direct my question to the police officer, desperate to get away from this claustrophobic scene. He nods.

'If the car is okay to drive, you can pull over here.' He motions to the kerb. 'If not, we can have a paramedic take a look at you next.'

'No, I'm fine,' says Dan. 'We'll pull over and wait.'

We go back to the car, inspecting the bonnet. The driver of the other vehicle is out now talking to the police and I wonder what he's saying, if he saw the girls on the pavement too. The damage to our car doesn't look as bad as the collision sounded and thankfully it starts easily. Dan's hands tremble slightly on the wheel. 'Christ, that was quite something,' he says, placing a hand on my thigh. It's warm and comforting. Even after ten years together, I still feed off his touch like a succubus, leeching calm from his body into mine. He's always had that effect on me. When we first got together I would lie with my head on his chest and breathe in his breath, warm and comforting. 'What an arrival. Are you okay?'

I nod absently. 'Quite something, yes,' I murmur back. I look at the young girls still standing with the police officer and the paramedic, a mother so quick to accuse a young girl of attempted murder and one who made no move to defend her child from the accusation.

What kind of place have I brought us back to?

5

Imogen

The only chip shop on the high street stands out like a nun in a nightclub. Chrome-fronted, with LED letters proclaiming *Oh My Cod*, and a silver cut-out of what I'm sure is supposed to be a fish winking, it is a far cry from the last time I saw the place. Then, the white paint was weathered to a dirty grey, peeling and flaking away from the wooden sign, on which faded blue letters almost begrudgingly announced *Chip Shop*. I wonder who was responsible for the facelift and the trendy rebranding – surely not Roy, the podgy, slack-faced manager from my youth. I smile as I imagine the look of disgust on his surly features as the winking fish was hauled into pride of place in his determinedly unfashionable establishment.

But to my amazement, Roy is standing behind the counter, not looking a day older than he did fifteen years ago, as though he was dragged into the word as a fully formed fifty-year-old and has stoically refused to age a day since.

'Nasty business back there.' I start at the voice from one of the four shiny silver seats behind me. Turning, I see a woman so grey she almost melts completely into the trendy Farrow and Ball wall. Her hair, face and clothes appear to be completely devoid of colour. I attempt a smile to cover my surprise.

'Could have been a lot worse,' Dan says in his best jovial voice before I can reply. He gives my hand a quick squeeze. I wonder if he can feel that I am still shaking slightly. 'No more than a grazed knee, as it turned out. And a dent in my bonnet.'

'Yes, that was some emergency stop you did there, son,' Roy pipes up. His voice has a kindness that I don't remember ever hearing as a young girl. Then again, I don't exactly remember an abundance of kindness from anyone round here, except Pammy and her family. 'Could have been a much nastier crash.'

'All's well that ends well,' I mutter, trying to put an end to the conversation. The grey woman, however, ignores the hint.

'That Harper girl was lucky it was you. Plenty round here that wouldn't have been quite as quick to react. But then,' and there is a steely glint in her eyes as she continues, 'you hardly expect to see a girl that age push another young 'un into the road, do you?'

Dan gives me a sideways look and I know he is silently pleading with me not to be drawn in. Don't bite, Immy. Not your circus . . .

'She didn't push her.' I hear my husband's small exhale of breath. He knew I wouldn't be able to resist. 'We saw it, didn't we, Dan?'

Dan nods. 'Yeah, she didn't push her.'

'Ah, but that's where you're wrong.' The woman gives a sly smile. 'That girl, she doesn't have to touch you to get the job done. I was sitting right here. And I saw what she did.'

My brows furrow. 'I don't understand. Are you saying she pushed her without touching her? That's crazy.' I look back

21

at Roy, expecting him to laugh or roll his eyes at the old woman, maybe twirl a finger around his temple to show that she's batshit. Instead, he stands frozen, avoiding my eye and flipping a fish over and over on the hotplate. I speak directly to him so that there is no way he can ignore me. 'Who is that girl? Ellie, is that her name? Who is she?'

'That's Ellie Atkinson.' The woman gives a chuckle. 'She's a foster child.'

'Oh, and I suppose that makes her—' I stop short as I feel Dan give a sharp tug on my arm. The door clangs open, and in the doorway stand Ellie and the woman I now know must be her foster mother. The teenage girl who came to her defence in the street trails in behind them.

The old woman breaks the silence with a chuckle, and Dan clears his throat.

'Two mini fish and a large chips, please,' he says to Roy, who nods as though the last few minutes haven't taken place.

'Five minutes for the fish,' he mutters, and we take a seat on the opposite side of the shop, as far away as we can get from the creepy old lady. Ellie's foster mother orders their food, then walks over to us.

'I just wanted to say thank you for standing up to that awful woman.' She looks weary, defeated almost. Her mousy brown hair is scraped back into a messy ponytail, tufts of it sticking out at odd angles from her head, as though she is the one who was nearly hit by our car. 'And obviously for not hitting her daughter,' she adds as an afterthought.

'Don't worry about it.' I smile with what I hope is caring sympathy rather than demented lunacy. Do they know what people are saying about Ellie? *That girl, she doesn't have to touch you to get the job done.* 'I hope you're okay?'

I direct my question at Ellie, who is standing with her head bowed, her eyes fixed on the floor. She doesn't move.

Her foster sister gives her a nudge, and when she still doesn't move, the older girl mutters, 'She's fine, thank you.'

Dan snorts and I shoot him a glare. The grey woman in the corner shuffles out of her seat, watching us all the while.

'Mrs Evans.' Ellie looks up, addressing the woman's retreating back in a low, clear voice. The first time I have heard her speak, and it doesn't sound natural.

The woman hesitates, almost as though she doesn't want to look at the young girl. Eventually she turns, faces her head-on. 'Yes?'

'You really shouldn't tell lies. In the olden days, they would have cut your tongue out.'

6

They walk down the street, a distance of only a few feet between them, but it may as well be miles. She glances up at the woman's hand, just dangling by her side, and longs to reach up and slip her own hand inside it. Just to see what it feels like. She's seen plenty of other children doing it, holding hands with their mums as though it is the most natural thing in the world to reach out and connect with the person they love. And Imogen does love her mother, even if her mother can't bring herself to love Imogen back.

Mother – she hates Mummy; makes you sound like a whiny little baby – looks down, and it's like she knows exactly what Imogen is thinking, because she snatches her hand away and shoves it deep into her coat pocket. And just like that, her chance is gone.

'Get a move on,' snaps Carla Tandy, turning her head away from her only child. 'We don't have all day.'

7

Imogen

I stand looking up at the house I grew up in, and in one moment it's like the last twenty years of my life have melted away as though they never existed at all. Welsh stone surrounds the heavy wooden door; ivy snakes its way around it like an alien trying to possess a host. The sound of this very door slamming behind a fifteen-year-old me is still like a whip cracking, a gunshot that echoes in my ears, so much so that the slamming of the car boot sends a shock through me, making me jump with fright. Dan is at my side in seconds. He probably thinks I'm still upset about what happened in the town, and I am: the thought of that woman screaming at poor Ellie, the frozen look on the girl's face as though she had no idea what had just happened. But that isn't what has me unable to reach out and slide the key into the front door of a house I left behind in my teens.

'Take your time,' he murmurs. 'I know this must be hard for you.'

He's obviously picked up more than I give him credit for. I've never given my husband enough credit.

'I'm fine.' I shake my head to dislodge the memories. 'Come on, let's go in.'

*   *   *

We finally manage to get the stiff front door open and practically fall through it with the effort. I prepare myself for the onslaught of memories to hit me like a freight train, but the hallway is so different from the one I remember that for a second I wonder if we've come to the wrong place. Nana Tandy's musty-smelling red and gold swirl carpet has been ripped up and replaced by polished wooden floors, a beige and navy striped carpet runner leads up the stairs, and the walls are a fresh light yellow instead of the grubby taupe they once were. It feels like a new house masquerading as the one I remember so well from the outside. But no, it may have had a facelift, but the bones of this house are still the same. The new paint hasn't managed to hide the small cracks of subsidence I once ran my fingers up and down, sitting on the stairs waiting for my mother to come home. Sometimes I would sit there waiting so long that the cracks became shadows, threatening to yank me in. Sometimes I wanted them to.

'This is nice,' Dan remarks as he hauls both of our bags over the threshold. 'I thought you said it was a bit of a dump?'

'She must have decorated,' I reply. *She* being my mother. I'm both relieved that it looks nothing like I remember and irritated that she spent the effort making herself a decent home only after I'd walked away. All those years we lived with peeling paint and flourishes of black mould as she wandered around the house like some kind of ghost, pretending she couldn't see how our house and our lives were decaying.

'Well that saves us a job.' He grins and goes to push open the door to the living room. This is moving too fast for me. I don't want to look like a totally irrational female, but I'd hoped I could take things a bit slower. Maybe if I'd confided even the smallest part of my past life here to him, my reticence would be more understandable. As it is, I'm reduced to pretending to inspect the large pile of post that carpets the wooden flooring in order to postpone leaving the comfort of the hallway. Looks like bills, bills and more bills. Mum left enough to cover her funeral costs, a funeral I organised but never attended. I feel a pang of something that might be shame at my final fuck-you to the woman who never cared about me enough to ask me to stay.

'There's something here addressed to us,' I mutter, but Dan has already gone right through the front room into the kitchen. I can hear him opening and banging shut cupboards, occasionally saying things like 'What's that supposed to do?' Considering he's barely been in a kitchen for the past five years, I wouldn't be surprised if he's discovered the oven.

The envelope addressed to us is bright pink, making solicitors or HMRC unlikely. I tear open the flap and a smile crosses my face when I see who it's from.

Hey, city slickers. I've left you a care package in the back garden under the coal shelter (that's the black thing made of tin, in case you've been in the big smoke long enough to forget). Come see me as soon as you can. Bring wine. Hope this isn't weird for you.
    Pam xx

'That's nice of her.' Dan reappears at my shoulder. 'Shame she didn't have keys to let herself in and do some cleaning. The place has at least an inch of dust.'

'Give you something to do while you wait for your muse to catch us up.' I smile, kissing the tip of his nose. 'Do you mind if I take a look around on my own? It's a bit overwhelming, being back here with Mum gone.'

'Of course.' Dan nods outside. 'I'll get the rest of the bits from the car.'

*   *   *

I spend the next hour wandering around the distant memory that is my family home. So many things have changed, yet just as I think this isn't going to be so difficult after all, I find the clock from the living-room mantelpiece, now sitting on a wooden shelf, a hidden relic waiting to thrust me back in time. My throat constricts when I see it, remembering the hours spent staring at this clock waiting for my mother's return with equal parts trepidation and excitement. Wondering if today will be the day she strikes up a conversation, or brings us a chippy tea; knowing that it won't be.

I pick up the clock and turn it over in my hands. A lifetime of sorrow has been reflected in that face. Its hands are frozen in time, and the bizarre notion that it stopped working at the exact moment my mother died strikes me. Don't be ridiculous, I tell myself, but I can't shake the idea that it knew its job was done; there was no longer any need to count the hours until my mother's return. She was never coming back.

I put it down and blink a few times to stall the tears that threaten to overcome me. Crying never solved a single thing, Imogen. One of the only pieces of advice she ever gave me. And she was even wrong about that. On the day I left, I waited until I was safely inside the squalid student digs I'd managed to get ridiculously cheaply before breaking into ugly, noisy sobs until my lungs almost burst. When I woke the next morning, my eyes swollen and puffy and my head feeling like I'd downed a quart of vodka, I felt surprisingly cleansed. And I promised myself not to shed another tear over a woman who had never once, in fifteen years, told me she loved me.

8

The sunlight has drained away and the garden has been painted a gloomy palette of lilac and grey, yet still the sky refuses to give in to the darkness. Sarah has been sitting with her legs folded up on the garden chair scrolling through Facebook on her phone for so long that she has barely noticed the shadows folding in around her, the warmth of the day ebbing away to be replaced by the chill of twilight, until a gentle breeze ripples across her bare arms, making her look up and blink in surprise.

'Bloody hell,' she mutters. 'What time is it?' She glances back at her phone. Ten past six. The girls and Billy should be coming in for something to eat by now. She's surprised they haven't already started on at her – kids are perpetually hungry, she has come to learn. Well, except Ellie, of course, but Ellie is the exception in most cases.

Speaking of the children, where are they? They were messing around in the ramshackle playhouse at the end of the garden what, half an hour, forty minutes ago? Couldn't be much more than that, although she's spent far too long arguing with Mark's cousin Tina over an article she shared on her wall that said women over forty were selfish to have babies. She must have known that Sarah would see it, but she still acted all 'soz hun didn't know ud b upset xx' when Sarah told her how insulting it was. Silly cow knew exactly what she was doing. Anyway, even if Sarah couldn't see the kids, she could hear them. Only now the garden is in silence.

'Mary? Billy? Ellie?'

Nothing. Sarah sticks her head around the side of the playhouse just in case, but the kids are nowhere. She shouts into the house and is met with resounding silence. Where are they?

Trying not to panic, she quick-walks back into the garden, her eyes scanning furiously. It's only small: a tree, the play-house against the fence, and beyond that a small patch of disused waste ground . . .

The waste ground. Why didn't she think to check there first? The kids are always sneaking through the gap in the fence, although usually she can hear them ploughing through the undergrowth, laughing and shouting. Today the air is still and silent.

'Mary?' Sarah calls as she approaches the broken panels. 'Billy? Ellie?'

It's a squeeze, but Sarah isn't a large woman and she manages to push herself through, her T-shirt snagging on the rough splinters and her hair catching in the branches of the unruly hedge that lines the fence.

The waste ground is a small patch of uncleared land that joins Sarah and Mark's property to two others surrounding it. It is a mass of untamed scrub and nettles; no one is really sure who it belongs to – if anyone – so it has remained orphaned and untended for as long as the Jeffersons have lived in Acacia Avenue. To them it's an eyesore; to the kids it's an adventure paradise.

She sees them instantly, the three of them kneeling in a triangle in the only clear patch the waste ground offers. All three have their eyes squeezed shut, and Mary and Billy are swaying slightly backwards and forwards. Ellie sits statue-still, only her lips moving furiously as she mutters a low incantation.

Sarah feels the hairs on the back of her neck stand as a shiver takes hold of her. She has found the children, they look unharmed – so why are goose bumps rising on the skin of her arms?

'Kids?' She moves closer. It's impossible for them not to hear her, and yet none of them so much as stirs at her voice. She pushes through the thorns and branches and walks out into the clearing to stand beside Ellie.

'Kids!' she practically shouts, and reaches out a hand to grasp at Ellie's shoulder. Before she makes contact, Ellie's lips stop moving and all three pairs of eyes snap open at once. Later on, Sarah will find herself telling Mark it was as though they had been released from a spell.

'Mum,' Mary says, her eyes widening. 'What's going on? What are you doing out here?'

'I was shouting from the garden. No one answered. What are you doing? What the hell is going on?'

'Just playing, Mrs Jefferson.' Ellie looks up at her, her dark eyes fixing on Sarah's face. She is the only one of the three who doesn't look confused and disorientated. Billy's eyes are darting between Ellie and the waste ground itself, as if trying to decide how on earth he has ended up there.

'Billy?'

'Just playing, Mrs Jefferson.'

'Then why did none of you hear me shout? I was standing right there.'

Ellie's eyes don't move from Sarah's. She looks far from guilty; her jaw is set in defiance.

'For goodness' sake,' Mary snaps, breaking the silence. 'Does it matter? You've found us now. Come on, you two.'

31

Ellie and Billy get to their feet and follow Mary out of the clearing, squeezing through the gap in the fence with much greater ease than Sarah herself did.

It isn't until they are back in the house and Sarah is alone in the bathroom that she lets out the terrified sob she has been holding in.

9

Imogen

I stare into the fire, watching the flames grow and die down, crackling and spitting. I smile up at Dan as he hands me a mug of hot chocolate piled high with whipped cream. 'Thanks.'

'Thank God for Pammy and her care package,' Dan remarks. We found my old best friend's box in the back garden and I was amused to see wine, Hobnobs, prawn crackers, hot chocolate and whipped cream alongside a bag of logs, a bundle of sticks with a note attached announcing them as 'kindling', and a pack of firelighters.

'Anyone would thing we were suburban idiots,' Dan joked, but I could tell he was secretly pleased that the hard work had been done for him. I'm looking forward to tomorrow, when I'm going to show him the log shed where the axe is kept.

Earlier, I moved through the house like a woman without sight, touching the walls, the furniture, trying to bring any kind of feelings to the surface that I could muster. But so much has changed – I have changed. I no longer feel like the lonely, miserable girl who sat in my bedroom on my heels praying to a God I didn't believe in that a mother I barely knew would open the door and fold me into her arms. Opening the door to my mother's room, where we would be spending the night, was the strangest thing of all. I was never allowed in there as a child, although that didn't always stop me, and I had only the vaguest memory of what it looked like. As I crossed the threshold, I got a chill imagining how furious my mother would be if she caught me in there. Don't be ridiculous, Imogen. You're not a child any more. Still, I didn't linger. I haven't yet been able to bring myself to open the door to my old bedroom.

'You're quiet,' Dan remarks, lifting a lock of my hair out of my face and tucking it behind my ear. 'Are you still thinking about what happened earlier, or is it something else?'

'Just earlier,' I lie. This subject is much easier than talking about how I haven't yet been able to push open the door to teenage Imogen Tandy's bedroom for fear of opening gates I can't close again. 'It's still playing on my mind, if I'm honest. The way they were with that girl. I mean, did she look as though she was the type of girl to push someone into the road?' But even as I'm saying the words, I know that no one can predict the type of person to commit violence against someone else. Least of all you, a nasty little voice reminds me. Your track record in that department is hardly gold star, is it?

'She was pretty creepy in that chip shop,' Dan replies. 'I mean, how many children do you know who would threaten to cut someone's tongue out? And how did she know that woman had been talking about her? They were nowhere near the shop when she said those things.'

I give a dismissive wave. 'She didn't threaten to cut her tongue out – she was just quoting something she'd heard at school or somewhere. And I got the impression that it wasn't the first time Mrs Evans had spread her ridiculous theories.

She could have been talking about another set of lies. Her foster mother was mortified, wasn't she? I don't know whether she was more embarrassed at Ellie's words or you laughing when you heard them.'

'I know. Bloody brilliant timing, don't you think? I probably shouldn't have laughed. Broke the tension, though.'

'She was nowhere near that girl,' I muse, ignoring the grin on Dan's face. He doesn't need any encouragement to turn every situation into a joke. 'You saw, didn't you? They were at least a foot apart. We would have seen it if she'd pushed her.'

'Actually, I didn't see,' Dan admits, a sheepish look crossing his face. 'I didn't even notice them, to be honest. They were on the pavement. I clocked that they were there but not what they were doing.'

'But you told the police officer—'

'I know.' Dan cringes. 'Don't be mad at me. I just agreed with what you said. That woman was being so horrible and I really wanted to back you up. When he took my statement, I said I'd seen the girls and I didn't see one of them push the other. Which is true,' he says quickly as I open my mouth to speak. 'I didn't see anyone push anyone. But I couldn't swear that she *didn't* push her either. I wasn't watching.'

I think back to the seconds before the car screeched to a halt. I was so certain at the time that I'd seen them standing feet apart, but that was when Dan backed me up, when he said he'd seen the same. Can I really swear that I didn't look away for a second? Would I testify in a court of law that Naomi had fallen? I try to replay the moment in my mind like a video, but there is no way of forcing myself to visualise what happened.

'Im, forget it. Seriously, no one was hurt and it doesn't look like that crazy woman is pressing charges against the kid. So let's not let it ruin our first night.'

That is so beautifully Dan. We almost ran a child over today but we wouldn't want that to ruin our night, would we? He's right, he's always right. What good will overthinking it do? No one was hurt. Both mothers took their children home today and that's the best outcome we could have wished for. So why do I still feel so uneasy about the whole thing?

10

Whole-school assembly seems like the perfect opportunity. Once she's made the decision to do it, once she's squared away the notion of 'cheating' in her mind as simply giving Yasmin the best chance she can have of passing, it's fairly simple. Far more so, in fact, than Florence would have you believe. The flaw in the head teacher's anti-cheating measures is that no one ever expects someone to actually try and cheat, so there is never really a great deal of thought that goes into trying to stop them. They want you to think it's impossible – locked drawers and sealed papers – when in actual fact there are three senior members of staff who have the key to the filing unit, and any one of them will lend you their supply-cupboard keys with that very filing-unit key on the same ring, not in a million years thinking that you might slip it off to be used later in the week. And even if they noticed it was gone, their first thought would be that it had fallen off the ring. No teachers in their school steal, or lie, or cheat. The problem with Florence is that she would much prefer to think her teachers are incompetent enough to lose a key than clever enough to steal one.

Hannah has at least twenty minutes before the children

spill out of the hall and normal classes resume. That's plenty of time to snap a quick picture of the maths resit that her niece will be taking next month. Yasmin was gutted when she failed last year and Hannah just wants to be able to make sure she revises the right things. She isn't going to tell her the exact questions, of course, that would be wrong, but knowing what areas to practise, knowing which equations to review, that sort of thing isn't real cheating. Yas has four weeks before the exam – plenty of time to learn what she needs to know.

Hannah glances back and forth along the corridor. It isn't exactly deserted; every now and then a teacher who has managed to make an excuse not to be in assembly emerges from their room, or a child who desperately needs the toilet dashes out of the hall looking frantic. No matter, she isn't breaking any rules by being in the supply cupboard, and what she needs to do will take seconds. If a child wandered in, it was unlikely they would even know she was doing anything wrong – for obvious reasons they don't tell the students where the exam papers are kept.

The supply cupboard is dimly lit and a total pigsty. Hannah herself has never even attempted a clear-up, but she knows several other teachers who have spent days in the holiday trying to organise it, to no avail. You won't catch her giving up her holiday to sort out other people's mess. Some of the staff are worse than the bloody kids. The filing unit that holds the exam papers is at the back and is low enough that Hannah has to hunch over it. She wrestles with the flimsy key, and after what feels like an eternity slides it open.

The papers are kept shrink-wrapped in alphabetical order, so finding the stack of maths GCSE resits takes a matter of seconds. The shrink-wrap is another simple obstacle to be overcome. Hannah pulls out a Stanley knife from the resist-ant-materials department that she hid behind a stack of pencil sharpeners yesterday and slices a thin line into the creases of the wrapping. Despite her earlier pep talk to herself that nothing will go wrong, that this is a simple two-minute job, her heart is thumping dangerously. Bloody hell, Hannah, calm down, she chides. It would hardly do to give yourself a heart attack and be discovered in here clutching a stack of exam papers, would it? She allows herself a small smile as she slides out one of the papers and clicks off a couple of photos on her phone. Jesus, these look harder than the original exam – thank goodness she had a look. Yas would never have revised half of this stuff.

Slipping the paper back in through the top, she slides the pile back into the filing cabinet. She isn't concerned about the split in the wrap – she made it in between the folds of the shrink wrap and no one is likely to notice it when they slice into it. Just to be on the safe side, she'll volunteer to be on the set-up team for the resit and open that one herself.

Locking up the cabinet, she congratulates herself silently on a job well done. She doesn't feel guilty; if they really expected no one to take a peek, they would make it harder. Probably half of those piles have slits in from other teachers having a nose. She slips the Stanley knife into one of the boxes of art supplies that litter the floor and turns to make her way back to her classroom. Her heart plummets. Standing silently in the doorway is Ellie Atkinson.

'Ellie.' Hannah plasters on her young-children smile. This child is more than slightly creepy. Hannah has heard all sorts about how her parents were killed in a house fire, Ellie the only survivor. She'd been moved on from two foster families before the Jeffersons took her in, and the woman from Place2Be who had been tasked with helping her settle in mysteriously quit just three weeks after meeting her. Hannah squares her shoulders. She's just a kid, she tells herself. What can she possibly do to me? 'What are you doing out of assembly?'

Ellie says nothing, just watches Hannah in that clinical way she has, as though she is appraising her and finding her disappointingly lacking.

'You should be in assembly,' Hannah repeats, but her voice sounds less certain to her own ears now. She isn't sure, but she thinks she hears Ellie mutter something.

'What was that? What did you say?'

Silence. Ellie has deep chocolate-brown eyes and they are fixed on Hannah, who feels frozen to the spot.

The hallway bursts into a cacophony of sound as the assembly spills out, breaking whatever spell Hannah's feet are under. She gives a disgusted little snort and grabs a pack of rulers from the shelf, waves them at Ellie muttering, 'Just getting these,' and pushes past her out of the cupboard. Ellie turns and slides into the crowd of children, leaving Hannah to lock the door with trembling fingers.

11

Imogen

'You look amazing.' Dan lets out a low whistle and gives my backside a squeeze. For months after I was fired, all my husband saw me in was my pyjamas or workout leggings – not that I did any working out. I barely moved from the sofa for days at a time, only shifting position to receive the meals he brought me. It's nice to be feeling more like a human being again. 'Are you nervous?'

'A little,' I admit. 'It's just strange being back here after so long, and now starting a new job. I'm not going to mess it up this time, though. You don't have to worry about what happened at Morgan and Astley happening again.'

'I'm not worried about that,' Dan says, but I see the momentary flicker of relief on his face. 'I'm worried about what being back here is doing to you. You've been pretty quiet since we arrived. Last night you stayed up until stupid o'clock to avoid going to bed in your mum's room. You know we could have sold this place, stayed where we were.'

'And how long would that have taken? We couldn't have afforded the rent on that place much longer, Dan, not with me not working. We were haemorrhaging money. Knowing that I was the reason our meagre savings were dwindling was difficult. Nana left this house to Mum mortgage-free; now it's ours. Plus I applied for about forty jobs in London and was turned down for every one. This was our only option and you know it.'

'We had other options,' he says gently. I know what our other options were.

'I wasn't about to take your parents' money.' My voice comes out harsher than I intended, but Dan just shrugs.

'They wouldn't have minded.'

'*I* would have minded.' I struggle to keep the edge out of my voice. I know his mum and dad wouldn't have minded. Dan is their only son and they – well, his mother to be exact – have always been desperate to keep me on side, lest I pack up and take my ovaries with me. His mum brings flowers and wine every time they visit – last time she turned up with a crocheted pen holder, a peach woollen tube that looked so obscene that when Dan had caught my eye I had to excuse myself to the kitchen and laugh until I sobbed into the fridge.

'It's like you said, a fresh start. We've gone from renting a place we could no longer afford and me being unemployed to owning our own home and me having a new job. This is important to us.'

'It's important to you,' Dan replies, kissing my hair. 'You are important to me. And I know you don't want to talk about your mum,' he holds up his hands in surrender at my look, 'and that's fine. You know me, Im, I'd never push you. But one day I hope you can get past whatever happened. For the sake of our family.'

My mouth suddenly feels as though it is filled with sand. I nod once, then look away.

'I'd better get going,' I say. 'Don't want to be late on my first day.'

12

The classroom is silent, all the children going about their work, and Hannah pulls out her iPad ready for at least half an hour on Facebook. Maybe she'll buy some new shoes, something for the weekend.

They're only five minutes into the task she has set them when Ellie raises her hand. Hannah resists the urge to sigh. 'Yes, Ellie?'

'Miss, I wanted to ask you a question about morals.'

Hannah feels the dread rise in her chest. This instantly feels like a trap.

'Go on.'

Ellie smiles, a small movement that makes the hairs on Hannah's arms tingle. 'I just wanted to know what you think someone should do if they thought they'd seen someone else cheating.'

Fuck. She knew Ellie had seen her in the cupboard. But how had she known what she was doing? Unless she knows where the tests were kept – and it's unlikely the Year 7s would know, let alone care – it would have just looked as though Hannah was getting supplies.

'I think you'd have to be very sure of what you saw, Ellie.'

'But would you say they should tell someone?' Ellie pushes. 'Like the head teacher?'

Hannah winces. 'Without any proof I'd certainly be wary. It might look like you were trying to cause trouble for the person. You're welcome to talk to me after class if you'd like?'

Ellie smiles that smile again. 'I don't think that's necessary, miss, thanks.'

13

Imogen

My new office is so far removed from my old one that it may as well be on a different planet. Completely open-plan, with pinboards between desks that barely rise above the occupants' foreheads and don't quite manage to pull off the illusion of privacy. There are twelve people in this office when it is up to capacity, or so I was told this morning, but most of them work from other offices half of the week and it is rarely full. Still, it is such a far cry from my private office with its tasteful decor and above all its silence that I already feel as though I might struggle to breathe in here. There are seven people in today and that is enough to maintain a steady buzz of conversation, like an air-con unit in need of a service.

'It's great to have you here finally.' Lucy has been given the unenviable task of showing me around, giving introductions and generally initiating me in the ways of the public sector. So far this morning she has covered tea funds, cakes on birthdays and communal lockers. She smiles at the emphasis on 'finally' to show me it's not me she's getting at. 'You'll soon find out what this place is like. Why do something in a week when you can stretch it out to three months?

45

Not that we got any notice of the vacancy, but still, it took them over a month to put the post out. That's the reason for the backlog.

'Anyway,' she takes a breath when she registers the look on my face, 'I'm scaring you. It's not that bad really, just public sector for you. Your last place was private, wasn't it? Can't imagine why you wanted to leave that for government work. I'd give my eye teeth for a job in the private sector, me.' She gives a self-conscious giggle and I try to fix my grimace into a smile. Is everyone here like this? I'm really not used to such a them-and-us approach; neither am I used to colleagues who tell you their life story before you even sit down at your desk. I was at Morgan and Astley for six years and I barely knew anything about my colleagues' personal lives.

I dig my fingernails into the flesh between my thumb and forefinger to quell the rising nausea. What have I done? Have I really thrown away my career and ended up here? The whole idea seems ridiculous now, as though I was really drunk and can't remember anything I did, or my reasons for doing it. *You're lucky to have a job*, I tell myself, *especially one as good as this. Place2Be is a fantastic organisation, providing mental health support in schools all around the country. We actually help children who need it, not just rich kids who have gone off the rails. Kids like . . . no, don't think about him now.*

'The stationery cupboard is just down the hall, next to admin. Joy keeps the key but it's only so people don't dump all their crap in there. I'll take you down there in a bit to kit your desk out. Looks like it's been raided since Em left.' She casts an apologetic glance at the bare desk; it's made of oak veneer, a giant chip in one corner and a cup-sized hole rimmed in plastic towards the back. My old one was . . . Never mind. It's someone else's now. Probably Fat Matt – he'd had his eyes on my office for years. I scowl at the thought of him rubbing his blubbery rolls all over my leather chair and replacing the light smell of incense with his rancid body odour. 'IT will come and set up your computer at some point today.'

Nothing like leaving it till the last minute, I think, but say nothing. They've known I was starting today for weeks now. But I'm not about to start complaining on my first day.

Joy is an aptly named smiling woman, one of those people who instantly make you feel better in their presence.

'Morning, love,' she says when Lucy herds me into the office. It's so strange, being presented around like a new kid at school. 'Nice to have you on board. Has Lucy been treating you well?'

She says this with such a fond smile at Lucy it makes me feel even more like an outsider. 'Yes, she's been lovely, thanks.'

'We've come for your secret key,' Lucy tells her, and Joy makes a mock-horrified face. 'Don't worry, we're not fly-tipping.'

'I've nothing to tip yet.' I smile. 'It looks like Emily took everything with her.' I wince, immediately regretting the insinuation that their ex-colleague is a thief.

Lucy and Joy exchange a look. 'Yes, well, we can hardly fire her now, can we?' Joy jokes. 'Here you go, stock up.' I sit for most of the morning at my new desk, watching as IT plug and unplug bits of hardware and try unsuccessfully to get my log-in credentials to work. At one point a photograph-sized piece of paper flutters to the ground when the IT apprentice struggles to pull the desk away from the wall. I pick it up; it is a close-up of a smiling young woman about my age, arms wrapped around a good-looking bloke. They look as though they are on holiday, bare arms and fresh tans.

'Is this Emily?' I ask, spinning on my swivel chair to show Lucy the picture. She turns and cranes her neck.

'Yes, that's her. Pretty, isn't she? And that's Jamie, the bloke she left to get married to. He's a right dish.'

'Loaded too, I presume?' I ask, cringing at how gossipy my voice already sounds. One morning in a communal office and I sound like a different person.

Lucy's face is a puzzled frown. 'I don't think so. Why do you say that?'

'Well, because who quits work to get married these days? I mean, unless she moved away to live somewhere else . . .'

Lucy shakes her head. 'She didn't say. To be honest, I was surprised too, but I never got the chance to ask her. She went off sick and didn't come back.' She lowers her voice. 'That's what most people here do if they're looking for a new job. We get full sick pay for six months.'

I nod as though this makes perfect sense, although I've long given up trying to work out how the minds of adults work. Why someone can't just look for a job while they're still in their current one is beyond me.

'So how did you know she got married?'

'HR told us. It's weird, though, she hasn't changed her name on Facebook, and she took us all off her friends list. Not that I really care, but I thought we were quite good mates. At work, at least.'

'All ready.' The IT apprentice taps the top of the computer and I swing around to face him.

'Thanks,' I say with a grin. 'Better do some work now, I suppose.' I glance at the clock – half an hour to get myself set up before my first meeting with my new boss, so for now the gossip will have to wait.

14

Ellie

The house is unnaturally silent for this time of night, and Ellie likes it. In this new life of hers she so rarely has time to bask in the quiet that she never even realised that she enjoyed it before. Or maybe she didn't; maybe it is only now, now that everything is always noise and colours and constant people, that she has learned to really appreciate the silence.

Her foster carers, Sarah and Mark Jefferson, are with Billy the Mean at parents' evening, leaving Ellie and Mary home alone. Mary is fifteen, and so she's allowed to be in charge of Ellie for a few hours, or so Sarah says, even though Ellie is sure she won't mention it at the social worker's visit. Billy is sly and vindictive and almost certain to get a glowing report at the school; they are all too stupid to see what he can be like when there are no grown-up eyes on him. The school, Sarah and Mark . . . only Ellie knows what he's really like; even Mary says he's just harmless – mixed up and sad – but that's Mary for you, always trying to see the best in everyone.

Tap.

Tap.

Tap.

When she hears the sharp clinking against the window pane, Ellie isn't afraid. The worst has already happened to her – she is nearly impossible to scare. She imagines that it is the long hooked talons of a scaly black-eyed demon strumming a rhythm on the glass.

Let me in, let me in, little Ellie, he is saying. *Let me in and I'll be your best friend. Let me in and I'll never let anyone hurt you again.*

Why should I trust you?

Well who else can you trust?

It is when she hears the voices that Ellie realises it isn't the clicking of a demon's fingernails against her window. It is the sound of stones snapping against the glass. She gets out of bed, crosses the room and peels back the curtains.

Underneath a street lamp on the pavement outside stands a group of seven girls. It's dark, and Ellie doesn't recognise any of their faces – she hasn't been at her new school long; she barely knows anyone, since none of them will even speak to her. But she knows that these girls are not here to make friends with her.

One of them looks up, sees her face at the window and points. Through the glass Ellie hears the girl hiss, 'There she is. The witch.'

The rest of them look up as one. One of them shouts, 'Come down, witch!' and they all begin to laugh and chatter, all except one, who is staring up at the window, her face blank and unreadable. Now Ellie recognises her. Naomi Harper. Of all the girls there, it is she who sends goose bumps up Ellie's arms. There is a real meanness in Naomi's eyes, a meanness Ellie has seen to a smaller degree in Billy. Even from this distance Ellie knows that she is here tonight to cause harm. She won't go down, she won't give them what they want. But what if they come up here? Is she certain that Sarah and Mark locked the doors when they went to parents' evening earlier?

It is Naomi who starts the chant, low and quiet at first, then louder as the other girls join in, all staring up at the window as they sing.

'One, two, Ellie's coming for you. Three, four, better lock your door . . .'

Ellie recognises the tune and words from a rhyme she heard in a scary movie back in her old life, when Jessica George invited her to a sleepover and they sneaked *A Nightmare on Elm Street* out of her dad's DVD collection. They barely made it halfway through when, screaming, Jessica ejected the DVD and threw it out of the window into the garden beyond. That seems like a lifetime ago now, the fear they had then so childish and innocent.

Ellie bangs loudly on the window to make them stop, and one of the girls screams like she's been struck. The noise is such that it brings Mary in from her own bedroom and she rushes over to the window to see what's going on below.

'What is it, Ellie?' she asks, peering out. 'Oh for fuck's sake.'

She disappears from the room as fast as she came in, and Ellie waits to see if she will emerge from the front door into the street below. She prays Mary won't do anything stupid in her defence. She would rather these children were here all night singing their stupid song than that Mary got hurt trying to defend her. She is a full four years older than Ellie, but a couple of these girls look older too, and there are more of them.

The front door doesn't open and Mary doesn't emerge onto the street below. Instead she pushes her way back into Ellie's bedroom, hauling a washing-up bowl, water slopping over the sides and landing on the carpet.

'What are you doing?' Ellie asks, watching her in fascination.

'I'm going to teach them a lesson,' Mary tells her. 'They need to know that they can't mess around with you, otherwise they'll be doing it all year.'

She balances the bowl precariously on the windowsill and then, realising she can't let go of it to open the window, gestures with her head at the handle. 'Open that, Ellie.'

Ellie fumbles with the window and then pushes it open as wide as she can. As quick as a flash, Mary hurls the water out at the girls on the street. Screams echo as it hits the pavement, soaking one, splashing the rest, and the two girls in the room turn to one another, both grinning.

'Now piss off!' Mary yells out of the window. 'Or I'll be throwing something worse than water at you little cowbags.'

The girls scatter and then run away, shouting over their shoulders as they do so, 'Witch!' Naomi stops halfway down the street and looks up directly up at where Ellie is looking out of the still-open window. Her expression is no longer unreadable; it is now one of fury.

'This isn't over, witch!' she screams.

Ellie places a hand against the cold window pane. Her features feel as though they have been carved from stone. She stares at Naomi Harper and sees the expression on her face change from hunter to hunted. Her eyes widen in shock and she stumbles backwards, just as she did in town. Ellie jerks her head forward as though launching an attack, and Naomi turns and runs into the night.

Mary places the empty washing-up bowl on the floor and pulls Ellie into a hug. 'They're just being horrible because you're different,' she tells her, squeezing her tightly. 'You don't talk much and your background is all mysterious. If they don't have all the facts, they start making them up. And the stuff they make up is usually much more inventive than the truth.'

'They were saying that I'm a witch,' Ellie says, and her

voice sounds detached, as though she is hearing snatches of a conversation through a closed door.

'It only takes one of them,' Mary explains. 'That's the way it works. It only takes one mean little bitch like Naomi Harper to start some rumour, and it's like a huge game of Chinese whispers. They are stupid little idiots. All they've heard is that you survived a fire when your parents and brother died. And who else survives fires? Witches. That's how pathetic they are. That's all it takes for them.'

'Stupid girls,' Ellie spits, and she is talking more to herself than to her sister. 'Witches don't survive fires. Witches *burn* in fires; that's how they used to kill them when they didn't drown.'

'That's what I mean, Ellie, about you being different. Normally eleven-year-olds don't talk about people burning alive. They hear you survived a fire and they think of witches. They don't know all the details of the Salem witch trials.'

'My mum told me about them,' Ellie explains. 'She said that a long time ago one of our ancestors was burned at the stake. The villagers didn't trust her because she used to heal people with herbs. That was enough for them to think that she was a witch.'

'And the fact that you're a bit quiet, and people don't know a lot about your past, is enough for them to decide that you're a witch now,' Mary says with a shrug. 'Not much has really changed, has it?'

Ellie thinks about this, about the women her mother told her about, put on trial for witchcraft for simply being different to everyone else. She never imagined for one second that people would be that way now. Or that it would be her put on trial for being a witch.

Mary strokes her hair, cups her chin and lifts Ellie's face to meet her gaze. 'Listen, Ellie, don't worry about it. Hopefully they'll go home soaking wet, and think about what happened tonight and realise how stupid they've been. Or at the very least realise that you've got someone on your side who won't stand for them treating you like that. And if anything is said about this in school, I'll kick their asses myself. I won't have them treating you like this, Ellie. You're my little sister now and I'm going to look after you.'

Ellie tries to smile, but the anger inside her runs too deep. 'Yes,' she murmurs. 'Like you said, I'm sure they'll get bored of it eventually, I'm sure they'll find someone else to focus their attentions on.' If they know what's good for them.

'Well if they don't,' Mary says, 'if you get any more trouble when I'm not around, you just try your best to stick up for yourself. You know you can do it. And then tell me and I'll make sure it gets sorted out.'

'Shall I tell Sarah what happened?'

Mary shakes her head. 'Not yet. Let's try and take care of Naomi ourselves first, hey? When adults get involved, things just seem to get messed up.'

When Ellie was little, her mother gave her a worry monster. She would write all her worries down and stick them in his mouth, and then in the morning they were gone. She wishes she had her worry monster with her now. She imagines its pointed felt teeth morphing into gleaming fangs, watches in her mind as they sink themselves into Naomi Harper's throat, bright red blood dripping from the deep puncture wounds. She knows that tonight she will dream of Naomi.

15

Imogen

'Imogen, I'm so sorry I'm late.'

I've been in the meeting room for ten minutes when Edward Tanners bustles in clutching a dog-eared A4 notebook and a mug of something hot. I didn't have time to get a drink – I was too afraid of not being able to find the room and being late to stop at the canteen on the way. Edward, to his credit, notices my glance at the mug.

'Oh, do you want one? Has someone shown you the canteen? I'm so sorry I haven't been around much this morning; I've been in partnership meetings back to back since nine. If I never hear the words "performance targets" again it will be too soon.'

I smile politely. 'I'm fine, honestly. Lucy has shown me where everything is and IT have me all set up and ready to go.'

'Christ, you must have the magic touch – IT is usually day four or five at least.' He smiles in a way that screams #jokingnotjoking. 'And I'm glad Lucy is helping you settle in; you'll be working quite closely with her and the rest of the team. We're all supposed to have our own caseloads here, but it's not like the private sector: there's four of us to do the work of six, and for a while there's only been three of us. We have to be a close team and luckily we have a really good one.' He smiles genuinely this time and I get the impression that this, at least, is true. For all the differences here that will take getting used to, the team's easy, relaxed nature towards one another is going to be one of the more positive ones.

'It seems great. I'm looking forward to working with everyone.'

'Speaking of working . . .' Edward opens his notebook and jots the date at the top; I follow suit. 'We take referrals from several out-of-town schools as well as Gaunt. You and Lucy will take on the school referrals, Jemma and Charlie the vulnerable-adults cases, but you can expect to move between the two when necessary. Does that sound okay?'

'Perfect. How do we allocate the cases?'

'We have a planning meeting every second Tuesday to divide the workload, but if urgent cases come in between them, we tend to take them on an ad hoc basis depending on who's free.'

I take that to mean 'whoever picks up the phone' and nod. 'Okay. Are there any outstanding cases you would like me to take on from my predecessor?'

Edward hesitates for a second. 'There are a couple of referrals the team haven't managed to fit in; I'll email the details over. The team tend to manage their own diaries, and we'll show you the case file program we use to keep everyone updated in case someone wins the lottery and ups and leaves.'

I smile, trying to look super-duper keen. 'Well at least you don't have to worry about me running off to get married.' I hold up my hand. 'Already done and I'm still here.'

Edward looks confused. 'Why would getting married make you leave work?' His face falls. 'We don't frown on marriage here.'

'Oh, sorry,' I falter. 'It's just that I thought that's why Emily left. I was just joking . . .'

Edward nods enthusiastically. 'Of course, I see what you mean! Ha! It does seem a bit odd, doesn't it? I'd almost forgotten.' He pushes his chair out. 'Right, I'm sorry this is a short introduction, but I have meetings all afternoon as well – it's coming up to the end of the month.' He shrugs as if this explains everything. 'Tammy from HR is going to do all the boring health-and-safety stuff with you this afternoon, and I've arranged for you to shadow Lucy on a couple of her visits later on in the week. I'll send over those cases for you to have a look at, and just give me a call or drop me an email if you need any extra info or you're unsure of anything at all.'

He stands and I do the same, feeling a little blindsided by the abrupt ending to the meeting.

'It's great to have you on board, Imogen. We're really excited to have someone of your experience and background on the team.'

'Thanks,' I reply to his retreating back. 'Great to be here.'

16

Imogen

'How did it all go today?' Dan hands me a mug of tea and arranges himself on the sofa next to me. 'No salt in your tea? Cling film on the toilet seat?'

I grin. 'It wasn't my first day at school, Dan. They were all really nice to me.' I pretend to look over my shoulder. 'Unless they stuck a "kick me" sign on my back that I didn't notice.'

'I peeled it off when you came in,' he jokes. 'The urge to kick you was too tempting with it there.'

I swat at him with my mug-free hand. 'How about you? Get any best-selling novels written today? What with your inspiring change of scenery and all that.'

'Two.' He reaches out and pulls my feet up onto his lap, begins massaging one of them. I let out a groan of appreciation and shift to get myself comfortable. 'You were right about this place, it really is a perfect country town.'

I wince inwardly, sure that I've never used the word 'perfect' in all the times I've described my home town. I think of how often I felt out of place here in the past, all the times I dreamt of escaping Gaunt for good. Then when I finally did, I ended up being drawn back here like a moth to a flame. I'm telling myself it was a necessity – who pays to rent when they have inherited a home in the country? But being back here, I'm wondering if it wasn't something more. A matter of unfinished business.

'And a great place to raise a family,' Dan adds when I don't speak. 'Did you look at the maternity policies?'

'Oh yeah,' I retort, not even trying to keep the sarcasm from my voice. 'The first thing I did when I got to my desk was print out the whole staff handbook and double-underline the maternity benefits.'

'Okay, okay, very funny.' Dan shifts, lifting my other foot closer and pushing his thumb into my sole. The pressure on my tired feet feels amazing. This move has completely exhausted me – God only knows how tired I would be if I'd had to do it all whilst organising a family. I was sick with nerves this morning and I can feel my eyelids drooping even now, and it's only 8 p.m.

'Maybe leave it a week or so before you tell them about the colossal brood you intend on producing.' He says it as though he is joking, but I suddenly get a horrific image of myself in a grubby pinny surrounded by seven or eight filthy babbling children, poking one another in the eye and pinching chubby flesh. I give an involuntary shudder.

'Are you cold?' Dan asks, moving to stand up. He beats his chest comically. 'I could do us a fire?'

'No, no, I'm fine, thank you. I might just finish this and head on up to bed, if you don't mind? First day and all that.'

'No, of course not.' He reacts immediately to the mention of an early night. 'Do you want me to come up with you?'

I shake my head a little too quickly. I know Dan's idea of 'come up with you', and it doesn't involve me resting my eyes. 'Not tonight, babe. You'll only be up at the crack of dawn if you go to bed this early. I'll get some sleep and I'll be fine tomorrow – back to fighting fit.'

17

Ellie

If she closes her eyes, Ellie can remember the first time she was here, in this very office. Unfamiliar clothes hung from her, reminding her that they didn't belong on her and that she didn't belong anywhere. She'd been placed in emergency care following the fire – her nana had flown over from France and was sitting behind that very door there, the one marked *Private*, even though Ellie, sitting with her back to the glass could hear every word they said: 'Not the best environment for a child . . . better for her to stay in her own country . . . auntie and uncle . . . three kids already . . .'

Now she is sitting here again, only this time she is not alone. This time she, Billy and Mary sit in perfect silence as they strain to catch even a snippet of the conversation that is taking place behind the glass.

'Did she just say "feet and alcohol"?' Ellie asks.

Mary pulls a face. '"Feet and alcohol" doesn't make any sense.' She scowls and holds up a finger to shush Ellie as the voices start again. 'I'm sure that was "court case".'

Ellie pushes herself as close up against the wall as she can without actually climbing through it. She and Billy asked Sarah and Mark countless questions about this meeting, about why they were going to social services, about whether it was to do with Ellie and how long she was staying with them. But they remained silent, shooting each other the occasional smile and saying, 'You'll have to wait and see.' Mary didn't say a word.

'Do you three want anything to drink?' A woman appears from the next office. She is tall and thin, with sharp features but a big smile on her face. She looks like one of those women who tries her best to look friendly but always looks as though she wishes she were somewhere else.

'I do,' Billy says rudely.

'No thank you,' Ellie replies.

'Sssshhh,' Mary hisses, completely ignoring the woman. 'That was definitely "court case". And "six months". Maybe you're staying another six months, Ellie, or maybe . . .' She shakes her head. 'No, I shouldn't say. It's mean to get your hopes up.'

'Maybe it's me,' Billy interrupts. 'Maybe I'm staying here. Maybe your mum is adopting me, Mary.'

'You really shouldn't be eavesdropping, you know,' the woman says, gesturing towards the closed door. 'It's adult stuff; if they wanted you to know, they would have let you go in there with them.'

Mary looks as though she would like to slap the woman in the face. 'Yeah, well maybe they don't realise how much their decisions affect the rest of their family,' she says, flashing the woman a furious look. 'It might be adult conversation, adult issues, but the kids always have to deal with it in the end.'

The woman looks as though she wants to engage further with them, but thinks better of it. Instead she gives a small nod, then turns around and walks away muttering, 'Well, I'll go and get that drink.'

'What were you going to say?' Ellie asks Mary when the woman is out of earshot.

'I was just going to say that maybe they're talking about adopting you.'

Ellie stays silent.

'Would you like that, Ellie? Do you want to be part of our family for good?'

'Her?' Billy looks incredulous. 'They would never want to adopt a weirdo like her. It's probably me.'

Mary shoots him a look that shuts him up as effectively as a punch in the mouth.

'Ellie?'

Ellie shrugs. She hates Gaunt, she hates school and all the other kids, but who is to say anything would be better in another school, another place? She can't see why the Jeffersons would adopt her; she doesn't think Sarah likes her all that much, and Mark seems pretty indifferent. But at least Sarah has never been mean to her, and Mark . . . well, she'd rather he was indifferent than like the foster father in her last home, with his greedy, hungry eyes following her everywhere she went. Who followed her into the bathroom to check if she needed more towels, and stroked her face as he tucked her into bed and kissed her good night.

No, there are far worse places she could be than with the Jeffersons. And what was it they said? Better the devil you know? Ellie isn't entirely sure what it means; her mother used to say it all the time about her father when they had fights. What she basically thinks it means is that it's better to stay where you are than go to something worse. And at least she has Mary. If she went somewhere else, she might be completely on her own. The school might be one where you were forced to eat maggots if you didn't get full marks in a test, or do push-ups if you were late and stand on one leg in the corner for an hour if you forgot your homework. One of the teachers at her old school told them about these other schools one time when they were complaining about a full-class detention they had been given, her voice full of relish as she recounted all the awful things that could happen to them,.

'Earth to Ellie?' Mary gives her shoulder a small shove. 'I said would you like it if my parents adopted you? Do you want to stay with us forever or don't you?' She takes Ellie's hand in hers. 'We could be real sisters.'

'I suppose,' Ellie says. The fact is that she can't imagine growing up in this strange place, surrounded by these people, her foster sister her only real ally in life, but she can't imagine growing up anywhere else either. If this doesn't work out, if the Jeffersons don't want to keep her, will she be sent to France after all to live with Nana? Or perhaps they'll force Auntie Pauline to have her, and she'll have to go and live in Derbyshire with Pauline's three horrible children – Ike, Tristan and Wagner or something equally stupid. She'll have to have piano lessons and she'll turn into a spoilt little shit – that was what she heard her father saying to her mother one time when they thought she wasn't listening: 'Those kids are spoilt little shits.' And still, none of those lives seem like they should be her real life. Like they are just temporary, fleeting existences until they find her real mum and dad again. While they find a way to bring them back to her, so that her proper life with her mum, her dad and her baby brother can start up again.

'You don't have to sound so enthusiastic,' Mary says solemnly, releasing Ellie's hand. She kicks at the chair leg, bored and impatient. 'I'm going to be out of here in a few years anyway,' she adds, looking at Ellie for a reaction. 'As soon as I'm old enough. I'm going to skip this town, and you won't catch me coming back.'

'Where you going to go, Mary?' Billy asks, balling up a leaflet from one of the nearby tables and tossing it at her. Mary scowls.

'Mind your own business.'

'You could take me with you, couldn't you?' Ellie asks, hope surging in her chest.

Mary laughs. 'And what would I do with you? You'll be fifteen, max. You won't be able to get a job or pay your way. You'll still be in school. No,' she studies her fingernails intently, 'where I'm going, you can't come with me. But it won't be long, only about seven years, until you can come yourself. Six if you grow up real good and can look after yourself by the time you're seventeen.'

'Seven years is a lifetime,' Ellie declares. 'Almost my whole lifetime again. I can't possibly stay here that long without you.'

Mary looks as though she's about to say something else when the handle squeaks and the door opens. In a flash, Billy is sitting up straight and pretending.

'Were you three listening?' But Sarah's voice isn't cross, or reprimanding. She is beaming. 'Come on, how much did you hear?'

'Nothing,' Mary admits. 'Are you going to tell us what's going on?'

'Why don't you come in.' Sarah gestures inside the office, where the social worker is still sitting behind the desk and Mark is still sitting on one of the chairs opposite her.

'Is this about Ellie?' Mary demands.

'If you just come into the office, we'll tell you.'

Billy is inside and sitting in one of the chairs before Ellie and Mary have a chance to move. Mary puts out a hand to squeeze Ellie's shoulder, and Ellie follows her into the office.

'Now I'm sure you must be wondering why you're here,' the social worker says, steepling her hands to a point on her desk. She peers at them intently in turn. 'But we have some good news for your family.'

'What is it?' Billy asks impatiently. Ellie longs for Mary to tell him to shut up. She wonders if Mary really is hoping that her adoption is on the table. Does she want to be her sister that desperately?

'Well, kids, we were going to tell you this at home, but Sandra thought it might be better to give you the news while we're here, in case you have any questions or concerns.'

Sandra nods sagely.

'You see, you know how long your father and I have wanted a baby, Mary?'

Ellie is knocked sideways by this. She isn't really sure where it's going . . . a baby? Is Sarah pregnant? Mary nods, but her face has gone from jubilant to confused as well.

'The opportunity has come up for us to foster a baby. She will be about six months old and we will be fostering her with a view to adoption. So there's going to be a little baby around the house, isn't that fantastic?' Sarah beams and Mary and Ellie nod automatically, although Ellie feels as though all the air has been let out of her, like she has been deflated there and then in her seat.

'Oh yes, just wonderful,' Billy comments, wrinkling his nose. 'A nice screaming, puking, ugly, wrinkled baby to look after.' Sarah looks at him in shock. Whoops, thinks Ellie. Billy the Mean is showing.

'I thought you were going to stop fostering?' Mary says quietly. 'I thought after Ellie . . .'

Sarah cocks her head to one side sympathetically. 'I know this is hard for you, love. But if we adopt this baby, then there'll be no need to foster any more. And that's what you want, isn't it? A stable family.'

'And what about Ellie?' Mary spits out. 'What's going to happen to her? Where does she fit in to our perfect family?'

Sarah looks uncomfortable and glances at Mark, looking for some help.

'Well, Ellie knows this was only ever a short-term solution.

And I don't suppose she wants to stay with us anyway.' Sarah looks at Ellie to back her up. 'I'm sure she wants a more stable life too, to be adopted by a family who can give her the proper . . . care and attention she deserves.'

'Oh yes,' Mary replies sarcastically. 'I'm sure that's what she wants more than anything in the world, to be shipped from one place to another, never being able to settle, being passed over for six-month-old bloody babies. I bet that's just the life she had in mind.'

Sarah's eyes widen. 'We're not passing anyone over in favour of the baby, Mary. I think you should watch your attitude. We've always discussed having a baby in the house, and Ellie is welcome to stay for as long as is needed. The least you could do is pretend to be happy about our latest addition. About what might be your new sister.'

'So where is the little shitbag?' Mary asks. Ellie hears Billy gasp, and Sarah looks as though she might explode with fury.

'Mary Jefferson, I did not bring you up to speak that way to your parents. And if you think you can get away with it because we're in company, you have got another think coming. The baby won't be with us for six weeks – there are a lot of official things that need to happen before she leaves her birth mother.'

Mary looks incredulous. 'Six weeks? But we've never had a baby before! They need loads of stuff. When Lola's mum had a baby, she said the house was just full of prams and cots and baby bouncers. We haven't got any of that.'

'These things can sometimes happen much quicker, overnight even.' The social worker speaks quietly. 'It's not ideal for first-time foster carers of very young babies, but there is no one else available. This has all been a bit of a rush, I'm afraid.'

'Well you're right about one thing,' Mary snorts. 'It's not ideal. Not for anyone – and least of all that baby.'

18

Imogen

It's only mid-afternoon, but my eyes sting and my entire body aches. The office is unusually quiet, but I'm pretty sure they will still notice if I have a nap under my desk. Maybe I should at least save that for week two. Stifling a yawn, I pull up the email I received from Edward following our meeting yesterday.

Hi, Imogen,

Hope you're settling in. Here are the cases that Emily was working on when she left. If you could do some file research and arrange appointments to meet these clients in the next week or so, it should give you enough to be going on with until our first planning meeting next Tuesday. Any problems, you can get me on Skype most of tomorrow or Friday (meetings the rest of the week – aargh!). Anything urgent, drop me an email – I'll check them while I'm playing solitaire in senior transformation board (joke!).

Kind regards,

Ted

I double-click the attachment on the email and an Excel spreadsheet opens up, password-protected. I curse under my breath and Lucy turns around.

'You okay?'

I point at my screen and Lucy wheels her chair over. 'Edward has sent me this caseload of Emily's to follow up, but it's passworded.'

'Oh, they're all just CAMHS#22. I think it was supposed to be a funny Catch-22 thing but no one really got it.' She leans over and types it in and the file pings open. She scans the list and her face hardens.

'What? What is it?' I ask, noting the look that my colleague has quickly replaced with neutral and scanning the list. 'Did I get one you wanted? I'm happy to swap if there's something you want to work on.'

'No, it's fine.' Lucy gives a tight smile. 'I just thought Ted was taking on a couple of those, that's all.' She hesitates as though unsure whether to say what she's thinking. 'If you need help, if any of them give you bother, come to me first, okay? I'll help you work out what to do.'

I feel my stomach plummet. 'Is there something I should know about these cases, Lucy?'

She shakes her head a little too quickly. 'No, don't be silly, I just meant in general, if you need any help with anything. That's what I'm here for, isn't it?'

'That's not how it sounded.' I lower my voice. 'Does it have something to do with why Emily left?'

Lucy's face colours. 'Emily moved away to get married. Look, I know this job is boring, but if you're looking for mysteries, you're in the wrong place.'

She spins her chair to face her computer screen and doesn't look back.

19

Ellie

Ellie's first few weeks at her new school have got off to a shaky start, and what happened in the town with Naomi has just made things worse. Everyone seems to know that Naomi's mother accused her of trying to kill her daughter, and the other children have given her a wide berth. She tries not to think about the new school she would have been starting in her old life, the local senior school where all her junior-school friends would have been navigating the long corridors and huge classrooms for the first time together. She was allowed to speak to some of her old friends over the summer break, but it felt like they had already closed over the Ellie-shaped gap in their lives so efficiently that she knew she wouldn't ask to call any of them again.

'Young girls are resilient, Ellie,' Sarah told her, not unkindly though. 'They adapt quickly to changes. You mustn't feel badly about it.'

But Ellie doesn't feel very resilient, just numb, as though her heart has been replaced with a mouldy potato.

Today the corridor is full of people and yet Ellie could be completely on her own for all the notice anyone takes of her. Usually she prefers to be unseen, to wander the halls as though she is a ghost, transparent and inconsequential. Today, though, with only her misery for company, she feels as though she would give anything for someone to look up, smile at her and wave, say hello and ask how her day is going. But she doesn't fit here, in this school, in this town, and the scene outside her foster parents' house two nights before is still sitting heavily at the front of her mind. She thought she saw one of the girls standing outside her English class just before they were let out, her mouth twisted in an evil smile as she watched Ellie through the glass pane in the door. But when she left the classroom, the girl had disappeared, and Ellie wondered if she had ever really been there at all.

Her next class is history, tucked away in a small classroom underneath the stairs to the art rooms and the library. Her history teacher is a quirky little man who always wears a waistcoat at least two sizes too small for his rotund belly and says 'ahem' at least once every two words. But he is kind, and this term they are learning about Nazi Germany, a subject Ellie finds disturbing and fascinating in equal measure. On the wall is a poem she has memorised word for word, written by a man whose name she can't pronounce. She repeats it now in her mind as she walks the corridor as a ghost.

First they came for the Socialists, and I did not speak
    out –
Because I was not a Socialist.
Then they came for the Trade Unionists, and I did not
    speak out –
Because I was not a Trade Unionist.
Then they came for the Jews, and I did not speak
    out –
Because I was not a Jew.
Then they came for me – and there was no one left
    to speak for me.

The poem is a warning, tacked on the wall for everyone to see, and yet no one heeds its words. It is like Ellie herself: seen and instantly discarded; not worth the time or attention.

She is almost at the door to her history class when her desire to be noticed is realised. Be careful what you wish for, Ellie Atkinson.

Naomi Harper is in front of her, blocking her path before Ellie even sees her approach. She appears so suddenly that Ellie stumbles, her foot jamming down on Naomi's toe.

'Ow!' Naomi shrieks as though Ellie has set her hair on fire. 'You did that on purpose!'

'I didn't, I'm sorry.' Ellie hates herself for her urgent, pleading tone, hates the way she sounds like a victim. She's desperate to tell Naomi to fuck off and ram the sharp end of her compass into the little bitch's arm. But she has promised Sarah that she will try and stay out of trouble. If she's going to stay here, she needs to keep her nose clean.

Naomi mimics her, sniffing and whimpering, 'I'm sorry,' in a humiliatingly good impression of her voice. Then, without warning and as quickly as she swiped the plimsolls off the stand that day in the school-uniform shop, she grabs Ellie's arm and yanks her into the shadows beneath the art-room stairs. Ellie's history room is only yards away – if she screams, her teacher will surely hear her. The door opens and the other children file in, but they don't even look in her direction. Ellie thrashes and wriggles, but Naomi has a firm hold on her arm.

Naomi is not the only person under the stairs. She shoves Ellie roughly into the waiting arms of an older girl – one of those who was outside her bedroom taunting and chanting. The girl grabs both her arms and hisses into her ear, her breath warm on Ellie's cheek, 'Hello, Ellie, remember us?' She nods towards the other girl waiting under the stairwell – the girl who was watching Ellie as she sat in her English class just a few minutes before. She must have been the lookout. 'If you scream, I'll break your pretty nose.'

The corridor is empty now – Ellie is late for class and she desperately wills her teacher to come out and look for her, but the door remains treacherously closed.

'Fucking hell, Ellie,' Naomi sneers, and Ellie is sure the other girl can see her trembling, can hear the thudding of her heart through her chest and smell the sweat that is beginning to trickle down her back. 'You look as though you're about to piss yourself.' The three girls cackle as though this is an in-joke, a joke with her as the punchline. Naomi looks at the third girl.

'What are you waiting for? Do it,' she snaps, and the girl holding her arms pulls her closer, holds her tighter, as though she knows that whatever is happening will make Ellie struggle. And struggle she does. She bucks and writhes wildly, but the older girl is too strong.

'What are you doing?'

'Teaching you a lesson. Do you know what my mum did to me for lying about your little mind-fuck stunt in town? She grounded me for two weeks. I have to miss Tanya's sleepover this weekend. Do it!' she snaps again, and this time the other girl doesn't hesitate. Ellie feels rough hands yank at the waistband of her trousers, the elastic of her knickers pulled roughly aside, and she lets out a squeal as cold liquid splashes against her buttocks, soaks into the crotch of her knickers and spreads down her thighs. The sharp smell of urine fills the corridor, and her eyes burn with tears. The girl releases her and Ellie sinks to the floor, hugging her wet knees with her arms.

Naomi's face is bright with triumph. The other girl deposits the canister that held the urine into a plastic shopping bag and stows it in her school bag.

'Get up,' Naomi commands, and with rising panic Ellie

realises that her punishment is not yet complete. Naomi is not going to let her slink off home in shame.

'Please,' she whimpers. Naomi aims a kick at one of her legs and she winces in pain.

'Get up,' Naomi commands again. When Ellie still doesn't move, the older girl grabs her by both arms, lifts her to her feet and shoves her towards Naomi.

'Ew!' Naomi shrieks and giggles. 'Don't get your pissy knickers on me!' She grabs Ellie's arm and steers her towards the history room. The older girls hold their hands up in farewell as Naomi shoves open the door, linking arms with Ellie and pulling her alongside her into class.

'Sorry we're late, sir,' she says politely as all eyes in the class turn to them. 'We were going to go to the toilet but Ellie didn't want to be even later so she said she could hold it. Oh.' Naomi's eyes widen as she pretends to notice the stain on Ellie's trousers for the first time. 'I guess she couldn't.'

Ellie closes her eyes as the entire class erupts in peals of laughter and excited chatter.

'She's pissed herself!' she hears one of them shriek, and a chorus of 'Ew!', 'Gross!' and 'Oh my God!' echoes around the classroom.

'Oh goodness . . .' When she opens her eyes, Mr Harris is at her side looking flustered. 'Ellie, go and sort yourself out. That's enough!' he hollers at the hysterical class. Naomi has joined her peers and is holding her nose, laughing.

Ellie doesn't stop to be told twice, and turning her back on them all, she runs from the classroom, her heart beating a furious tattoo inside her chest.

20

Imogen

The office is getting dark. As the only one there, it's down to me to move often enough to alert the light sensors to my presence, so the sole light on is the one directly above my desk. I've spent hours poring over the case notes on the tracking system; some of the stories have sucked time from me like a sponge. So many damaged children – probably more that we don't even know about. In my old job I was a child psychologist, dealing with privileged children; my office was a revolving door of posh pampered princesses and overprivileged mummy's boys, followed faithfully by mothers who looked as though they had been ripped from the pages of a Boden catalogue, with their carefully coiffured hair, nautical stripes, gilets and brown leather calf-length boots. I knew what to expect every time I saw the name Portia or Sebastian on the referral form. Until the last time. We'd taken on a certain amount of pro bono work, and the last case was a referral much like the ones I'm looking at now. My one and only chance to really help a child who needed it, and it all went horrifically wrong. Not this time, though.

I glance again at the email containing the list of cases Edward has assigned to me. One of them in particular stands out this time, just as it did the first. The name, the age, they both fit with the little girl who allegedly pushed her school friend into the road on our first day in Gaunt.

Ellie Atkinson. Eleven years old, currently in foster care following the death of her family in a tragic house fire. I remember the look on her foster mother's face. Frightened and unsure. The other mothers I've dealt with in the past have all been defensive of their children, ready to pounce at anyone who dared suggest that precious Tyler or Isabelle might be a precocious little shit. This woman was different, unwilling or unable to pin her colours to the mast.

I open up the case file Emily started months back. The school has done well, calling Place2Be as soon as they knew Ellie would be joining them after the summer. Emily took the girl on three visits to Gaunt High School that seemed to go well, and she met with the family on a couple of occasions, noting that Ellie had settled in to the Jeffersons' as well as could be expected, that Sarah and Mark Jefferson had noted some concerns about how withdrawn and quiet Ellie was and that there had been a couple of angry outbursts following arguments with the other children in their care. Emily put a note on the file to ask Ellie about her relationship with a boy called Billy, although she never noted the outcome.

So how has Ellie Atkinson gone from slightly quiet and withdrawn to being accused of attempted murder in the street? I already know this is the case I will be taking on first. It's as good a case as any to come out of the gate with, right? Nothing to do with what that weird old woman in the chip shop said, or the haunted look on the girl's face, obviously. Could this be the child I make a difference for? Is Ellie Atkinson my redemption?

I click on the interested-parties tab and note down the number of the headmistress, Florence Maxwell. Wow. Twenty years ago, Florence Maxwell was a fresh-faced twenty-something PE teacher, always beaming, as though trying to get thirty sullen teenagers to enjoy rounders was the highlight of her day. Now she is running the school, and I wonder as I pick up the phone to call her if she is still smiling.

21

Ellie

Ellie did not go back into school the day of the incident with Naomi. Instead she ran straight back to the Jeffersons' house, waited until she could see that Sarah was preoccupied in the study – probably ordering more baby junk – and let herself in as silently as possible through the back door. She changed into a fresh pair of trousers, shoving the old ones in a Morrisons bag down the back of her bed. Then, giving herself a quick spray of deodorant, she went back downstairs and let herself in again, noisily this time. When Sarah came to see why she was home so early, Ellie burst into tears – that hadn't been part of the plan; she just couldn't help it. The image of her entire class pointing and laughing was burned into the inside of her eyelids – she saw it every time she closed her eyes.

Mary had heard, of course – although she didn't know what had really happened. As far as everyone at school was concerned, Mary included, Ellie Atkinson was a pants pisser.

'Oh Ellie,' she said when she arrived back home, gathering her into such a warm, motherly hug that Ellie began to cry again. 'It'll all be forgotten in a few days.' But they both knew that wasn't true. Things like this were like crack cocaine to bullies; even the nice kids found pant-wetting hilarious.

Ellie insisted she could never go back there – that she was going to tell Sarah what had happened and she would have to find her a new school, or else she would ask to be moved to new foster carers.

Mary gave her arm a little squeeze. 'Oh El, do you really think social services have nothing better to do than move you around the country until you find a school where you're Little Miss Popular? I'm not trying to be mean,' she said quickly when Ellie's eyes hardened. 'But what if this happens again somewhere else? You'll be in exactly the same position as you are now, only you won't have me. No, what you need to do is go in there, head held high. If anyone says something, you just ignore them – do you hear me? No getting upset, or running away. Say something smart if you can think of it – it's always harder to be smart when you're on the spot – but either way you need to fight back somehow, even if that just means ignoring them and getting through the rest of the term. Kids hate it when they don't get a response; it annoys the hell out of them and they get bored and give up. You have to show them you don't care, Ellie. You have to fight back.'

It is these words – *you have to fight back* – that follow her into school today. It's project day in PHSE, and although Ellie doesn't even know what PHSE stands for – and doesn't care enough to find out – she's made a real effort on her 'Pets At Home' project. An effort that Past Ellie would be positively proud of. When she carries her A2 cardboard sheet up to the front, she smiles as widely as she can manage, doing exactly what Mary has instructed and ignoring the giggles and smirks from her classmates. She's found she can tune out quite effectively the whispered taunts – she has been tuning out real life for some time now.

'I've done . . .' Her voice, although loud and clear in her head, comes out of her mouth as a croak. A few of the other students giggle. Ellie clears her throat, not because there is anything clogging, it but because she's seen adults do it when they are about to give an important speech. 'I've done my project on spiders,' she announces. 'Spiders are not, as many believe, insects; they are arachnids. There are about thirty-eight thousand species of spider; however, scientists believe . . .'

Her teacher, Ms Gilbert, smiles at her, but it's a tight, thin smile, the kind adults think looks patient but actually looks a bit constipated. Ms Gilbert hates Ellie. Ellie doesn't feel this in the way many children fresh from the mothering environment of junior school feel; she knows it to be true. And she hates the teacher in return. Hannah Gilbert is a cheat and a liar.

'That's very interesting, Ellie,' Ms Gilbert says, as though her spider facts are the least interesting thing in the world. 'But spiders aren't really a pet, are they?'

'Yes they are. Lots of people have spiders as pets. A girl at my old school had—'

'But they aren't household pets, are they? Not common household pets?'

A boy at the back, a boy whose name Ellie can't remember, speaks. 'They are, miss. My brother's got a spider as a pet. It's wicked cool.'

Ms Gilbert's cheeks colour.

'Well that might be so, Harry, but the spiders in this project,' she points to Ellie's picture board, 'are the common household type, and you wouldn't keep those as pets, would you? They would just run out of the cage.'

There are a few giggles. Ellie's face flushes red, her neck burning hot. 'Well I've got other pictures . . .'

'Very good, Ellie. Let's move onto the next one. Oh thank

goodness, Emma, parrots, a proper pet. I was beginning to think nobody in the class understood simple instructions.'

Ellie sits down, her heart deflated like a withered balloon. She did her very best on this project. And still it isn't good enough.

She hears Mary speak as clearly as though she is sitting beside her. *You have to fight back.* She remembers that day in town – the day she forced Naomi Harper into the road just by willing her to go away – and she knows that her sister is right. She has to fight back.

22

Imogen

I suck in a breath when I spot Pammy's house – a gorgeous barn conversion so close to the far edge of Gaunt that it barely qualifies as being part of the town. Is this her version of escaping? Or am I the only one who sees Gaunt the way I do?

When the door opens, Pammy stands behind it holding a tea towel and wearing leggings and a baggy T-shirt, still looking glamorous. Her shiny blonde hair looks freshly highlighted and I self-consciously finger my own neglected mousy brown mop, feeling a stab of shame at just how far I have let myself go.

'Immy!' Pammy practically throws herself through the front door and wraps her arms around me in a tight bear hug. 'I wondered when you were finally going to get round to coming to see me. Look at you, you look amazing!'

I step back, overwhelmed by her response. We only saw one another a few months ago, just after my mother passed away. Pammy had travelled to London to sit with me. As the only person who knew the complex relationship I'd had with Mum, her presence meant more than she'd ever know. Of course she thought Mum's death was the reason I looked such a state – she had no idea about my breakdown. Compared to the Imogen she was with then, I suppose this me is a vast improvement.

'No I don't,' I laugh as she steps back to allow me through the door. 'You don't have to pretend to me. That's why I haven't put a photograph on Facebook for years.'

'Well I think you look great, all things considered. How are you?'

'Great, thanks. Look at this place, Pam.' I sidestep the question, knowing she's expecting to talk about Mum, and look around. 'It's lovely. Bet you never thought you'd end up here.'

'Ha! Never thought I'd end up married to Richard Lewis either.' She grins. 'Do you remember how much I used to hate him?'

'No-dick Dick, wasn't it?' I can't help grinning back. Things with Pammy have always been so easy – what's that they say about a friend? Someone who knows everything about you and still likes you. Although Pammy doesn't know everything about me – not any more. One day I'll tell her what happened in London; it'll be good to have someone other than Dan to talk about it with, and I know I'll be relived to get it off my chest. But that's not what today is about. Today I have something else on my mind and I need to tell someone before I lose the plot altogether.

'Come on, I'll get you a glass of vino,' Pammy says, leading me through to a huge, completely white lounge.

Now. Tell her now.

'How's Dan?'

Dan and Pammy have only met a couple of times, and I was relieved that they seemed to get along. I hope that now we can properly rekindle our friendship, a real friendship rather than the long-distance kind where you only seem to talk when one of you is in mortal peril. I don't really know

Richard the adult – I must remember not to call him No-dick to his face – but if he can put up with Pammy, he's certain to be able to get along with Dan and me.

'He's good, like a kid on some kind of adventure. He's such a city person that moving here is like every Enid Blyton book he swears he's never read.'

Pammy swings open the door of a huge silver fridge. It reminds me of our Smeg back in London, ice-maker in the door, and I feel a pang of longing for our stylish money pit. 'I don't think it's hit him yet that we actually live here for good now. I keep catching him trying to set the central heating with his phone.'

Pammy sniggers. 'I'm surprised that place of yours actually has central heating. Are you really going to stay there? It's a bit of a change from the penthouse.'

I give her arm a shove. 'Was not a penthouse. And it wasn't even ours, remember? All that money and nothing to show for it. But yeah, we'll stay at Nana's for a bit, try and smarten it up before we sell.'

Pammy holds out a wine glass in question. I shake my head.

'Not for me. Bit early.'

She shrugs. 'Suit yourself. It's five o clock somewhere.' She pours herself a generous slug. 'Shall I put the kettle on?'

'I'll do it.' I busy myself filling the space-age see-through kettle.

'He still trying to convince you to re-create *The Waltons*?'

'Yup. I ran out of flippant remarks. I've resorted to running the tap loudly in the bathroom while I pop my pill out of the foil.'

Pammy sucks air through her teeth. 'Oh what a tangled web we weave.' She takes a seat at the kitchen island and gestures for me to do the same. 'Don't let him talk to Richard. He'll be telling him tales of loose pants and tepid baths.' She smiles at my raised eyebrow. 'Got to look after the sperm, apparently. They only have one job, but turns out they're a bit like men – have to have the exact right conditions or they do fuck-all.'

I screw up my face sympathetically. 'Still not working for you guys then?'

'Nope.' She grimaces. 'Low sperm count.'

I don't know whether it's sitting here like a teenager with my best friend, or the way she says it, exactly like you'd announce that you've got the flu, but a snort escapes my nose, instantly making my cheeks redden.

'God, Pammy, I'm sorry . . .'

'You can laugh, you bitch.' She grins and tosses a balled-up piece of kitchen roll at me. 'Richard is very sensitive about his diminishing swimmers.'

'Pam, I'm so sorry, I wasn't laughing, I just—'

'Honestly, don't apologise,' Pammy laughs. 'We can't even say the word "sperm" without arguments. It's horrendous. I'm not sure either of us wanted kids that much before we found out we probably weren't going to have them. Now even the subject of other people's children sets off a row.'

I feel a pang of guilt at her words, the knowledge of what is growing inside me burning like a guilty secret. How can I deny Dan a family knowing that people like Pammy and Richard want one so much? I've told myself time and again that I'm thinking of the child – I know first-hand what it's like to feel unloved and unwanted. What if I feel the same way about my child as my mother felt about me? It's hardly ideal to wait and hope for the best.

'Hey.' Pammy leans forward and touches my hand. 'Are you okay? You and Dan, you're okay, aren't you?'

'Yeah, we're fine.' I feel myself begin to well up. Bloody hormones; I've never been this emotional before. 'It's just . . .' I sigh. In light of what my best friend has just told me, this is the last thing I want to be saying, but I have to tell someone. I feel as though the words are swelling up inside me and I'm going to choke on them if I don't spit them out. 'I'm pregnant,' I say.

Pammy lets out a breath. 'Shiiiit,' she says. 'Are you okay?'

Her words are like a trigger opening the floodgates for the tears I've been holding back since I took the test this morning. How could I have been so stupid? I've been taking my pill religiously every night, but I had a sickness bug a few weeks ago and wasn't able to ask Dan to use extra protection for the week afterwards – how would that have looked when we were supposed to be trying for a baby?

'No,' I whisper. 'I don't think I am.'

Pammy envelops me in a hug and I allow myself to sob into her shoulder. When I am hoarse from crying, I sit back and wipe my eyes on my sleeve.

'I'm so sorry,' I say, as Pammy gets up to reboil the kettle. 'After what you've literally just told me about how much you and Richard want kids, and here I am bawling that I got myself knocked up. After all these years, I bet you're wishing I hadn't bothered coming back.'

'Don't be stupid.' She makes my tea and hands it to me. 'It's decaf,' she says, 'two sugars. We've all got our problems. Mine don't make yours any less shit for you. Have you thought about what you're going to do?'

'I only found out this morning; I can't be more than a few weeks. I've been feeling dizzy all the time, being sick for no reason. I put it down to stress at coming back here. We almost had a car accident on the way . . .' I wave away Pammy's concerned look. 'It turned out to be nothing, but when I felt faint, I put it down to shock. Then a few days ago I realised I'd skipped a period. It's taken me this long to work up the courage to take the test.'

Pammy lays a hand over mine and I feel a rush of warmth.

Thank God I have her to talk to. Ever since this morning I've been going crazy pacing the house while Dan tapped away on his laptop upstairs, oblivious to the life-changing event that has just taken place. I'm not sure he even knows what day of the week it is when he's this deep in first-drafting – he sounded so surprised when I called up to tell him I was coming to see Pammy that I'm sure he thought I was at work.

'I'm guessing it's a stupid question, but have you told Dan?'

I laugh. 'You're right, that is a stupid question. If I'd told Dan, you wouldn't be able to see me for all the bubble wrap.' I take a sip of tea and pull a face. 'Seriously, this is what decaf tastes like? You can't even have good tea when you're pregnant? Bloody baby isn't even ten weeks old and I'm making sacrifices.'

'Does that tell you something?'

'No,' I say firmly. 'It tells me nothing. What tells me something is that I have the one piece of news that my husband has been waiting for for over a year – the one thing that would make the love of my life the happiest man on earth – and I would rather stick pins in my eyes than tell him.'

'Surely you can't get rid of the baby? It would break his heart.'

'He would never know,' I reply quietly. 'If I choose not to go ahead with this pregnancy, Dan must never, ever know I was pregnant to start with. It would break his heart and I don't think our marriage would survive.' I feel so awful saying this to her, talking so candidly about aborting a baby when she so desperately wants one. But I have no one else. It sounds so selfish, and I suppose it is.

'And if you lie to him and terminate his baby, could you live with that? Would your marriage survive that kind of secret?'

I sigh. 'I don't know. What if I have a baby I don't want just to please my husband? Can a marriage survive *that*? It just seems like whatever I choose, we're doomed. At least the secrecy route doesn't ruin some poor child's life.'

'This is your problem, Im, this thing you have about not being a perfect mum. No one is a perfect mum. Everyone makes mistakes, loses their patience, says things they don't mean and inadvertently screws up their children. What if everyone suddenly decided that the only way to resolve that was to not have kids? The population would die out in no time at all.'

'Most people don't have the genetic proclivity to damage their offspring,' I argue. 'Most people don't have—'

'Blah blah blah, bad childhood, blah blah blah, negligent mother, blah blah blah, bad genes.' Pammy looks as though she might cry herself. 'The fact is that you are not your mother. You make your own choices, and if you choose to love your child and do the best you can do, then you will be a good enough mum. And that is all anyone can try and be. Not perfect, just good enough.'

'You don't know that,' I snap, and instantly feel bad. But she doesn't know what kind of mum I'd be. What kind of danger I would be. Because the last child I failed ended up dead.

23

Imogen

The school smells exactly the way it did twenty-five years ago, and it throws me the instant I step inside. How can an unidentified smell linger for decades? The old carpets have been changed for colours that match the school's new academy status, the walls are freshly painted, and yet the feelings of fear and inadequacy that the long corridors always threw up in me remain unchanged. Instantly I'm eleven years old again.

I never imagined I would walk back through these doors. The reaction feels physical, like all the air has been sucked from the corridor. More so even than my childhood home, here I feel like I am swimming through treacle.

I pass the pen back to the school secretary, who barely looks up at me before muttering, 'Up the stairs to the left.'

'I know, I used to go to this school.' I offer a smile, but there's no point; the plump silver-haired woman has already turned back to her computer screen behind the pane of glass.

That's new as well, the banking-style security screen that shields the staff from having to get too close to visitors, although it's a change I can well understand. The school environment has changed since I was young; everything is designed for maximum safety should the worst occur. It's a constant reminder that the world we are living in is evolving, for better or for worse.

Taking the stairs two at a time, I swallow back the dread rising in my chest. Don't be ridiculous, I tell myself. You're an adult. A professional. Not some wayward teen being summoned to the head's office.

Not that I ever was a wayward teen; even the idea of it makes me smile. Any time I went up these stairs, it was to talk about the other girls. Girls who shoved me, pulled at my uniform and pretended to catch fleas from walking past me. These stairs don't only lead to the head's office – they also lead to the school nurse.

I face an office door the colour of red wine and take a deep breath, placing a hand against the jamb to steady myself. I can hardly expect Florence Maxwell to have confidence in my abilities if I walk into the office a puce-faced nervous wreck. Counting backwards from ten – a trick the school nurse taught me, as it happens – I feel better by the time I've reached three and give a knock on the door, pushing away the image of my eleven-year-old self doing exactly the same thing.

'Come in.'

The woman behind the desk rises as I enter, leans forward and offers her hand.

'Florence Maxwell. You must be Imogen.'

Florence Maxwell is nothing like her predecessor. Mr Thorne was as prickly as his name suggested, a spindly creature made up of thin lines and sharp edges. My only memory of him smiling was after the rugby team won the finals in my last year. By contrast, Ms Maxwell looks every inch the PE teacher I remember, someone who has accidentally found herself behind the head teacher's desk and is still perplexed as to how. Her sandy blonde hair is cropped short, her cheeks have a slightly pinkish look, as though she's just come back from a run, and she is athletically built. The only thing she's missing is a tracksuit. She is wearing a flowery black and red blouse and plain black trousers that only add to her out-of-place look in this office. She shows no indication that she remembers me.

'Thank you for coming. Drink?' She inclines her head towards a sleek, shiny coffee maker.

'I'd love a coffee, thanks.'

It looks like the door and the large desk are the only things that have stood the test of time. The walls have been repainted in a pastel yellow and blue colour scheme, and there are photographs on every available surface of Florence and people I presume to be other teachers, along with Ofsted certificates declaring the school to be satisfactory. I find this odd; to be proud that it has been basically proclaimed the equivalent of a shrug and 'all right', but maybe satisfactory means something different to Ofsted than it does to me.

She passes me a steaming mug of coffee and takes a seat opposite.

'Now, down to business, I suppose. Oh, wait . . . I had the notes here somewhere.' She opens a drawer and starts to shuffle around inside it, and once again I find myself wondering how she found herself in the position of head teacher. Perhaps I'm being unfair; people in authority don't have to look stern and unyielding to be effective leaders. And the school hasn't burned down yet, so she must be doing something right. I pull out my own notepad.

'Ah, okay, here. Sorry.' She places a thin brown folder on the desk and opens it up. It barely contains a dozen sheets of paper. 'Okay. Ellie has been with us for a few weeks now. Her parents and baby brother died in the fire that destroyed their family home. They never even woke up – not one working smoke alarm in the entire house. If Ellie hadn't got up to use the toilet, she'd be dead too. Firefighters heard her shouting from an upstairs window; she'd managed to get it open and had used the curtain to shield herself from the smoke.'

'Any problems here so far?'

'She's not settling in as well as hoped, but it's early days. It's unfortunate that her former Place2Be contact left in such a hurry; we're hoping that the integration will be smoother with your intervention.'

My face reddens. 'Presumably she had counselling following the death of her parents?'

'Naturally.'

'And is that ongoing?'

Florence scrunches up her face in a disgusted scowl. 'No. Funding means she was allocated six months of sessions, with a further follow-up if needed. The grief counsellor determined that she was dealing with the situation as well as could be expected and I understand the sessions were gradually phased out after eight months.'

'How's her work? Is she performing at the expected age levels?'

'Ms Gilbert will tell you more about that. I've asked her to give us some time today; she's teaching Ellie's class now, as a matter of fact. Perhaps if we make our way down there?'

The headmistress leads me along corridors that look so much smaller now that I'm an adult. The chairs, the doorways – it all seemed so monstrously big back then. Now it just looks like any other school in any other town and I tell myself that it's going to be fine. I can come here and I can be an adult and I can do this.

It's only as we get closer to the classroom that we hear the scream.

24

Ellie

The police came to her foster family's house a week after the unfortunate event to assure Sarah and Mark that no charges would be made against Ellie for what had happened in town with Naomi Harper.

'Well I don't know why he had to come all the way here to say that,' Mary hissed, holding Ellie's hand as they sat at the top of the stairs. 'You didn't do anything wrong. That woman from the car said so herself – she saw everything. That Naomi is a bloody cow to say you made her fall into the road. As if you could do that just by telling her to go away.'

'You saw it too,' Ellie hissed. 'You saw I didn't push her too. You said so.'

Mary cringed. 'Um, well I didn't exactly see what happened.' She looked guiltily at Ellie and put an arm around her shoulder. 'I just said that so that horrible woman would stop shouting at you. Really, it's no wonder Naomi is such a bitch if that's what her mother is like.'

'So how do you know I didn't push her?'

'Are you kidding?' Mary held her at arm's length and

looked straight in her eyes. 'I didn't need to see what happened to know that you wouldn't do that.'

'I bet you're the only one,' Ellie replied.

Ms Gilbert sits down at her desk and looks around for her beloved class planner.

'I'm sure it was here before break time . . .' Ellie hears her mutter, and she yanks open her desk drawer.

A blood-curdling scream issues from the teacher's open mouth. The entire class looks up in alarm, and in seconds it feels like all hell has broken loose in the classroom. Ellie cranes her neck to see what is wrong, and without meaning to, she breaks into a grim smile.

A writhing black mass seems to ooze from the gaping mouth of Ms Gilbert's drawer, and with a gleeful realisation, Ellie sees that the desk is alive with hundreds of black spiders, clambering over one another in their fight to escape the confines of the drawer, fat black bodies and evil spindly legs reaching out towards her.

The classroom is alive with the hysteria of the other children now. Ms Gilbert has frozen as shrieking students climb onto their chairs as though the floor is teeming with mice. Girls cling to one another and boys inch closer to the desk, egging each other on to put their hands into the seething mass of arachnids.

One of the spiders falls to the floor, and as though the sight of it breaking free of the desk has flicked a switch, Ms Gilbert leaps into action

'Quiet!' she shouts, moving around the front of the desk, determinedly ignoring the spiders still scurrying across it. 'For goodness' sake, girls, they aren't poisonous snakes.'

She hesitates for an instant, as though considering the possibility that they *might* be poisonous, then points at the door.

'Line up, we're going to lunch early.'

The children run to the door, all except Ellie. She packs up her things, slowly, fully aware that most of the eyes of the class – including Ms Gilbert's – are on her. She has a sick feeling in the bottom of her stomach. Somehow she already knows that she is getting the blame for this.

'Not you, Ellie. You are coming with me.'

25

Imogen

'There weren't even a hundred spiders,' Florence says, her voice matter-of-fact. 'But I'm sure to the children it seemed like much more.' She rubs a hand across her face and gives a weary sigh. 'Ms Gilbert was quite put out, I'm afraid. She's refusing to teach Ellie any more, which is ridiculous, because there is absolutely no indication that this was Ellie's doing. But Hannah is convinced that because she was less than glowing about Ellie's pets project, she put the spiders in her desk to get back at her.'

'And do *you* think that?' I ask, trying to keep the incredulous look from my face, thinking about what just happened.

By the time we reached Hannah Gilbert's classroom, the screams had subsided and instead we were greeted by a cacophony of excited children's voices as a classroom full of students burst out into the hallway. Hannah spoke in low tones to Florence, who nodded and shepherded me into an empty classroom, leaving me sitting wondering what on earth was going on.

'I'm not sure what to think, if I'm honest. Ellie's been through so much, I wouldn't be surprised if she was acting out.' Her voice rises at the end, making it sound like a question rather than a statement. 'I don't want to believe that any of them could have done this, but it's clear one of them did. Those spiders didn't get into Ms Gilbert's drawer by themselves. And the fact is that Ellie's project was about spiders. Is it just unfortunate timing? Or something more sinister? Where would an eleven-year-old girl even get that many spiders? And how would she put them in there without anyone noticing?' I'm not sure whether she's asking me these questions, or herself. I don't bother trying to answer them.

'What you going to do about it?'

'There's not much I can do, without any evidence. I'm going to speak to the entire class, tell them that what happened today is unacceptable, and if I catch anything like it happening again, the consequences will be very severe. I suppose that's all I can do. I don't think I should get the police involved.' She shakes her head. 'No, let's not make it a bigger deal than it needs to be.' She looks at me and I can see fear in her eyes. Florence Maxwell is scared and I don't know if it's fear of getting it wrong, or of something much worse.

26

Imogen

Ellie's teacher, Hannah Gilbert, is on her feet, pacing back and forth across the empty staff room, when Florence and I walk in. At the sound of the door, she flinches and swings around to face us, her shoulders sagging when she sees who it is.

'Florence, thank God you're here. I didn't know what to do.' Her hand shakes slightly as she rubs it across her face. 'It was horrible, they were everywhere. And I had to hold it together in front of the kids. I don't even know how I managed it, I was terrified. And I . . .' She stifles a sob.

'Please, Hannah, sit down. This is Imogen Reid. She's here from Place2Be.' Florence places a hand on the teacher's arm and guides her gently to one of the sofas. 'Can I get either of you a drink?'

'Coffee, please,' Hannah replies, as I say, 'Water, please,' and sit down on the sofa opposite. We wait in an uncomfortable silence until Florence walks over and places our drinks in front of us. I don't suppose either of us expected our first meeting to be like this.

'What happened?' I ask.

'There were spiders everywhere. In my desk. I put my

97

hand in there, I touched them.' She shudders. 'Ellie Atkinson put them there.'

I start to speak, but Florence beats me to it. 'How do you know it was Ellie?'

Hannah scowls, her pretty face becoming ugly in an instant.

'The class had some homework, a project on pets. Ellie did hers on spiders.' She spits out the word and shivers as though reliving the memory of the eight-legged creatures clambering over one another in her desk drawer.

'Was there a problem with Ellie's project?'

'Household spiders are not pets,' Ms Gilbert says firmly. She looks as though she is ready to argue the point if pushed, and I wonder why she's being so defensive.

I sigh. This woman is an idiot, and I almost hope Ellie Atkinson *did* put the spiders in her desk. It would serve her right for being so bloody inconsiderate. I spent the time on my own in the classroom reading through Ellie's file and I already know something this woman has failed to realise after weeks of being Ellie's teacher.

'Does Ellie have a pet she can talk about, Ms Gilbert?'

Ms Gilbert shrugs. 'It's Hannah. And how would I know? That was the point of the assignment, to get to know the kids' home lives. They usually love it.'

I have to fight every urge I have not to get angry with this petulant woman. 'But you know Ellie's home situation? Presumably you know that she's in foster care, and therefore any family pet is unlikely to be hers? And presumably you could have found out – since it's in this file in front of me, handed to me by Mrs Maxwell less than an hour ago, that Ellie's family pets, both her dog and her hamster, perished in the fire that killed her entire family? So it makes perfect sense, to anyone who bothered to look, of course, that Ellie might not want to choose a conventional family pet to base her homework on, and certainly wouldn't have a plethora of pictures of her own dead animals.'

'Well,' stammers Hannah Gilbert, flustered by the anger I haven't quite managed to hide. 'That doesn't excuse what she did! And how did she know I have a fear of spiders? That girl,' she grits her teeth, 'that girl knows things. She knows things she shouldn't know.'

'Oh come on,' I say, shaking my head. 'Let's say for a moment that it *was* Ellie who put the spiders in your drawer – and you don't seem have any clear evidence to prove it – that doesn't prove that she knew anything about your phobia. The majority of people are scared of or dislike spiders. It's hardly the highest evidence of psychic ability, is it?'

Hannah looks ready to argue again, but Florence interjects.

'Ladies, I don't think this is getting us anywhere.'

'No, you're right,' I agree. I don't want to get into an argument with the teacher on my first day on this case, but sometimes I can't help myself. Dan calls it passion. 'I apologise, Ms Gilbert.'

Hannah Gilbert nods in acceptance. 'Yes, me too. I've had a bit of a shock. Of course I wasn't implying . . .' She trails off, unable to enunciate what it was she wasn't implying. She looks embarrassed now, as though she's let her mouth run away with her and is regretting it already. Despite her anger, I'm glad she's spoken candidly; it's given me an insight into what Ellie is facing in this school. Does Florence Maxwell know about the run-in Ellie had with Naomi and her mother in the town? Does Hannah Gilbert? I know I should mention it – if the police come to the school, my name will be on the report, which they'll discuss with at least the headmistress – but given what's just happened, I don't feel like Ellie will come out of it looking good.

'So where do we go from here?' Florence asks, relieved

that the disagreement isn't going to escalate. 'With regard to Ellie and her care?'

'I'd obviously like to speak to Ellie as planned,' I say. 'But perhaps today isn't the best idea. If she associates me with what's happened today, she might feel like I'm here as some kind of punishment. I'd prefer our first meeting to be under less emotionally testing circumstances, if that doesn't put you to too much trouble?'

Florence shakes her head. 'Of course not, you're probably right. I should call her foster parents, get one of them to collect her, and we'll start again tomorrow.' She looks at me as though for clarification, and I get the sinking feeling once again that the headmistress has no idea how to deal with circumstances like those she's found herself in today. Indeed, if my own time at this very school is anything to go by, then she probably doesn't. Gaunt is a small place, with very few problem children – the bullying I experienced was ignored or swept under the carpet, which is indicative of how the place deals with its problems by and large. I stopped noticing, after a while, how people treated me and my mother when we were in the local shops or down the high street, looking straight through us as though we weren't even there, in the way you ignore a child having a temper tantrum, or a fart in a lift.

'Can I ask something?' Hannah says.

'Of course,' replies Florence, regarding the teacher sympathetically. What kind of relationship do they have? Are they close?

'Well it's like Imogen says, if we send Ellie home now, then won't it seem as though she's been singled out? We have no real proof that it was her – although I still believe it was,' she adds quickly. 'But if we want to make sure she doesn't feel unfairly persecuted, then she shouldn't be treated any differently to the others.'

'Yes, okay, I see your point.' Florence nods quickly. 'I had thought she might feel uncomfortable staying in school, but you're right, Hannah, let's just see how the rest of the afternoon goes, shall we? Now, I'd better go and talk to her, let her go for some lunch and then back to classes.'

Hannah stands quickly as Florence rises.

'Can I go?' she asks. Her face reddens. 'It's just that I was a bit sharp with her before . . . the shock . . . I, I'd like to apologise.'

Florence positively beams. I try not to narrow my eyes and let my suspicion show on my face. Hannah Gilbert was so furious when we walked in, so certain that it was Ellie who was responsible for scaring the wits out of her and making her look foolish in front of her class. Furious enough to practically accuse the girl of bloody witchcraft, for goodness' sake. Now she's going to slink off with her tail between her legs and apologise to the person she still believes responsible?

'That's a fabulous idea, Hannah. I'm sure it will make Ellie feel better to know that there will be no bad feeling between the two of you.'

You're paranoid, Reid. Hannah Gilbert is no more Lady Macbeth than Ellie Atkinson is Sabrina the Teenage Witch. I try for a warm smile to cover my suspicion. Hannah nods in my direction.

'It was nice to meet you, Imogen,' she says. 'I'm just sorry it was under these circumstances. I look forward to working with you.'

'And you,' I lie.

As the door swings closed behind her, Florence Maxwell turns to me.

'I'm sorry about that. Hannah isn't a bad person – she's a good person and a good teacher – but when it comes to Ellie Atkinson, she seems to be a tad blinkered. I'm not sure what else has gone on between them – Hannah has always maintained that Ellie just has a bad attitude. You seem to have got through to her, though. I'm glad.'

I highly doubt that's true, but I don't want to appear disingenuous. Anyway, I'll have a much easier time keeping an eye on Hannah Gilbert as her friend than her enemy.

'Yes, well we can all overreact a little when we've had a shock. It was nice of her to offer to go and speak to Ellie.' I stand. 'I really have to go back to the office – it's my first week and I have an awful lot to get through.'

Florence nods. 'Of course.' She offers me her hand. 'It was lovely to meet you, Imogen. Thank you for coming. Shall I email you to arrange your meeting with Ellie?'

'That would be good, thanks.' I search the other woman's face for any sign that she has recognised the scrawny, grubby girl who once avoided her PE lessons, but it is obvious that Imogen Tandy has been long forgotten by the school – perhaps by the whole town. A stab of sadness takes me by surprise. Am I really upset that a town I hated could have forgotten me? Or is it just sadness that fifteen years of a girl's life could mean so little?

'Oh, just one more thing?' Florence Maxwell speaks as I am halfway through the door. I turn back.

'Did Emily say anything about Ellie before she left? In her handover?' There is a forced casualness in her voice.

'We didn't have a handover,' I reply. 'She was already gone when I arrived. Apparently she was in a bit of a rush to dash off and get married. I have her notes, but to be honest, I didn't get the feeling she'd managed to get very far with Ellie.'

Is that relief that briefly crosses the head's face, or have I imagined it? Either way it's gone by the time she speaks. 'Right, yes, well hopefully you'll get a little further.'

'I'm almost certain I will,' I reply. Only I'm not certain of anything at the moment, and haven't been since the minute we drove into this town.

27

Ellie

The door to the classroom swings open and she looks up, feels her stomach clench when she sees the face of her teacher, Ms Gilbert, approaching. She shoots to her feet, her words tripping out all over the place before she can catch them.

'It wasn't me, okay? I'm telling you . . .'

'Listen, Ellie.' Ms Gilbert advances towards her and perches on the edge of one of the tables. 'I know that you are responsible for what happened today.' Her voice is low and calm, almost as if she's informing Ellie of a change in her timetable or the menu choices for lunch. 'I can't prove it, and therefore no further action is going to be taken. But know this. If you pull a stunt like that again, I will have you thrown out of this school and I will make sure those foster parents of yours send you back to social services.'

Ellie just out her chin. 'I'm telling you now I didn't do it. This wasn't my—'

'Wasn't your fault? It seems like a lot of things happen to you that aren't your fault.' Ms Gilbert lets her last sentence hang in the air and Ellie knows exactly what she means. The fire. 'Only I'm not as blind or as naïve as some of the teachers in this school. Our headmistress might refuse to believe that the string of bad luck that follows you around is anything more than that, bad luck, but I know the truth. Bad things happen to bad people, Ellie, and I want you to know that you don't fool me. I don't know how you pulled that stunt with the spiders, but I do know that I am going to watch you every single day of your time here. And I'm going to make sure that's as short as possible.'

Ellie fixes her dark eyes on Ms Gilbert and throws every ounce of hatred she is feeling at that moment into her words. 'That's fine,' she says. 'You watch. But just be careful, Ms Gilbert, because I have a feeling I'm going to be around here much longer than you are.'

28

Imogen

'How did it go today?'

'God, Dan, it's just horrific how they're treating that girl!' I shudder at the thought of what I saw that day. It's 7 p.m., I've only just walked in and everything aches. I've heard the early stages of pregnancy can be exhausting, but this is ridiculous. Does growing a baby really have to make you burst into tears because the toilet is out of soap? Dan hands me a mug of green tea, and as I look at it, my stomach turns. I'd kill for a glass of wine right now.

'The teacher, Hannah Gilbert, is bloody mental,' I tell him, putting the tea on the counter. 'It's like she has a grudge against this girl, this eleven-year-old girl. I've never seen anything like it.' My face crumples and I fight tears of exhaustion.

'Hey, calm down. Come here.' He folds me into his arms and I bury my head in the warmth of his chest. Without warning, I'm sobbing into his jumper. After a few minutes I pull back and wipe my face on my sleeve.

'And the notes, they're all a mess, just a jumble of papers. This Emily woman was a bloody maverick and a lazy cow. She clearly got by doing the least amount of work humanly possible, then ran off to get married leaving the shit-tip to someone else. Which they are all really weird about, by the way. Who leaves a job to get married? I think she was fired and everyone is too afraid to talk about it. Which is a joke, because they talk about everything else. Constantly. I never realised how hard it would be to work in an open-plan office.' I sigh. 'Have I made a massive mistake?'

Dan shakes his head. 'Of course you haven't. You just have to rebuild your faith in yourself after everything. Do you think you can help this kid, this Ellie?'

'I didn't even get the chance to meet her,' I admit. 'But yeah, I'm going to do my best, of course I will.'

'Then it's not a mistake, is it? Even if this job means you help one kid who wouldn't have got the help before, then it can't be a mistake.'

I think back to my own time at school, how different my life might have been if there had been just one person there to give me the kind of help I can offer Ellie. 'You're right. You're always right.' I smile and reach up to kiss him. 'Thank you.'

'That's what I'm here for. Drink your tea and I'll give you a foot rub. This place was supposed to relax you, not be more stressful than your old job.'

My shoulders sag. 'I know,' I sigh. 'I'm sorry. I'm sure it will be fine once I'm up and running. The position has been vacant a while and no one's done anything from what I can gather.' I hold up my hand as Dan tries to hand me my mug of piss-smelling nettle water. 'Oh please, Dan, I don't want a bloody green tea, for God's sake. I can go back to being a good little baby machine tomorrow.'

Dan looks crestfallen. I immediately regret my harsh tone, but I can't find the words to apologise. I could tell him the real reason I'm so crabby, all the hormones that are causing this foul temper, and he'd be so delighted that he'd forgive my snappiness in a heartbeat, but I just can't bring myself to say it.

Damn it, Imogen, I berate myself as he nods and walks from the room. My head thumps. How is it you can spend so long trying to fix others and you still can't bring yourself to give him what he wants?

29

Ellie

Ellie sits on a bench in the far corner of the playing field and pulls out a notebook. Lunchtimes are excruciating. Worse perhaps than classes, when she can at least convince herself she is in her old school with her old friends, passing notes with the names of boys they fancy covered in hearts and doodles.

She looks out over the field now, watching the boys playing football and the groups of girls giggling and watching the boys. Why doesn't she have any friends? Why can't this be easy for her, like it was before? Before the fire, before . . . everything. Maybe what they're saying, what they whisper when they think she can't hear, is true. Maybe she *is* evil. Can you make something happen just by wanting it? And if that's true, did she want her parents to die? She was mad at them, it was true, but she never imagined a life without them.

The thought that everything is somehow her fault is almost more than she can bear. And if it is true, if she is some kind of evil freak-show, then she will never be able to get close to anyone as long as she lives. Because what if she's already hurt them before she has a chance to make friends? No, it's easier just to stay away from people, not to make friends and definitely not to love anyone for now. Just until all this is sorted out. Probably not forever, she thinks, although she doesn't for the life of her know how long it's going to take – or how she is going to fix herself.

30

Imogen

I peer though the one-way glass panel on the door to the health and social care suite. The young girl sitting on the chair outside is unmistakable as the girl who was accused of pushing her school friend into the road a week earlier. She is smaller than the other eleven-year-old girls I saw around the school, and looks skinnier, although I'm not sure why that would be – she isn't in the care system through neglect, and as far as I can ascertain from the case notes Florence Maxwell sent me, there have been no issues with neglect before or since the fire. Her long dark hair is clean and her nails look trimmed, no visible signs of being unwashed, and yet she just doesn't quite fit.

I open the door and give my most welcoming smile. 'Ellie? You can come in now.'

The girl has the air of someone visiting the dentist, or being forced to do something equally unpleasant. I am used to this; council workers are seen by children as equal to doctors, teachers or police. To be feared until you knew you're not in trouble.

I realise as I get a closer look at her why Ellie seems small – her uniform is at least a size, maybe two, too big. Not quite enough to swamp her, not so you'd even notice straight away, but it gives the subconscious the illusion that she is smaller in stature than her peers. My heart breaks at the thought of someone this young losing everyone and everything she loves – everything that at that age seems a certainty: your family, your house, your clothes. No eleven-year-old expects all those things to be pulled from under them so cruelly.

'Do you want to sit on these sofas? Or would you be more comfortable at the desk?'

Ellie nods towards the desk and I nod back. 'No problem. Take a seat. Can I get you a drink?'

The girl fixes her eyes on her lap and says nothing. I remember the words I heard her speak after the incident in town: *You really shouldn't tell lies. In the olden days, they would have cut your tongue out.* Seeing her again brings back the chill I felt that afternoon. I pour myself a glass of water and return to the desk to sit opposite her.

'Ellie, do you remember me from the other day? From the accident your friend had in the town?'

Ellie nods. 'She's not my friend.'

'How are you feeling about what happened now? Have you been okay since?'

Silence. I decide not to push the issue – we can get back to it in later sessions.

'Do you know why I've asked to chat with you today?'

'The spiders.'

'No, I was asked to see you before any of that happened. You've spoken to counsellors before, haven't you?'

Ellie nods. 'They all just wanted to talk about my feelings.'

'Well I'm hoping you're going to be the one talking eventually.' I smile, try to look encouraging, but she gives nothing back. 'I want you to know that I'm not going to force you to talk about anything you're uncomfortable with. I'm not here to report back to your teachers or carers. These sessions are to provide somewhere safe for you to express how you feel without thinking you're going to get into trouble. This isn't about assigning blame about certain things that have happened. I'm not a teacher. Or a detective,' I add.

The girl stares blankly at me, not giving any indication whether she believes me or not. I plough on, unperturbed.

'Is there anything you'd like to talk about, Ellie?'

When she doesn't speak, doesn't shake her head or nod, I speak even more gently.

'How about we start with school? Do you like school?'

'I used to.' Her voice is low, as though she is testing it out for the first time. I wait a few seconds.

'But you don't now?'

She shrugs. After a long pause, she says, 'They don't like me here.'

'The children?'

'The teachers.'

I sit forward. 'What makes you think they don't like you?'

'Because I'm not like the other idiot children they teach.'

I give a slow nod, trying not to show any shock. The sad thing is she might be right; it is often the most intelligent children who are the most misunderstood.

'Can you think of one teacher that you feel doesn't like you – you don't have to tell me who it is, but I'd like you to think about how they act around you that makes you feel this way.'

'The way she looks at me. Like I'm different. Like . . .' she pauses, 'like she's scared of me.'

I have a good idea of who Ellie is describing. I still recall the fearful look on Hannah Gilbert's face when she spoke of the girl, the idea I had that there was something she didn't want to say.

'Why do you think your teacher would be scared of you?'

'People are always afraid of things they can't understand. That's not my fault – it's theirs.'

'That's quite true, Ellie, it's not your fault and you must remember that. Can you tell me about things at home?' I ask.

Ellie scowls. 'I don't have a home now. Nobody wanted me.'

I was afraid of this. After the fire, social services tried to place Ellie with relatives, but it seemed she had very few in England to choose from, and the ones she did have were less than receptive to having an eleven-year-old girl thrust upon them. Her only living grandmother, her father's mother, lives in France and travels regularly – no life for a young girl who needed stability, she said – and her uncle lives in New Zealand with a family of his own; he's never even met his niece and didn't travel back for his sister's funeral. Her parents had many acquaintances but few close friends, and none in a position to take on a child. Her mother's sister has three kids of her own and was reluctant to take care of another that she hardly knew. It's surprising how often children find themselves in care because everyone around them thinks someone else should take responsibility.

'Now I know that isn't the case,' I tell her. 'These things are a lot more complicated than you or I could understand.' I lean forward conspiratorially. 'I'm not even sure the people who make the rules understand them half of the time.'

'I don't think you have any idea what I understand.'

I force another smile, trying to remember how abandoned Ellie must have felt when no one around her stepped forward to take her in. How alone. No wonder she is feeling hostile. 'How are things where you live at the moment? How do your foster carers treat you?'

'They treat me as you would treat a poisonous snake,' she replies. Her dark eyes are fixed on me and I shift uncomfortably under her intense gaze. 'Like they are interested in me but they don't want to get too close. Like Ms Gilbert, but with less of the meanness.'

I think about how Ellie's foster mother didn't rush to defend her that day in town. What was it she said? *What did you do to Naomi?* She couldn't defend her because she believed that Ellie had pushed Naomi. That would explain the relief on her face when I swore to the police officer that I had seen the girls standing feet apart moments before the accident. And the older girl backed me up . . .

'Who was the other girl with you when I saw you on Saturday? Was that . . .' I glance briefly at her notes, 'Mary?'

Ellie nods.

'And how do you get on with Mary?'

'She's the only person who doesn't treat me like an idiot.' Ellie shrugs. 'And she hates Billy as much as I do.'

'Billy?'

Ellie scowls. 'He lives with us too but he's not Mary's real brother, he's like me. His mum is a complete waste of space and nobody wants him either. I'm not surprised, though, because he's horrible.' She stops suddenly, as though she's realised she's said something she shouldn't.

'It's okay.' I smile. 'You don't have to look so worried. Like I said, you can say what you like to me and I won't tell anyone. I'm not allowed to – I'd get into real trouble.'

'You people always say things like that, but I know you'd have to tell someone if I told you I'd done something bad.'

'Okay, here's the deal with bad stuff. I'm a bit like a priest. Have you ever met a priest?'

'I'm not allowed into church,' Ellie replies. 'In case I burst into flames.'

I can't stop the gasp. Then I see the glint in Ellie's eyes and my mouth drops.

'Ellie Atkinson, was that a joke?'

She shrugs, but I see a shadow of a smirk. She really is quite pretty when she isn't being so intense.

'Well I'm a bit like a priest, only younger and more attractive . . .'

'And not as bald,' Ellie says. I laugh.

'Yes, definitely not as bald. And like with a priest, you can tell me about bad stuff without getting in any trouble. Though if it's really bad, if I think you might have hurt someone or you might hurt someone in the future, I would have to tell my boss. Because there are some things that are too important to keep to yourself, aren't there?'

Ellie says nothing. She seems to be thinking carefully about what I've said, running it through her mind as though it is a contract she might want to sign.

'So for example,' I continue, 'if you were to tell me you had put those spiders in Ms Gilbert's desk—'

'Which I didn't,' Ellie replies indignantly.

'It's just an example.' I put my hands up. 'Okay, how about . . . if you told me you'd put itching powder in Ms Gilbert's pants . . .'

Ellie rolls her eyes.

'Or slugs in Mr Harris's wellingtons . . .'

'He'd probably like that. What if I swapped all the sugar in the staff room for salt?'

I screw up my nose. 'Well I would definitely need you to tell me that – I use the sugar in my tea! If you told me that thing about Ms Gilbert's pants, though, I'm not sure I could promise not to laugh, but I promise I wouldn't tell anyone. On the other hand, if you told me you'd dug a pit in her garden and covered it in leaves . . .'

'You would have to tell the police,' Ellie finishes.

I nod. 'Or at the very least Ms Gilbert and her cat.'

'Okay.' Ellie nods back. 'I'll think about it.'

'That's all I want, for you to think about it.' I smile. 'Can

I just ask you one more question before you go back to class?'

Ellie looks suspicious again, gives a small shrug.

'Well you said that Mary is kind to you, right?'

Another nod.

'I was just wondering, can you speak to Mary about things that happen at school? Maybe if you need someone to talk to before you see me again, you could talk to her?'

'I could,' she concedes. 'But what's the point?'

'Sometimes it's just nice to have someone to tell things to, even if nothing changes straight away. It sounds unbelievable, but just saying how you feel to someone can make you feel better.'

'I know what would make me feel better,' Ellie replies, as though the answer has been there all along. 'If every single one of them was punished.'

31

Imogen

I pull up in front of the terraced house and cut the engine.
I sit for a moment in the car, looking at the unruly front
garden, where a plastic toy that has faded to white lies abandoned underneath a white UPVC windowsill. I take a couple
of deep breaths and try to picture the people I'm going to
find behind those walls. Then, steeling myself, I get out of
the car, stride up the short path to the front door and rap
sharply.

After a few minutes, when nothing happens, I try again,
then again. Eventually the door swings open, and the teenage
girl I first met that day on the high street is standing there.
She smiles when she sees me; has she recognised me as the
woman who stuck up for Ellie that day? I'm glad now that
I spoke out, even if Dan is always telling me I should hold
my tongue more often.

'Hi, are you Mary? My name's Imogen, I'm here to see
your mother.'

The girl nods and opens the door wider. 'Yeah, sure, Mum's
inside. She would have come to the door herself, but . . .
well, never mind, come in.'

She turns to lead the way through the hall and into the

kitchen, where Sarah Jefferson is frantically wiping the surfaces down. She turns when I enter, looking flushed and harassed.

'Good morning.' She wipes her hand on the front of her jeans and shakes the one I hold out to her. 'Sorry about that, we had a bit of an incident.'

From the acrid smell of burnt plastic and electrics it seems like more than just a bit of an incident to me, but I'm not here to judge. I've never had to look after one child, let alone three – two of whom are bound to be challenging – so for all I know, incidents like this are commonplace in any family. Sarah must have noticed my frown, as she immediately offers 'Blown fuse,' with a wan smile.

'I'm Imogen Reid,' I say weakly. Poor woman looks like the last thing she wants is a council worker in her house.

'Sarah Jefferson.' She gestures to the small dining table in the corner. 'Please, sit down. Would you like a drink?'

'Coffee would be lovely – actually, do you have any decaf?'

From the look on Sarah's face, I may as well have asked for a litre of cider. 'No, I don't think we have, sorry. I can send Mary to get some?'

I shake my head quickly. 'No, really, tea would be fine if you have it.'

The kettle is already boiled and I get the impression that Sarah was completely prepared for the visit before whatever happened in the moments leading up to my arrival. As she sets about making two mugs of tea, I watch her, taking in her smart but casual appearance, her clean nails and tidy pinned-back hair. Aside for the recent stains on the wall, the kitchen is clean and neat, everything completely respectable. It looks like a normal family home, the kind Pammy grew up in and a million miles from the one I myself was raised in.

'We've met before,' I say as Sarah carries the teas to the

table. 'In the town, do you remember? My husband narrowly avoided hitting one of Ellie's school friends with our car.'

Recognition dawns on Sarah's face and her cheeks colour.

'Of course, I'm sorry, I didn't recognise you straight away, though I thought you looked familiar. That day was a bit . . .' She trails off, searching for the word.

'Intense?' I suggest. 'Yes, it was rather. I felt awful about what happened.'

'Well it wasn't your fault.' Sarah scowls. 'That woman . . .'

'Naomi Harper's mother?'

'Yes, well, she made rather a big deal out of nothing, I think. The police even came round to say they'd spoken to Naomi again and she'd been quite clear about the fact that she'd lost her footing on the kerb. Messing around, I bet; you know what kids are like. And Madeline reacted quite terribly, I thought.' She looks embarrassed, like she doesn't want to sound uncaring. 'I mean of course she was upset; if your husband hadn't reacted so quickly, God knows what could have happened. Anyone would be the same, I suppose.'

Not everyone would have accused an eleven-year-old girl of attempted murder, I think, but I just nod. 'It was an emotive situation. Was Ellie okay afterwards?'

Sarah hesitates. 'She was quiet, she barely spoke about it. She's like that, you see, she bottles things up until . . . Well, she doesn't talk about her feelings.'

'Until what?' I press. 'You said she bottles things up until . . .'

Sarah shakes her head. 'It's nothing. She has these little outbursts, but we expect that, given what she's been through.'

'Is she ever violent?'

'No,' Sarah answers quickly. Too quickly, I think. 'I've never seen her do anything violent.'

I note the careful choice of words but don't comment. 'You know why I'm here, Mrs Jefferson? The school thought

Ellie would benefit from talking to someone, a professional. There have been some incidents . . .'

'Please, call me Sarah. And I take it you're referring to that thing with the spiders?' She scoffs. 'Ridiculous to say that was Ellie. I mean, where would she get that many spiders from? It's not like you can just walk into a pet shop and buy a few hundred house spiders. Or do they think she summoned them like the Pied Piper? Perhaps that teacher thinks she's the spider whisperer now as well.'

'As well as what?'

Sarah looks wrong-footed. 'Well, it's that teacher they need to have a word with, Hannah Gilbert. Trying to make everyone think Ellie is some kind of delinquent. Telling everyone in town that she's strange and that she makes up stories. Ellie has never even said anything about her – God knows what she's done to get under her skin. She's been through so much already, it's hardly fair to make her out to be a problem child in her first few weeks.'

'How does she get on with the other two children here? Mary and Billy, isn't it?' I remember how Ellie had described Billy in our first meeting. *He's horrible* . . .

'Fine,' Sarah answers, then, catching the sceptical look that must be on my face, she qualifies her answer. 'I mean, they bicker, but what children don't? There's always a bit of that with these kids, vying for attention and all that.'

'Have you had many foster children in the past?'

'Oh yes,' Sarah peacocks. 'We've looked after about twenty children in the last five years. Some stay longer than others, but we think of them all as our own while they're here. Some have been much more troubled than Ellie,' she confides. 'Which is why I was a bit surprised when the school called in Place2Be for her. We've dealt with a few anger issues in children before.'

'It's not just the anger issues that we're here to deal with,'

I say. 'Obviously Ellie's situation is slightly different from children who have been removed from their parents' care. It's my personal opinion from speaking to her teachers and Ellie herself that she didn't receive adequate grief counselling after the death of her family. That's not your fault,' I add quickly at the crestfallen look on Sarah's face. 'She should have been receiving the extra counselling way before she even came to you. I've checked her files and she seems just to have slipped through the net somehow.'

I don't add that it happens more than anyone could imagine. With the NHS stretched so thin there are more holes than ever before, it is easy for a quiet young girl with no history of abuse or behavioural issues to fall through one of them.

'My first recommendation will be that Ellie gets some more one-on-one counselling from a qualified grief counsellor.'

'Can't you give her that?'

'Well technically I'm qualified to offer counselling; however, it's not in my current job description. I used to work as a private child psychologist,' I add, cringing at how important it is to me that this woman knows my full credentials. Notice that you didn't tell her why you're not doing that any more. 'I'm just here to make recommendations and referrals.' It sounds pathetic even to my ears. It is sickening to realise how much I want to be able to help this family. I don't want to write Ellie's name on a list for further counselling only to have it continually passed over in favour of other children who are deemed to have been through worse, or are posing a threat. 'I'll make sure she gets the help she needs,' I add weakly. 'I promise.'

'But Ellie told us she'd already spoken to you, that you promised to speak to her again. I think she liked you, although she doesn't give much away.' For someone who believes that Ellie is no danger, for someone who has seen much worse,

Sarah Jefferson sounds awfully keen that the girl receives immediate help. My heart sinks as I remember how I promised I would speak to Ellie again. I'm so used to taking cases on a long-term basis rather than my new conveyor-belt-style role that I barely registered myself making the promise.

You knew exactly what you were doing, a sly little voice in my head tells me. There is something about that girl that made you want to help her, and you made that promise on purpose.

'Well I can certainly have another chat to her if you'd like,' I find myself saying now. 'As part of my current job, I mean.' I've already got enough information to give the referral she needs; there's no reason for me to speak to Ellie again. But I also know that no one at the office will raise an eyebrow if I put another meeting in the diary with her case reference on it – no one keeps watch over how many sessions it takes to close a case, or asks for minutes or even notes on these sessions. 'But I can't take her case on the way I would have done in my old job.' Which I fucked up beyond all recognition, I remind myself. In truth I'm not sure I'm going to be able to stand seeing this side of life, these nice normal people who need the extra help more than anyone and will probably never receive it because their bank balance is a few zeros short of being able to pay for it and their case file a few arsons short of being a priority. On the other hand, we can't afford to move away and rent again; that's the reason we're here. I have to make this work.

'That would be great.' Sarah's voice pulls me back to the kitchen table. 'If you wouldn't mind? Between you and me,' she looks around as though she is checking for some kind of recording device, 'I feel as though I've failed her a bit. I had such high hopes when we heard we were getting another little girl, a sister for Mary. It's what we always wanted – well, it's what we had, actually.'

She reaches over to the fridge behind her and pulls off a photograph, passes it to me. The picture is of a baby, just a few days old by the looks of it, swaddled in a pink blanket.

'That's Mia,' she says, pointing unnecessarily at the picture. 'She was our second baby. She was born when Mary was three. We lost her a few days after that photograph was taken. She got an infection that her little body couldn't fight.'

'I'm so sorry.' I hand the photo back as quickly as I can without looking rude or uncaring. Another family that has lost what I'm considering throwing away. Say it how it is. Aborting. My hand goes automatically to my stomach, and when I realise, I snatch it away, hoping she hasn't noticed.

'She would have been about the same age as Ellie now,' Sarah says, a wistful tone creeping into her voice. 'So maybe you can see why I was hoping that Ellie would begin to feel like another daughter to me. But right from the start she was so cold, so aloof.'

'She has been through an awful lot,' I murmur.

'Of course. It's not like I expected it to happen right away,' Sarah acquiesces. 'I just thought that eventually . . .' She sighs, lifts her mug to drink the dregs of her tea. 'She's just nothing like I ever imagined Mia would be. She's so quiet, so strange at times. I'll find myself wishing I could hear what she's thinking, and then the look on her face will change and I'll be glad I can't.'

'How do you mean?'

Sarah leans forward. 'I mean that she scares me. Sometimes,' she qualifies quickly. 'Only sometimes. We've had a lot of children here,' she repeats, 'and some of them have been damaged, in here, you know?' She taps her head. 'And some of them have been violent, and like Billy, some of them can be a bit sly. It's the way they've been raised, or haven't been raised with most of 'em. Left to fend for themselves, rely on themselves or older siblings for food or to get them to school. They come here and they're not sure what to do in a normal house with normal parents. But Ellie, she's different. It's as though she knows exactly how to be on the outside, but on the inside, there's nothing. Like she's hollow. And the things she comes out with – she sounds older than me sometimes.'

I nod encouragingly, but to my horror, I feel my mouth water and nausea rise in my throat. Oh God, please don't let me be sick here.

'And she has the most horrific nightmares,' Sarah continues, oblivious to my discomfort. 'She screams and screams, and even when we wake her up, she's still screaming, as though she can still see whatever she was seeing in her nightmares. And then after those nightmares, that's when it happens.'

'What happens?' I swallow, desperately trying to keep back the overwhelming feeling that I'm going to throw up. This was what I came to hear after all; not the party line that I'm sure was trotted out to my predecessor, but the crux of what is actually going on in this house, at the school.

'Just bad things. It's something different every time: a dead bird in the back porch, something electrical blows up. My hairdryer, the blender . . .' She gestures at the blender on the counter. 'Last week Billy went to the cupboard to get me a saucepan, and when he pulled it out, it was full of earthworms. Worms!' She lowers her voice and leans closer to me. 'I mean, how the hell does a saucepan get full of worms, for God's sake? They don't just crawl into the house and make themselves at home in your cupboards, do they?'

'What makes you think Ellie was involved? I mean, if it was Billy who found the . . . them . . .' I try not to picture a pan full of slimy, pulsating worms wrapping themselves around one another. 'Sorry, I'm . . . I . . . Do you think I could use the bathroom, please?'

'Top of the stairs.' Sarah looks surprised at this sudden interruption, but I don't have a chance to explain as I push my chair backwards and flee from the room.

32

Imogen

I sit back on my heels and wipe my mouth on my sleeve. Pushing my fringe from my eyes, I squeeze them shut to stop the tears from forming. This is a nightmare. Not only have I always hated being sick, but now it's making me look unprofessional, and probably damaging my chances of ever finding out more about what's going on with Ellie. It took Sarah long enough to start blaming every little thing that went wrong in the house on the eleven-year-old girl – longer than it took Hannah Gilbert, who was very forthcoming with her wild theories – but eventually off she went. I can see quite clearly what the problem is, and it isn't Ellie Atkinson.

Standing up and checking myself in the mirror, I try to work out my next move as quickly as possible. I have to keep this woman on side if I'm going to be allowed further access to Ellie, which means humouring her a bit, trying not to look incredulous when she suggests that Ellie's bad dreams are making her blender blow up. I smile at the thought of it, but it's not funny, not really. It's little things like this – people putting two and two together and making five – that lead to long-term harm, sometimes even abuse. They've obviously decided to blame Ellie for everything that's gone wrong in the house, overlooking the fact that two other children live here, both of them equally capable of blowing up blenders with their minds – although I'd put money on Billy for the earthworm stunt; kids usually want to be around to see the fruits of their hard work.

Pushing open the bathroom door, I glance into the room next to it, hoping to see Ellie. Instead I see the girl who answered the door – Mary – sitting at a desk covered in funky stationery, writing on some cute apple-shaped sticky notes.

'Hi,' I say, glancing down the stairs to check that Sarah isn't coming to find me. 'Mind if I come in?'

Mary looks up, shakes her head. 'Are you here because of Ellie?'

I nod. 'Yeah, your teachers think she's struggling a bit to adjust. You seem to know her pretty well, what do you think?'

Mary looks momentarily shocked that someone has bothered to ask her opinion, then scowls. 'I think that if they would give her a break and stop blaming her for everything that goes wrong in the world, maybe she'd actually talk to them a bit more.'

I'm saddened, but not surprised, that the most mature insight into the situation has come from a fifteen-year-old.

'So you don't think Ellie is to blame for the things that have happened? The spiders in her teacher's desk? The blender blowing up? The worms?'

Mary snorts. 'If Ellie wanted to get back at Gilbert for ragging on her project, do you think she would have been stupid enough to choose the very thing her project was about? She's only young, but she's smarter than that. And we all know it was Billy who did the worms, but me and Ellie are too nice to tell on him. We saw him covered in mud the day before he "found" them in the pan.'

'And the blender?'

Mary looks at me pityingly. 'Don't tell me you think Ellie has the power to blow up electrical equipment with her mind too? Okay, so we've had a few fuses go, but believe me, it is not because my foster sister had a bad dream. It's a bit pathetic really, all the whispering and the frightened looks people give her in the street round here. They're supposed to be grown-ups. And now I see my mum's joined in – telling you every single problem we've had with the electrics in the last year. She should be on the phone to the council, not the social workers.'

I smile and touch her on the arm. 'Thank you for your time. You're a very good friend to Ellie, I can see that. She's lucky to have someone like you on her side.'

I turn to walk out of the room and Mary speaks again. 'And you?' she asks in a small voice. 'Are you on her side? You won't just abandon her, will you?'

I turn back and look at her. Her eyes are silently pleading – here is a girl who has seen far too many social workers, far too many government officials come and go, leave without a backwards glance.

'No,' I say, already hoping I won't live to regret my words. 'I'm not going anywhere.'

33

Ellie

Ellie runs as fast as she can down the corridor, arms pumping and her school bag slapping uncomfortably against her side. She can still hear them. The laughter and the taunts . . . and then the screams.

She still isn't entirely sure what happened. One minute Tom Harris was teasing her about her scuffed shoes and her second-hand bag; the next, he was on the floor, writhing in agony. The huge canvas mural was propped up in the corridor ready to be put back up on the freshly painted wall; then, as her anger sizzled and bubbled, scorching her insides, it fell on top of him. Can it have been her? She can still hear his voice now, teasing, goading. And when he asked her if she'd been a gyppo before her mum and dad died, that was when she really lost it. She started screaming and screaming, the wailing noise like a siren echoing off every wall in the corridor, and then she realised it wasn't the echoes of her screams she could hear – everyone else was screaming too.

When she opened her eyes and saw what she had done, she bolted from the corridor and just kept running. Now she slams into the glass doors at the end of the corridor and out into the fresh air, leans over with her hands on her knees and gulps in big deep breaths. This is it, now she's done for.

She has no idea how long she's been sitting huddled on the cold, wet grass underneath the tree. Once she stopped running and calmed down, she realised with sickening clarity that she had nowhere to go and ended up in the patch of land reserved for the infants' school to collect bugs and do tree rubbings. The area is overgrown and unruly – it is the only place in the school Ellie feels calm, even though they aren't strictly allowed in there. She assumes that is the least of her worries today.

It is Miss Maxwell who finally finds her, freezing cold and shivering, silent tears cutting like ice down her cheeks. She can't have been gone long, but it feels like an eternity on her own. The head teacher kneels down beside her in the wet grass, puts a hand on her shoulder and says gently, 'It's time to come back to school, Ellie.'

She shakes her head furiously. She isn't going back there. Not ever. 'They hate me,' she says. 'Everyone hates me.' *And I want to hurt them all.*

Miss Maxwell shakes her head. 'No one hates you, Ellie.' She is speaking slowly, quietly, as though to a very small child. 'We just want to help you.'

'I didn't hurt Tom,' Ellie says, realising as she says it that she doesn't know that this is strictly true. 'At least I don't think I did. I didn't mean to if I did.' She knows she is making herself sound even guiltier. What kind of nutcase doesn't know if they have pushed a wooden-framed canvas on top of someone? 'Is he okay?'

'Let's talk about this inside,' Miss Maxwell urges. 'Come on, Ellie, please; it's cold out here. You won't have to see anyone, I promise, we will go straight to my office and talk in there.'

Ellie shakes her head again, more firmly this time. 'I don't want to talk to you. I don't want to talk to any of you. I know what you all think of me. I want to talk to Imogen.'

Miss Maxwell looks almost relieved. 'If that's what you want, I'll call her right away, if you just come inside. You've only got a T-shirt on and you'll freeze to death out here.'

A frozen child to go with her burned parents, Ellie thinks. Ice and fire. Maybe that's how it's supposed to be. Maybe her heart is frozen permanently now and she's supposed to lie here on the grass until her dead parents come to get her.

But then the school bell rings and Miss Maxwell stands up.

'Come on, Ellie, time to go inside. We'll go through the back of the staff room – you don't want the other children to see you out here on the grass, do you?'

Ellie's heart plummets and she gets to her feet. Not today, Mum. I know I'll be with you soon, but not today.

34

Imogen

'It's a bit of a mess, I'm afraid.' Florence Maxwell paces up and down her study, biting the inside of her cheek and every now and then shaking her head. She looks paler than the last time I saw her, and if possible, more harassed. 'Tom Harris's parents have gone straight to A and E just to be sure, and Ellie's foster carer is on her way here. I really appreciate you getting here so quickly. She only wants to talk to you.'

'It's nothing,' I reply, wondering whether it really is nothing. When Florence called the office, I barely took the time to lock my computer before grabbing my handbag and rushing out. I'm almost certain that Edward would be fine with me leaving the place unattended to come here – Florence made it sound like an emergency, after all. 'What happened?'

'It's hard to tell; the children are in shock and none of them seem to agree. All we have established is that Tom was teasing Ellie; he was being pretty mean by the sounds of things, although no one has told me exactly what he was saying. Then Ellie got mad and the mural fell on Tom. You know what kids are like; some are swearing blind she pushed it, others are saying it fell by itself. They can't even agree on where she was standing. Even the ones who are convinced she pushed it remember her being on the other side of the corridor. Either way it's a nightmare for the school – that mural should never have been left propped against the wall where it had the potential to fall on a child.'

'Can't be a dream for the boy, either,' I mutter, and Florence has the good grace to look embarrassed.

'No, of course.'

A thought occurs to me. 'I hope you didn't call me here to try and get a confession out of Ellie. You know that's not my job.'

Florence looks as though it has crossed her mind but she has already resigned herself to me having that exact reaction. 'Yes, I understand that. With a complete lack of any evidence that this is malicious, I've decided to treat it as an accident – provided that speaking to Tom and his parents doesn't provide any enlightenment.' She sighs. 'Really I just want to make sure Ellie is okay – although right now, I'm unsure as to whether I should be more worried about her or about everyone around her.'

35

Imogen

'I didn't do it,' is the first thing Ellie says when I walk into the health and social care suite. She was on her feet as soon as I entered the room and is now standing with her arms crossed defiantly across her chest. Still, even with her tough-girl stance, she looks so tiny that I want to give her a massive hug. I know what it is like to go days, weeks, months even without something as simple as a grown-up's embrace; hugs are one of those things that regular kids from regular families take for granted. *The rules are there for a reason, Imogen*, that voice in my head warns me. Then, against any better judgement I might have – and I don't think that's a lot right now – I cross the room and wrap my arms around Ellie's shoulders, pulling her so close and holding her so tightly that I can feel the little girl's body tremble.

'I know you didn't.' I break the hug and hold her at arm's length. 'This wasn't your fault. That painting should never have been where it was. It was an accident, that's all. An accident.'

'You don't know that.'

'If you say you didn't that's enough for me. Honestly Ellie, what can I do to make you believe that I trust you?'

'I just don't know why, that's all.' Her chin juts out and she reminds me of someone. She reminds me of me. 'Why would you trust me? No one else does. Maybe they're right and you're wrong. Maybe you shouldn't trust me either.'

She's just being pedantic, testing me to see how far my loyalty to her goes, and I *know* that but still her words sound more like a threat than a childish strop and they send shivers up my arms.

'Well that's a risk I'm going to have to take,' I say slowly, watching her face. She gives no sign of what she's thinking, staring straight back at me so unflinchingly that I am the one to break and look away first. I turn to walk towards the desk, perch myself on the edge. Ellie turns to study the spines of the books on the shelf behind her. When she speaks her voice is casual and I almost don't catch what she is saying.

'You shouldn't be taking risks in your condition.'

If it's possible for a heart to skip a beat, mine does. 'What did you say?'

Ellie turns and looks at me, her face full of an innocence that I can't tell if it's real or fake. 'I said you shouldn't take risks in your position.'

I nod, feeling foolish at my overreaction. Of course I'd misheard, there was no way she said 'condition'. Because that would mean she knows about the baby. And that would be impossible.

36

Ellie

Ellie watches the moth's wings batter furiously against the inside of the glass and wonders if it will die soon. At eleven years old, she has experienced more death than anyone she knows, but she isn't afraid of it. No, her parents are dead and they aren't suffering now, are they? They are either in heaven, together with her brother, or they are nothing, dust, ash. Even nothing has to be preferable to the life she's living now. Anger surges up inside her. She feels like the moth, beating its wings against the glass. And everyone outside the glass is just watching, interested to see what she will do next. When she doesn't even know herself.

She lifts the glass slightly, just enough to let some air in, just enough to let the moth breathe a little. She isn't ready to let go of the only thing that can't leave her, but she knows that sooner or later she is going to have to let it fly free. It isn't going to be easy to watch the moth flutter happily through the window when she remains stuck here in this life, but she isn't sure she can leave it to suffocate. After all, she's never killed anyone, anything. Not yet, anyway.

She thinks back to dinner that evening, when Billy the Mean spent the entire time poking her with his fork and hoping she'd retaliate, get into trouble. He never seems satisfied unless someone is in trouble; he doesn't even seem to care if it's himself. He was a mild irritation this evening, like when Riley used to cry because he was tired instead of just going to sleep, but when she refused to rise to his stupid immature behaviour, he upped his game. At first he just hissed things at her about having no family, no friends, nothing worse than the kids at school said, and Mary shoved his arm and gave him a warning look. At least someone realises what he's like. Sarah thinks the sun shines out of his backside

Then, when dinner was almost over without event, Billy turned to Sarah and said, as sweetly as could be, 'Would you like me to load the dishwasher?'

She beamed as though he'd offered to clean the whole house for a week.

'Thanks, Billy, if only the girls were that helpful!' She laughed as though she was joking, and Mary turned to Ellie and rolled her eyes. Ellie grinned, pleased to be in on the joke, pleased to feel like an insider in the family, until Billy walked past her and hissed, 'Better not let Ellie do it. If she's as stupid as her mother, we'll all be dead by morning.'

The anger burst through her so hard it nearly knocked her off her feet. Anger like she'd never known it was possible to feel, anger she had never felt in her entire life. Before she'd even thought about what she was doing, like her body belonged to someone else entirely, she launched herself at the boy, wrapping her fingers around his throat and shoving him so violently against the dinner table that the whole thing shook. It didn't matter that she was two years younger than him, or half his weight soaking wet; in that moment alone she had the strength of a fully grown man. Billy's eyes widened in fear as he seemed to realise that he had gone too far.

'You want to shut your filthy little mouth,' Ellie hissed, her mouth so close to his face that a small glob of spittle landed on his cheek. Her voice didn't even sound like her own and she felt as though this new Ellie, this other Ellie, could crush his windpipe just by thinking about it. 'Before someone shuts it permanently.'

The entire table, just seconds ago stunned into silence, now burst into life. Mary was shouting, 'Ellie, stop!' while Sarah screamed at her to let Billy go and Mark flew to her side, pulling her fingers from around the boy's neck. Billy slumped to the floor, gasping, and in an instant Sarah was at his side, holding his head close to her chest as though he were a baby. Ellie blinked and looked at the scene in front of her in shock. What had happened? Where had that come from? She looked down at her hands, which seconds ago had been so strong and were now shaking furiously.

'You get to your room, young lady!' Sarah screamed, rounding on her. 'And don't come out until morning!'

Ellie fled the room without a backwards glance, shoving past Mary, who was standing in the doorway, fear and shock etched on her face.

37

Billy opens his eyes and for a second wonders what it was that startled him awake. Was it the sound of his door closing? Probably just Mrs Jefferson come to wish him goodnight, give him one last kiss before bed. She always does that; it's a bit weird, he thinks, and he's not entirely sure he likes it. His own mum never did anything like that, just left him to put himself to bed after he'd made tea for him and his brothers. It feels strange to have these people around him who don't expect him to do everything for himself. It's almost like it's too good to be true, and he knows that it won't last; it never does. He'll be moved on before long, when these people get fed up of him.

He just can't ever seem to get it right, to fit in the way the other kids seem to be able to. He's never been taught to be in a normal family. He longs for things to be like the old days, when he and his brothers would tease each other and play-fight. They'd be mean and nasty to each other some-times, but they loved each other really, and they all knew that if they ever needed one other, they would be there. The strange people he has been put with are nice; they give him everything he needs – he has hot food, a nice warm bed and he never has to lie on smelly sheets or sleep on the floor if he's forgotten to put the bins out. So why does he miss his mum so much? If this is the perfect life, why does he want to go home? And go home he will. If he is horrid enough, they will decide no one wants him and that he'll be better off back with his real family. His mum might be useless, but she is familiar and safe. He never felt like he didn't belong when he was at home.

What time is it? His lips feel dry, like when he has a cold, and he puts out his tongue to lick them. Only his tongue won't run over his lips, won't come out of his mouth at all. It's like when you've been sleeping all night and you have so much sleep in your eyes that the next day they won't open properly. Only it's his lips that won't open. He pulls at them with his fingers, wincing in pain and panicking as tiny bits of skin begin to peel away. He tries to scream, to shout for help, but without being able to open his mouth, no real sound comes out. Hot, panicked tears sting at his eyes, and he flings himself out of bed, races towards his bedroom door and onto the landing.

The house beyond is silent. Just the dull echo of voices coming from the TV in the front room downstairs. Mr and Mrs Jefferson are still awake. He runs for the stairs, pulling in deep breaths through his nose, but he doesn't seem to be able to breathe fast enough. If he doesn't get more air into his lungs, surely he will die. He trips on the third to top stair, loses his footing and clatters down to the bottom, his head smashing against the wall and exploding in pain. He feels a thin line of warm blood trickle down from his mouth. The door to the front room flies open and Mrs Jefferson stands there.

'Billy!' she screams. 'What the . . .?' She kneels down next to him, takes in his frightened expression. 'Why is your lip . . .?' She runs a finger along the line of blood on his chin; there is a look of horror on her face as realisation dawns, and it's that look that scares Billy more than anything else. When adults get that look, you're really in trouble.

'Mark!' she screams. 'Mark, get out here now! Call an ambulance! Do something!'

38

Imogen

I've arranged to meet Sarah at the only coffee shop in town – a strategic move on my part because I knew exactly what she was going to say from the moment I took her call. I'm clutching a mug of decaf tea as insipid as the worn-out plastic gingham tablecloth like it's a protective charm.

'It was her, I know it was.' She rubs a hand wearily over her eyes. 'You don't believe me, do you?'

'Why does it matter to you whether I believe you or not?' I gaze out of the window at the two girls sitting miserably in the car outside, waiting for Sarah. 'If you have a reason to believe it was Ellie, you need to speak to her social worker, and possibly the police.'

As it happens, I don't believe her. The Ellie I know would not superglue a young boy's lips together; she just wouldn't.

'You barely know her,' Sarah accuses. 'She's said nothing to you, has she? You have no idea what she's really like. What was the point of Florence even getting you people involved?'

I sigh. The incidents with Ellie are much more frequent now, and I know I'm going to have to hand the case over – this new claim is way beyond anything Place2Be is designed to deal with. But I promised myself I would help her, and so far I feel like I've done nothing for the girl.

'Florence Maxwell referred Ellie to Place2Be on the advice of Ellie's social worker to provide Ellie with the support and guidance she might not be getting elsewhere.' If Sarah notices the barb, she doesn't comment; I get the impression she is so wrapped up in her own problems that I could have outright accused her of failing Ellie completely and she would have responded with 'hmm'.

'This is not fair. Something has to be done about that girl, and if no one in authority will do it . . .' Sarah lets the sentence hang.

I hold up a hand. 'Please do not finish that sentence in front of me. Look.' I sigh again. 'Mrs Jefferson, according to the hospital, Billy had been playing with superglue earlier that evening. There were traces of it on his hands and he admitted he couldn't be sure he hadn't wiped his mouth and got the glue on his own lips. As difficult as this might be for you to accept, especially given that Billy shouldn't really be messing about with superglue unsupervised . . .'

'Didn't you hear what she said to him at dinner?' Sarah ignores the implication that Billy's accident is most likely due to her own negligence. There seems to be nothing I can say to make her realise that she is going to have to accept some responsibility for what happened two nights ago. 'Have you asked her about that?'

'Ellie said there had been a disagreement . . .'

'Yes – where she told him to shut his mouth before she shut it permanently. Then he wakes up with his lips stuck together! Tell me that's a coincidence, Mrs Reid.'

'It was an unfortunate choice of words, certainly . . .'

'Oh, forget it.' Sarah snatches her mobile phone off the table and stands up so quickly her chair almost falls over. Her face is flushed and her jaw set in a hard line that gives me the impression that she is clenching her teeth to hold her words in. 'You're clearly on that girl's side.'

'I'm not on anyone's side, Mrs Jefferson,' I say, for once keeping my cool. 'This isn't about sides. My job is simply to get Ellie the support she needs.'

'And what about the support *we* need?'

'I won't say anything to Ellie's social worker about what you've told me today,' I say. 'This is clearly an emotional time for you. However, when I write my report, I will be recommending that Ellie moves foster carers. On the basis of what you've said to me today, I don't feel a hundred per cent confident that she should be in your care any longer.'

Sarah looks shocked. 'Are you saying she's not safe with us? Are you trying to imply that we would hurt her?'

I fix her with a stony stare. 'Your words exactly were "Something has to be done about that girl, and if no one in authority will do it . . ."' I let the words hang in the air, just as Sarah did moments before. They hit their target.

'I didn't mean . . . I wasn't saying that . . .' she stammers. 'I wouldn't hurt her, obviously.'

'I would have thought you'd be pleased that my recommendation is that Ellie be moved. Isn't that exactly what you want?'

If I'm not mistaken, I see something like fear pass across the other woman's eyes. 'It's just that, in the past, when people have upset her . . .'

'You're not suggesting that if Ellie gets moved on, she might do something to hurt you? You do realise how ridiculous that sounds? She's an eleven-year-old girl.'

Sarah points a finger at me. 'Don't you tell me what's ridiculous,' she snaps. 'You haven't seen it first-hand. You haven't been there.'

I smile, ready to say something condescending.

'Don't you dare smirk at me!' Sarah shouts. A few people

in the café turn to look at us now. 'You sit there like you know all there is to know about the world when you're barely out of training bras. Well one day you *will* know, one day you'll find out exactly what she's like and you'll be back to apologise to me. I just hope it won't be too late for you.' And she turns on her heels and stalks from the table, leaving me sitting there alone, stunned and bewildered.

39

Ellie

Ellie sits in the back seat, her head resting against the cool glass of the window. She can see her foster mother talking to Imogen inside the café. As she watches them, she feels the hope inside her slip away, like it's a tumour that has been cut out of her. She wonders what her foster mother is saying to the woman; whatever it is, she knows it can't be good. Sarah still blames her for what happened to Billy, despite what the doctor at the hospital said.

'She's never going to help me now,' Ellie mutters. From the front of the car, where Mary is sitting wearing her head-phones, the older girl turns around.

'Did you say something, Ellie?' she asks.

Ellie shakes her head. 'No. It doesn't matter,' she says miserably. 'It was nothing.'

But it wasn't nothing. When Ellie was with Imogen, she finally felt like there was some hope back in her life. Like someone was on her side. The woman made her feel like she couldn't possibly be responsible for the things that had been happening since she moved to this town – like there was no such thing as evil and that bad thoughts didn't always make you a bad person. Now, thanks to Sarah, that is over and everyone who matters thinks she is rotten to the core. She will be abandoned again; there is no chance left for her here. Like a snake twisting and writhing inside her, the anger rears its head.

40

Imogen

The darkness draws in around me and the cold comes hand in hand with it. I give an involuntary shiver, pull my coat tighter around myself and walk a little faster. The trees and bushes that line the path either side of me make dusk feel like midnight, and I wish, not for the first time, that I'd chosen the lighter path. It is an extra ten minutes on my journey home, but the chances of shadowy creatures lurking in the bushes, or me losing my footing and ending up in what was once a canal and now resembles an overgrown swamp, are smaller. I regard the luminous green algae resting on top of the black water and resolve that from now on, I won't be so impatient to put my feet up with a cup of tea. After what happened this morning with Sarah Jefferson, I wish more than ever that I could pour myself an extra-large glass of wine. Just another thing I have this baby to thank for.

The silence that solidified around me the moment I noticed it is broken by a cracking sound in the bushes to my left. I pause momentarily, sneak a furtive look at where the noise came from and, on seeing no immediate danger, pick up my pace once again. My feet are numb inside my impractical high-heeled shoes and I will them to move faster. There is nothing to be afraid of, I tell myself. There's nothing there. Just don't come this way again.

Another snap in the bushes and I let out a small gasp. I've always been fascinated by how easily the mind can be influenced by a person's surroundings, and I try to concentrate on the psychology of it. Thinking about the autonomic fear response focuses my mind and calms my thumping heart. That doesn't help when I hear the voice.

'Imogen.'

It's a low whisper from somewhere behind my left shoulder. I spin around, relieved to have someone I know to walk the rest of the way home with, but the path behind me is empty. My heart banging against my chest, I peer into the bushes for any sign of someone playing a trick on me, but the silence seems even thicker than before and the path around me is still. Stupid woman, I curse myself. Stupid woman hearing things.

Still, I dig my hand into my pocket, lace the thick plastic fob of my car keys between my fingers and wish to God that I had my car here now instead of letting Dan drop me off at the coffee shop this morning. My makeshift shiv firmly in place, I turn on my heel and stride purposefully on, embarrassment at my own fear propelling me forward.

'Help me. Please help me.'

A child's voice sounds small and helpless from the dark trees beyond. I wince. Is this in my head as well? My own fear battles against the knowledge that if I'm not imagining the voice, if a child is in trouble and I do nothing, I will never forgive myself.

I pause, waiting for the voice to speak again, to pinpoint where it's coming from. As I wait, I pull out my mobile phone from my coat pocket and press Dan's number on the call log. I keep it away from my ear until a voice in my hand says, 'Hello? Immy?'

'Dan.' I put the phone to my ear and whisper my husband's name. 'I'm walking back along the canal path . . .'

'Fuck's sake, Im, I told you not to walk that way. Remember that woman had her purse stolen there last—'

'I know, but I'm here now,' I hiss, cutting him off. I'm annoyed at myself for choosing to walk this way when Dan expressly told me not to, but also annoyed at him. If he hadn't been telling me what to do as usual, I probably would have come to my own conclusion that this path was a bad idea. As it is, part of my decision to come this way was to prove to him I'm not a child. And see how that turned out, I think ruefully.

'Look,' I continue, 'I heard a child's voice, in the trees. Asking for help. I've got to go in and have a look, but I wanted to let someone know where I—'

'You absolutely will not, Imogen.' Dan's voice is livid and I can picture how red his face will be. 'Just keep walking. I'm getting my coat and coming to meet you now.'

My face burns. 'I don't need you to come and get me, Dan. I'm thirty-two years old. My mother stopped walking me to school before I was ten.' Any fear I felt just a few minutes ago has dissipated at the sound of my husband's voice. Now I just feel annoyed.

'You do realise that there are gangs who use children to lure women into the woods so they can rob them and . . . Just keep walking, Imogen, please.'

His last plea sounds so desperate that I can't help but soften. 'Okay. I can't hear anything now anyway. It was probably just some local kids playing hide-and-seek or something.' Even as I say it, I know that's not likely. Kids playing are noisy and boisterous, shouting and crashing about. Not quietly imploring. Still, when Dan replies, he sounds so relieved that I know I'm doing the right thing not venturing into the woods.

'Thank you. Shall I still come and meet you? We can grab some supper from the chippy on the way back.'

'Mmm, sounds lush.' I start walking again, Dan's voice a comfort in my ear.

'Okay, just leaving now. How far down the canal are you?'

I glance around. 'Past the old bench. Just coming up to—'

My words catch in my throat as the thump on my back reverberates through my chest, and I am knocked off balance into the filthy, freezing water of the disused canal.

41

Imogen

I cough violently and try to push myself upwards. My lungs burn and I struggle to pull in fresh clean air, but I am drowning, drowning in stagnant muddy water. Algae claws its way down my throat, wrapping itself around my windpipe and dragging me further under the surface. I can't open my eyes; they are thick with sticky brown mud, and I claw desperately at my face to wipe it away. But every time I clear it, more of the filth closes in to take its place. I feel the last of my breath expel from my lips, and I know in that instant that this is it, I am dying. As my body fights with its last ounce of strength, I hear a voice, the voice that dragged me down into the depths, the voice of a young girl. 'I only wanted help,' it chants, and now I can't tell whether it is a girl or a boy. *The* boy . . . 'I just needed someone to help me . . .'

'Imogen!' Firm arms grab me around the shoulders and clutch me tightly. I cough again; my fingers stretch out for the arms holding me and I grab them, clinging on to stop myself being dragged down to the murky depths of the disused canal.

Except, I realise, I'm not wet any more. And my eyes are

no longer thick with mud. My lungs still burn but they aren't filled with water; they are filled with air, clean air.

'Imogen, can you hear me?'

I open my eyes, then snap them closed again when the bright white lights hit my retinas. I bury my head in Dan's chest and let him rock me gently until the pounding behind my eyes subsides and my breathing slows. Within a few minutes another voice speaks, female this time.

'Imogen? Imogen, my name is Dr Harding. Can you hear me? Can you open your eyes, Imogen?'

42

Imogen

I turn over in bed and shift around to get comfortable. I fluff up my pillow, punch a dent in the middle and try to sink back into it. Closing my eyes, I try to zone out, refocus my mind so my thoughts aren't so close to the surface, but just as they begin to sink downwards, as they fade into a dull drone, the words slide through my mind and they are back in focus: *I just needed someone to help me.* I am awake, alert again, hear them as keenly as if someone has whispered them in my ear. But there is no one in the room with me, I know that, and I know that those words are ingrained in my subconscious, along with the feeling of thick dirty water clogging my throat. The water is just the memory of a dream, and yet still I swear I can feel the cold wet mud and the reeds snaking their way down my windpipe, wrapping around my lungs until I can barely breathe.

Throwing my legs out of the warm covers, I pull myself to my feet and put on my dressing gown. Feeling my chest relax a little and my breathing returning to normal, I pad across the hallway, flicking the light on as I go.

The clock in the downstairs hall shows 9.15 p.m. – I've managed to grab a couple of hours then – but I have no idea what woke me so abruptly. Dan left at 7 p.m. to meet the editor of the local paper for drinks at the pub; he had approached the man to talk about an idea he'd had for a regular column about the glamorous life of a novelist, and it turned out the editor has read a couple of Dan's books and considers himself a fan.

'I thought we didn't need to worry about money now I'm working again,' I questioned when he mentioned it earlier. It's not that I object to him working on other projects – it's great for him to have something else to focus his mind on, and this might open doors for him – but the idea of being at home alone since the incident in the canal leaves me cold.

'It's not about the money, baby, it's just that . . . well, I'm a bit lonely stuck here all day while you go out to work.' He looked sheepish, as though admitting to needing company was a stupid weakness. 'I thought this might get me some human contact every now and then.' I felt selfish and rotten when he quickly told me that if I wanted him to stay in then of course he would; this feature wasn't as important as I was – it could wait until another time. I know enough about the world of journalism, though, to understand that 'another time' is about as reliable as 'one day' or 'in the future'.

'No, of course you have to go,' I said with a smile that I hope wasn't as fake as it felt. 'I'm absolutely fine. I'll be going back to work in a couple of days, and without me to fuss over, you're going to need something to focus on.'

I have to admit that my husband would have made an incredible nurse. He's looked after me tirelessly since my release from the hospital the morning after my fall into the canal. They kept me in overnight – for observation, they said, but I knew it was more a case of not having anyone around at that time of night to sign the release forms – but the next morning they declared that I was fit to return home as long as I was well taken care of. Dan took to the task as though he'd signed his name to it in blood, almost to the point of smothering me. Thank God he was out making a phone call when they told me the baby was fine.

In the kitchen, I flick on the light, then look around, blinking. Everything is normal, exactly how I left it when I went upstairs to nap. So why do I feel so uneasy? There is nothing obvious down here that could have woken me, no dishes slipped down into the sink or recycling fallen over. It isn't a comforting thought that I was probably woken by my own nightmares.

Stoically ignoring the solid darkness outside the kitchen window and silently reminding myself to buy some blinds at the next opportunity, I pull open the fridge door and lift out the carton of orange juice Dan brought back from the shop earlier especially for me. Full of vitamin C, he said proudly. Taking a swig straight from the carton, I resist the urge to giggle at my insubordination – Dan would shudder at the mere thought. If I'm going to take the rest upstairs, I need to pour it into a glass so I don't get told off.

I push the fridge door shut firmly with my elbow and glance up. The carton slips through my fingers. Cold, sticky orange juice explodes onto the floor, soaking my feet, but I barely notice. I let out an ear-splitting scream as I see the pale face pressed up against the kitchen window.

43

Imogen

The face moves away from the kitchen window and towards the back patio doors. I let out a yell and yank down on the back-door handle – locked. I run through to the dining room. The curtains are closed across the double doors. I have no idea whether Dan locked them when he left, but I can't force myself to pull back the curtain and face whoever is standing outside. I grab my handbag containing my mobile phone from the dining room table and close the door behind me. Standing in the front room, I look around for something to barricade the dining room door with – even if the patio doors are open, I can stop whoever is outside from coming through the house.

Who is it out there? I try to picture the face at the window, pale and bloodless, with sunken black eyes – although that could have been my imagination, or the reflection from the glass. I jump as I hear a pounding on the patio doors. My heart thumping, I attempt to pull the large mahogany dresser across the dining-room door, but it is laden with Nan's old trinkets and won't budge. At least if they're knocking on the doors it must means they're locked. When the pounding stops, I check the front door – that's locked too.

Outside, there is silence, which is worse than the pounding on the glass. Without the sound, I have no idea where the intruder is, and therefore where I should be. Pulling my mobile from my bag, I thumb through my recent call log until I find Dan and click call, feeling my heart sink as the pre-recorded answerphone woman invites me to leave a message after the tone.

'Dan, it's me. Don't panic, but can you give me a call when you get this, please?'

I hang up and stare at the phone in my hand. Should I call the police?

And tell them what – that there's someone knocking on the door? I imagine the humiliation of the police turning up at my front door to find Dan outside having left his keys at home and his phone battery dead. Or Pammy, or Lucy from work returning my purse or my cardigan, or something else equally innocuous. I take a few deep breaths in and out, knowing that I am going to have to find out who's outside before I can call for help. Even my call to Dan makes me feel a bit stupid now, like a helpless teenager in a horror movie. Steeling myself, I push open the dining-room door, half expecting someone to be on the other side with a carving knife.

You've watched too many scary movies, idiot.

Yeah, and if I was watching myself in one now, I'd be screaming at me to call the police, not to open the frigging curtains.

Still, this isn't a scary movie, and even I have to admit that the likelihood of being carved into tiny pieces in my own home is slim.

There is no one in the dining room. Before I open the curtains to face whoever is on the other side, I go cautiously back into the kitchen – avoiding looking at the blindless window – and draw a knife from the knife block. Chancing a glance at the window, I see nothing but an inky black square and my own face reflected back at me. I take the knife back through to the dining room, switching off all the lights as I go. I don't see any reason to backlight myself if there is someone still out there.

I take another couple of deep breaths, then, holding the knife out in front of me, rip the patio door curtains open.

The back garden looks empty. No sign of anyone outside. I press myself up against the window, searching the blackness for signs of movement, but there is nothing. Releasing the breath I have been holding, I let the curtain fall back into place. Whoever was outside is gone.

Still clutching the knife, I go back into the front room. My mobile lies unblinking on the mahogany dresser – Dan must not have got my message yet. As I'm about to sink down into the sofa, there is a bang on the front door.

I am there in an instant. I've had enough of being scared now – I just want to find out who is stalking around my house at this time of night. Kids, trying to scare me? I fumble with the security latch, and when the chain slides into place, I pull open the front door, stepping back when I see the figure standing on the porch.

'Mrs Reid?' Hannah Gilbert emerges from the shadows. 'I'm so sorry I scared you. I shouldn't have gone to your kitchen window, but there was no answer at the front and I . . . I'm sorry.'

I feel my pulse slow. There's nothing threatening about the teacher and I feel slightly stupid as I close the door and take the chain off. Opening it wider, I realise I'm still clutching the knife. Hannah Gilbert sees it before I can hide it.

'Oh God, I really did scare you,' she says, putting a hand to her chest. 'I'm so sorry.'

'Don't be,' I say, sliding the knife onto the telephone table behind the front door. 'New house, middle of the countryside – I'm still a bit jumpy. Used to living in the city, I suppose. Is something wrong?'

Hannah looks beyond me into the hallway. 'I, erm, I was hoping to have a word. Would you mind if I came in?'

'Please do.' I open the door all the way and gesture for her to come inside, though I can't resist peering out into the darkness beyond, just in case.

Inside, and with the door firmly locked, I see just how jittery Hannah Gilbert looks. No wonder her face scared the life out of me – even in the light of the hallway she is pale, dark purple circles beneath her eyes. I might be the one who narrowly escaped drowning in the canal two days ago, but Hannah looks as though she has been through a near-death experience of her own.

'Can I get you something to drink?' I ask in an attempt to break the awkward tension. It seems that now Hannah is inside, she doesn't have the slightest idea what to say. 'Tea? Coffee? Wine?'

Hannah nods. 'A glass of wine would be great, thanks.'

I lead her through to the kitchen, and pour her a glass of white wine and myself a glass of water, noticing how her hand shakes slightly as she takes the glass.

'You're not having one?' she asks, bringing it to her lips and taking a gulp. I shake my head.

'Painkillers,' I offer by way of explanation.

'Yes, I heard what happened at the old canal. Are you okay?'

I nod, wondering who else has heard of my embarrassing fall. 'Yes thank you,' I reply. 'Silly accident.'

'Hmm,' Hannah says, but doesn't push any further. We go into the living room and I gesture for her to sit down.

'Is your husband out?'

'Yes, he's at a work meeting. What is it you want to talk to me about?'

Now that she has my full attention, Hannah seems almost too embarrassed to speak.

'I'm not really sure how to say this,' she begins.

'Why don't we just speak candidly, Hannah – if you don't mind me calling you Hannah?' She nods. 'And please call me Imogen. Why don't we forget the work issue and you just tell me what is troubling you enough to come to my house late at night.'

She seems to consider this, then gives a small nod. 'Okay, fine. I came because I heard about what happened to you. And I heard about your, erm, your discussion with Sarah Jefferson in the café just hours before that.'

'Well, news certainly travels fast in this town.' I fight to keep the barb from my voice. This is one of the things I never came to terms with when I lived in Gaunt before – the idea that your business is everyone else's business. It isn't like that in London – you can shoot someone on their front doorstep and as long as the blood doesn't splatter the neighbour's windows, no one else notices a thing.

Hannah has the good grace to look embarrassed. 'I know a lot of people.'

Why, when she says this, do I get the feeling she is doing more than replying to my comment? I hardly need reminding that Hannah knows more people in this town than I do – even the ones I knew once upon a time don't know I'm back and wouldn't care a jot if they did.

'What does my discussion with Sarah Jefferson have to do with me falling in the canal?'

Hannah takes a sip of her wine, preparing what she is about to say next. After a pause pregnant with tension she replies, 'Are you sure you fell?'

I was expecting this, but still I redden with shock at the other woman's bluntness.

'It was stupid of me to walk on my own in the dark. I

don't know the area well and I didn't realise how close the canal is to the path. It's overrun with grass and weeds . . .'

'Do you know how many people have accidentally fallen in that canal in the past eight years? One. Some kid who was trying to jump across it for a dare. And you're trying to convince yourself that you fell in, completely sober, the same day as having an argument with Ellie Atkinson's foster mother?'

'Are you suggesting Sarah Jefferson pushed me into the canal? What, she just snuck up behind me without me seeing or hearing a thing and shoved me in because I wouldn't declare her foster daughter insane?'

'Not Sarah, no.' Hannah's muddy brown eyes are locked onto mine, her voice steady.

'What?' I scoff. 'Ellie, then? Can she turn herself invisible now, on top of reading minds?'

I say nothing of the voice I swear I heard before I fell. I realised afterwards, while I was recuperating in hospital, and later here at home, that it was a ridiculous manifestation, my mind playing on my fear of the dark, unfamiliar route.

'I know you're fond of Ellie,' Hannah says, ignoring my mocking words. 'But even you have got to see that bad things happen to the people who cross her. I thought that once you'd experienced it first-hand, you'd realise . . .'

'Realise what? That she's possessed? The devil? You know how ridiculous this sounds, don't you? Ellie is an eleven-year-old girl! What you people are doing to her, what you're making her out to be – it's inhumane!' I can feel weeks of anger and frustration building up within me, rearing up and bucking like a beast. 'Ellie needs saving all right, but not from myself – from all of you! I've never seen anything like it in my life.'

Hannah stands up, places her glass on the table too force-fully, her cheeks so flushed with anger or humiliation that

I wonder if she will lash out. Let her try and I'll smash her face in.

'I can see this is doing neither of us any good,' she says, clearly struggling to keep her tone measured. 'I hoped we would be able to have a civilised conversation. That after what you've been through, you'd be able to open your mind enough to consider the possibility that you might be wrong about that girl. But no,' her voice is rising now as she loses her own fight with her emotions, 'you are clearly too blind, too ignorant and arrogant to see that there might be things going on in this town that are beyond what can be understood and what can be proven. Things that can only be felt and believed if you are willing to feel and believe them. I expected more of you, Mrs Reid, I confess. I was sadly mistaken.'

She strides across the room as she speaks, and is at the front door when my phone begins to ring from the dresser. I ignore it and stalk after her.

'Sadly mistaken?' I scream. 'Damn right you're sadly mistaken if you thought I was going to join your little witch hunt against a girl who has already been to hell and back! You people sicken me, and I will do everything I can to make sure Ellie is kept safe from you!'

Hannah Gilbert stops in the middle of the driveway and turns back to face me, her heels crunching on the gravel. She walks back up the drive until her face is inches from my own. I refuse to move away, don't even flinch. My heart is pounding as she speaks through clenched teeth.

'I pity you, Mrs Reid. I pity you and your small mind. I came here to warn you that no one is safe from what that girl is capable of, but I can see that my concern is falling on ignorant, deaf ears. Let me tell you this: you need to be very careful. You need to watch your back, and above all, do not upset Ellie Atkinson. Because when you do – and that's *when*, not if – your ignorance and your refusal to consider anything outside of your perfectly ordinary world will come back to haunt you. You had better hope you live to regret not listening to me.'

And before I can formulate any kind of response, Hannah Gilbert stalks off into the night.

44

Ellie

Ellie can see that Mary is fidgety and restless. She moves from the floor to the bed, the bed to the chair and back to the floor again, picking up a photo of her and her parents and moving it from one end of her desk to the other with no real purpose. Mary's room is tidy and ordered, everything has its place, and the photo frame looks strange in its new position.

'What's wrong with you?' Ellie asks eventually, noticing how Mary cringes at the sudden noise that breaks the silence. 'You're acting crazy.'

Mary makes a squeaky noise in her throat, as though she can't believe that Ellie is calling her crazy. 'Nothing,' she croaks. 'Everything's fine.'

Ellie has heard that before; her mum used the same pinched tone whenever her dad said something useless. *I'm fine. It's fine. Leave it, Martin.* Her dad knew better than to push the issue then, and Ellie knows better now. When they have sat in a thick, foggy silence for a little while longer, Mary will start speaking herself, like the words are drip-drip-dripping into a clogged-up sink and eventually, if no one unblocks it, they will spill out over the top. And sure enough, the words come.

165

'I heard Mum talking about that social services woman,' and like water, the words won't stop spilling, and they can't be put back in the sink. 'The one who came to the house – Imogen. She had an accident.'

Ellie sits up poker straight on the bed. So this is why Mary has been so itchy tonight. 'What kind of accident? When?'

Mary turns to face her now, like it is difficult to do and she has been building herself up to it. Her eyes bore into Ellie's as though there are lasers attached to them and her words don't sound like Mary at all now but like Ms Gilbert and Sarah when she thinks no one else is listening. 'Have you been having the dreams again, Ellie? Have you dreamt about Imogen?'

'No.' The word is out before Ellie can contemplate whether it is a lie. If she is going to be honest, she doesn't remember her dreams; she wakes in a cold sweat, her chest rasping from the effort of fighting to breathe against smoke and fumes, but sometimes there is more. Sometimes the faces of people she knows now break through the flames, people who have upset and mistreated her, people she would gladly see suffer in her dreams. But in real life? She wasn't even able to kill the moth, instead sobbing as she opened the window and watched it fly feebly to freedom.

45

She can't see any flames, but that doesn't mean she is safe. Thick plumes of smoke claw at her throat and sting her eyes as though trying to claim her, possess her. She tries to cry out to her mother for help, but the sound catches in her throat. The air is searing hot and every inch of her feels as though she is the fire herself.

Where is everyone? Have they all escaped, Mum, Dad, Riley and Plum? Did her parents even try to look for her? Or did they think only of themselves and the baby they love so much?

She can see nothing now. Not her bed with its turquoise, pink and lilac bedspread, or the desk her dad sanded down and painted white. It is all concealed by the smoke, hidden as cleverly as though someone has taken a grey marker and coloured it in. Stumbling forward, she reaches out a hand to steady herself and catches fabric in between her fingers. The window! She has made it to the window! Tearing open the curtains, she looks out upon the back garden in all its darkness. Everything looks so normal, pitch black and still as a drawing. How can that be? How can everything be so ordinary when inside the house everything is ending?

Ellie bangs the window, knowing even as she does that it is no good. There is no one in the back garden, no crowds of watching *people or firefighters come to save them. It is as though she is the last person left in the world.*

The smoke is taking over now, filling her lungs with every breath she tries to take. If only she could plug her mouth; soon she will be so full of burning air that there will be no room inside for breath. She is a clever girl; at eleven years old she knows what happens when there is no room left for air. She pulls at the curtain, holds it in front of her mouth and nose to stop the smoke from getting in, and bangs again on the window.

She doesn't know what time it is; she woke in the night to go to the toilet and wondered why the room was so warm, saw the wispy tendrils of smoke curling under the door. Her first thought was to open the door, to see where the smoke was coming from, but the thought of opening it and seeing hellish orange flames terrified her so much that she stumbled backwards, tripping, falling against her bed. Now it is too late; the smoke has overtaken the doorway and the window is her only hope.

Her hands, slick with sweat, slide over the handle of the window as she attempts to yank it upwards. As she fights to keep her grip and try again, she realises with dread that it is locked. Her mum keeps all the windows locked, terrified that her children will somehow climb out and fall to their deaths. Now it will be the thing that kills her. At the thought of her mum, Ellie lets out a sob, and then a scream. Why aren't they coming? Why have they abandoned her now?

One foot on the bookshelf, she launches herself upwards toward the small window at the top. These are the ones Mum opens when she wants to let some air into their rooms. Not big enough for a child to fit through, they are rarely locked, and tonight is no excep-tion. Ellie nearly breaks down in tears as the window opens and she pushes herself higher to greedily gulp at the fresh air it allows in, but it is as though her lungs are smaller now; the bad air has taken over and they have less space for good air. Her throat burns and her scream comes out as a croak as her fingers slip against the plastic of the window edge, threatening to let her fall back into the smoke-filled room.

In the distance she hears the wail of sirens. They are coming! Her mum and dad must have escaped the house and raised the alarm, and the fire brigade are coming to save her. She doesn't let herself wonder why her parents didn't just open her door to get her on the way down, or why she hasn't heard them scream or shout her name. It will all be okay when she is back in her mum's arms; everything will be explained at the hospital while they check to see that she is okay and replace the bad air with good again.

The sirens are right outside the house now and the world seems to have come back to life. Lights are pinging on in the houses around them, people opening their curtains to see what is going on. Within seconds of the siren stopping, there is a crash at the front door, muffled voices on the stairs. She wants to run to her bedroom door and throw it open, but she is terrified to leave her only source of good air.

The fingers holding her up against the windowsill tremble, threatening to betray her, but still she clings on. This thin gap is her only connection to the real world, keeping her from the nightmare one that has taken over her house. When the man in the black jacket and yellow trousers with a mask over his face bursts into her bedroom, he has to prise her screaming away from her lifeline, but at last she falls against his chest and squeezes her eyes tightly shut against the hell beyond her bedroom door.

46

Hannah shivers and pulls her sleeves down over hands that feel like ice. Why didn't she wear her bloody gloves? She was in such a hurry to get out of the house, away from her husband and all his sodding questions. Luckily she remembered to put a coat on in her haste. No worries: she'll be inside soon and there is an oil heater in the flat – and other ways to keep warm.

She gives another shiver, but this one is from anticipation rather than the wind that bites at her even through the jacket she is wearing. This, this thing they have – Hannah hates the word 'affair', it's so damning – has only been going on a couple of months, and every time they meet it is still so exhilarating that things like crawling into an abandoned building in the dead of the night – something she would never even have considered doing with her husband – don't bother her in the slightest. In fact it is wildly exciting. She feels a flash of guilt that had she been a bit more open to adventure with Sam, this might not be happening, but she ignores it, determined not to let her husband ruin this for her.

She pushes aside the black bin liner that has been taped across the broken window – the tape has worked loose in the wind and is flapping against the grimy once-white plastic still – and peers into the dark room beyond. The first time she did this, jamming her foot against the broken drainpipe and hoisting herself up onto the sill, she was petrified that it was going to give way and she'd end up with a broken leg, or worse, be discovered wedged in the window, one leg in, one leg out like a grotesque ballerina. Now she is well practised, and even with the sill slick with rain and grime she manages to pull herself up and over with little fuss. One time she slipped halfway in and smacked her knee against the frame – she winces now at the memory of the sharp pain followed by the dull throb that plagued her for days. On the other side of the window is a dust-filled pouffe – another of her trial-and-error ideas after having to jump to the ground the first time – and relief courses through her when her foot connects with it. One more push and she swings her other leg through and climbs down.

If there's one thing Hannah has never got used to about these night-time meetings, it is the absolute darkness that greets her inside the abandoned flat. If Evan gets there before her, he usually turns on the battery-operated tea lights dotted around to light their way, but for nights when she arrives first, she has learned to bring the brightest torch she owns. Tonight is one of those nights, and she flips on the torch and swings it around looking for the tea lights. Flicking them on one at a time, she remembers fondly how she teased him about his sensible approach to the flame-proof lighting, but when he turned them on and they flickered like real flames, she had to admit they were quite romantic. Now, though, much to her annoyance, only three of the ten actually work.

'Fuck's sake,' she mutters, all her sentimentality gone. Well, Evan will have his torch anyway, and as long as the lights upstairs work, it makes little difference to her whether down here is lit.

When Evan first showed her the abandoned block of flats, Hannah was impressed and a little surprised at his daring. She had hardly expected something this out-of-the-ordinary from the shy, awkward maths teacher. His eyes lit up when he told her about how it had been condemned, and every single tenant evicted overnight, most having nowhere to go, making transportation and storage of their belongings impossible. So now here it is, like the *Mary Celeste*, a macabre snapshot of the lives lived in this small slum-like building.

Hannah crosses to the door of the flat she's entered, cursing as her foot connects with a mug that has been left on the floor next to the sofa. It rolls across the laminate floor, its rattle cutting through the silence.

A thump from the hallway makes Hannah jump.

'Evan?' Hannah stands in the doorway of the flat, reluctant to step out into the cold empty stairwell alone, and looks upwards. 'Hello?'

Another soft thud echoes through the stairwell, the sound of a door closing quietly. So he is up there. Hannah frowns. Evan has never struck her as the game-playing type, but then she never had him down as an explorer of abandoned buildings either. 'Idiot,' she mutters, but she gives a quick smile and heads for the staircase.

Most of the doors to the other flats are still locked, although the odd one or two has been kicked open by local youths for parties and, judging by the paraphernalia littered all over the floor, drugs. That's why she and Evan use one of the flats on the top floor – it's too much of a trek for any of the other people who utilise the empty block. One time they were in the flat when they heard a group of kids climb through the same window they had climbed through an hour previously. They were frozen in fear – if they were discovered, it was more than their dignity at stake. Ms Gilbert and Mr Hawker hiding in a derelict block of flats? Hannah shuddered at the thought of the urban legend that would have been created within the close-knit community. They would both lose their jobs, and probably their marriages. They had to wait it out for two hours while the kids – plenty of whose voices she recognised – got louder and cockier, at one point exploring the flat right underneath theirs. Hannah thought Evan was considering throwing himself from the window rather than be found.

Stepping into the stairwell feels like walking through a wall of ice. How is it possible for it to be colder inside than out? The darkness is less dense in here, the moonlight casting dusty light in streaks onto the wall. As she climbs the stairs, darkness closes in on her between each level.

Her breath catches in her throat as she hears the sound of footsteps on the stairs directly above.

'Stop messing around, Evan,' she calls up into the stillness above. 'I'm about two seconds from turning around and going back home.' She hopes she sounds like she means it, even if she doesn't. She hears what might be a giggle, or a snort, or maybe even a cough, and for the first time since climbing in through the broken window, she falters. What if it isn't Evan upstairs? What if this behaviour is so unlike him because it *isn't* him? The tea lights weren't lit, after all, and now that she really thinks about it, something else is missing. Evan's smell. In these musty, stale corridors, whenever he is here, his scent pervades every inch of the flat, laying out his path like a trail of breadcrumbs. Tonight, she can't smell him at all.

'Evan?' Her voice is more of a loud whisper than a shout. Met with silence, she feels for the banister to make her way back down, and as she turns, a clear voice echoes off the walls above her.

'Hannah.'

She freezes. The absolute swine! She grins and carries on

back upstairs to where he is waiting, smirking at how scared she was just seconds before. What was she thinking? No one else knows she's here tonight – and if the flats have been taken over by squatters, they're much more likely to have set up residence on one of the lower floors; what kind of squatters enjoy climbing flights of stairs?

The top floor is as silent and still as the grave. Flat 17 stands as though waiting for her, the door half an inch ajar, the way it has been since the first time Evan showed her around. He'd had to break in, he told her, although the thought of her lover shoulder-barging the door open is as amusing as the idea of an army of Spandex-clad squatters using the stairs for warm-up routines.

'Okay, you can come out now.' Hannah steels herself for Evan to leap out and surprise her. It would be so embarrassing for him to see her jumping at shadows. She stands for a second in front of the flat door, takes a deep breath and shoves it open.

'Ha!' she shouts into the empty hallway beyond. 'Oh for fuck's sake, Evan,' she mutters, thoroughly fed up of the game now. She only has a few hours before Sam begins to question where she's been, and Evan knows that. Why waste precious time playing hide-and-seek? She is sure Emma will cover for her if Sam ever asks, though she would prefer not to have to test that theory.

She starts at the sound of voices in the front room beyond. No, not voices, music. The wind-up radio Evan brought here when the electricity was finally cut off on their second visit. Until then it had been like meeting at a hotel, albeit the grubby hostel variety; there had been lights at least, but no TV, though they hadn't been there to watch Netflix. The music produced by the small radio is low and tinny, but it is better than silence. She walks towards the front room, but when she enters it is empty, only the radio singing its slow ballad. She crosses the room and switches it off. Turning to leave the flat, she resists the urge to look back. She's going home – Evan can just get his rocks off without her tonight. She is about to close the front door of the flat behind her when she hears the music start up again.

47

Imogen

I wipe the corners of my mouth and push my hair from out of my eyes. Shoving my hands under the cold tap, I splash water onto my face then bury it in the warm towel hanging on the heated towel rail. I lean back against the bathroom wall to take a minute before I rejoin Dan in the front room. The fire is blazing – Dan is really getting the hang of country life – and the heat nearly takes my breath away.

'You okay?' Dan asks as I fold myself onto the sofa next to him and try to look normal.

'Yeah, it's just pretty hot in here. I got used to having to wear a few more layers in our old place.'

'I know.' He grins proudly. 'Our heating bill will be minuscule this year. I could get used to this kind of life though, couldn't you?'

'I'll have to, won't I?' I reply absently. 'My job's here now. We'll have to get someone to value this place.'

Maybe that's what is wrong with me, I think as I watch Dan pick up the TV remote and start to flick. Maybe I'm just stressed at the thought of house sales and permanent moves. Having seen how well Dan has taken to life in the country, I am coming to accept that this isn't a trial run any more;

he loves it here and wants to stay. Maybe it's the stress of a pregnancy I can't tell my husband about. Maybe that's why I'm hearing voices and falling in canals.

A ringing from deep within the house makes us both jump. Dan frowns.

'Is that ours? Bit late for cold callers, isn't it? Have you given work the number?'

'I can't even remember the number,' I reply, getting up from the sofa. 'I don't know where the bloody phone is. Where is that coming from?'

'It sounds like it's in the hallway.'

I throw open the door to the hallway and with a sinking heart remember that the phone socket is in the cupboard under the stairs.

There is a cupboard under the stairs in my house. It has a light, the bulb so weak and encrusted with dust that the most it will emit is a faint glow, two threadbare cushions that I found in a skip outside next-door-but-one's house, four books and a thick crocheted blanket that my mother gave me. But the absolute best thing in my hideaway is the photograph.

They sit on an ageing wooden bench, its once bright blue paint weather-worn and chipping away. His arm is slung so casually around her shoulder that I can hardly believe it is the same woman who flinches at her daughter's touch. Dressed for the summer, they are both wearing shorts, she in a salmon-pink vest top, he in a white polo shirt, and holding towering ice creams with Flakes sticking out like miniature flagpoles. Every time I look at it, I can almost feel the sunshine on my back, smell the sea air, taste that ice cream. The breeze has whipped up my mother's hair slightly at the back, but either she hasn't noticed or she doesn't care because she is smiling – no, she is positively beaming – and it is this that makes the photograph my most treasured possession. Even at my young age I feel sad that my favourite thing in the world isn't even mine, I found the photograph amongst a stack in a box in my mother's wardrobe and couldn't stop my fingers from slipping it into the waistband of my trousers.

'Hello?'

The line is silent. I curse bloody automatic call centres and their multi-dial computers. My hand is still shaking from the memory of the days when I used to hide under the stairs as a young girl, and crouching in here once more is making my legs feel weak. As I'm about to hang up, I hear a soft voice whimper, 'Imogen?'

My heart thuds. 'Yes? Hello? Who is this?' But for no reason I can explain, I know it's Ellie Atkinson. 'Ellie?'

'There's a girl. She's running. She's afraid, so afraid.' Her voice is raspy, coming in short bursts, a staccato gunfire of words.

'Who's running, Ellie? Is this someone you can see? Where are you?'

I don't ask how she got my number, or why she's phoning me rather than the police; those are questions for after. The urgency in her voice frightens me.

'There's a man in a mask and he's chasing her. I can see the stairs but she doesn't think she'll make it. She's going to die. She's going to die!'

'Who, Ellie? Who thinks she's going to die? Where are you?' I don't know what to do. I can't hang up, but because it's a landline I can't rush out to find Ellie either. I have to calm the girl down, get her to safety before I can put the phone down long enough to go and find where she is.

'I'm outside. She's not here, she's somewhere else. Somewhere dark. I can't see my face. I'm frightened.'

Somewhere else? 'How can you see her, Ellie? Where are you?'

'I don't know. It's a house. I can see her in my head.'

Her voice is calmer now, a monotone, as though she is in some kind of trance. I feel my pounding heart begin to slow. Is she having a dream? Has she woken from a nightmare?

'Is there anyone else there with you, Ellie? Someone close by who can help you?'

'I have to go home,' Ellie intones, and I can hear the confusion in her voice. 'I have to get back, get away from here.'

'Okay, good,' I encourage. 'Where are you now? Are you near home?'

'There's a tree. I'm in the back garden, I think. Of Sarah's house. It's okay, they will come and get me. They're inside.'

'Can you still see the girl? The man in the mask?'

'No.' She pauses as though she is looking around her. 'I think they're gone. I must have got away this time.'

'This time? Have you seen her before?'

'I think so. I think so.'

I hear a voice in the background, hear someone calling out Ellie's name. A girl's voice – Mary? Relief floods though me. If Mary's there, she'll get her to safety.

'I have to go,' Ellie whispers. 'Don't tell them I saw the girl. They'll think I'm mad. They already think I'm crazy.'

'You're not crazy, Ellie. You need to tell Sarah what you saw. I'll help you. They can get you some help.'

There is a pause, and I think for a second that Ellie has dropped the phone, or hung up even. Then she speaks again. 'I don't need help. I have you.' And the line is dead.

48

Hannah hears the quiet thump of feet behind her, too light to be those of a grown man. Spinning round, she catches a glimpse of someone running down the hallway. Fucking kids! She dashes to the door, hoping to spot whoever it is descending the stairs, but the landing outside is deserted. Screw this, she isn't staying here to be made a fool of; it might teach Evan not to play stupid games in the future.

As she stands at the top of the stairs, she hears a low hiss from one of the doorways behind her. Before she can turn, a shoulder hits her square in the middle of her back, sending her crashing down the first flight of stairs. Her head slams against the last step, sending pain shooting through her skull. She is lying on the cold landing, a dull pounding of blood in her ears, but she cannot force herself to her feet. Move, she tells herself urgently. Fucking move. Whoever is upstairs doesn't just want to scare her; they want to hurt her.

She uses the stairs to push herself unsteadily to her feet; grasps the handrail, her hands slick with sweat. It's fine, there's no one behind her now – no one who wants to risk being seen anyway – and she stumbles down the next few steps towards the second landing, where more flats lie dormant, waiting. A sudden thought makes her stomach roll – what if there is more than one of them? What if there's someone waiting on this level too?

She sways, steadies herself against the wall and takes a few more steps. The darkness is complete here; all the doors to the flats on this floor are closed and no sliver of moonlight seeps through to light her way. She doesn't even hear her pursuer behind her this time; just feels hands on her shoulders, shoving her forward. Her foot catches on the edge of the stair, she pitches forwards and she is powerless to stop the weight of her upper body propelling her downwards. Her arm flails sideways, grasping for the rail that she knows is there, but even when her hand connects with the smooth surface, she is falling too fast to grab on. She hits each stair as she tumbles, her shoulder, her shin, her face. She feels her nose explode as it connects with the edge of a step, her arm splinter as it twists at an unnatural angle beneath her.

For a second she thinks she has stopped falling, that her feet have grounded her and she is standing again. She is in pain and she needs help, but she is alive! There is a moment when she is frozen in time, the single moment she's certain everything will be okay, before her back explodes with a pain like she didn't know it was possible to feel. She doesn't look down; she doesn't see the copper pipe protruding from her chest, thick rust-coloured blood dripping from the end and pooling at her feet, which are suspended an inch from the floor. Blood gathers inside her mouth and trickles down her chin; her eyes glaze over and her limbs go slack.

It takes less than three minutes for Hannah Gilbert's body to go into shock, another two hundred seconds for her heart to stop pumping her blood out onto the floor, a total of six minutes and twenty seconds for thirty-seven years of life to be extinguished entirely.

49

Imogen

I have my coat on before I even return to the sitting room. Dan looks up as I enter, frowning when he sees what I'm wearing.

'Where are you going?' he asks, standing up. 'Who was on the phone?'

I relay the phone call as quickly as I can, pulling on my boots as I talk.

'So you're going over there?'

'Of course I'm going over there,' I reply. Is he being deliberately stupid? Didn't he hear what I just said? 'How can I not?'

'Let me see, some eleven-year old Carrie White calls you late at night to say she can see a man chasing a girl in her head and you feel the need to rush over to her house?' Dan grabs my arm. 'Repeat after me – "not my circus, not my monkeys".'

I pull away in annoyance. 'She sounded scared, Dan, and she was outside. What if I leave her and something happens? What if she doesn't go back into the house and wanders off somewhere, goes missing? How is that going to look at work? How am I going to live with myself then?'

'Fine,' Dan replies, striding over to the sitting room door. 'But I'm coming with you. And how did she even get this number? Did you give it to her?'

'I have no idea,' I admit. 'It didn't come from me. I'd say she could have got it online or from the phone book, but I've never told her where we live.' Even as I say it, Hannah Gilbert's words came back to me, making me shiver. *That girl knows things. She knows things she shouldn't know . . .*

'Come on.' I pull out my keys before he can argue or try to convince me that I shouldn't be going. 'If you insist on coming, you can drive.'

50

Ellie

When Ellie opens her eyes, her entire body is frozen in fear. She can't feel her legs or arms; if she couldn't see the outline of them in the inky darkness, she'd think they were gone completely. She squeezes her eyes closed against the sudden images that flood her mind, but she can't shut them out completely; neither can she close her ears against the screams that echo through them. Her screams? Or someone else's?

Where is she? Her back is against something rough and she is shivering from the cold. She flexes her fingers and they grasp at wet grass, slide into soggy mud. She is outside, and when she eases her eyes open for a second time the images are gone, replaced by a row of lights from the windows of houses beyond. Her vision adjusts to the darkness and she realises that she is in the back garden of her foster parents' home. Only she has no idea how she got here. She is wearing a pair of tracksuit bottoms and a vest top covered by a badly fitting hoody – what she was wearing when she fell asleep on top of her covers earlier that evening. Her mobile phone is in her pocket. The daylight was only just retreating when she last looked out of the window of her bedroom – that must have been hours ago, but the time between then and now is a black pit in her mind. Was she speaking to someone? She can almost remember hearing the sound of her own voice.

She needs to get up, go back inside where it is warm and safe, but her frozen legs can't find the strength to lift her up, and in all honesty she lacks the motivation to save herself. She thinks about staying here and letting herself slip away into nothing. Maybe no one will find her until it's too late, until her body has sunk into the mud and her spirit has already left it behind. Just as she thinks that this is exactly what she wants, to not exist any more, to take the easy way out and lie here until it is over, she hears the soft click of the back door closing.

'Ellie?' Mary's voice cuts through the silence, but Ellie doesn't answer. She's hardly hidden, it won't be long until Mary finds her, but maybe she'll have enough time for her heart to give up. Maybe Mary will go back inside when she doesn't answer.

'Ellie, what are you doing out here?' Her foster sister's voice is coming closer now, her panic clear. She kneels down next to Ellie and places a warm hand on her arm. Ellie turns her head to look at her. 'What's going on?' Mary says. 'What's wrong?'

'I don't know,' Ellie whispers, her throat burning with the effort of speech. 'I don't know, Mary.' A sob escapes. 'I don't know why I came out here. I don't remember. I'm scared.'

Mary puts her arms around her and pulls her close. 'Can you come with me? I need you to come inside before you catch pneumonia.'

'I just want to stay here. My mum and dad are going to come for me. They told me to wait for them here; if I go anywhere, they might not be able to find me.'

Even in the darkness, Ellie sees Mary's confusion. She doesn't understand, and Ellie doesn't blame her. How can she understand when she has her parents here, when she has her whole life right where it's supposed to be?

'Look, you have to come inside. Your mum and dad . . .' Mary hesitates, 'they'll still know where you are. They can see you all the time now, remember? And if you stay out here, I'll have to get Mum and she'll probably take you to the hospital. You don't want that, do you, Ellie? To go to the hospital?'

Ellie shakes her head. She spent enough time in the hospital after the fire that she never wants to go back to another one as long as she lives.

'You don't have to tell your mum,' she whispers. 'You could just go back to bed and forget you saw me. Leave me here, Mary, I'm not afraid. You don't have to feel guilty – I want this.'

Mary stands up, and for a second Ellie's heart soars. She understands! She closes her eyes and is sinking back against the tree when she hears Mary say, 'I'm going to get Mum.'

'No!' Her eyes shoot open and Mary turns back to face her.

'Then you are going to get up and come with me. I'm going to take you to my room and get you changed and warm and you're going to sleep in my bed with me. And if I hear one objection, then I'll call for Mum and she'll take you straight to the hospital.'

Ellie sighs and gives a nod. She's tired, scared and defeated, but in some way her heart is warmer for the care Mary has shown her. She puts out a small hand and it is taken by one not much larger than hers, but it feels strong, and when Mary pulls her to her feet, her legs hold her up and together they make their way back to the house.

51

Imogen

We drive through the winding country lanes in a tense silence, the few metres in front of the headlights all we can see. I can tell that Dan's annoyed at being dragged from our nice warm house so late in the evening because of what he muttered was 'probably some kid prank-calling you', but he won't hold a grudge – he'll thaw before we get home – and he wouldn't have dreamt of letting me go alone.

It's one of the things that irritates me about my husband – I love a good argument every now and then, but he avoids conflict like a hostage negotiator. Not just with me; Dan is one of the most laid-back people I've ever met. When we first got together, it amazed me how much of a calming influence he was on me. It's near impossible to argue with someone who refuses to argue back, but instead of testing how far I could push him like I'd have done in previous relationships, I found myself bending to his ways, my fire not so much extinguished as redirected. I took the passion that I had always had for a good fight – all the screaming, the name-calling and the sharpened words that couldn't be put back in once they had been thrown – and I channelled it into my work. And truth be told, as much as he doesn't understand my need to rescue Ellie Atkinson, he won't condemn it or try to stop me. He won't even say 'I told you so' if it all blows up in my face. Just like he didn't last time.

This is nothing like last time, I tell myself. Nothing at all like last time. Ellie called me. She asked for my help. It would be negligent not to follow up on this phone call. Even as I repeat the words, I wonder if I'm trying to convince myself or practising to convince Edward should this trip ever come to light at work.

'Left here.' I point to the turn coming up, and within five minutes the road is lined with street lamps illuminating the sign for Acacia Avenue. 'Left again.'

'It's not that bad down here.' Dan sounds surprised, as though he expects Ellie and her foster family to be living in a stereotypical broken neighbourhood.

'Ellie is a nice girl.' I say it a little more firmly than I meant to, still smarting from Dan's Carrie White remark. I haven't told him about Hannah Gilbert's visit to the house, or her wild claims about Ellie; when he asked about my panicked voicemail I told him I'd heard noises in the back garden that had turned out to be a cat. I wonder if he'd still be driving me to the Jeffersons' house if I'd told him the truth. 'It's the last house, that one there.'

As we pull up at the end of the driveway, I glance upwards to the small room at the front that I know is Ellie's. The Jeffersons have extended over their garage, so where I imagine the rest of the houses on the street are three-bedroom, this one has four. Ellie's curtains are drawn and her light is off, but a small lamp shines through Mary's curtains above the garage. My mouth feels as though I've gargled with rice, and I swallow to try and build up some saliva. Now that I'm here, I have absolutely no idea what I'm going to say. Sarah is probably still furious with me after our last encounter at the coffee shop. Will Ellie be in trouble if I walk up to the front door and say she called me? Will Sarah call my boss, accuse me of being unprofessional?

'Are you okay?' Dan asks, and despite his annoyance at me, he puts out a hand and squeezes my shoulder. 'Your call. I can turn around and we can leave . . .'

'No.' I unclip my seat belt. 'If anything has happened to Ellie, how could I . . .?' I let my sentence hang there for a moment, then push open the car door. Whatever this might mean for my incredibly short career at Place2Be, Ellie chose to call me, to reach out to me. I can't let her down.

The air outside the car is thick with moisture, and I hope to God that Ellie is inside the house, tucked up safely in bed, her earlier nightmare replaced by boys from her class or the bands that young girls have splashed across their bedroom walls.

The hallway beyond the front door is in darkness; no light shines from around the edges of the front-room curtains. Apart from the small spot of lamplight in Mary's room, there are no signs of life anywhere. I pull out my phone and light up the screen: 10.25 p.m. Is everyone in bed? The girls should be, certainly, but maybe Sarah and Mark are too. It doesn't matter. I've come this far and I can't go home without checking Ellie is okay.

Taking a deep breath, I bang on the front door and wait. Nothing happens. What do I do now? When the house beyond stays swathed in darkness, I knock again, harder this time, more insistently. After a brief pause, a light at the top of the stairs flicks on and I hear from deeper within the house the thud of footsteps that get louder as their owner approaches.

The downstairs light comes on and a figure appears through the frosted glass.

'Imogen.' Sarah greets me with what I'm sure is fake joviality. How could anyone be pleased to see one of the mental health team at their front door after ten at night? Especially after the row we had the last time we spoke. I just pray that she really does have Ellie's best interests at heart. 'Is something wrong?'

I plaster on a smile and put on my best 'I'm so sorry about this' look.

'No, at least I don't think so, but I got a call from Ellie, about forty minutes ago. I think she was on her mobile and it sounded like she may have had a nightmare, but we got cut off. I'd have called the house, but my files are at work and I didn't have your home number. I wasn't entirely sure what to do, to be honest, after that day in the café, but I couldn't have slept until I'd checked she was okay . . .'

Sarah looks embarrassed. 'Oh God, I'm so sorry. What a bloody inconvenience for you! Ellie is in Mary's room, I'm sure I heard them chatting as I came to answer the door. They do that sometimes, sneak into one another's rooms, and I haven't put a stop to it because Mary doesn't mind really and it's good that Ellie has someone to chat to. They—'

'Would you mind checking?' I interrupt. 'I hate to ask, but I'll sleep much easier if I know I've done all I can.'

'Of course,' Sarah replies. 'No problem. Do you want to come up and talk to her?'

'No,' I say quickly. 'I'd prefer she didn't know I'd been here. I don't want her thinking I've betrayed her confidence.'

'Right, yes, I see what you mean. I'll just pop my head in and ask if she's okay – although she might have seen your car or heard the door.'

She turns and takes the stairs two at time, I hear her knock quietly on Mary's door and then low voices.

Glancing around the front hall, I clock two pairs of children's trainers by the door, the bottoms of both covered in fresh wet mud. Ellie's and Mary's? Would the mud still be wet from earlier in the day, or is it from tonight?

Sarah appears again.

'They're both in Mary's room. They seem fine. I said I thought I'd heard the door and wanted to see if they were both in bed. Ellie's hair is wet, but when I questioned it she said she'd been in the shower. Mary mouthed that she'd wet the bed. Her bed has been changed.'

'Does that happen often?'

Sarah shakes her head. 'It's not unheard of with some of the kids we've had, but it's never happened to Ellie before. She was quiet and I didn't want to push her. Without asking specifically if she'd called you . . .'

'No,' I say quickly. 'Don't do that. It's fine, she probably just had a nightmare. She sounded a bit distant when she called; she might have just woken up.'

Sarah frowns and glances again up the stairs. 'Have you given her your phone number?'

'No,' I admit. 'I'm not sure how she got that. But it was the house phone and I guess it wouldn't be hard to find. I haven't mentioned where I live, but at the same time it's not a huge secret and it's a small town.'

Sarah nods. 'Well, I apologise for the inconvenience of you having to come out here at this time of night.'

'Really, it's nothing,' I assure her. Now that I know Ellie is safely inside, I just want to leave. I can practically hear Dan's voice: *Remember what happened last time you got too involved.* And Pammy's, more frank: *Get the fuck out of there and look after your job, you idiot.*

'Thank you, all the same. It can't be easy, getting involved with children like this.' She gives a mirthless laugh. 'I of all people know that. I appreciate you coming to check. And I wanted to apologise, about that day in the café. I was out of line.'

'Don't worry about it. Emotions running high and all that. Well, I won't take up any more of your time,' I say, turning

191

to the door. As I put my hand on the handle, Sarah speaks again.

'You won't have to tell anyone about this, will you?' Her voice has a slight tremble to it.

'No.' I wonder if I'm going to regret this even as I say it. 'As long as Ellie is safe and you keep an eye on her in light of the nightmares and possible bed-wetting situation, I don't think anyone needs to know that she called me tonight, or that I came here. She was a bit confused, but she was at home and not in any danger.' I open the door and Dan starts the car.

'Thank you,' Sarah says, and I nod, trying not to look at the mud-covered shoes on my way out.

52

Ellie

They hear the front door click closed and Sarah's footsteps on the stairs again. Ellie lets out the breath she's been holding.

'Where were you all that time, Ellie?' Mary's voice is gentle as she rubs Ellie's hair with the towel. She has helped Ellie change into a pair of her fleecy pyjamas and a dressing gown, and they are sitting on her bed. Ellie shakes her head.

'I don't know. I don't know how long I was outside or how I got there. It's like I sleepwalked or something. How did you know I was gone?'

'I came to give you this,' Mary indicates a mug of hot chocolate on her bedside table that has long gone cold, 'but you weren't there. I looked all around the house, then I got dressed and went into the back garden. You weren't there either. I went inside again and the security light came on in the back porch. When I went back outside, you were just sitting under the tree. I was so scared.'

'Why were you scared?'

'I thought someone had hurt you. I thought you were . . .' She lets the sentence trail off. 'Then when I got to you, I saw that your eyes were open but you still didn't look like you were here, in this world. You looked like you were somewhere else completely.'

'I think I was,' Ellie tells her, but she doesn't even know what she means. She's scared; scared of the screams that woke her, screams that she knows now were inside her own head. She's scared of where she went and why she can't remember leaving her bed, and she's scared of what she might have done.

53

Imogen

The dirty grey sky is pregnant with rain; moisture hangs in the air, making the faces of the mourners damp with more than tears. Groups of people clad in black stand huddled together, the women jiggling and stepping from foot to foot to keep warm. There is fear in the air, making itself known in the faces of the bystanders, in the eyes of the congregation, in the way they keep their voices low when they talk. Everyone in the town knows how Hannah felt; everyone knows the accusations she made against Ellie. Do they think Ellie did this? Not necessarily, I suppose, but they don't believe it was an accident either.

Evan Hawker, the maths teacher Hannah was having an affair with, came forward about their meetings in the flats the minute he found out about her death, but he furiously denies sending her a message about meeting that night. The police investigation is ongoing, but nothing has been found on her phone, or in the hollow in the tree in the school grounds where they apparently hid notes for each other, and yet according to Evan, Hannah wouldn't have been at the flats for any other reason. Her death has ripped the community in two. People are shocked at the news of her affair, and Evan hasn't been able to show his face at the funeral. The fact that she had a lover is bad enough, but for her death to have been so gruesome – two scandals in one event – is more than people can cope with. Florence Maxwell has asked me to take extra shifts at the school to make sure the children are coping with the loss of their teacher, and Edward has gladly released me from my other cases for the time being.

Most of the Year 11 kids that Hannah taught have been allowed to come to the funeral today, but the younger children have been kept away by concerned parents. Sullen teenagers line the kerb kicking stones and staring at their shoes; for once, none of them are telling jokes or discussing their sex lives. They look sad and respectful, and yet I wonder . . . who was really responsible for Hannah Gilbert's death? Her lover? Her husband? One of her students? I know what some people will be saying: Hannah got on the wrong side of Ellie and now she has paid the ultimate price. All ridiculous, of course. Ellie was at home when Hannah was at the empty flats. No one saw her leave the house; there's no reason to believe she wasn't exactly where she said she was. I was there just a short while after Hannah was alleged to have been killed; too short a time for Ellie to have made it back from the block of flats. I just hope she won't end up being used as a scapegoat for a small-town mentality of paranoia and fear.

I turn at the sound of tyres on gravel. The funeral car rolls slowly through the crematorium gates, and people gather to take their places in line. I wonder if half the people here even knew Hannah, if they liked her. Scanning the crowd, I see some familiar faces, including Florence Maxwell standing with a group of other teachers.

The car pulls to a halt outside the crematorium, followed by another, and then a third. Men in top hats and tails step out to open the doors for the people in the back. Hannah's husband Sam and a young girl who must be her daughter get out of the second car. Sam has his hand on the small of the girl's back as though steadying her, helping her to walk. He looks haunted by something more than grief. He sees Florence Maxwell and steers his daughter in her direction, the young girl collapsing into the head teacher's arms.

From the third car emerges a frail old woman: a sight that should never be seen – a mother burying her daughter. I feel a pang of grief. However I felt about Hannah Gilbert in life, death changes everything. And Hannah's was a particularly undeserving fate. A middle-aged woman – Hannah's sister, perhaps – steers the frail old lady to the front of the line, assisted by Florence Maxwell. She and Hannah must have been close for the head teacher to take her place with the family like this. And indeed, the way that Florence embraced Hannah's daughter suggests they knew each other very well.

What was it that made Hannah Gilbert hate Ellie so much? And all the talk about evil? For all her faults, Hannah really believed in what she was saying. I'm determined to find out why she felt that way. Not today, though, not now. Today we have someone to bury.

54

Imogen

'I wanted to talk to you about what happened with your teacher,' I say slowly, looking at Ellie to gauge her reaction. She doesn't look up, keeping her eyes on the dirt beneath her feet. The two of us are walking along the canal path, the same canal that I fell into what feels like a lifetime ago. Now it's daytime and the place doesn't scare me in the light, although I've not risked walking home in the evening this way since my impromptu dip.

'What about it?' Ellie asks, still refusing to meet my eye. 'I don't know what happened.'

'I'm sure you do,' I say kindly. 'It's a small town and people talk, especially in school. I wondered whether anyone had said anything to you?'

'No one ever says anything to me,' Ellie says, almost sulkily. 'They hardly talk to me at school at all, unless it's to call me names. That doesn't mean I don't hear things, though,' she adds. 'I hear more than people think.'

I feel a stab of foreboding. 'What have you heard, then?'

Ellie looks up at me. 'That Ms Gilbert and Mr Hawker were having an affair. They were having sex behind everyone's back.'

It's not the first time I've heard something like this from one of the children, although none of them has put it quite so candidly.

Ellie kicks at a stone in her path. 'So if they were betraying people they were married to, maybe one of them killed her. To punish them.'

I stop walking and Ellie finally looks up at me. 'What?'

'No one killed Ms Gilbert, Ellie. What happened was a tragic accident.'

'It wasn't an accident. She was stabbed through the chest with a—'

'That's enough.' My voice comes out sharper than I intend. Where do these kids get their information? And how is it so startlingly bloody accurate? I know the details of Hannah Gilbert's death through my work contacts; I told myself I wasn't being nosy, but in order to help the children through what had happened, I needed to know the details so I wouldn't be shocked at anything I heard. It obviously hasn't worked, though – hearing such things from a mouth as young as Ellie's is pretty shocking.

'I'm sorry,' I say gently, trying to dull the impact of my words. 'It's just not a very nice thing to talk about. The children at school don't know the details, so they are embellishing to get a good story.'

'You don't honestly think what happened to Ms Gilbert was an accident?'

We are approaching the town now; I can see the tops of the buildings over the trees that line the canal. The path curves round into a huge park where the canal joins the river; in the summer I can remember it being so full of teenagers sunbathing and picnicking that it was hard to imagine where they all went in the winter months, hard to picture Gaunt and the surrounding villages having enough houses to store all these children away. Then once a year the fair would come to town and Pammy and I would sneak down to the park after dark – well, Pammy would sneak; my mum really couldn't have cared less where I was any time of the day. Even now, after all these years, as we round the corner into the wide expanse of green I swear I can smell the burgers and doughnuts, the sweat mixed with suncream, and hear the music and the screams from the waltzers and twisters.

'Sorry, what?'

'Ms Gilbert,' Ellie presses impatiently. 'Do you honestly think it was an accident? That someone didn't do it on purpose?'

'Yes, I do,' I say firmly. 'There was no evidence that anyone else was with her at all.'

'No evidence, right. So you don't think someone could have done it without knowing?'

I give her a curious look. 'What a strange thing to ask, Ellie Atkinson. How on earth would someone hurt a person and not know they've done it?'

'Like if they were in a trance or something, maybe.'

'You mean like hypnotised? Really, Ellie, you should be a writer with an imagination like that. Look, let's cut across here.' I gesture to the grass; it will save us a long walk around the outside of the park. It's damp but not muddy, and our feet leave trails in the dew behind us.

'Not hypnotised then; maybe sleepwalking?'

I laugh. 'Are we still on this? No,' I look her firmly in the eye, 'nobody hurt Ms Gilbert, with or without knowing it. She fell, that's all. Do you want to talk about how you feel about her being gone?'

'You said this wasn't a session, remember?' Ellie points a finger at me. 'You said it was a weekend and I didn't have to talk about feelings.'

'You don't,' I promise. 'I was just checking.'

She's right. When I called Sarah and Mark Jefferson's house the previous evening and asked if they would mind if I took Ellie out for lunch, Sarah agreed almost instantly, relief painfully apparent in her voice. She didn't even ask whether it was entirely appropriate for me to be taking one of my cases for a day out – it isn't – or if my superiors knew – they don't. She just called to Ellie, who agreed almost as quickly as Sarah, on the condition that she didn't have to talk about 'any of that feelings stuff'.

We spend the next hour wandering around the shops, Ellie trying on clothes and jewellery, me watching in delight as she whirls in and out of changing rooms. She looks so delighted with one of the trendy outfits she puts on that on impulse I ask the assistant to take the garments to the till when she is finally finished.

'Are you sure?' Ellie gushes, her eyes sparkling. I smile and nod.

'You can't leave something that nice behind. How about we go and find you a necklace to go with it?'

I know I shouldn't – I'm breaking every rule in the non-existent rule book back at the office – but the look on Ellie's face and the way she throws herself at me in a huge hug makes it absolutely worth any trouble I might get into if Edward finds out.

'I'll look just like the girls at school,' she remarks, and something in her voice makes my heart hurt. The thing about Ellie is that she is nothing like the majority of girls at that school; the fact that she is so desperate to fit in is heartbreaking.

55

Ellie

If anything good can be found in all this foster-baby mess, it's that in a few weeks' time Billy is going to be leaving the Jeffersons for good. They say it isn't because of the baby; Billy is going back to his mother – just those words stab at Ellie's heart; how come a monster like Billy gets to go home to his mum when Ellie will never get to? – but as soon as they heard the news, Sarah was measuring up his room for the cot that was sitting flat-packed in the dining room.

'I told you what was going to happen,' Mary remarks miserably as the three of them sit on the old rusting swing set in the back garden, gently drifting back and forth. From here they can see Sarah going in and out of Billy's room, carrying bits of furniture, a stupid grin plastered on her face.

'Well actually you said it would be me they got rid of,' Ellie replies. 'At least that hasn't come true. And Billy wants to go back to his mum, don't you?'

'Better than staying with you,' he remarks, and Ellie sticks out her tongue, but she doesn't care. He's leaving and that's all that matters.

'You wait,' Billy warns, his voice low and ominous. 'You're next.'

'I bet he's right,' Mary agrees. 'I'm telling you, they'd send me packing and just have a house full of babies if they could. She's been obsessed with it for years.' She nods up at the window, where Sarah, spotting them, gives a happy wave. 'Ever since my little sister died.'

'You had a sister who died?' Ellie asks.

'Well yeah, but I didn't hardly know her. I was really little when she was born and she died right away. Mum was so broken, it's like she's been trying to replace her ever since. Like she's got a jigsaw missing a section and she thinks she can just grab a different jigsaw and make one of those pieces fit instead.'

Mary says this matter-of-factly, but to Ellie it makes so much sense of the way Sarah has been since she arrived here. Like she had a play all written in her mind and Ellie is getting her part wrong because she's never seen the script. Billy didn't matter all along; it was a little girl Sarah was trying to replace.

'That poor baby,' Ellie whispers.

'Huh?' Mary frowns. 'That poor baby will get everything it could want – I wouldn't feel too sorry for her if I were you.'

'She's going to spend her whole life trying to live up to a baby who never lived long enough to be anything but perfect,' Ellie says, staring up at the window.

'I didn't think of that,' Mary replies, following Ellie's gaze. 'Looks like me and Lily will have something in common after all.'

56

Imogen

I laugh as I watch Ellie try to fit the entire top of the mountainous mint-chocolate-chip ice cream into her mouth at once. When she finally manages to get her lips around it I ask, 'So, how are things going at school?'

She pulls a face, her mouth full of gooey ice cream.

'Mmmm mmm mmmmm,' she says earnestly, earning a rapturous laugh from me. She swallows and grins. 'You did that on purpose,' she says, ice cream covering her upper lip and the tip of her nose.

'Would I?' I grin.

It's wonderful to see this side of Ellie. The intensity that burned inside her the previous times I've been with her seems to have melted, revealing the intelligent, funny young girl I always hoped was in there. She was right when she said I'd never met a girl like her before. And Hannah was right when she said that Ellie knew things she shouldn't. But she was wrong about the evil in her heart, I'm sure of it. Ellie knows things because she is by and large ignored, transparent. People let themselves open up when ghost children like her are around; they let their masks slip a little because they barely even notice their existence. Add to that her high intelligence, and it's inevitable she will notice and realise more than a normal kid her age does.

'But seriously, things any better?'

Ellie nods. 'A bit. Since I've been talking to you, I feel less klutzy. I don't stand out as much any more and I think they're bored of picking on me now I don't get mad and set people on fire.' She laughs at the shocked look on my face. Did I mention her wicked sense of humour? It's like talking to a girl twice her age. 'Seriously, though, since I've been holding my temper, I'm no fun any more. And I've been looking at those YouTube videos you showed me.'

I frown. 'I didn't show you those so you could use them yourself,' I chide, remembering how Ellie told me she wished she could be more like me, wished she knew how to do make-up and dress nicely. I confided in her that I used to be terrible at those things, until a friend of mine – Pammy – told me about the YouTube tutorials and I spent hours learning how to put on foundation and blusher, which brushes to use and what hairstyle complimented my face shape. I was trying to show her that that kind of knowledge doesn't come naturally – that no one is just naturally 'cool', even if they pretend to be. Instead she convinced me to show her what I meant, and I stupidly fell for it.

'I wouldn't worry. Sarah doesn't care if we wear make-up, as long as we don't look like clowns. She's so busy preparing for the baby that she wouldn't notice if I left the house looking like Ru Paul.'

I cackle. 'And how does an eleven-year-old girl know who Ru Paul is, anyway?'

Ellie shrugs. 'I heard my mum talking about him once so I googled him. Actually, what she said was that Auntie Abigail wore so much make-up that she looked more like Ru Paul than Cindy Crawford. She was right,' she adds mischievously.

'And home?' I'm almost afraid to ask. My argument with

Sarah in the town café seems to have been forgotten by everyone but me. When I told my boss about it, he looked concerned, but told me that ultimately we're not social services, and that it isn't our place to interfere in the foster system unless we suspect abuse. 'Foster carers are hard to come by, you know,' he added.

'Sarah's excited about the baby?' I ask when Ellie doesn't reply. My hand unconsciously touches my stomach. I'm certain I've begun to feel the beginnings of a bump in the last week; it feels harder than it did before, although it's probably too soon for all that and I'm just paranoid. I mentioned period bloating to Dan just in case he noticed, and I wear baggier tops to work. With every day that passes, I can hear the clock ticking inside my head. I know I have to make a decision about the life growing inside me – say it, Imogen: *your baby* – but every day I manage to tell myself that I will make a decision tomorrow.

'Yup. It's all she ever talks about.' Ellie jumps down from the back of the bench where she was perched and dumps the remainder of her ice-cream cone in the bin. I pat the seat next to me and she sits down sideways, facing me with her feet tucked up on the bench, her knees close to her chest. I don't think I've ever seen her looking so relaxed. 'Mary is furious.'

'Why's that?'

'She doesn't want a baby in the house,' Ellie replies matter-of-factly. 'Keeps saying that all they do is cry and that Sarah won't have time for us any more.'

'It's understandable for her to feel that way. She already shares her parents, but a baby is a different kettle of fish. Are you worried about that too?'

Ellie shakes her head. 'Nah. I don't really want Sarah's attention, you know? And I know I'm not staying there forever, although I'd like to keep Mary as a kind of sister. It doesn't feel like home, though. It's like I'm just a lodger.' She shrugs. 'Which I guess I am.'

'Do you think it's just that you don't want to settle in? So it won't be so hard when you have to move on?'

Ellie eyes me suspiciously. 'You're doing the counsellor voice again.'

I grin. 'Well that's what I'm supposed to sound like, Ellie Atkinson. You can't keep getting free passes from talking about your feelings just because you buy me ice cream.'

'*You* bought the ice cream,' Ellie reminds me. 'And now I see why.' Her face is mock stern. 'Yeah, you're probably right. I dunno. I just feel like my forever home will be different. Like it will immediately feel right. Like when I'm with you.'

My stomach lurches. I've been afraid of this; the little voice in my head has warned me that I'm letting Ellie get too close, too attached. I pushed it away because I'm so sure I'm doing something good, Ellie is progressing so well, but there's always the fear that I'm going to screw something up again.

'But Ellie, you know—'

'Oh yeah,' Ellie cuts me off, saving me from having to find the words to let her down gently. 'I know you can't be my new mum or anything. You've got enough on your plate.'

I'm about to ask what she means by that when I see her face go tense. I turn in the direction she's looking and see Naomi Harper and two girls walking towards the bench we're sitting on, seemingly oblivious to our presence.

'That's the girl who accused you of pushing her into the road, isn't it?' I say quietly. Ellie nods.

'Do you want to go? We can walk that way.' I nod across the park, a route that would take us clean away from the girls – they might not even notice us leave.

'No.' Ellie shakes her head firmly. 'I'm not afraid of her.'

I don't know whether to be proud of her or scared for

her. I'm not afraid of a little shit like Naomi, and I very much doubt she will try anything while I'm around to witness it, but that doesn't stop my heart thumping dangerously fast as I watch the girls approach.

When Naomi notices us, it seems to be genuinely for the first time. She locks eyes with Ellie, her face darkening.

'Hi, miss, hi, Ellie. Nice day for an outdoor counselling session.'

'Yes, it is,' Ellie replies, and there is a slight tone of defiance in her voice. Naomi looks as though she's about to say something else when she catches sight of Ellie's canvas bag lying on the bench at her side.

'Is that Limitless? I didn't know anyone else even liked them.' There is genuine surprise in Naomi's voice, and was that a note of respect? 'No one I know has even heard of them.'

'Oh, er . . .' Ellie looks caught off guard, as though she has been preparing for barbed comments, or even for the girl to strike out. 'Yeah. My mum knew one of their dads so we used to go and watch them play sometimes.'

'That's really cool,' Naomi says, a small but seemingly genuine smile playing on her lips. 'I might have been wrong about you. Your hair looks nice today. Actually, when you're not in clothes three sizes too big, you look really pretty.'

Ellie shrugs her thanks, playing it cool, and although Naomi's words were insensitive I get the impression they weren't meant to sting. It's true, I noticed the first time I met Ellie that her hand-me-down clothes and frizzy hair set her apart from the other girls. Today she's wearing the outfit I bought for her and her hair is sleek and straight. She even has the smallest amount of make-up on – although nothing to give Ru Paul a run for his money.

Perhaps this Naomi girl isn't as bad as she seemed the first time I met her; after all, she had just fallen in front of a car.

Besides, it was her mother who was the nightmare that day; Naomi herself barely said a word.

'Well, see you in school.' Naomi raises a hand in a goodbye and gestures to her friends to keep walking. Ellie looks as though the other girl has just named her prom queen.

'She seems all right,' I offer when Naomi is far enough away not to hear us.

'She's actually been pretty mean to me,' Ellie admits, watching the girls retreat. 'But she's right, that school uniform makes me look like such a loser. I'm not surprised I stand out a mile. And then after what happened in town . . .'

'What did happen, Ellie?' I venture. I've never asked her about that day, choosing to trust what I'm certain I saw with my own two eyes instead, but today she seems in the mood to open up.

'I didn't push her. I already told you that. You said you saw it.' Her words are sharp and accusatory, the Ellie I met on that first day resurfacing in an instant.

'I know you didn't,' I say, back-pedalling quickly. 'Let's forget all about it. Did your mum really know one of these boys' parents?'

Ellie grins and all is forgotten. It strikes me how fast she can go from intense to normal and back again. Which one is real? 'Nope. Made that up. She seemed impressed, though. I might offer to get her a signed T-shirt or something. It might make up for having to wear a clown uniform,' she adds darkly.

'Look,' I say, getting to my feet. 'Come with me. We'll see if we can't pick you up a new shirt and trousers for school, a set you don't have to pin at the waist. You'll have to keep them clean and tidy, mind you,' I warn, and Ellie nods eagerly, her face bright with gratitude. I don't even give the small voice in the back of my mind time to tell me it's a bad idea as we set off into town.

57

Imogen

'You seem bright and breezy today,' Dan remarks, coming up behind me and planting a kiss on my cheek. 'Was that humming I just heard? Or was your growl malfunctioning?'

I swat at his face with the sponge I'm using to wash up, and he ducks and nips playfully at my neck. I squeal and shove him away.

'Sod off.' I smile. 'I'm not that grumpy that a hum is a news story, am I?' My husband purses his lips and turns his head in a mock 'I'm saying nothing' gesture.

'Oh God, I'm sorry, Dan.' I chuck the sponge in the sink, wipe my soapy hands on my jeans and turn to face him. 'This was supposed to be a fresh start for us, to get away from you having to look after your mentally fragile wife.'

'You are mentally one of the strongest women I know.' Dan wraps his arms around me and pulls me to his shoulder. 'What happened was nothing to do with your mental state. It happened because you care too much. Which is why I was getting a bit worried about how concerned you are about this Ellie girl.' He leans back to check my reaction, one eye closed, still mucking around. I smile.

'Well you really don't have to worry,' I assure him,

extracting myself from his arms. 'Ellie is coming on leaps and bounds. Today I was practically—'

'Today?' Dan frowns. 'You said you were just nipping into town today.' His face darkens. 'Imogen?'

'It was a spur-of-the-moment thing,' I lie quickly. 'I decided to pop in and see how she was getting on and asked if she wanted to go out for ice cream. Her foster mum said it was fine.' I'm aware of how defensive I sound, but it's true. Sarah Jefferson was distracted by something – baby arrangements by the sounds of what Ellie was saying – and agreed instantly, and by the look she cast Billy, she was probably wishing I had come to take him too. I make a mental note to check when I'm back at the office that Sarah is using her respite sessions.

'Well, I suppose if she agreed then it can't do any harm. And you think she's improving?'

'Oh yes.' I beam. 'And we saw a couple of girls from her class. One of them said her hair looked really pretty and she was pleased as Punch. I think she's really made a break-through.' I don't mention the new uniform I bought Ellie, or the hug the girl gave me when I dropped her off, squeezing me tightly and whispering in my ear, 'I wish you were my foster mum.' Or the way it felt to be making a real difference in someone's life.

I made a decision on the way home from my morning with Ellie. I have nothing to fear from the life growing inside me. I am nothing like my mother; I am going to be a good mum. I am going to make sure my child never goes to school in the same uniform for two weeks in a row, or is so hungry that they wait outside the back doors of the kitchen until the breakfast club leftovers are put out. I've come to the conclusion that actually my childhood taught me exactly how to be a mother, by showing me all the things that are really important. Not the latest gadgets or the best TVs, but being tucked in at night and kissed before you fall asleep. Or warm baths filled with bubbles and cheese spread on crackers when you get in from school. A mum who forces you to do your homework before you play on your Xbox and punishes you if you are rude or unkind because she cares about how you turn out when you're older. And I can provide those things, I'm sure of it. When you've grown up without love, it's almost as though it fills up inside you; nowhere to direct it, but it's still there, waiting to give to someone. That's why I was so obsessed with helping the boy, and why I've got so attached to Ellie. I love Dan, but it's not enough. I need to give my love to a child. I am going to have Dan's child.

I'm going to tell him tonight. When I realised what was missing from my life, I decided that sooner was much better than later – before I talked myself out of it, or fear overtook me again. I went four miles out of my way to the super-market to pick up all Dan's favourite things for dinner, and a pregnancy test. If I'm going to do this, I don't want him to know that I kept it from him, even for a minute. I'm going to tell him at dinner that my period is late and we will do the test together.

58

Imogen

The food is in the oven and I'm upstairs applying the finishing touches to my make-up. My face is red and blotchy from nerves and I've opened and closed the drawer with the pregnancy test in four or five times at least during the day. If it's possible, I'm more nervous this time than I was the first time I did one.

'This looks amazing,' Dan comments as he sits down at the dinner table. 'And so do you.' He frowns. 'Wait, have I forgotten our anniversary?'

I smile. 'If you'd forgotten our anniversary for the second year in a row, you would be wearing that dinner, not eating it.'

'Then what? You haven't got a promotion already? Or is it bad news? Is this buttering me up to tell me you've been fired?'

I laugh. 'I'll pretend I'm not insulted by the insinuation that I'd only cook you a nice meal and put lip gloss on because I've been fired.'

I pour him a glass of wine and top up my orange juice, wondering if the fact that I'm not drinking when there's a bottle open will be enough of a clue for him. After so long agonising over the decision to keep the baby and tell Dan, I didn't expect to feel this giddy with nerves. I was so sure earlier, but sitting here ready to pee on a stick, I feel my old apprehension resurface. Once I say the words out loud, there will be no taking them back.

'So, Mike phoned me today.' Dan's voice breaks into my thoughts.

'Mike?'

'From the newspaper. About the column?'

I nod through a bite of teriyaki chicken. 'Mmm, I remember.' I swallow. 'What did he say?'

'That he pitched the column to the team and . . .' When Dan smiles, his eyes are sparkling. 'I've got myself a job.'

'Dan, that's wonderful! I know you said we don't need the money, but it's great for you to be able to get out of the house for a bit.'

Dan chuckles. 'Well, it's a newspaper column, so I'll be submitting it from my trusty home office. But it means I have a few more contacts and it's something different, so that's great.'

'It is, really great.' And I have some more great news. Just say it, Imogen . . .

From the cupboard under the stairs the phone begins to ring. I groan and start to get to my feet. Dan holds up a hand.

'Let me. Probably cold callers. I'll tell them to fuck off – you'll engage them in polite conversation.'

He appears back at the table. 'It's for you. I think it's the girl.'

I freeze. There is only one girl Dan could be referring to. And the last time Ellie called the house, Hannah Gilbert ended up dead. *Don't be ridiculous*, I tell myself. *She's fine now. All that stuff is in the past.*

'Hello?'

'Imogen? I'm sorry . . .' Ellie's voice is breaking and I can hear her holding in the sobs.

'What are you sorry for, honey? What's happened? What have you done?'

'Done?' Ellie sounds confused. 'Nothing. I meant I'm sorry for calling your house. I got the number from the phone book . . .'

'So what is it, sweetheart?' I mentally kick myself for assuming that Ellie is calling because she's done something wrong. Way to show you trust the girl.

'It's Mary. We had a fight.'

'What about?' *Is Mary okay? Is she still alive?*

'Naomi added me on Snapchat and Mary said I was stupid for wanting to be her friend. She said Naomi only wants to get close to me so she can do something mean and awful. But that's not true, is it? Isn't Mary being horrid? She's jealous and she doesn't want me to have any friends. I want to come and live with you.'

My heart sinks. This is my worst fear; I knew I was letting Ellie get too close and I always worried that one day I would have to face this subject. And how do I tell her that Mary is probably right? That Naomi Harper is a troublemaker and girls like her rarely do anything to be kind to the strange new kid. I can see why Mary is warning Ellie to be guarded. She is just trying to look out for her in the only way a fifteen-year-old knows how – a little heavy-handed and ham-fisted, but her heart is in the right place.

'Ellie, hon, you know that isn't possible. The people in charge won't let it happen. People can't just go around adopting children because we like them; there is a whole system that has to be followed. And that's beside the point. You can't run away from a family every time you have a fight. Families fight all the time. You need to sort things out with Mary. She loves you.'

'No she doesn't.' Ellie's voice is sullen and sulky.

'You know that's not true,' I cajole.' She cares for you very much and has been a wonderful sister to you. And sisters fight a lot.'

'Do you have a sister?'

'No.' I think of all the times I wished I had a sibling, a comrade who understood what life was like for me when I was small. Someone else to bear the brunt of my mother's depression and her painful indifference towards me. Someone to talk to. 'But I always wanted one. And sometimes I'd make believe me and my imaginary sister had had a fight just so we could go on a make-friends outing.'

'What's one of those?'

'You know.' I smile. 'A secret adventure, just the two of you. That's what sisters are for, sharing adventures. And being best friends. Soooo, I think you should go and make friends with Mary. I'm sure she's sorry about what she said.'

I hope that is the case. Mary seems clever enough to realise that she might have gone about things in the wrong way, and hopefully now they have both calmed down, nothing bad will happen to her.

You need to stop thinking like that, Imogen Reid. You're as bad as Hannah Gilbert.

'Okay. But she's wrong about Naomi. She wants to be my friend, I know she does.'

'I'm sure that's true, sweetheart.'

Oh God, I *hope* it's true.

59

Ellie

'I got this for you.' Ellie holds out the T-shirt shyly, braces herself for the sniggers from the small group of girls. Naomi takes it, stares at it blankly for a second, looks confused.

This is it, Ellie thinks. She's going to pretend she's never heard of Limitless. She's going to make me look a fool in front of her friends.

'You got this for me?' Naomi says, quite stupidly. That's what Ellie said – why does she look so confused? 'But I . . . I've been . . .' Her mouth opens and closes like a fish. 'Thanks, Ellie, that's really nice of you.'

Ellie beams. She knew she was right about Naomi, and she knew Mary was wrong.

'It's signed,' she offers, pointing at the T-shirt. She knows she should just take the win and walk away, but she wants to bask in this moment a little longer. The warmth of Naomi's smile is like a thousand suns.

'Wow, thanks! You're really cool, you know that?'

Ellie feels like her face might crack from the width of her smile. She spent hours last night practising the signature of each band member, tracing the ones she'd found on the Internet in pencil, then going over them in pen before finally attempting them on the T-shirt. They didn't look great but she figured signatures would look different on shirts to paper anyway. That's what she and Mary argued about – her foster sister caught her practising the signatures and asked her why she was doing it. When Ellie explained that she'd stupidly told Naomi Harper she knew someone in the band and that she was forging the autographs to give the shirt to her, Mary overreacted ridiculously, telling her that she shouldn't be giving gifts to someone who had treated her so badly, how she was always going to be a doormat if she didn't stand up for herself and how Naomi would never change and not to trust her. Ellie was upset and furious all at once. How dare Mary be so cruel? She had no idea what it was like to spend every day lonely and outcast. Mary had plenty of friends, so who was she to tell Ellie not to make an effort?

'It's nothing.' She shrugs now, afraid to be too eager, afraid to play it too cool. 'I just don't know many other people who like them, so I thought you might like it.'

'I love it.' Naomi motions at a spare seat at the table. 'Do you want to sit with us?'

Ellie wants to sit with them more than anything; she wants to fit in and laugh and giggle and just have real friends again. But she is scared. This has gone perfectly, exactly as she played it out in her mind last night, over and over, imagining the best possible scenario – and sometimes the worst; she couldn't help it – and she's petrified that the longer she stays here, the greater the chance that she will say something stupid, and all will be lost. So instead, she plasters on a look of deep regret and shakes her head. 'Sorry,' she says, putting on her coolest voice. 'I've got lunchtime detention with old Fathead. He thinks it was me who let those frogs out in the biology room.'

'And was it?' Naomi asks, a faintly impressed look on her face. Ellie shrugs.

'I'm not admitting anything.' It wasn't her.

Naomi grins. 'Well thanks for the shirt. Maybe you can sit with us when you're finished being a rebel and all that.'

Ellie grins back. She has to turn away now or she might cry.

60

Imogen

'I really don't know what to say.' Florence beams. 'The difference in Ellie since you came to work with us has been phenomenal. And the extra work you've been doing with the children since losing Hannah . . .' Her words tail off.

'It's been a difficult time for everyone who knew her,' I say gently. 'But I'm glad I've been here to try to help. Is there any word on when Evan . . .?'

Florence shakes her head. 'I'm not sure he ever will return, if I'm honest. People in this town have long memories and strong opinions. The students, the parents . . . let's just say I've already had more than one complaint about his continued employment at the school.'

I frown. 'What exactly are you expected to fire him for?'

Florence sighs and shakes her head. 'I don't suppose they particularly care about the whys and wherefores. They see an injustice and expect it to be fixed. The fact that Hannah was meeting Evan behind her husband's back won't be forgotten in a hurry. And she's not here to blame, so I'm afraid poor Evan will bear the brunt of that legacy for as long as he stays here. Which I doubt will be much longer,' she confides, her eyebrows raised.

'Are he and his wife still together?'

'I have no idea. He hasn't been in touch since he told us he was taking some time off – his doctor signed him off and I told him to take as long as he needed. It's barely been a month; I don't expect him back any time soon – like I said, if he returns at all.'

'Florence . . .' I don't know if I should ask about Evan's possible involvement in Hannah's death – I still barely know Florence Maxwell, and the last thing I want after her singing my praises just moments ago is to lose her trust and look like a gossip, but I've been looking for a way to talk to her properly ever since Hannah's death, and I might not get another chance. Florence seems to sense what I'm going to ask and nods to the sofas in the corner of the office.

'Come on,' she says, motioning for me to join her. 'If we're going to get serious, we should at least get comfy first. Coffee?'

'Tea, please.' The request is automatic and I have to make an effort not to touch my stomach. After chickening out of telling Dan the other night, I can't afford for anyone to guess before I find the opportunity again. I want it to be perfect. I want to make up for keeping it from him for so long.

I take a seat on the sofa and Florence brings over my mug of tea.

'I like this,' I remark, touching a finger to a small statue of a Buddha sitting on the coffee table between us. 'I don't remember seeing it before.'

'It was over there.' She gestures at the shelves to the left of the office door. 'I got it down the other day to look at it. Hannah gave it to me.' She looks as though she is struggling not to break down.

'I'm so sorry about what happened,' I murmur. 'I can see how close the pair of you were.'

'It's a small town. We worked together, we socialised

together. I gave her the job here and we became good friends. Although not good enough for her to tell me . . .'

'To tell you about Evan?'

Florence looks past me, her eyes focusing on a point on the wall. A classic coping strategy in emotive situations. Does she blame herself? Does she suspect Evan Hawker?

'I never had a clue. And yet afterwards I found out just how brazen they'd been. Did you know they left messages for one another in a tree on the school grounds?'

'I had heard,' I admit.

'Don't you think that sounds unusually risky? Schools are full of the most inquisitive minds you can come across – teenage ones. To leave notes in such a blatant place, it's like they wanted to be found out.'

'Part of what makes an affair so much more exciting than a relationship that everyone knows about is the fear of getting caught. People take incredible risks. I'm sure Hannah and Evan justified it by saying to themselves that the hollow was too high up for people to see, or that no one would have any way of knowing who the notes were between even if they were found. It sounds much more like something a teenager would do anyway – it could easily be passed off as one of the students.'

'And yet someone did find them, didn't they?' Florence asks softly. 'Because Hannah was lured to that building. Apparently Evan told the police that the flat was their regular meeting place but he'd never left a message for her to meet him that night. The only reason she would have been there was if someone had left her a note purporting to be from him.'

'Unless she was there to meet someone else?'

Florence looks horrified. 'No way. Hannah and Evan – well, I can just about believe it. Now that I look back, there was always a certain degree of flirting between them, although

222

I still find it hard to believe that someone as socially awkward as Evan Hawker could lure one woman into bed, let alone two at the same time. No, Hannah might have convinced herself that she was in love with Evan to justify cheating on her husband, but there is no way she would have betrayed him with multiple partners.'

If she says so. Hannah managed to fool her friends, her family and her husband; who's to say she wasn't harbouring an addiction to infidelity? Although if she was seeing someone else, surely someone would have said something by now. Anyone she was involved with would be a suspect.

'Well if she hadn't arranged to meet someone else there, and they were convinced no one had rumbled their message system, then there was only one person who could have known that Hannah was going to be at the flat that night.'

'You mean Evan, don't you?'

'Who else is there, Florence? I know you want to think the best of your colleague, your friend, but—'

'Sam could have found out. Or Veronica.'

'Evan's wife? Do you think either of them is capable of murder?'

'No,' Florence says. 'But then I don't think Evan is either.'

'Is there any way it could simply have been an accident? Could she have slipped? Fallen down those stairs?'

'That's how the police are treating it,' Florence replies. 'As an accident. But no one can explain why she was there in the first place. What the hell was she doing in those flats that night?'

I shrug. 'We might have to live with the fact that no one but Hannah will ever know.'

'Oh I don't believe that for a second,' Florence says. 'Someone knows.' She lets out a huge artificial sigh, stands up and places her coffee cup on the table. 'Anyway, I'm sorry to have burdened you with all that. I didn't ask you here to talk about what happened to Hannah. I wanted to tell you that I'm going to request that you become our school advocate – if that's okay with you, that is?'

I frown. 'School advocate?'

'Gosh, sorry, I forgot you were new to all of this.' She smacks the side of her head in a mock 'silly me' gesture that doesn't suit her. 'We tend to use Place2Be quite regularly. The school doesn't have the budget for an in-house counsellor, but it's important to keep things consistent for the children, and I'd like to put in a request to your supervisor that when we use the service in the future, you are our first port of call. It's quite normal.'

I don't know what to say. After everything that happened in London, this small triumph feels like a dream come true. 'I . . . I'm honoured.' I touch a hand to my chest. 'You don't know how much it means to me to get a vote of confidence like this from you. It's wonderful, thank you.'

'Don't thank me.' Florence beams fondly at my over-the-top display of gratitude. 'You're the one who's gone the extra mile for this school. We need people like you here, Imogen. We need you like you wouldn't believe.'

61

Ellie

'You will not believe what happened to me today.' Ellie shoves open Mary's bedroom door without knocking and the older girl jumps up from the floor, a guilty look plastered on her face. 'What are you doing?'

'Nothing,' Mary snaps, and Ellie wonders if she's still annoyed at her after their argument two nights before. 'You should knock before you burst into someone's room. What if I'd been naked?'

Ellie's face flushes – Mary has never been this short with her before – but even her sister's temper does little to dampen her mood. 'Sorry. Aren't you going to guess?'

'You got asked to the dance by Tommy Ross,' Mary says, with something of a sneer in her voice.

Ellie frowns. 'Huh?'

Mary shakes her head impatiently. 'Never mind. What happened?'

'I gave Naomi Harper that shirt and she said I was cool. Me! I think it's the most anyone's spoken to me since I started school, except to be horrid to me. And she asked me to sit with her at lunch! Sit. With. Her. Do you have any idea what a breakthrough that is?'

Ellie stops to take a breath and notices the crestfallen look on Mary's face. 'What?'

Mary sighs and rubs a hand across her face. For a second she looks much younger than fifteen; Ellie has never seen her as vulnerable as she is now.

'What?' she asks, starting to panic. 'What is it, Mary?'

'It's nothing, Els. Just promise me one thing, okay?'

'You're not going to ruin this for me, are you? Please don't tell me that the only person who has been friendly to me since I got here is trying to trick me, because I won't believe you.'

Mary's eyes fill with tears. 'The only person who has been friendly to you? Haven't I been friendly to you? Haven't I been the best friend you've had here? I've looked out for you – I'm looking out for you now! All I'm asking you to do is not to let Naomi Harper get too close. Please, Ellie, you can't trust her! I'm not even asking you not to be friends with her; I want you to have friends. I'm just saying keep your guard up.'

But Ellie is only eleven, and although sometimes she feels decades older, she wants more than anything just to be able to make friends and let her guard down.

'I'm sorry. Of course you've been the best friend I have here. You still are; you're the best sister I could have asked for. But you're not in my year, and no one can survive school with just one friend. Some days I'm so lonely that I help the dinner ladies clean up the canteen for someone to talk to. And now I might not have to do that any more.' Tears cut wet tracks down her cheeks. 'I just want so badly to be normal.'

Mary crosses the room, knocking half a dozen school books from her bed to the floor and throws her arms around Ellie, pulling her into her chest. Ellie leans her head on Mary's shoulder and sobs into her school jumper. Mary strokes her hair, whispering into her sister's ear.

'Shush, shh, it's okay. It's okay, Ellie-bean. I was just trying to look out for you, but I can see how convinced you are that Naomi is a good person and you want to give her the benefit of the doubt. Maybe I was wrong about her.'

Ellie gives a watery smile. 'Here, let me pick that stuff up for you.' She reaches down to pick up the books from next to the bed, but Mary jumps as though she's had an electric shock.

'No!' she shouts, and Ellie pulls her hand away. There is a sheaf of papers poking out from under Mary's bed, and Ellie pulls them out.

'What's this?'

Mary looks devastated as Ellie's eyes wander over the A4 pieces of paper. They are crumpled, with Sellotape at the top and bottom, and they look as though they have been ripped down from whatever they were taped to. Ellie takes in the content, feeling her stomach lurch at the crude drawing of a little girl, a puddle of water at her feet and the caption *Smelly Ellie smells of piss* scrawled at the bottom. 'Mary?'

Mary lets out a sigh and sinks to the floor next to Ellie, puts an arm around her shoulder.

'I pulled them down from the bus stop earlier, before you came out of class. I got all the ones I could see and I don't think many other people saw them.'

Ellie thumbs through the stack; there are ten in total, all identical copies of the first. 'Do you think Naomi did this?'

'I did,' Mary admitted. 'But after what you said about her being so nice to you, it can't be her. I didn't want you to see them, Els, I'm so sorry.'

Ellie sits in silence, staring at the picture, unable to pull her eyes away. The picture is childlike but undeniably Ellie, and her name is on it of course. Whoever wrote the words dotted their i's with little hearts, and Ellie recognises it as Naomi's signature handwriting. She's seen her doodles all

227

over her notebooks, and remembers thinking how adding the hearts must slow her writing down, at the same time wishing she herself was cool enough to pull that off. That doesn't mean anything, though: anyone could dot their i's with hearts to make it look like Naomi drew the picture. But in her mind's eye she sees Naomi's friend holding her tightly as the other girl poured fresh piss into her trousers, thinks about how that must have been planned in advance: bringing the canister, going to the toilets and one of them weeing in it, giggling as they did so about smelly Ellie smelling of piss. How could she have been so stupid? How could a couple of kind words be enough to erase those images from her mind, even temporarily?

'It was her,' she whispers, and she knows it as surely as she has ever known anything. She wonders what would have happened to her if she had sat down at Naomi's table at lunch. Did she, in her cowardice, unwittingly avoid another joke at her expense? She was stupid to think that she would ever make friends in a place like Gaunt, a town that chews up outsiders and spits them into the gutter. A town that proclaimed her evil but has the darkest heart she has ever known. 'She doesn't want to be my friend,' she murmurs. 'She never did. No one does.'

Mary squeezes her shoulder. 'You'll make friends, Ellie, I promise. You just have to be more careful who you trust. You're so lovely, you just want to think the best of everyone, but you have to toughen up a little. You have to show them that they can't treat you like this, or they'll carry on for as long as you're here.'

'I'm not going to let her get away with it,' Ellie vows, her voice tight and almost unrecognisable. 'I'm going to show her that she can't treat people like this. I'm going to show her, Mary. I'm going to show them all.'

62

Ellie

As always, Ellie is the first into her form room. She likes it; it means that she can sit and read her book, and everyone else can filter in and ignore her as though she doesn't even exist. Today is no exception.

The classroom begins to fill up, children wandering in in twos and threes, talking about what they did the night before, what TV they watched and who texted who and said what. Before long the hum is a buzz, and Ellie has neither spoken nor been spoken to.

Naomi Harper is one of the last to arrive. Her hair is wild around her head in a just-out-of-bed style that probably took her an hour to perfect, and she has a light dusting of make-up on her pretty face. She carries her school bag not with the uncomfortable slump of someone who is trying to fade into the background but as if it is an expensive handbag and she expects to command attention with every step. The other children greet her like a celebrity, and Ellie gives in and looks up, accidentally catching her eye. Naomi flashes her a small smile that just yesterday would have warmed Ellie's heart and given her fresh hope but that today makes the small knot of discontent in her stomach squirm.

Naomi takes her place at her usual desk near the front of the class and as always spins instantly in her seat to chat to the two girls behind her. Ellie watches her as inconspicuously as she can –

I HATE YOU I HATE YOU I HATE YOU

– as she tosses her hair and giggles coquettishly. She pulls something out of her bag and Ellie see that it is the shirt she gave Naomi the day before. Before she knew what she was. The girls around her ooh and pretend to look interested, taking it from her and holding it up, passing it around. Naomi smiles and says something, gesturing towards Ellie, and the girls all turn to look in her direction. Naomi holds up a hand in greeting and Ellie averts her eyes, pretends not to notice.

YOU WILL GET WHAT IS COMING TO YOU, NAOMI HARPER.

63

Ellie

Naomi hasn't asked Ellie to sit with her at lunch again so Ellie takes a seat at a table nearby. She hasn't seen any of Naomi's posters around school, even though she's looked for them – the ones that Mary took down from the bus stop might have been the only ones, but she doubts it. They are waiting somewhere, plastering the walls of the library or the gym, somewhere the entire class will walk in and see them. Every time she pictures the scene, Ellie can feel her blood physically boiling beneath the surface of her skin. She imagines it now: Naomi beginning to laugh and point, the whole class staring at Ellie and doubling up in peals of laughter, right up until the posters peel themselves off the walls, ripping and tearing at the Sellotape that holds them as though they have come alive and flying towards Naomi and her giggling friends, wrapping themselves around their faces, screwing themselves up into balls and flying down the throats of the stupid vacuous Harperettes and their evil queen.

Ellie's whole body is hot now. The blood that pumps through her veins is thick lava pounding a rhythm in her ears, thump thump thump, and she can no longer hear the giggling of the stupid girls or the incessant chatter and whooping of the boys, the yelling of the teachers to sit properly on the chairs or keep in line. Everything fades to muffled static.

The lights in the hall flicker and everything goes black.

64

Ellie

The dining hall is filled with screams. Ellie's eyes are closed against the darkness and she can feel that something bad is happening, but she's not afraid. It's not coming for her. The bad thing is coming straight through the darkness and it's getting stronger and stronger; she can feel it almost as strongly as if it *is* her, and maybe it is. Maybe it is part of her. She concentrates all the energy she has on sending it towards Naomi Harper and her friends.

The teachers are yelling, telling the children to calm down. Ellie opens her eyes and she can see them pulling at the strings that open the thick curtains concealing the high windows of the hall. Were they closed before? Or did she do that too? When she tries to remember the way the hall looked before the screams started, all she can see are the bright artificial lights – would anyone have noticed the curtains shutting out the natural light? Sometimes the teachers close them for drama practice to check the lighting on the stage; maybe someone forgot to open them.

No one forgot to open them. You did it. You knew this was coming . . .

Daylight spills into the hall as the heavy curtains ease

slowly backwards. The screams have died down now, replaced by a buzz of excitement and the voices of the teachers trying to calm down a hall full of excited teenagers. Nothing this exciting ever happens at Gaunt High School. Ellie can hear wild speculation all around her about how the lights failed, why the curtains were closed, but her eyes are fixed on one table in particular, one where the screams have not stopped.

'Miss! Miiiisssss!' One of Naomi's friends is on her feet, waving her arm desperately at the group of teachers. The other two are squatting down next to where someone lies prone on the parquet floor.

Teachers surround them in seconds, but not before Ellie catches a glimpse of Naomi lying serenely as though she is merely taking a nap.

It is as if Miss Maxwell feels Ellie's gaze upon Naomi and the surrounding chaos, because of all the children who are watching her now, it is Ellie whose eyes she locks on to. Ellie, not screaming or becoming hysterical, but watching intently. The head teacher's face clouds with fear and something in her snaps into action.

'Get these children out of here,' she barks at one of the others, an art teacher whose name Ellie doesn't know. 'And call an ambulance.'

One of Naomi's friends is crying, the loud, messy sobs of a truly overdramatic pre-teen. Another is muttering something over and over, and Ellie strains to hear her, milking every ounce of pleasure there is to be had from this mayhem. Didn't she say they would pay? Didn't she promise Mary that Naomi Harper would suffer? And here they are, screaming and sobbing and afraid, and she barely had to do anything at all. Simply imagine it. Granted, it wasn't as entertaining as she imagined – no dancing pieces of paper choking the life out of Naomi and the Harperettes – but still, she has achieved what she set out to do.

She still can't hear the girl's words, but she can read her lips. 'Her hair,' she's saying. 'What's happened to her hair?'

And just at the last minute, just as Ellie is herded from the dining hall by the art teacher whose name is inconsequential, she catches a glimpse of Naomi Harper's hair on the floor. Only it is no longer attached to her head. Now it lies separate, sheared away until only short tufts remain, sticking out at odd angles from her scalp.

A nice touch, Ellie thinks with a smile. A nice touch indeed.

The teachers don't know what to do with them. The whole school is so abuzz with what has happened in the lunch hall that the students are practically uncontrollable. No one knows whether Naomi is alive or dead, or how this happened, or why. But Ellie knows how, and Ellie knows why, and when she slips away during the confusion, no one even notices she's gone. Just like always.

She opens her bag and peers inside, smiles when she sees exactly what she was expecting. The scissors sit on top of her books, their glint an evil wink as though to say, 'We did it, Ellie, you and I. We got her.'

She walks quickly and with purpose, her excuse ready if anyone were to catch her outside of the school grounds: *I was afraid, I was afraid that whoever killed Ms Gilbert was coming for all of us.* There is a delicious irony in that excuse – whatever killed Hannah Gilbert *is* coming for all of them, and she is the only one who knows it.

When she reaches her destination, she reaches into her bag and pulls out the scissors, wipes them quickly with her sleeve and drops them neatly through the grid covering the drain.

65

Imogen

I stare at the grid, each square seeming to increase in size as I look at it. One, two, three, four, five, six, seven, eight, nine . . . nine weeks since my last period. That means I have three weeks until my first scan is due and I still haven't told Dan about the baby. I was so close that one time, until the phone started ringing, breaking whatever spell I was under. Standing in that cupboard, all my fears and insecurities came seeping back in, and when Dan asked again what the dinner had been in aid of, I stuttered that it was just because I loved him. Maybe it will always be this way, swinging between wanting desperately to have a baby of my own to love and being terrified of having a tiny human to keep safe and not screw up irrevocably. Does every pregnant woman feel this scared? It's a wonder the human race didn't die off a long time ago if so.

'Ready for you.' Edward's voice shatters my thoughts and I'm glad of the distraction. Florence Maxwell called me in yesterday to request my help following a major incident at the school. The police were called and a child was taken to hospital. I wasn't even that surprised when I heard the girl's name: Naomi Harper. I rushed to the school to talk to the children affected – apart from Naomi, of course, who was still being treated for head injuries – but Ellie wasn't on the list of those needing help. I didn't even have time between my sessions to seek her out, although I saw Mary when I left the suite for a toilet break.

'Mary!'

She jumped nearly a mile at the sound of my voice and swirled around. 'Oh, it's you.'

'Have you seen Ellie? Is she okay?'

Mary frowned. 'She's in class. Why wouldn't she be okay? She's the one . . .' She clamped her mouth shut.

'She's the one what, Mary? Are you saying she had something to do with this?'

Mary looked at me, disappointment etched on her young face. 'I was going to say she's the one person we don't have to worry about today. Not because she did this, but just because for once the bullies stayed away from her.' She looked intently at me. 'I thought you were on her side. I thought you believed in her?'

'I do.' I cursed my stupidity. It was one thing to have private doubts but another thing altogether to show them to the children. 'It's just with Naomi being the one who . . . and Ellie being so fragile . . . I didn't know if Naomi might have pushed her too far this time.'

'Naomi got what she deserved. And if Ellie did do something, well I wouldn't blame her.'

It was the first time I'd heard even the slightest concession from Mary that Ellie might be involved in any of this, but I didn't have time to process it there and then. I wonder now if I should have pushed harder.

'Imogen?' Edward's voice pulls me back to the small office. 'I wanted to find out how things went at the school yesterday. I've got a meeting scheduled with the head, but we've had to rearrange it a few times. I heard about what happened. Is everything okay?'

I thought back to the conversation in Florence Maxwell's office a few days earlier, the one in which she told me that I'd made a real difference in the school and that she wanted me to be the school advocate. Does she still feel that way now, after what happened yesterday? It's stupid of me to feel like it was somehow my fault – Place2Be are there to help the students talk, give them support if needed, not stamp out every incident of violence and bullying overnight, yet I can't shake the feeling that I should have been able to foresee this, that maybe my closed-minded view of Ellie is a factor in what had happened to Naomi.

I swallow nervously. I'm letting my imagination get the better of me. I'm letting the pressure of what happened last time I was wrong cloud my judgement in this case. Ellie Atkinson is no more the devil than I am Mother Teresa. When the curtains were opened in the lunch hall, she was sitting in exactly the same position she had been in minutes before. She's nothing to do with this – Naomi has obviously upset more than one person this year.

'As far as I'm aware, Florence is really happy with the work I've been doing at the school. Yesterday was an isolated incident unrelated to my case. Everything seems to be going perfectly. I don't think there's anything to worry about.'

66

Ellie

Ellie moves quickly through the wood, sometimes putting out a hand to steady herself against the cold bark of the broad oak trees. The light here is dim, so thick are the branches above her, even though they barely have any leaves left now. She is alone, on her way to meet Mary, but she isn't scared. Twigs crack beneath her feet and she hears the occasional rustle of birds landing in the trees above her. Her feet won't move as fast as she wants to go and the clearing seems a million miles further than it was last time Mary brought her here.

Mary's got something to show her. Something exciting. Ellie hasn't seen see her foster sister all day – she's been waiting ever since she got her text message at lunchtime and she raced here as soon as school finished – but she knows exactly which clearing Mary means; they have come here a dozen times before. What seems to be the biggest, most solid tree in the forest stands in the middle of the clearing, and it is lighter here.

Mary hasn't arrived yet, but that's fine, she's always late. The tree looks different, though: the base of it is surrounded by twigs and stuff, all piled up around it. Ellie tries to think what it reminds her of, but she can't conjure the picture her brain wants to show her. There's a stump off to one side and she sits down, pulls out her phone from her pocket and texts Mary.

Where are you?

It doesn't matter, though, she has no reason to be afraid. Ellie likes the clearing; it's quiet and peaceful, and no one bothers them when they come here. It feels like a special place for the two of them sometimes; it feels like they are the only two people in the world to even know it exists. The trees don't grow in this patch on purpose, it seems; they've left a space wide open for Ellie and Mary. Encircling them, closing them in, shutting them off from the world.

She hears a noise from the trees: at last! Her heart beats faster in excited anticipation. What is it that Mary has to show her? She loves the idea of something special that just the two of them will share. She loves the idea of being special to anyone, especially Mary.

The children emerge from the trees around her one by one, and suddenly Ellie *is* afraid. Some of them she recognises from school, others she's never seen before in her life. They seem to move into the clearing as one, oozing in like liquid, rather than walking. And they are all staring at her, each and every one of them. Ellie looks between them and the tree and she knows now what it reminds her of. The way the twigs and logs have been placed round the edge . . . it looks like a bonfire.

One girl stands forward, breaking free of the crowd, and for a blissful second Ellie thinks it's Mary, that she has nothing to be afraid of because her sister is here and these people are just here to see the secret thing too. But it's not Mary. It's Naomi Harper.

Naomi doesn't look angry, or as though this is a prank or some kind of joke; she doesn't seem to be having fun. Her hair has been cropped all over her head now, obviously as stylishly as her mother's hairdresser could make it, and seeing her scalp show through in one spot gives Ellie a small thrill. Naomi Harper has no idea what she's letting herself in for.

'What's going on?' Ellie's voice doesn't shake. She knows what will happen if she wants it to. She knows that despite Naomi's confident expression, she is the one in control. 'Go away.'

The girl steps forward and points at her. 'Grab her.'

Two more people step forward, boys this time. Ellie recognises one of them from her year. He's only eleven years old and has never said boo to a goose in class. She looks around, recognising more faces as she does so. How many children are here? Forty? Fifty? Enough for this to suddenly seem very real and very scary. Keep it together, Ellie, they can't hurt you.

'Don't touch me!' she snaps, but still they walk towards her. One of the boys seizes her arm roughly, dragging her to her feet.

'Who's got the ropes?' Movement in the crowd as a tangle of rope is shoved into Naomi's arms.

Ellie concentrates all her anger on the two boys holding her, imagines them flying backwards, landing with a thud against the tree, or bursting into flames and running screaming through the woods. Nothing happens. *Concentrate harder*.

'What are you going to do?' she asks, partly afraid, partly curious. She has never seen children act like this before. Part of her wants to know if they will actually go through with any of this.

'We know it was you who attacked me the other day in school. And we know it was you who killed Ms Gilbert.'

'I did not,' Ellie replies. 'I didn't touch you. And Gilbert fell. Everyone knows she fell.'

'She was pushed,' Naomi replies. 'You pushed her.'

'I wasn't anywhere near her! I wasn't anywhere near that place. I was, I was . . .' Ellie's sentence trails off. She doesn't know where she was, does she? All she remembers is the screams, those horrible screams, and then waking up in the garden. Did she kill Hannah Gilbert? Did one of these children see her? Is that why they are here, for revenge?

'See? You can't deny it.' The girl jabs a finger at her. 'We all know what you are, Ellie Atkinson. We all know you're a witch. You didn't need to be anywhere near Ms Gilbert to cause her death.' She steps closer now, close enough to touch Ellie, then reaches out and grabs a fistful of her hair. The boy at Ellie's side releases her arm and Naomi drags her forward. Ellie stumbles, trips and falls to her knees. Pain shoots through the side of her head; Naomi still hasn't let go of her hair. Now she pushes Ellie face-down into the dirt, leans as close as she can and hisses into her ear, 'And you know what happens to witches, don't you, Ellie? They get burned at the stake.'

Ellie opens her mouth to scream, but the second boy shoves his hand roughly over her lips. 'Don't even think about it.' He smiles at her. 'No one can hear you.'

The group watching them seem to be in some kind of trance. Only Naomi and the two boys move, dragging Ellie roughly to her feet and over to the large tree. One of the boys shoves her against it, and she feels the rough bark cutting into her arms and back. She pictures the ropes falling away as though her mind is a knife slicing into them, but still nothing happens. Has it deserted her? Is she just a regular girl now? Regular and defenceless?

'Here.' Naomi throws something at one of the boys and he catches it, his eyes widening.

'What's this for?'

'To keep her quiet, of course. Are you stupid?' Naomi

starts picking through the rope, looking for the end, and the boy shakes his head slowly.

'I don't know, Naomi,' he says. 'This is kind of horrible. I mean, are we going to put it in her mouth?'

'For God's sake, you just hold her still, I'll do it.' Naomi snatches the thing out of the boy's hand and marches to the tree where Ellie stands, her legs shaking.

'Open,' she says roughly.

Ellie looks at her dumbly. 'Open what?'

Naomi snorts. 'Open your bloody mouth.'

Ellie sees now what is in her hand: a tennis ball with a piece of fabric shoved through a hole in the middle. She clamps her mouth shut and shakes her head. Naomi pinches her nose roughly until Ellie is so desperate for breath she thinks her head might explode. As she gasps for breath, Naomi takes the chance to shove the tennis ball roughly into her mouth, knotting the fabric at the back of her head. From the crowd of children there is a gasp of horror. Someone, Ellie isn't sure who, shouts out.

'Naomi, you sure about this? She didn't say—'

'Shut up,' Naomi snaps. 'She attacked me! She killed Ms Gilbert. Are we going to let her get away with that? If none of the adults are going to do anything about it, then we need to stop her. We can't have witches in Gaunt.'

'She's right,' another child shouts. 'My mum said there's something weird about her. My mum said she had something to do with Ms Gilbert being at the flats in the first place.'

There's no point in arguing, she can't do any more than shake her head and even if she could speak they don't want to listen. Fear is growing inside her, but something else too . . . anger. Something bad is going to happen here.

She can barely breathe through the sides of the tennis ball Naomi has shoved into her mouth. Her eyes are still streaming with tears and her nose is getting clogged up now. If she doesn't stop crying soon, she's going to suffocate. She tries to push at the tennis ball with her tongue, but it makes no difference; it is firmly in place.

'Tie her to the tree,' Naomi commands.

Ellie starts to scream and struggle against the two boys, thrashing her arms wildly. 'Someone bloody help them,' Naomi shouts. She drags another boy from the crowd and pushes him towards them. Ellie recognises him immediately as Tom Harris. She looks up at him, beseeching him with her eyes to put a stop to this. But Tom regards her with fear and anger, then shakes his head and picks up the ropes.

'You brought this on yourself, Ellie. Why couldn't you just leave Ms Gilbert alone?' he hisses, handing the end of the rope to one of the boys holding her, then walking round the tree, wrapping the rope round her torso until she is held firmly against the trunk.

'Tie it up,' commands Naomi.

'How do you want me to do that?' Tom asks, sounding almost angry. 'I'm not a bloody Boy Scout.'

For just one second, Ellie thinks they might give up. That the fact that no one can tie a decent knot might put an end to this whole ridiculous mess. Then Naomi shakes her head again and grabs the end of the rope from Tom. Ellie watches as she weaves it expertly in and out of the other strands, each knot making it tighter and tighter. When she is finished, she gives the boys a smirk and steps forward to address the crowd.

'This girl,' she motions towards Ellie, who is frozen now, frozen in fear and by the ropes. She can't open her mouth to defend herself; she can't stop crying even though her blocked nose is threatening to suffocate her. 'This girl killed one of our teachers, and if we don't take care of her now, she will never stop until everyone who has done her any wrong is dead.' Naomi turns to face her. 'Ellie Atkinson, let this be a warning to you that we don't like witches in Gaunt. We will not tolerate evil here.'

She produces a piece of fabric from her bag and ties it roughly around Ellie's eyes. Ellie can see nothing now, but that doesn't mean she can't hear. She can hear the gasps from the crowd as Naomi rifles through her bag once again. She hears one of the younger girls shriek, and then another sound, a sound she knows well. The sound of the flint. Flick, flame, flick, flame, flick, flame.

They are going to burn her alive.

67

Imogen

'Imogen?'

I look up from my computer and blink my eyes. It feels like hours since I've spoken to another human being; I've been so deep in concentration trying to get these reports finished, trying to stop myself falling further behind with my work than I already am. 'Yes?'

The woman who called my name tilts her head towards the door. 'There's someone here to see you. A girl.'

'Okay, thanks,' I falter, realising I don't even know the woman's name. You have got to start making an effort with people here, I tell myself. Act as though you're staying. 'I'll be along in a second.'

A girl in reception? It must be Ellie. There aren't any other girls who would visit me at the office. My other cases are further out, and I'd be surprised if half of them even know my name.

What is she doing here? We have no appointment today.

I rise from my seat and cross to the foyer, but when I buzz myself into reception, it's not Ellie waiting there for me, it's Mary. Her eyes are red and puffy, her face wet with tears.

'Mary, what is it? What's going on?'

'I don't know!' She grabs my arm so hard it makes me start, and tries to pull me towards the doors. 'You have to come with me, you have to help me. I don't know what they're doing to her!'

'Whoa.' I put a hand on her arm gently. 'Just wait a second, slow down. What do you mean you don't know what they're doing to her? What's going on, Mary?'

Mary takes a deep breath. 'It's Ellie,' she says, clearly trying to control her impatience. 'I lost my phone at school today. And when I found it,' she pulls a phone out of her bag and hands it to me, 'this was on it. I don't know who sent it, but I know where they mean. I can't get hold of Sarah, so I need you to help me. I can't go on my own.'

I look down at the text message on the screen: *Meet me at the clearing tonight, straight after school.*

'The clearing?'

Mary nods. 'That's where we go sometimes, me and Ellie. It's just in Parry's Woods. There's nothing dangerous about it,' she adds, almost defensively.

'Then why are you so worried?'

'Because I didn't send her this message. And if I didn't send it, then who is trying to get Ellie into the woods? And why would they use my phone to do it?'

I nod. 'Okay, it doesn't look good. Let me get my bag.'

I let myself back into the office, already wondering what the hell I'm going to say to the rest of the team. As I walk in, Lucy raises her eyebrows enquiringly.

'Oh, there's been an emergency at home.' The lie doesn't exactly come out seamlessly, but it doesn't sound too forced either, and Lucy must believe me because she nods.

'No worries, Ted's already left anyway. Hope everything is okay, see you in the morning.'

I nod, relieved at how easy that was. 'Thanks.'

Back in reception, Mary is pacing the floor impatiently. 'Come on.' She grabs for my arm again but I sidestep her.

'Okay, calm down. I'm sure everything is fine.'

'Why would anyone want Ellie to go to the woods after school?'

'How would I know?' I ask. 'Have you any idea who could have taken your phone? How have things been at school lately?'

Mary shakes her head. 'It disappeared at lunchtime and I couldn't find it anywhere, so I went to look in lost property but it wasn't there either. Then, after maths, it just reappeared back in my bag.'

'So it must have been someone in your class?'

'Not necessarily. They could have put it in my bag in the corridor. It was just sitting in the top, as if it had been there all along.'

'And had Ellie replied?'

'Yes. She just said, "Okay, see you there."' Mary lets out a little groan. 'If anything has happened to her, it'll be my fault. I practically led her there.'

'Don't be ridiculous.' I motion to the door of my car and Mary lets herself in. 'You didn't send that text message, even if Ellie thinks you did. Have the other kids been giving her a hard time?'

Mary nods. 'A lot of them are saying she had something to do with Ms Gilbert's death. Ms Gilbert was quite popular in school – she was young and she got along with most people. It's ridiculous.' She picks at the dry skin around her thumbnail. 'There's no way Ellie could have had anything to do with Ms Gilbert being in that block of flats, or what happened to her there. She's eleven years old, for God's sake. She's not a killer.'

'Of course she's not.' My insides are churning. I thought we'd dealt with this. I thought things were getting better. Have I got it catastrophically wrong again?

We sit in silence for another few minutes as I instinctively navigate the roads to Parry's Woods. It's somewhere I've been hundreds of times with Pammy when we were just young girls, no older than Mary. What I don't know is who could have asked Ellie to go there, and why. What are they doing to her right now? Should I have phoned the police?

'You should try calling Sarah again,' I instruct Mary. 'Then maybe we should call the police.'

Mary shakes her head. 'I'll get into so much trouble. I'm supposed to be looking after Ellie. What if the police think that text message was from me?'

'The police aren't stupid, Mary. If it was really from you, then what would you be doing at my office trying to get me to go to the woods?'

'Can't you drive a little faster?' Mary urges. 'We'll get there before the police could anyway.'

We are already passing the high school. It's about a fifteen-minute walk from the school to my office, and Mary didn't set off until she saw the text message on her phone. It's a twenty-minute walk to Parry's Woods in the opposite direction, which means Ellie has probably been there for about ten minutes already with whoever was waiting for her.

'Nearly there now,' I promise. I reach out and place a hand on Mary's knee. 'Don't worry, nothing will happen to her. I'll make sure of it.'

'I just can't figure out who might have sent that text,' Mary says. 'I know the people here don't exactly like Ellie – they have this weird, crazy theory that she's evil. But it's not Ellie who is evil. It's this place.'

'What do you mean?'

Mary looks at me. 'Don't tell me you don't feel it,' she says. 'Don't tell me you can't sense the evil spreading outwards like mould. I don't know why anyone lives here. As soon as I'm old enough, I'm out of here and taking Ellie with me.'

'It's always been the same,' I murmur. 'It's always felt like that here.'

'What do you mean, always?' Mary asks. 'I thought you'd only just moved here?'

I could kick myself at my stupidity. 'I lived here when I was younger,' I admit. 'This is where I grew up, in Gaunt.'

Mary's eyes widen. 'You lived here? And you left? Why the hell would you come back?'

I shake my head. 'My mother died and I inherited her house. Then I lost my old job, so moving here seemed the logical conclusion.' I don't know why I'm telling this to a fifteen-year-old girl. 'But it's not just that. It's like you say, there's something different about this place, something that pulls you back even though you don't actually want to be here.'

'I'm sorry about your mother.'

'Thank you. We hadn't spoken for a long time. I didn't even go to her funeral. She wasn't like a real mother. Not like yours.'

'What, you reckon mine is the perfect mum?' Mary scoffs. 'You reckon taking in waifs and strays makes her some kind of saint?'

'She's got to be better than what I had.' I shouldn't be talking about this, discussing my past with a teenager. I gesture ahead as the woods come into view. 'Whereabouts do you and Ellie go in?'

Mary points. 'Just up there on the right; there's a little hole in a fence. We usually climb through that.'

I drive slowly down the lane until I see the hole Mary is talking about. I pull over, tucking the car in as tight to the edge of the woods as I could manage, and swing open the door. 'Come on then.'

Mary hesitates. 'Do I have to come with you?'

'I haven't got a clue where this clearing might be.' I pause.

I shouldn't be dragging a teenager into the woods after school. Although technically she is the one dragging me. 'I'd better call the police.'

'No!' Mary practically shouts. 'They'll take forever to get here. We're here now, we need to just go in and get her.'

We are at the fence, just about to climb through the tiny gap, when we hear the scream.

68

Ellie

She smells the burning twigs and begins to scream. The crackling, the smoke, just like before. Only this time there's no one to save her. This time she's going to die.

The clearing has gone quiet now, or maybe Ellie just can't hear anything over the noise of her own screams. Where are they? Have they left her here? Or are they going to watch as she burns, like the witch they believe she is? She thinks about her mum and her dad and her brother and hopes this will be over quickly. Hopes that she will see them again soon. But despite wanting to be with them, despite wanting to see them again, she can't help but fight against the ropes that bind her to the tree trunk. She can't help screaming as the heat rises and she wonders when the pain will begin. Why has the power deserted her now? Is it her fear that stops her from being able to break the ropes?

Tears run down her cheeks and into the gag over her mouth. Snot pours from her nose and she hopes that she will suffocate, suffocate quickly rather than burn. She's afraid, more afraid than she was in the house, more afraid than she's ever been in her life. Her bladder loosens and empties, warmth spreading down the leg of her trousers. Now she really is the smelly Ellie they already thought she was. But still the pain doesn't come.

And then she hears a voice. The voice of an angel, calling her name, but it's not her mother. It's a voice she knows well, it is Mary's voice. Mary has come to save her! And then there is another voice – Imogen! Surely they will save her, surely they will not let her burn? But the voices aren't close enough, they won't reach her in time. The smoke is filling her lungs and she can't breathe.

Then fingers grasp her arms. Naomi? One of the boys? But no, Imogen's voice is in her ear now, saying it's okay, Ellie, we've got you. And the ropes around her, the ropes that pin her to the tree, loosen, slackening enough for her arms to move, and then she is falling away from the tree. Her legs won't hold her up; they feel like jelly, useless. But strong arms hold her tightly, and it feels as though her mother is back, and she is being held in a way that she hasn't been held in a long time.

Deft fingers pull the tennis ball from her mouth, untying the fabric at the back of her head, and the cloth falls away from her eyes, but they are full of tears and they sting, and she can't see a thing. Yet still the voice keeps whispering in her ear, it's okay, I've got you. Imogen's voice.

Ellie's body is racked with sobs. Once the tears come, she can't stop them, loud, noisy sobs that feel like they will never end. But she is alive, and they will end, and she will be okay. Because Imogen has saved her.

69

Imogen

I stalk up the stairs, not bothering to check in at reception. When I reach the top, I bang loudly on the door in front of me. It swings open and Florence Maxwell stands in front of me, a concerned look on her face.

'Imogen, is everything okay?'

'No, it is not.' I barge past her into her office without waiting to be invited. She follows me back in.

'What is it? What can I do for you? What's happened?'

'Last night I had to deliver a hysterical young girl to her foster parents,' I tell her, fury building inside me with every word. Fury that had been bubbling inside me all evening, fury that had prompted me to text Lucy and ask her to cover my morning appointment so I could drive straight to the school this morning.

'Ellie?' Florence gestures for me to sit down, but I remain standing, where I feel more in control. That being said, control is not my strong point at this moment in time. I'm so bloody furious that I feel like every blood vessel in my body is about to burst, leaving a pile of skin and a river of claret where I stand. 'What happened to her?'

'A group of students from *your* school took it upon

themselves to tie that girl to a tree and pretend to set fire to her. Because they said she was a witch.'

'Oh Jesus.' The colour drains from Florence's face. 'Is she okay?'

'What do you bloody think?' I point a finger at the headmistress, and she steps back. 'Of course she's not okay! She's completely traumatised. Luckily there's no physical damage; they didn't set fire to her, just some twigs about a foot away. They wanted her to think she was going to be burnt alive. That's how evil these little bastards are. They accused her of attacking Naomi and murdering Hannah Gilbert.'

Florence shakes her head pathetically. 'Well I can assure you—'

'What can you assure me?' I demand, cutting her off. 'Because you can't assure me it won't happen again. You can't assure me they'll be dealt with. Ellie is so petrified, she won't even tell us who it was. She says she doesn't know.'

'I'll speak to them all, I'll get them in here one by one . . . I'll hold an assembly . . . I'll . . .' She doesn't have a clue what she is going to do. Florence Maxwell is well and truly out of her depth, and any fondness I had for the endearing, bumbling uncertainty is well and truly gone.

'You're lucky the police haven't been here. You're lucky they aren't crawling all over the place,' I inform her. 'Sarah Jefferson wanted to call them last night. Ellie begged her not to; she said it would just cause her more trouble. She is terrified of these kids. It's assault, plain and simple.'

Florence lets out a groan. 'How the hell did it come to this? What am I supposed to do?'

'Whatever you do, you need to do it fast. Because if anything else happens, if anyone even so much as says a word out of line to that girl, I'll go to the police myself and I don't care what Ellie says.'

Florence nods. 'Of course, of course,' she mutters. 'I'll

speak to the teachers. I'll have them keep an extra eye on Ellie in class, and see if we can't find out what's going on. Who was involved.'

'Mary said a group of them turned up at the Jeffersons' house a few weeks ago, shouting up at Ellie's window, calling her a witch. This has been going on for some time. And I think you know how it started.'

'Hannah?' Florence rubs a hand across her face. 'But Hannah is dead.'

'I'm not saying she had anything to do with what happened last night, obviously. But it's quite clear that whatever feelings she had towards Ellie have spread. The whole town is talking about it. About how she's different, how she's evil, all things that Hannah Gilbert said to me just a few nights before she died.'

Florence's eyes widen in shock. 'When did she say these things? I had no idea it was this bad . . .'

'She came to my house, ranting about how bad things have happened to people who upset Ellie. And obviously her feelings haven't died with her. Now the children have taken up the baton, ganging up against that poor girl, trying to make her life hell.'

'And you don't think . . .?'

'I don't think what?' I snap, daring her to say what I know is coming.

'You don't think there might be something in what Hannah was saying?'

I shake my head in despair. 'Ellie's family burned to death.' I stress each word and watch Florence flinch. 'And now the people who are supposed to be looking after her, the people who are supposed to be keeping her safe, are making her feel like a monster. Tell me, Florence, would you not be acting a little strange if that were you?'

Florence shrugs. 'I can't explain it.'

'No, you can't explain it because it's bloody ridiculous. And if you don't find a way to put a stop to all this, I'll be sending a full and frank report to the school board stating that Ellie is in danger under your care.'

I don't wait for her to reply. I don't want to hear any more about how this is Ellie's fault, or that the girl is different, or strange. I don't want to see grown adults acting like scared little children, giving in to mass hysteria. The way they are behaving is beyond reprehensible. And I have had enough.

70

Imogen

I know there is something wrong as soon as I walk into the office the next morning. It's too quiet, as though there's been a conversation going on and it has stopped the minute I arrive. When I say good morning, everyone replies, but they are all staring intently at their screens as though they hold this week's lottery numbers. Mornings are usually a loud, raucous affair, a cacophony of noise only settling to a dull murmur when everyone has made themselves their morning coffee and fully dissected last night's TV. Some mornings it's 9.45 before any kind of silence falls, as people filter out to meetings and home visits. It's one of the things that took me some time to get used to – in my old job, I barely spent ten minutes greeting my colleagues in the kitchen before closing the door on my quiet office – but now I prefer this bustling, sociable environment.

The stark contrast between the usual joviality and this tense, uncomfortable quiet fills me with unease, and a sense of pending dread settles over me as I turn on my PC and open my emails. A quick scan of the messages gives me no real clue as to what may have caused the thick atmosphere; no emails from HR announcing potential redundancies or budget cuts. Perhaps I should try the news – a local news-paper often knows when jobs are on the line way before the workers. I glance up from my screen. Lucy, who is usually the last person to settle to work, is deep in concentration.

'Lucy,' I hiss. The other woman can't have failed to hear me – even Tim a few desks away looks up – but she keeps her eyes firmly on her screen. 'Lucy!' I hiss again, louder this time, and I'm certain I see her wince. Slowly she looks up from her screen and I mouth, 'What's up?'

Lucy shakes her head slightly and looks back at her screen. Within seconds, though, I get an email: *Ted called us all in separately yesterday afternoon. Can't talk about it in here. He wanted to talk about you.*

I feel my stomach lurch. What was Edward asking about me? And more importantly, what did people tell him? For one awful second, the only thing I can think is that he knows about the baby.

But that is ridiculous. For a start, it would be a serious breach of procedure to ask my colleagues about a subject so personal, and Edward doesn't seem the type to invite that kind of trouble. Secondly, my colleagues know nothing about my pregnancy – I've managed to disguise my sickness well, and it's far too soon for anyone to notice any changes in my figure, especially people who have known me such a short time. No, whatever this is about, I'm sure it's not about the baby.

In that case, he knows what happened in London. Oh God.

I tap out a reply – *What about me????* – and cringe as Lucy's email tone sounds, certain that everyone will realise we are messaging back and forth. I feel as nervous as a teenager waiting for my crush to text me back, and click 'mute' on my PC's speakers. When Lucy's reply flashes up on the screen, I can't double-click fast enough.

He wanted to know if you'd asked us to cover your appointments.
I had to tell him about yesterday. It was like he already knew and
he was testing me. I'M SORRY :-(

My face flushes with embarrassment and fear. Obviously
everyone knows that Edward is questioning my work in my
first few weeks on the job. Do they think I'm going to get
fired? *Am* I going to get fired? I send a reply to Lucy – *Don't*
worry about it. I hope I didn't get you into trouble – and sit back
in my chair. But when the next email pops up on my screen,
it isn't from Lucy; it's from Edward himself.

I click on the message, almost wishing that I don't have
to, but it's better to know what's going on than to have
everyone else talking about it behind my back. It's a formal
request from Edward to come to his office when I have a
minute. It's obvious from Lucy's email that he knows she
covered a meeting for me yesterday while I went to confront
Florence, but is that really a sackable offence? I've seen the
others do it for one another countless times since I arrived;
I've even attended a planning meeting with the Safe and
Well team on Edward's behalf. So what else have I done? I
know I'm still behind with some of my paperwork, and I
forgot that one report on safeguarding at the school. Then
there was the time Chaz had to make an excuse when I
missed a follow-up appointment with Mrs Bethnal in community health . . .

I put my head in my hands and brush my fringe from my
face. Now that I think about it, there have been a few over-
sights – in fact my colleagues have been covering for me
continuously ever since I started. Well, to be more accurate,
ever since I started my sessions with Ellie Atkinson.

I suck in a deep breath, straighten my hair and stand up,
preparing myself for the worst. I pick up my notepad,
although I'm unlikely to need it – *We're sorry we have to let*
you go hardly requires writing down to be remembered – but

it feels like some kind of safety blanket, a shield against my failures. What are we going to do now? It took me long enough to find this job; I'll never find another one as close to our new home. Maybe it's for the best. We'll sell for a pittance, but at least we'll be able to afford rent on a flat somewhere for a while. But can we afford the baby?

As I walk through the office, nobody looks up; everyone seems stubbornly determined to avoid eye contact, as though I'm contagious and so much as a look in my direction will bring disaster upon them too.

In the kitchen, I make myself a cup of tea to take up to Edward's office – that is the done thing here; we carry around notebooks and hot drinks like accessories. As I wait for the kettle to boil, I wonder if maybe I've sabotaged this position on purpose, perhaps subconsciously. Do I want to be fired, so I can tell myself I gave it a go, but that this place has shunned and deserted me again as it did when I was a child? I wondered as we drove into the town if returning to Gaunt would turn out to be the worst possible mistake I could make. And maybe it has been.

71

Imogen

'Come in.' Ted motions for me to take a seat at the tiny round table in his office. 'Do you want a drink?' I hold up my cup and Edward picks up his own. 'Do you mind if I get one? I won't be a minute.' He hits the lock button on his PC and the screen shuts down. I sit myself at the table, staring up at the various Mental Health Awareness posters and the whiteboard full of notes between the team leaders, squiggled flow-chart processes and scrawled appointments. At the top, in Kim's untidy loping scrawl are the words *Ted – Florence from MA called – call her asap on 07345 879092.*

Edward returns to the office with a coffee in one hand and a packet of crisps and a chocolate bar in the other. Placing his coffee on the table next to me, he opens his desk drawer and shoves the latter two items inside.

'No lunch,' he shrugs by way of explanation. I try to smile but am certain it crosses my face as more of a grimace. Edward seems to sense my tension and sits down opposite me, ready to get straight to the point. I steady myself.

'Okay.' He takes a deep breath. 'I'm not going to drag this out, Imogen. The reason I called you in here is because I've had a complaint.'

Oh fuck. An actual complaint. One of the team? I glance again at the whiteboard bearing Kim's scrawled message.

'A complaint?'

'Okay, I suppose that's a bit strong. More of a concern, really.'

'From someone here?' I'm not sure what would be worse: the idea that one of my colleagues has gone to my boss, or the thought that it's something to do with that message.

'No. I spoke to your team.' Edward smiles, as though that will sweeten the blow he is about to deliver. 'I wanted to get some idea whether there was a real problem here. They all said that you are hard-working and conscientious. Which is what worries me about the concern that has been raised. That maybe you are a bit *too* conscientious at times.'

'I don't see how that can be a—'

'It's about Ellie Atkinson.'

I was expecting it, but still the words are like a knife in my chest. Stay silent. Don't say anything. Don't fuck this up. That was my downfall last time: my passion. My unwavering self-righteous belief in my own infallibility.

'The person who called me wanted to express that they weren't trying to cause trouble.'

I imagine Florence Maxwell's simpering voice. She was obviously on the phone to Edward as soon as I left her office after vowing to make a complaint about *her*. Now anything I do say will look like sour grapes. Well played, Florence, well played indeed.

Edward is still speaking. 'They felt that I should be aware of your growing relationship with Ellie Atkinson. Sh— they are worried that it is stretching the professional boundaries, and if I'm honest, after taking to your colleagues, so am I.'

I dig my fingernails into my palm to remind me not to react without thinking, not to lose my cool, not this time. I should have put an elastic band on my wrist like that psychiatrist suggested. Right before he prescribed me a shedload of drugs for my breakdown. The fact is that everything Edward has said so far is right; all I can do is try to trivialise it, make it seem like an overreaction on Florence Maxwell's part.

'I was just trying to do my job,' I say, keeping my voice low. 'I probably did hold on to the case longer than would usually be necessary, but that was just because I didn't feel Ellie was getting the help she needed quickly enough.' I don't mention the strange connection I feel to the girl; how, despite my numerous other cases, this is the one I think about day and night.

'And we appreciate that,' Edward replies. I wonder whether 'we' is him and Florence Maxwell. 'If I'm honest, we could do with having more people on the team like you. But the fact is, we don't. We don't even have five full-time members of staff to deal with a lot of vulnerable children and adults. Unfortunately that means that sometimes we can't dedicate the time we'd like to individual cases. We have to do what we can and then refer them on to the agencies who can give them proper, *regulated* care.' He emphasises the word and raises his eyebrows as he does. He knows about the shopping trips, then.

But how can I explain? How can I explain that I feel as though I've been compelled back here, to Gaunt; that everything that has happened over the past twelve months has led me to help this one little girl? That not one of the other people on my list of cases matters to me – I can't even remember half of their names.

'You can't just leave her there, in the care of those people. Do you know what happened to her two nights ago? Do you know what those children did? What the adults we pay to care for her are saying about her?'

Edward sighs, rubbing a hand across his face. 'Imogen, I hoped this wouldn't come up; I hoped you would just agree to stay away from this case and that would be the end of it. But I'm well aware of the wild accusations you have been making against Florence Maxwell and her staff, one of whom sadly passed away just a few weeks ago.'

I feel like he's slapped me in the face. 'The accusations *I* have been making?'

'Yes. About children in the woods, and witchcraft and the like. I've spoken to Florence Maxwell and she was very nice about the whole thing, very understanding; she's aware of how fond you have grown of Ellie and she is certain you believe you are acting in her best interests. However, these accusations against her pupils and staff have got to stop.'

'Have you spoken to Ellie? To Sarah Jefferson? She was there when I took Ellie home; she wanted to call the police, would have called the police if Ellie hadn't begged her not to.'

'I spoke to Sarah Jefferson myself this morning.' Edward's voice is sharper now; he's losing patience. 'She said there was a game in the woods, that Ellie and some friends had been messing around when you showed up out of the blue and dragged her home under the guise of rescuing her. She said she did indeed want to call the police, and that Ellie begged her not to because she didn't want you to get into trouble. Now, I . . .' Seeing the look on my face, Edward presses on. 'I have no doubt that you believed you were acting in Ellie's best interests when you went running off from work – citing personal issues, I might add – to look for her. But you must realise that you can't go chasing around after every eleven-year-old girl who doesn't go straight home from school. For a start, if you believed she was in any kind of danger, you should have called the police and stayed well out of it.'

I open and close my mouth like a fish out of water. How do I defend myself against lies? Why is Sarah doing this?

She saw the state Ellie was in when I brought her home. Has Florence been to see her? I shake my head. Clearly I underestimated the seemingly mild-mannered headmistress.

'So, you understand my position?' Edward asks, his sharpness ebbing away.

'I understand.' I pick up my notepad and my half-empty mug of cold tea. 'I'll get my things. Thank you for giving me the opportunity—'

Edward frowns. 'What things?'

I'm momentarily thrown off balance. 'Well I don't have much – my coat, my mug, a photo on the pinboard . . .'

'I . . . I don't think you understand. I'm not firing you – goodness, I'm not even reprimanding you properly. Please,' he waves his hand at the desk and I feel relief claw at my chest, 'sit down.' He sighs, as if he's suddenly realised this has all gone wrong. 'I'm sorry if I gave you the impression this was more than just an informal chat. The truth is that what I said before is true: we are lucky to have you. I'm aware that you come from a background of being able to do much more for the people in your care than we have the time or funds to manage here. But the fact is that we are limited in what we can do.

'And while the concern has been raised – don't look at me like that; you know I can't go into details about where it came from – I do feel that you have become too attached to Ellie Atkinson. I'll put it down to you being new at this, new and keen to help a young girl who has had an extremely bad hand dealt to her in life. That's admirable, of course, but it can't continue. This case has got in the way of your other work. I know, for example, that Lucy attended the regional meeting for you yesterday, and that she had to finish a report that you were supposed to be producing for Protection. I need you to refer Ellie on to the appropriate authorities and progress with your other cases. I have no doubt that you will continue to flourish in this department once you get used to the way local government operates, and that we will have no further need for discussions of this nature.'

The last sentence sounds more like a warning than a clarification of my position, but I nod anyway, feeling like I've dodged a bullet.

'Thank you,' I say quietly.

'You're welcome. Now,' Edward turns to log on to his computer, effectively closing the meeting, 'I don't want to keep you from your work any longer, so I shall see you in this week's planning meeting.'

I stand to leave, but something stops me. I don't want to push my luck, but . . .

'Edward?'

He turns to face me again, looking wary. 'Yes?'

'I really appreciate you not taking this further, and I understand what you're saying about Ellie. I will refer her on, just like you've said, but do you mind if I have one last meeting with her, just to let her know what will be happening? She's been let down so often that I would like her to understand that I've not just abandoned her.'

Edward's face softens. 'Of course,' he replies. 'I don't see that being a problem. Just as long as you make it clear that it will be your final meeting. We can't save everyone single-handedly,' he says, his words sounding kindly. 'As much as we may want to. Just remember to submit a full report with your recommendations.'

I nod, and leave the office. I feel as though I've just been in a battle, even though I barely spoke a word. I knew the day would come when I had to let Ellie go; the best I can hope for is that the poor girl understands why.

72

Ellie

Ellie doesn't understand. She thought Imogen was there to help her. Things between them were going so well; Imogen's the only person apart from Mary who doesn't believe that she is some kind of monster. She's seen the way everyone else here looks at her, with a fearful reverence, as though they are afraid that the demon bubbling inside her might burst through her skin any moment. Imogen never looks at her that way. Sure, she feels sorry for her – Ellie can see that mixture of pity and helplessness in the woman's eyes even now – and yet she doesn't mind that so much; she feels sorry for herself much of the time, so why shouldn't at least one of the adults feel the same too? No, pity is much better than fear and distrust. Pity can be used.

Imogen has always acted towards her like the adults in her old life did – as though she is just a child to be looked after, taken care of and protected from bad things. She even speaks to her like an adult sometimes, and spoils her a little bit the way her mum used to. Now she is telling Ellie it all has to be over, just like that. Dumping her like everyone else has.

'But you promised,' Ellie says, and she hates the way her

voice sounds so whiny and childish. She tries again, tries to inject some anger into her words, to stand up for herself like Mary is always telling her she should. 'You said you would help me.'

'And I feel that I have,' Imogen says, and she puts out a hand to touch Ellie's arm. Ellie jumps back as though she has been burned, and even at eleven she sees the hurt in Imogen's face, but she doesn't care. Why should she care when this woman obviously doesn't give a single spot of shit about her? 'Ellie, please.'

'Ellie, please,' she mocks in a spiteful voice that doesn't sound like hers, and she hates it but she can't stop it, just like she can't stop the anger flooding through her like someone has left a tap on in her brain, and now it's filling up and spilling over the sides, spilling hot raw anger into her arms and legs, up into her chest, and like water it is uncontrollable and there is no way to scoop it up and shove it back where it came from. The anger has a life of its own and it is making her whole head throb. There is enough of the old Ellie left in her to feel afraid for what she might say or do with this thick black anger pumping through her, but not enough to stop the words flooding from her lips.

'You're just like everyone else!' she screams, and she can feel her face turning red and ugly, feels the demon that Ms Gilbert told her is inside her rearing up. 'Except you're worse than them because you pretended to be different, you pretended to care! They all say that I'm the bad one, that I make those bad things happen, but maybe those things happened to them because they were bad people and perhaps bad things will happen to you and maybe I don't even care if they do!'

And now the tears are running down her face as if the black water has filled her up so entirely that there is nowhere else for it to go, and even as she wipes them angrily from her face Ellie doesn't want to look down at her sleeve in case they aren't the clear tears of a normal girl but the thick, sticky black tears of a monster.

'Ellie, you don't mean that.' Imogen wrings her hands together in anguish or prayer, Ellie can't tell which. She *should* pray, she should pray that those things the people of the town whisper when they think Ellie can't hear them aren't true. 'You're not a bad person, you are a wonderful little girl and I wish to God that we could work together and that I could help you, but I have a job to do and I've done as much as that job will let me.'

'Fuck your job!' Ellie shouts, and the word doesn't shock or frighten her. She knows bad things are inside her waiting to come out, and in this moment the anger has taken hold of her so firmly that she doesn't even care when they do. 'I trusted you!'

'And I'm glad you did; I hope you still do. Trust that the people I refer you on to—'

'That's all anyone ever does.' Ellie fights to calm her words but they are still filled with unbridled vitriol. 'Refer me on, move me around. Too much trouble for you? Too much hard work? That's fine, ship her on, move her to someone else's list, make her someone else's problem. Do you know that I wished you were my mum?' The sobs threaten to make her words unintelligible. 'I lay in bed praying to a God I don't even believe in that you could be my new mum and you could look after me and we'd move away from this horrible town and be happy together.'

Imogen shakes her head in sad desperation. 'Ellie, that's my fault. I should never have let you have hopes like that, I should never have—'

'Don't ruin it even more!' Ellie screams. 'Don't you tell me it was a mistake! I was happy with you!' She wants to throw something, to hurt Imogen like she's hurting now.

'Well I'm glad you're not my mum.' She spits the words like gunfire, each one a direct hit. 'Because my real mum would never have given up on me like you are. You don't deserve to be a mother, you don't deserve that thing that is growing inside you. It would be better off dead.'

And before Imogen can react, Ellie leaps to her feet, runs from the room, and flings her skinny little body into the arms of her waiting foster mother.

Imogen

I stand alone in the office, my hands covering my face and trying not to cry. This has all gone so wrong. I should have known that Ellie would feel this horrific betrayal so keenly. Edward was right, Florence Maxwell was right – this is what happens when you get too close. Just like last time. And look how that ended.

73

Ellie

Mary strokes a hand down Ellie's long dark hair and cups her chin in her palm, lifting it so that Ellie is looking into her eyes. 'It's okay, Ellie. Don't cry, please. I hate it when you're sad.'

'You didn't see her, Mary.' Ellie chokes back the sobs; she'll do anything to please the only person she has left. 'It was like she didn't care at all. And the things I said to her were terrible – just the worst things you could say to a person. I feel horrible, all twisted up inside my belly, like everything inside me is tied in a billion knots.'

'I'm sure she does care, Els.' Mary lowers her head so that her eyes are level with Ellie's. 'It's just that she's a grown-up. And you know what grown-ups are like, don't you? We've talked all about this before. They've forgotten what it's like to feel all alone, to feel as though you have no one to rely on in this world. They are so worried about looking after their own jobs and families and lives that they forget what it's like for the children they're screwing over.' She lifts a lock of Ellie's hair away from her face – it is wet with tears and tries to cling to her cheekbone – then tenderly wipes a thumb under her eye. 'But I won't forget.'

'You won't leave me, Mary, will you? Even if I get moved to a different family, you'll still be my friend, won't you?'

'Of course I will, silly,' Mary promises. 'We're more than friends, aren't we? We're sisters. You can't take that away, even if you want to. Which I don't.' At the look on Ellie's face, she lifts her little finger. 'Pinkie promise.'

'I said she didn't deserve her baby. I said it would be better off dead.' Ellie speaks these words in a whimper, certain that Mary will be disgusted. 'I wish I hadn't said that.'

Mary shrugs, although Ellie is sure she sees a little recoil of horror. 'It doesn't matter, Ellie. They're just words. And words can't hurt someone, can they?'

Ellie feels shrunken and miserable, like the tiny, sad little girl she truly is, and Mary gives her a tight hug. 'But if you want her to pay for what she's done to you, for how she has hurt and betrayed you, you know you can do that, don't you? You know what you can do.'

Ellie's eyes widen at the look on Mary's face. So she knows after all. She knows all about the anger, and the dreams, and the demons, and she loves her anyway. And when Mary gives her an encouraging smile, Ellie replies with a tiny nod. Because Ellie doesn't really want to hurt Imogen Reid. But she doesn't want to let Mary down either.

74

Imogen

I take early leave from the office that afternoon; to his credit, Edward, who saw my face on my arrival back at the office, was the one to suggest it. 'You've done some extra hours this week,' he told me, placing a hand gently on my shoulder. 'And you've had some tough decisions to make. Take the afternoon off and come back refreshed tomorrow.'

Tough decisions? I thought with a trace of bitterness. Except it wasn't my decision to make, was it?

I have barely let myself back into the house and thrown my bag on the floor when Dan appears at the top of the stairs. 'How did it go?' he asks, a genuine look of sympathy on his gentle face.

'It was awful.' I wander through to the living room, unsure of what to do with myself. I want to call Sarah Jefferson, explain what happened with Ellie, check that she's okay, but I know I can't. I have to take a step back now, let the family deal with Ellie's issues the way I should have done in the first place.

I don't even notice Dan standing behind me until his hands are on my neck, rubbing my shoulders gently. God, that feels good.

I let out a deep breath, my muscles unclenching. My husband's strong arms wrap themselves around my waist.

'It's not your fault,' he says soothingly. 'It wasn't your decision.'

I sigh. 'You didn't see her face, Dan. She was devastated. She was angry and upset, and I can't blame her. I'm all she has.' I shrug off his arms and pace the room irritably. 'That fucking woman! All because she isn't doing her job properly and decided she'd discredit me before I had a chance to tell people how useless she is.'

'But if Edward thinks you should refer Ellie on,' Dan says in his most reasonable voice, 'then maybe it is for the best. It's a new job and you've got other things to be thinking about. We've got other things to be thinking about too.'

'What's that supposed to mean?' I round on him, desperate for someone to take my anger out on. It's unfair and unkind, but I'm furious and devastated and all he can do is swing the conversation around to what he wants again. 'That because you want me to get pregnant, I can't be any good at my job? Like that's all I can think about?'

He hasn't said anything like that and I know it, but the truth is I'm scared that the baby he doesn't even know about is already making me crazy. Is this what happened to Mum? Is that why Dad left her as soon as I was born? Because she went crazy? Mental illness is hereditary, after all. Why wouldn't I be just like her?

Dan backs away, putting up his hands in a gesture of defence. 'I didn't say that, Im, and you know it. I would never question your ability to do your job. You're good with these kids; you'll be good with our kid. And I thought it was what we both wanted?'

I turn away from the hurt look on his face and want to scream in frustration, glad now that I haven't told him about the pregnancy. If he's like this now, what would he be like if he knew? He's probably hoping I'll quit work at the appearance of the two blue lines and start knitting booties. I hear Ellie's words throb through my mind. *You don't deserve to be a mother.*

'It is,' I say. 'I just don't see why everything always has to come back to us and our family. This is my job, Dan. And what I was doing with Ellie, that was important to me. It's not all about us.'

'What if it is?' Dan's face darkens. 'What if you're not going to be able to give the same level of care to these children once you've got your own? What does that mean for ours? You get so close to these kids. You have to learn to take a step back; that's why we came here in the first place.'

Take a step back? Is he for real? Does he even know anything about me at all?

'I don't need to talk about this now, Dan.'

'When, then?'

Turning to look at him, I can see that he is angry, that the months of denying him his dearest wish is pushing him further and further from me. Guilt sears through me; the knowledge that I have inside me the one thing he really wants, the thing that would make him the happiest man alive, and yet I still can't bring myself to tell him. Because then it will over – my choice in the matter will be taken away. And I feel so cruel and selfish, but right now, in this minute, I don't want to make him happy because *I'm* not happy.

'When do we talk about it if not now? When we've been here a year? When you get a promotion and it's sorry, Dan, it's not the right time? Because frankly, Imogen, I'm starting to think you'd rather talk about anything but having my child. And I'd say I understand, that I don't want to pressure you, that I don't want children unless you're ready, but you've spent the last year assuring me that a family is exactly what you want, that once you have a less demanding job and a house in the country and whatever other insurmountable obstacles you can think of to throw in the way, then we'll do it, and I've gone along with it all, I've given you everything you wanted, and you still don't want to start a family. Tell me what it is, Imogen. Tell me what's going on inside your head.'

'Did you ever stop to think that I might not want to give up my career, my body, my life? It's so simple in your world, isn't it? You don't have to sacrifice anything; you carry on doing exactly what you're doing now, only with a cute little baby to coo over and play with, when I'll be the one who is fat and exhausted and stuck changing nappies at one a.m. and—'

'I'd help with all that, Immy, you know I would. I work from home, it's not like I'm out long hours, and I want to do the night feeds and—'

'Oh stop trying to fucking fix everything!' I scream. 'Stop trying to persuade and cajole and bloody second-hand-salesman me into doing something it's patently obvious to anyone with half a brain that I DON'T WANT TO DO.'

Dan steps back, shock flooding his beautiful face, and I want to take back the words and throw my arms around his neck and tell him I'm having his baby, but the words won't come. The cruel, selfish part of me who has known all along that I can't be allowed to be a mother holds me back as effectively as if it were a separate person, stronger than the Imogen who loves her husband and wants to make him happy more than anything in the world. That Imogen has been trodden down so often by her evil twin that I'm not even sure she has a voice any more.

'I just thought . . . you always said . . .' His voice trails off, these new, uncharted waters of our marriage too black and treacherous to explore.

'Well now you know. I won't give you what you want, Dan; you may as well pack your things and go.'

Pushing past him into the hallway, I stand at the bottom of the stairs, squeezing my eyes shut at the image of the devastated look on my husband's face. I wait, one, two, three seconds, but he doesn't try to come after me.

75

Imogen

The sound of running water blocks out any noise from the rest of the house so that I can't hear whether Dan is following my awful suggestion or not. I've locked the door to the bathroom to run myself a bath, but it doesn't matter; he hasn't come to look for me, hasn't tapped lightly on the door and pleaded that we talk about this like he usually would. I've gone too far this time. I have pushed him and pushed him until the wall that I've built around myself is insurmountable, and now I'm going to lose him. So why can't I bring myself to just go and say sorry? Because I can't bear to be the one to show weakness. It's the thing that frustrates Dan the most about me; he has always been the one to apologise, always the first to break. I am stubborn and self-protecting, having been taught at an early age that to admit you are wrong, to say sorry, is to show weakness. Even now, even though it might lose me the one person I can't bear to be without, I'm not able to break the habit.

Leaning over to turn the cold tap on, an excruciating pain shoots through my stomach and I bend over double with the force of it. I clutch my middle in agony and scream for Dan. I can't catch my breath; I can't scream again. I'm dying,

I know I am, and I was such a bitch and now I'm never going to be able to say sorry. The pain pulses through my stomach over and over again, and I reach out for something to hold me up. My flailing hand hits the sink, but it is wet and slides against the shiny enamel, sending me crashing to the ground.

I've never felt pain like this; what is happening? A thought crystallises in my mind – the baby. As I lie sobbing on the floor in agony, I hear Dan's shout through the locked door, but I can barely raise a whimper in response. Ellie's words echo through my mind over and over again, a loop of prophecy: *You don't deserve to be a mother, you don't deserve that thing that is growing inside you. It would be better off dead.*

76

Imogen

My eyes are too sore to open, but even without looking, I know I must be in hospital. I'm not lying on the bathroom floor any more, yet the bed isn't comfy enough to be mine, and my arm is pressed against cold plastic. My hand throbs. Cannula. The excruciating pain I felt before I blacked out is gone. Instead there is a warm haze in my head, but apart from that, numbness. I open my eyes slowly, the hospital lights above me stark and unpleasant. I get a glimpse of Dan sitting in a chair beside my bed before I screw them shut again. He's the only person I need, and the absolute last person I want to face as I ask the question.

'The baby.' My voice comes out as a croak and my throat screams.

There is a pause, then my husband's equally strained voice. 'No,' he whispers. 'The baby didn't make it.'

My shoulders crumple against the hard mattress; I didn't even realise that I was stiff with fright. The baby didn't make it. The baby is dead. My baby. Dan's baby.

'How long have you known?' The words come from Dan but they don't sound like him. I open my eyes. His face is so full of pain that I want to reach over and pull him into my arms. We should be coping with this together, it shouldn't be like this – and yet it is, because of me. Because I never even told him about the baby, and my first instinctive question upon waking was about the child I can no longer claim to know nothing about.

'A couple of weeks.'

Dan winces as though I've slapped him.

'You weren't going to tell me.'

'I was,' I lie. Was I? I thought I would, I planned to, but I will never know now what decision I would have made. It has been made for me. I should feel relieved, but I don't. 'I was looking for the right time.'

'After the conversation we had today, I think we both know that's not true. Tell me, Imogen, had you already booked the termination? Were you planning to abort my child without ever telling me it existed?'

'You don't understand, you're making it sound all wrong . . .' But he isn't, not really. He's making it sound exactly as it was. Because of my selfishness, he never had the joy of knowing he was going to be a father.

'I'm sorry.'

'Are you? You got exactly what you wanted and none of the guilt that goes with it. You should be bloody ecstatic. Or maybe you are – I don't even feel like I know what you're thinking any more.'

It doesn't feel fair, that the husband who has supported me through every choice, every difficulty that I have faced in the last twelve months could sound so cold now, when I need him the most. *You did this*, I remind myself. I have taken a loving, patient, kind man and torn him into little pieces, until the only way he can rebuild himself is into stone.

'I'm sorry,' I repeat, too exhausted, too broken to say any more.

'I've called Pammy,' he says by way of reply. 'She'll be here in about an hour. I'll stay with you until then, then I'll go home and pick up some things for you; they want you to stay in at least overnight. And I rang work, said your appendix had ruptured and you wouldn't be in for a couple of weeks. The doctors say you need rest, and when you're feeling better they can run some tests so they might have a better idea of why the . . . why it happened. But sometimes this really does just happen. Sometimes there is no explanation.'

'Dan . . .' I let the word tail off, not knowing how to follow it up. Dan sits back in the chair without looking at me.

'You should sleep.'

I close my eyes and rest my head back against the pillow, thinking of the tiny life that only hours ago was growing inside me. The tiny life that has been washed away in a haze of pain and blood.

77

Imogen prises open her eyes groggily and for a split second panics at the darkness that envelops her. Is she blind? Why is it so black? As her eyes adjust to the darkness and the things around her begin to emerge, so does her memory. She was in her hideaway, reading Jane Eyre for the millionth time, when her eyelids began to feel heavy so she closed them, just for a minute.

Her stomach lurches in panic. What time is it? She has always been out of the hideaway by the time Mother gets home, blankets and pillows stored in the old meter box, books behind the disused ironing board, the picture . . .

She lets out a mixture of a sob and a gasp. The picture of her mother and father is no longer on her knee where she is so sure it was before she fell asleep. She fumbles around in the darkness, her small fingers finding dust-covered trinkets and piles of old magazines, but no photograph. With a heart as heavy as if it were carved from stone, she gets to her feet and pushes open the door.

Mother is sitting on the sofa, staring at the cupboard door as she emerges. Clutched in her fingers is Imogen's photograph.

'I'm just going up to bed,' Imogen stutters. When her mother doesn't answer, she starts towards the living-room door.

'Come here,' her mother instructs, her voice low. Imogen turns slowly, knows that her face is ash grey. Placing one foot in front of the other as though every step causes her great pain, she does as she's told and comes to a halt in front of the sofa.

'Sit down.'

She knows better than to argue.

'This picture,' Mother holds up the photograph – Imogen's photograph – and shakes it at her, 'was taken a couple of months before I got pregnant with you. Can you see how happy we look?'

Imogen nods silently, trying to stop tears forming at the corners of her eyes. Of course she can see; it's one of the reasons she loves the photo so much – it shows a side of her mother that she has never seen in her short life.

'We were so in love,' her mother continues, as if Imogen isn't even there. 'Your dad was the best husband I could have asked for.'

Imogen is listening intently now. Her mother has never talked about her dad before, and she's frightened to look too eager in case she puts her off. 'He was caring and attentive, he loved me. And he wanted children above everything. Two, three even. I wasn't so sure; we hadn't been together long and I thought we should concentrate on each other for a while. But he was insistent. He kept on and on until I agreed. I thought that if he was happy then I would be too.'

Imogen's heart is doing somersaults inside her chest. Her father wanted her! She was wanted! But she knows this story can't end well. What did her mother do? Why isn't the dad in the photo – the man who wanted her so much – here with her now?

'He was brilliant when I got pregnant with you,' Mother carries on. 'It wasn't an easy pregnancy, but he was there, rubbing my feet and holding my hair back when I was sick.' Her eyes have a shiny, faraway look. After a minute of silence, she shakes her head and looks at Imogen as if she's only just realised she's still there. 'Anyway,' she says brusquely, 'that's that. Now go to bed.'

Imogen feels like a deflated balloon. 'What happened?' she asks, her usual fears all but forgotten. She hasn't been this forward with her mother since she was a small child, since before she knew better than to pester and ask questions.

'I said go to bed.'

'But Mum . . .'

'Fine!' In that instant Imogen knows she has pushed her mother too far, but it's too late. 'You want to know what happened next? You happened.' Mother's eyes burn with fury and hatred, and ten-year-old Imogen Tandy recoils. 'You were born and all you did was cry and eat and cry and shit. You sucked up all my time and all my love until there wasn't any time or love left for anyone else and your father couldn't handle it! He couldn't cope with not being the centre of my universe any more and so he left. He left me alone with a screaming, selfish, ungrateful child who goes into my bedroom and steals from me and demands to know about a man who HASN'T GIVEN A SHIT ABOUT US FOR TEN YEARS!'

She is screaming louder than Imogen has ever heard her before, and angry tears are streaming down her face. She lifts the photograph into the air and rips it savagely in two, straight down the middle, then hurls the pieces into the cold, disused fireplace. Imogen springs to her feet, her legs trembling so fiercely she isn't sure they will even hold her, and runs from the room, up the stairs into her bedroom, where she slams the door behind her.

78

Imogen

Pammy sits beside the bed, looking at me with unabashed worry on her face. She asked how I was feeling the moment she walked in, barely acknowledging Dan as he shuffled past her muttering unheard excuses. I didn't know what to say, so I said nothing.

'Have you ever not known you wanted something, Pam, until it was taken from you?' I ask eventually.

Pammy reaches over, places a hand on my leg. 'Nah, not me. I've always been pretty good at knowing what I want,' she says with a rueful smile. 'But I know a man who has.'

'Richard?'

She nods. 'He had no desire to have kids, or at least was in no rush. They weren't high on his list of priorities. I suppose he always assumed he had all the time in the world. He agreed to start trying for my sake, really, but when we found that it wasn't working as easily as it should for healthy people our age – well, it became an obsession for him. I don't know whether it threw his manhood into question or whether he just didn't know how much he wanted kids until he was told it might not be an option.'

'He started trying because you wanted them? What about

what he wanted?' I don't mean to sound cruel, but Pammy flinches.

'I didn't try and pressure him – it wasn't that he didn't want them, he just wasn't in the kind of rush for them I was. My clock started ticking and suddenly it was all I could think about.'

I nod and lie back on my pillow, shifting restlessly. Why can I not get comfortable in this bloody bed? I hate it here, surrounded by mothers and their screaming babies. They've put me in a private room at the end of the maternity ward, clearly to try and spare my feelings, but it just makes me feel like a leper – unfit to be around the normal, good mothers. The ones who kept their babies safe and loved. How can I explain to Dan that this was inevitable? Sooner or later I would have screwed something up – it's in my DNA. Surely it was better to find that out now? And if that's true, why do I feel such a gaping hole where my heart once was?

'Are you trying to say that you wanted the baby?' Pammy asks, leaning closer. 'Surely that's normal, Im, to be scared and unsure. Maybe you wanted it all along, you just didn't know.'

'I think I did know,' I admit. It's a relief to be able to talk to someone removed from the situation, although I'm painfully aware of Pam's desire for a baby of her own. Selfish Imogen, always thinking about what you want, what you need. 'I convinced myself I didn't want a baby because I was so certain it would ruin my relationship with Dan, that I would end up resenting it . . .'

'Like your mum,' Pammy finishes. That's why I needed Pammy here. She knows about my upbringing. She knows about this place and what it does to people, the hold it has. I'm just surprised she's considered bringing children of her own into it.

'You, Imogen Reid, are nothing like your mum. And I know how you feel about Gaunt, but none of that has anything to do with how you would be as a mother. That's inside of you; not in your DNA, but in your heart. And if you tell anyone I said anything that soppy, you'll need to book yourself another bed in this place.'

I try for a smile, but fail. It's like my face has forgotten how. 'Thank you. Although I don't think it matters any more – I'm pretty sure my marriage is finished.'

Pammy sighs. 'For someone quite clever, you can be so stupid sometimes. Your husband loves you, anyone with half a glass eye could see that, and despite the fact that you've done your best to push him away, he has just spent the whole evening sitting by your bedside before rushing off to get you whatever you need from home. And before you say it' – she raises a hand to stop my reply – 'he doesn't have to do that. If you give up on him and let him go, Imogen, well, there aren't any pills to fix that kind of stupid.'

I don't even attempt a second smile. 'I'm not sure I have the energy, Pam. I just feel like I could sleep for a thousand years.'

'Well I'm not surprised, given what you've just been through.' She lowers her voice, even though no one else can hear us. 'Have the doctors said why it happened?'

I shake my head, a thumping rhythm beginning even at the thought of it. 'They're booking tests in.'

'Well I just want you to know I'm here for you.' She twists the bedcovers in her fingers and I actually get the impression she's nervous. I'm not sure I've ever seen Pammy nervous before. 'Because I've been where you are.'

'Oh God, Pammy, I'm so sorry. Why did you never tell me?'

She shrugs. 'I dunno. I didn't want to put it on you, I guess. You were so far away, living this perfect life in the city with your amazing career and your perfect flat, and I didn't want to burden you with my small-town crap.'

'It doesn't feel like small-town crap right now.'

Pammy winces. 'Oh shit, I didn't mean that. I'm just awful at this.'

'You are not. And I'm sorry you didn't feel like you could talk to me.' I take a deep breath. 'Maybe it's time I told you the truth about this perfect life of mine.' My fingernails pick absently at the loose skin around my thumbnail. 'The real reason I left my last job was because there was a complaint about me. I was given the option to leave before they fired me.'

Pammy is watching me intently and I can't meet her eye. My cheeks burn in shame. When she says nothing, I carry on.

'There was a boy,' I say. 'Not much older than Ellie; in fact he'd only just turned twelve. He was referred by the hospital as part of the pro-bono work we did. The boy . . .' I take a deep breath. 'God, I haven't said his name in almost twelve months. Even during the inquiry I just couldn't bring myself to say it.'

Pammy gives my leg a squeeze.

'He had just turned twelve. His parents brought him to me because he was hurting himself. He was covered in bruises, and they said that he would punch his own arms and kick his shins against the furniture, scratch himself and hit himself in the face when he was angry or upset. We worked together for a long time and I . . . I felt like I got to know him very well. He was kind, and funny, and so clever for his age. But the whole time we worked together he never spoke once about the episodes of self-harm. It was as though he wanted to avoid the topic completely.

'Then one day he came to me and his arm was in a sling, and his hand in a cast. His mother said he had thrown himself down the stairs in a fit of rage and broken his wrist and fractured a bone in his elbow. When I asked him to tell me what happened, he shrugged and said he wasn't sure. He looked nervous and I could see that the situation made him uncomfortable, but I didn't want to leave it alone – not like I normally did when I asked about his injuries. By that time I had a suspicion and I wanted him to confirm it for me. So I asked him outright: "Are you causing your own injuries, or is it someone else? Are you protecting someone?"

'He didn't answer straight away, just sat in silence staring at the desk in front of us. Then eventually, after what seemed like an eternity, tears began to roll down his cheeks. I told him he didn't have to be scared, that anything he told me in these sessions was between the two of us. I said that even though I knew that if he was being hurt by someone, I would have to tell; I knew I was probably lying to him. There and then, sitting in that room, facing that sad little boy, all I wanted was to get to the truth. So I lied. I broke one of my own rules and lied to a patient.

'He sat in silence for a little while longer, and then, eventually, he nodded. Just a small nod, just the slightest inclination of his head, and I *knew* that what I had been thinking was true. I knew he was protecting someone, probably his parents, and I knew there was more to this than anyone was telling us. So I vowed I would help him, and I meant it. Together we went through every one of his injuries and I encouraged him to tell me how they had really happened. We drew pictures together: a picture of his father shoving him, him hitting his arm on a dresser. A picture of his mother standing at the top of the stairs while he tumbled down. We did word associations, and every time I said words like "caregiver", "parent", "guardian", "mother", he would write words like *fear*, *hurt*, *pain*, *confusion*.

'After a few of these sessions, I felt like I had enough to

go to my supervisor. He sat down with me and went through every session, listened to the tapes, analysed the drawings. Then, after seeing and hearing the exact same evidence as me, he made the decision that there wasn't enough in what we had to go to social services. He suggested that I'd asked leading questions, encouraged the boy to give the answers that I wanted to hear, rewarded him for making up stories against his parents. I was furious. I believed unequivocally what that boy was telling me. It wasn't something you heard in the sessions or something you could see from the drawings; it was a feeling you got from being around him. It was a hunch, it was instinct. But instinct isn't something you can prove, and so it was mine and his word against his parents'.

'My supervisor and the board decided that there would be no action taken against the parents. That unless he decided of his own accord to make a complaint against them, there was nothing further we could do. I was livid, hurt, confused. You see all these stories about children being taken away from their parents because of a bruise on their leg and here was this boy telling us he had been abused and they were just going to ignore him. I was ordered to give up the case, and his parents were told that they should find a new psychologist. But I couldn't leave it there. I couldn't leave him on his own with those people, knowing what they'd been doing to him, knowing what might happen to him if I didn't take action. So I went to the police.'

Pammy puts a hand to her mouth, as though she is trying to stop herself from interrupting, and I know that if I don't carry on now, I will just clam up and never speak of it again. But I want to tell someone, and so I push on before she can say a word.

'I showed them everything: the drawings, the statements; I spent hours in a tiny grey room outlining every injury the boy had sustained, every brutal attack I believed the parents had committed against this child.' I'm speaking faster now, and tears are tumbling down my cheeks at the memory. I can still see the boy's face, so confused, so betrayed when the police turned up at his house with me by their side.

'They took the boy's parents, they interviewed them for hours; they took him too. But he said nothing. He refused to give any kind of statement against his parents, and when faced with the recordings of our sessions he said that I had made him say those things, that he had said them because he wanted to please me, because he knew that was what I wanted to hear. He said that when the tapes weren't rolling I told him that he couldn't possibly have given himself those injuries, that someone else must have been to blame. He said I pushed and pushed and pushed until eventually he just agreed with me to make me stop.'

I brush the warm tears from my cheeks and shake off the hand Pammy places on my shoulder. I don't want her pity; I want her to *understand*. 'Eventually the police had to let the parents go. There was literally no evidence; without the boy's statement, they had nothing on them. I had been waiting in the reception of the police station in case they needed me, in case he needed me. I thought that after his ordeal he might want someone to speak to and I would be there for him. Instead I was faced with his parents. The mother had her arm around the boy's shoulders and pulled him closer to her as they passed me. Then, as they were about to leave, she turned on me, shouting and screaming that I was trying to ruin their lives and take their child away from them. That I was a liar and a bully and that I was to leave them alone and never speak to them again. He didn't look at me once.'

I take a deep breath. 'When I got back to work, the supervisor called me into his office. He was furious that I had gone against the wishes of the clinic, and that I had released confidential case notes without their permission. The boy's parents had made a complaint against me that had to be investigated, and were it to be upheld, the clinic would be fined a considerable sum. The parents said they were going to sue; they said they were going to take away my licence and that of my supervisor. The only way around it was for the clinic to settle out of court, and I was to have my own separate hearing with the General Medical Council.

'I couldn't stand the thought of the publicity – not for me, but for the boy. He was a juvenile, so the papers wouldn't be able to name him, but I was frightened that people would find out who he was, that this would make his life more difficult. So I quit. Not just my job, but psychology altogether. I told my supervisor I would go quietly, there would be no need for a lengthy investigation, no need for the clinic to be brought into disrepute. I begged them to give me a reference so that I could move away, get a new job. My supervisor agreed, but said that the only way they could give me a reference was if I never practised as a psychologist again.

'The worst thing about all this? The absolute worst thing was that I still believed, I still believe, that I was right. I still believe that we sent that boy back to his parents knowing the damage they had inflicted on him, and there was nothing I could do about it. After I left, I went to his house, I sat outside in my car. I only wanted to see if he was okay, but his mother saw me there. She must have watched me for over an hour, recording me on her mobile phone, although I didn't know it until the police turned up. I was told that if I didn't stop stalking – that was the word they used, stalking! – the family would press charges against me. I was to stop calling the house, even though I'd only rung once or twice to speak to the boy, and I wasn't to write him any more notes. I'd had no idea she'd found the note I'd given to one of his classmates, imploring him to tell the truth, telling him that was the only way I could help him. The police rang Dan to come and get me and I was forced to tell him what I'd done.'

'Oh Im,' Pammy breathes. 'What did he say?'

'Well, he was typical Dan,' I reply, remembering how he nursed me back to health as though I was a child myself. 'He was worried about me, he fussed around and tried to get me to see a doctor. He was the perfect husband, all the while not understanding anything.'

'How did you expect him to understand, Im? How did you expect him to know that the reason you were so desperate to save that boy from a life of abuse and neglect was because no one saved you? Because everyone saw the way your mum was and no one did a damn thing about it. Because you know that's what it was, don't you? And you know that's what it is with this little girl. You're desperate to do for them what no one would do for you. But your past gets in the way of you thinking clearly. I mean, I get it, really I do, and you know I love you like a sister, but turning up at the kid's school? Giving his friends notes to pass to him?' Pammy shakes her head. 'You are the stupidest clever person I know.'

I groan. 'I know. Don't you think I don't know? Once I was out of it all, I could see it clearly, how crazy I'd been. I was so certain, so sure I was right.'

'Like you were certain about Ellie?' Pammy asks gently. 'You don't think you got so involved in this case because you couldn't help that little boy?'

'Maybe,' I reply. 'But what if I was? Does that mean I'm wrong? Does one mistake mean I should just give up my convictions completely?'

'It means you should be more careful,' Pammy advises. 'It means you shouldn't get so involved that you lose your mind. It means you can't afford to ruin your life a second time. And that's exactly what you're in danger of doing.'

'That's not everything.' If I've come this far I need to tell her the rest. The real reason why I was so unsure about giving Dan the baby he craved, the real reason I had slunk back to Gaunt at the first available opportunity. Exactly what I'd been running from. 'The boy I'm talking about, he's the one that was in all the newspapers; Callum Walters.'

Pammy's eyes widen and I know that she knows exactly who I'm talking about. 'The one who . . . ?'

'The one who committed suicide after his parents were falsely accused of abuse.'

79

Ellie

'Was it you?' Mary grabs Ellie's arm excitedly, her eyes are shining. She's been looking at Ellie weirdly throughout dinner, and now, at the first moment when the others aren't around, she rounds on her.

'Was what me?' Ellie asks quietly. 'I don't know you what you're talking about.'

'Everyone is talking about it,' Mary says dramatically. 'That woman that was coming here, working with you, Imogen Reid.'

'What about her?' Ellie interrupts.

'She's been off work for a few days; she was taken into hospital. Maisie King's mum works with her at the social. Says she lost her baby.'

Ellie takes in a sharp breath. She remembers Imogen's face when she spat out the words at their last meeting.

You don't deserve that thing that is growing inside you. It would be better off dead.

'So was it you?' Mary asks, echoing Ellie's thoughts as clearly as if she's read them. 'Did you do it? To teach her a lesson, like we discussed?'

'Of course I didn't. That's horrible, I would never do

297

anything like that.' Her voice comes out sharper than intended and Mary narrows her eyes.

'But you can, can't you, Ellie?' Her foster sister is looking at her intently. 'Maybe you did it by accident, without meaning to.'

'I already told you I didn't,' Ellie snaps. 'I'm going up to bed.'

She gets up and pushes her chair back under the table, wincing as it squeaks against the floor. Sarah appears from the kitchen. 'Where are you going, Els? There's pudding.'

'I'm not really very hungry,' Ellie lies. 'I thought I'd just go and read in my room for a little while.'

'Erm . . .' Sarah looks backwards into the kitchen at Mark. 'Well, okay then, if you're sure . . .'

And then Ellie realises that the reason Sarah hasn't left her alone all day, the reason she has consistently suggested that they do things together, spend more time as a family, is that she knows about Imogen. And she wants Ellie where she can see her.

'Me too, Mum,' Mary agrees, jumping up from the table and pushing her own chair underneath. 'We've got tons of homework this year.'

But as they go upstairs, Mary doesn't head into her own room; she follows Ellie into hers.

'So,' she says, throwing herself down on Ellie's bed, 'how did you do it?'

'I'm telling you, I didn't,' Ellie insists, gritting her teeth. For the first time since arriving at the Jeffersons', she wishes Mary would just go away. Mary is the only person who has made her feel properly welcome here, she has stuck up for her at school, she has shared her clothes and her make-up, but right now Ellie just wants to be alone.

'It's so cool,' Mary says, folding her legs underneath her. 'I wish I could do it, I wish you could teach me. To be able to just make anyone suffer, anyone who upset you or pissed you off. I know a few people I'd use it on.'

'It's not like that,' Ellie insists. 'I don't do any of this stuff on purpose. I don't even know I'm doing it. It just seems to . . . happen.'

'Okay,' Mary relents, but Ellie can tell she doesn't believe her. 'But don't you think you could learn to control it? Don't you think that if you really tried, instead of fighting it, you could harness it, you know, like use the power? You could get whatever you wanted. Imagine, eventually they'd have to make you prime minister or something.'

'Or stick me in a zoo,' Ellie replies, which she thinks is much more likely. She's seen the X-Men; no one was rushing to put them in charge of a country. 'Or a mental hospital.'

'I wonder if that woman . . . that Imogen . . . I wonder if she knows it was you? I don't suppose she'd be able to prove it, even if she suspected.' Mary is talking to herself more than Ellie now.

Ellie wonders when it happened, when Imogen lost her baby. When was the chain of events set in motion? What is it that triggers these awful things? Maybe if she can pinpoint that, she will be able to control it, like Mary says.

Was it her words? Was it when she actually said the words 'You don't deserve that thing that is growing inside you'? Or was it because of all the thoughts running through her mind at that very second, clashing against each other, clamouring for space in her brain. Angry, horrid thoughts that she should never have had. Maybe that's when it was decided. Because certainly, by later on that evening, by the time she went to bed, she had calmed down quite considerably. Or maybe it was in her sleep, in her dreams like it was with Ms Gilbert. Ellie can't remember dreaming the night of her argument with Imogen, but that doesn't mean she didn't. Dreams are spectral, elusive; once you wake up, there is almost no chance of remembering them if they don't want to be remembered. So maybe that's when it happened.

'We could do an experiment,' Mary suggests, breaking the silence and once again giving the impression that she has managed to read Ellie's mind. Or maybe Ellie is just so transparent. 'To see how you do it, I mean. To see how it works.'

'I don't think I want to . . . I think . . . I'm scared to,' Ellie admits. Imagine if they prove that she has this power. What will that mean for her? She won't be able to fool herself any more that the things that have been happening might be coincidence.

'I know it must be scary for you, not knowing what you're capable of, not being able to control the anger you have inside you, or what it does to people. That's why I'm here. I'm here to help you. But I can't help you control this thing unless we learn about it,' Mary says gently, patting Ellie on the arm. 'And anyway, we need proof.'

Proof. Proof that Ellie stuck Billy's lips together, proof that she made thousands of spiders appear in Ms Gilbert's drawer just by hating her. Proof that she killed Ms Gilbert, and Imogen's baby.

'Why?' she asks. 'Why do we need proof?'

Mary smiles, a smile Ellie has never seen her use before. It is the kind of smile Ellie imagine the demons to have in the books she has read, or the bad guys in the films they sometimes watch. The kind of smile that is a little bit twisted.

'Of course we need proof, silly,' Mary says, still smiling. 'Without proof we will never get anyone to be afraid of you. Without proof, people will just keep treating you the way they have been all along. And you don't want to be treated like that any more, do you, Ellie?'

No, no, she doesn't. 'Okay,' she says, giving one hard nod. 'I'll do it.'

80

Imogen

'I'll sleep in the spare room for now,' Dan says, his voice quiet as he opens the car door for me. 'Let you get some rest.'

I don't want rest, my mind is screaming, I want my husband back. But of course I don't say that; he's got every right to be mad at me. I just wish I knew the time limit on his anger – like if I knew it was going to be six days and three hours, it would be a lot easier to bear. Then there's the part of me that wonders if he's ever going to forgive me, or if this will be the wedge that drives us apart for good. I know what I did was wrong, but I had no idea it was going to end like this. I thought I had time to tell him when I was ready.

He's so cordial I could scream. I want him to scream. I want him to tell me I'm a fucking bitch and he hates me; I'd give anything for my husband of five years to lob something at my head, for Christ's sake, anything but this cold indifference. I know that as soon as I am well he's going to pack his bags and leave me. It's only ever been a matter of time; there was only ever going to be so much a loving, caring, patient man like Dan could take from a monumental

301

fuck-up like me. I feel a million times better after telling Pammy about Callum, after saying everything out loud – telling my side of the story, like I've ripped off a scab and let the blood flow. The papers hadn't named me, the details of the case had been minimised by the practice, by the BPS, by the police even. I had already been asked to leave Morgan and Astley by that point, Callum's history of self-harm had overshadowed the accusation and only the less reputable tabloids had even reported it. Still, it was there, in my mind, every time I thought about having children, every time I thought about taking on a new case at Place2Be. I'd been mostly honest with them when I'd gone for the job – I'd told them that I'd gone against my employer's instructions in what I believed was the best interests of a patient. I'd never told them what had happened next and unless I have to I never will.

Dan is upstairs now, and I can hear him opening the door to my old bedroom – the one place I have yet to go. I didn't know what would be worse – if I went in there and it had been redecorated, like the rest of the house, or if I went in and she'd left it exactly the same. Now, though, it doesn't seem to matter; it feels like all my feelings, about my life here with mum, even about Callum, have been trapped under a glass dome: I can see them, I can remember them but I can't access them. I make us both a cup of tea – decaf doesn't seem like such a chore now, and I choose it automatically – and take them up.

'I brought you this.' I hold out the tea as though it's a white flag.

'Thanks.' Dan gestures around the room. 'It's been cleared out in here.'

I take a tentative step through the door and look around. 'No it hasn't.'

The room looks exactly the same as the day I left. The

walls are a muted peach; bits of Blu Tack from where I took my posters down have hardened over the intervening years and look like miniature pebbles stuck to the paint. A rickety desk sits in the corner next to a canvas-covered wardrobe. I cross the room and run a finger through the thick layer of dust and cobwebs on the desk.

'I'd say she never came in here once I left.'

'That's crazy.' Dan looks around. His eyes meet mine and I can see him searching for signs of pain. Sorry, Dan, all dried up over here. 'Did you live like this, Imogen?'

'Well it's not the Ritz, I can see that.'

'It's not funny. Is this why you never spoke to her? There was no falling-out, was there? You left because you had no home to begin with.'

'I had a roof over my head.' I don't know why I'm defending her now, after all these years of hating her and her frozen heart. 'Which is more than some kids get.'

'Come on, Imogen, even I know this isn't right, and *my* mum used to knit all my friends cock-blankets as gifts.'

I think of Dan's prim-and-proper mum, sitting in her knitting group producing her flaccid peach pen holders, oblivious to the fact that they are basically obscene, and I can't help it, it's an automatic reaction, I smile. Not the weak offering I've been using to reassure people the last few days that I'm not having a breakdown, but a real grin. Dan catches my eye and smiles back, and for a moment everything is all right. He looks around and I can see him thinking about his own room back at his parents', kept like a shrine to the boy he was: shelves and shelves of paperbacks I'm certain his mother read to him every night before bed, trophies celebrating various sporting achievements and other memorabilia of a happy childhood.

'Well, it is what it is.'

His expression transforms into one of absolute pity. 'Is this why . . .? I wish you'd talk to me about things, Im. If I knew, if I understood . . .'

He places a hand on my arm, and for once I don't shrug it off or move away. I just let his touch comfort me as I begin to cry.

81

Imogen

I have been staring at these four walls so long that I swear I can feel them drawing closer, just an inch at a time, pushing quietly inwards. Dan has been the perfect nurse, bringing food and drink and pills, placing them on the bedside table, asking if there's anything else I need. There has been the slightest change between us in the two days since I sobbed into his arms in my old bedroom; it's less like he can't forgive me for what I did and more like he's giving me time and space to come to terms with everything. I'm relieved that he's thawing, obviously, but I'm not sure I'll ever understand the unfairness of it all. What did I do to deserve this? All I ever did was try my best for Ellie. If anything, all I'm guilty of is trying too hard, getting too close to the wrong person. Again.

I've tried to rest – doctor's orders, after all – but every time I close my eyes and begin to drift downwards towards sleep, my mind is filled with images of Hannah Gilbert, her face blood-encrusted, filthy fingers covered in mud reaching towards me, whispering, 'Didn't I warn you?' and children, scores of children in black hooded robes, all carrying dead babies, throwing them one by one into a pit. Ellie Atkinson stands at the front, holding my baby. She lifts it high over her head, looking straight at me with eyes that burn red like the fires of hell themselves, and casts my unmoving child into the pit below, calmly telling me, 'You don't deserve to be a mother.' I scream, but I am frozen in place, a spectator unable to stop this murderous coven. Then the picture changes and I am back at the canal, my head submerged under the filthy cold water, only this time I can feel tiny hands in my hair holding me down until I am sure I will die.

I wake gasping for breath, certain that I can taste the muddy water retreating down my throat. The murderous image hovers on the edge of my conscious. Will Ellie be content with killing my child, or is she coming for me next, grasping for me through my dreams? How will they explain it when they find me drowned in my own bed? Of course it will be too late; there will be no one left to connect it to Ellie. Perhaps Sarah Jefferson will know, but she will be too scared to try and tell anyone the truth, too scared that no one will listen. Too scared of the monster living under her roof. If only I'd listened to Hannah Gilbert, if I hadn't been so closed-minded, so bloody convinced of my own absolute rightness. If I'd bothered to give her the time of day, maybe I would be lying here with my husband next to me, his palm resting gently on my stomach as we talk about names and colours for the nursery.

Except you didn't want the baby, did you? asks the voice in my head. *Not until you knew it was gone.*

I wasn't given that choice, I reply silently. She took it away from me. And I don't know how she did it, but I'm going to find out.

I pull myself up out of bed, wincing at the objection from my legs. I don't care what the doctors or Dan say, I'm fed up of resting. What I need is to put right what I got so very wrong and make sure this never happens to anyone else.

I dig my iPad out of the drawer and take it to the comfy armchair in the corner of our room. Opening Google, I type in the word 'telekinesis' and wait for the pages to load.

Even typing it into a search engine feels ridiculous. Telekinesis. Yet it's all I've been thinking ever since I woke up without my baby inside me. The night I miscarried is a black hole in my memory. I went from being a married mother-to-be running myself a bath to a soon-to-be divorcee whose baby will never breathe its first breath, and yet all I can remember of the moment things changed is Ellie's voice loud and clear in my mind. *You don't deserve to be a mother, you don't deserve that thing that is growing inside you. It would be better off dead.* It couldn't be a coincidence. Not another one. Not after Tom Harris and Naomi Harper. Not after Hannah Gilbert. If I'd listened to her, would she still be alive?

My stomach cramps violently, and I close my eyes and tip my head back, trying to breathe through the pain. Tears form at the corners of my eyes and I ball up my fists, shove them in my eye sockets until pinpricks of light dance in my vision. When I open my eyes again, the web page has loaded.

Psychokinesis (from the Greek ψυχή, 'mind', and κίνησις, 'movement'), or telekinesis (from τῆλε, 'far off', and κίνησις, 'movement'), is an alleged psychic ability allowing a person to influence a physical system without physical interaction.

There it is. It's followed by pages and pages of 'evidence' and anecdotes from people who believe they have witnessed this phenomenon first hand. I click on one after the other, my eyes scanning accounts of children with the ability to move objects, to control electricity and to influence things with their minds. Dan's jokey words about Carrie White float back to me.

It was easy to laugh it off back then, the idea that this innocent-looking eleven-year-old girl was exacting her revenge on people around her using her mind alone. But that was before; before I experienced first-hand the anger, the cruelty. All the things she said to me about wanting to punish the people who had treated her badly. I think back to the night Hannah Gilbert was killed, the night I received the phone call from Ellie sounding scared and talking about screaming. Had she heard Hannah Gilbert screaming? Had she known what had happened to her because she was there, perhaps not in body, but in mind?

I press the home button on my iPad and throw it onto the bed in disgust. This is ridiculous, I think. I'm acting like a fucking idiot – one of those crazy tinfoil-hat types you see on late-night television – rather than an intelligent thirty-six-year-old woman.

But when I open the iPad an hour later, the webpage is still there, and I find myself scrolling through story after story. As I read one particular account from 1978, my heart pounds a rhythm in my chest.

Abigail Sampson, ten years and four months old, had suffered a deep trauma, a car crash that killed both her parents, leaving her an orphan. She had been taken in by her maternal grandmother, who had alerted social services saying that she couldn't keep the child because she was strange and dangerous. Nothing was thought of the woman's words; she was regarded as old and senile, incapable of looking after a ten-year-old child. Abigail was taken to live with foster parents, who for several weeks reported that she was a happy, well-adjusted child. Then, after they had taken on a second foster child, a five-year-old girl, they began to note that Abigail's demeanour and behaviour had changed. She became quiet and withdrawn, prone to angry outbursts. On these occasions, certain electrical abnormalities were noted within the household. Lights would flicker, TVs would turn on and then off and then on again. One particular time, after a nasty argument with her foster mother, the household microwave burst into flames.

I rest my hand on my chest, remembering the time I turned up at the Jeffersons' house to find Sarah cleaning up after an incident with the electric blender. I can still smell the burning wires. Had she argued with Ellie that day? Had she angered the child in some way? And what would I have said there and then if Sarah had told me that Ellie had caused the blender to explode through the power of her mind? I know what I'd have said: I'd have laughed, perhaps made a recommendation that Sarah Jefferson wasn't mentally fit to be a foster carer. And am I mentally fit now? Would anyone believe me if I told them what I've been thinking, or would they just see me as a damaged woman struggling to come to terms with a tragedy?

The members of the household began to notice other strange phenomena occurring when Abigail was around. They centred on her foster sister in particular, the five-year-old girl who had triggered this behaviour. One time she took a tumble down the stairs while Abigail was in the kitchen with her foster mother. Clutched in her hands was one of Abigail's toys that she had been sneaking out of her room. When Abigail's foster mother screamed on finding the little girl at the bottom of the stairs, Abigail simply said, 'She really shouldn't have been stealing my things.'

Afraid that no one would believe them, Abigail's foster family gave up fostering, sending both girls back into the care of social services. It wasn't until years later that they spoke about their time with Abigail, after other carers had come forward with similar accounts of her behaviour. 'We kept trying to come up with rational explanations for what was happening,' said her foster mother, 'but there were just too many instances, too many coincidences. No one wanted to say the words, no one wanted to say "evil", or "witch", but that's what we were all thinking.' It wasn't until one of Abigail's foster homes nearly burnt to the ground, with her foster parents still in it, that the truth about her alleged psychic abilities came to light.

Fire. I picture flames engulfing the Atkinson household. Did Ellie start the fire that killed her parents?

So many questions to answer. I skim-read a few more articles, the same sorts of things cropping up over and over. Trouble with electrics, mysterious unexplained happenings, people worried they won't be believed. And then, on one of the pages, I find the telephone number of a doctor in Brighton who claims to have seen psychic phenomena at first hand, saying that he has real evidence and asking anyone else with proof to get in touch.

The article is three years old; it's unlikely that the number even works. So when I find myself closing the bedroom door tightly so Dan can't hear and dialling the number on the website, I'm surprised when it is answered on the fourth ring.

'Hello?'

'Is that Dr Benson?' I close my eyes, not quite believing I'm actually making this call.

'Who's calling, please?' The voice is clipped and unwelcoming.

'My name is Imogen Reid. I'm calling because I need your help . . .'

82

Imogen

I arrive at Greenacres early the next morning. The air is cold and crisp, and when I get out of my car, I can see my breath in front of me. I researched the unit on the Internet after my conversation with Dr George Benson, and so the huge sprawling stately home with its emerald-green gardens comes as no surprise to me. It looks more like a hotel than a psychiatric hospital; it's no more than six years old, pale-bricked and vast, with pillars announcing the front door. The trees surrounding the house are bare, but I know from the pictures I have seen online that they are usually strikingly different shades of green.

There are no other cars on the drive; staff parking is signalled to be on the left-hand side, visitor parking to the right. I look around – no sign of Dr Benson yet – so I pull out my phone and flick to the Facebook page I found the day before.

Emily Murray is a pretty girl, around twenty-five, with jet-black hair and striking blue eyes. There are no signs of any wedding pictures on her page. I look again at the message I composed yesterday.

Hi Emily,

I hope you don't find this inappropriate but I'm doing your old job at Place2Be, working with Ellie Atkinson and the Jefferson family. This might sound strange, but I have been wondering why you left. Please forgive me for being so forward, but it feels like it might be important to me.

Hope things are going well for you.

All best,

Imogen Reid

Trying not to think too deeply about it, I click send. There, it's done now.

'You must be Mrs Reid?'

I jump. An elderly man stands in front of me. In his sixties, his hair thick and white, he is carrying a few more pounds than look natural, and his forehead is creased with frown lines. His eyebrows are white and bushy and his nose is veined and red – a sign of alcohol dependency? He was reluctant to say why he was no longer practising when I spoke to him on the phone yesterday. But he has kindly eyes, and I can see that he was suited to the role of doctor, at least once upon a time. Now his shoes and coat both look as though they have seen better days.

I nod and hold out a hand. 'And you must be Dr Benson?'

'Well, yes, but I don't really call myself that now I'm no longer practising.'

'But I thought even retired doctors still called used their title?'

Benson looks sheepish. 'Well, technically I'm retired, but . . .' He shakes his head. 'Come on, let's go inside. They know we're coming. I asked for a meeting room.'

I walk alongside him to the front of the house and up the steps to the front door. Although the place has been designed to look old, it boasts a brand-new security system, and when

Benson presses his finger to the buzzer, a wall-mounted security camera turns to face us.

'They have video monitors,' Benson explains. 'Nothing but the best security here.'

A tinny voice sounds from the intercom. 'Good morning, George.'

The door buzzes and Benson pushes it with the palm of his hand. I feel slightly self-conscious as I follow him into a large reception area, where a friendly-faced woman sits behind a desk.

'Morning, Patricia,' Benson greets her warmly. 'Bit chilly out there today.'

'Don't I know it. We've had the heating on full blast here all morning and I still can't get warm.'

I can see why. Despite its modern appearance, Greenacres looks as though it will always have a chill to it.

'Hetty said you wanted a room?' Patricia inclines her head towards a door off the reception. 'We've only got Beech free today; I hope that's going to be all right?'

Benson nods. 'Of course, yes, that's fine. It's really very nice of you to be so accommodating.'

'Anything for our favourite visitor.' Patricia beams. 'If you could both just sign in here . . .' She indicates a large visitors' book open on the desk. 'I'll get you some tea or coffee sorted out.'

'Oh no, don't you worry yourself, Patricia.' Benson holds up a hand. 'I know very well where the vending machines are; we'll go through and get our own.'

Patricia hesitates, then gives a small nod. 'Of course, yes, you've been here plenty of times. I'm sure it's fine. Just don't go wandering around too much. Most of the patients are still in bed anyway.'

Benson signs us both in and takes my elbow, hurrying me towards the doors before Patricia can change her mind. 'I'm not technically supposed to have free rein at this place,' he admits. 'I'm just a visitor myself these days, but I've got to know a few of the staff over the years, and they really are all right. Not the sort of jobsworths you often get in this type of place.' He lowers his voice. 'I offered to get our own tea and coffee because I wanted to show you around a little bit.'

The inside of Greenacres is more like a school than the stately home it resembles from the outside. I peer through doors as we pass, looking into classrooms with brightly coloured displays, artwork and encouraging slogans emblazoned across the walls. Some rooms contain nothing but comfy chairs, and as we pass a closed door, Benson gestures towards it and says, 'That's the office. It's where the staff spend most of their time between shifts and when they're not needed. It's a living area in itself really.'

'So this place is manned twenty-four seven?'

Benson laughs. 'Why yes, of course. These children are vulnerable, they need constant supervision. And some of them can be . . . dangerous. Although usually just to themselves.'

'And Gemma?' I ask. 'Is she dangerous?'

Benson looks around as though someone might be listening. 'We'll talk more about that in a minute. Let me show you this place.' He leads the way through a set of double doors into what looks like a large canteen. Although it isn't like any canteen I ever had at school. It contains a recreation area, with comfortable sofas, beanbags and a wide-screen TV with a stack of DVDs next to it. There is also a kitchen area and a couple of vending machines. The walls are decorated with posters of teenage actors and singers.

'This is the common room,' he says unnecessarily. 'You see, it's really very nice here. It's not like a hospital really.'

I wonder why he's trying to justify the place to me. And

what this little tour is really about. 'Yes, it looks lovely,' I reply, because I know that's what he's expecting. In truth, no amount of slouchy sofas and posters can disguise the fact that these children are not in some trendy hostel or back-packers' retreat. The locks on the cupboard doors, the absence of sharp edges, and the security cameras in the corner of each room give that away.

We help ourselves to coffee from the machine, Benson producing a handful of tokens and slotting them in one by one. 'Visitors can buy tokens for the machines; the kids get them given to them. They aren't denied anything,' he adds quickly.

'I can see that.'

He looks momentarily embarrassed. 'Come on, we'd better get back to our room or Patricia will send out a search party.'

He leads us back through to the reception, where Patricia is indeed looking a little twitchy. She smiles when she sees us, the relief evident in her voice when she says, 'Ah, fantastic, you're back. If you'd like to go on through . . .'

Inside the meeting room, Dr Benson sits down and undoes the first few buttons of his coat. He doesn't take it off.

I remove my own coat, sit down opposite him and place my hands on the table.

'You said on the phone that you might be able to help me?'

'Well,' Benson looks sheepish now, 'I'm not sure how much help I can actually be. You see, it's like I said in the car park, I'm not a practising doctor any more. I . . . well, I resigned before I could be fired.'

'I see,' I say evenly, despite my shock. 'And can I ask why you didn't feel the need to tell me this yesterday?'

He at least has the good grace to look embarrassed. 'I wanted the opportunity to explain the situation in full, in person. And I must say, I was quite excited about what you told me. I thought that maybe you wouldn't meet me if you knew the full story.'

I instantly feel deflated. A liar and a quack, just as I feared. But he's right, I'm here now and I may as well hear what he has to say.

'Go on,' I say, taking a sip of my coffee. 'I'm listening.'

Benson smiles and nods. 'Okay, as you already know, I am . . . I was a doctor. A psychiatrist, in fact. A long time ago. I dealt with children with a wide range of illnesses, from eating disorders to schizophrenia. Much like this place does. But I'd always been interested in the paranormal. I know, it sounds odd, doesn't it? A doctor, a man of science, effectively believing in ghosts and ghouls. Those two parts of me never sat well together. My education, my career battled against my curiosity about the unknown, about those things we couldn't explain through science. I never discussed such matters with my colleagues; they were all men and women of science themselves, and none of them would have wanted to indulge in that kind of debate. And who can blame them? There are a lot of people who admit to believing in the paranormal when directly questioned, but in everyday life most people scoff at anything they can't explain, anything they haven't seen with their own two eyes or felt themselves. Even when confronted by absolute evidence, they still shake their heads and claim there must be another explanation – even if they can't give it themselves! It often frustrates me how closed-minded people can be.'

I shift uncomfortably in my seat, remembering how I myself scoffed at Ms Gilbert when she sat in my living room imploring me to open my mind.

'Surely you can see how people would be sceptical when there is so little evidence of the paranormal?'

'Ah!' Benson bangs his hand on the table and points at me delightedly, as though I have just proved his point. 'But that's just it! There *is* evidence, there always has been evidence, but people refuse to see it. They assume it is faked, or that there are rational explanations, as if the thought of there being things in this world that we cannot explain with science is just too much for them to bear. Yet despite all the scoffing and the naysaying, we as a race are fascinated by the paranormal. You only have to look at our TV shows and our films to see that. We are intrigued by what cannot be explained and yet we refuse to believe these things could happen in real life.'

With every word he speaks, Benson's face gets redder, his voice climbing higher and higher. It is obvious that he is passionate about the subject, and despite his caginess about the fact that he was forced to resign psychiatry, I find myself believing in him – and hoping that he might believe in me.

'And so,' he sits back and clears his throat, 'and so I continued to be fascinated by the paranormal, albeit secretly. Until I was asked to take on Gemma Andrews.'

I look up at the corner of the room, expecting to see one of the many security cameras focusing in on us at the mention of one of the patients. Benson catches my glance.

'It's fine,' he assures me. 'This is a private interview room. It's soundproofed; we can't be overheard in here.'

I nod. 'Can you tell me about Gemma?'

He drops his eyes to the table. 'Not my finest case, I must admit. I'm rather ashamed, as it goes, of how it turned out. As you've probably guessed, Gemma is the reason I quit psychiatry. And what happened is the reason I still come here every week to visit her.'

I say nothing, waiting for him to fill the silence. As a psychiatrist, he must be familiar with the trick, but it still works.

'Gemma's parents contacted me in the spring of 2009. They were concerned about some of her behaviour following a car crash the year before in which they had lost her younger sister.'

Loss and trauma, I think, just like Ellie, but I dare not interrupt.

'Go on,' I urge.

'Gemma had become prone to angry outbursts. On several occasions she had destroyed her bedroom in a rage. And yet this behaviour was wholly out of character for her. Ninety per cent of the time she was a mild-mannered, studious, polite and well-brought-up young girl. Before the loss of her sister she had never been in trouble at school, barely ever said a cross word.'

'But surely some of those kinds of behaviours are to be expected following such a loss?' I point out. 'That just sounds like the textbook guilt/anger stage of grief. Guilt that she was still alive internalised until the anger demanded an outlet.'

'That's exactly what I thought at first.' Benson nods. 'And I agreed to counsel Gemma, to help her deal with her grief and to help her family provide acceptable outlets for the anger. Unfortunately, my initial thoughts were somewhat under-informed. It wasn't until my third session with Gemma that I realised I might be dealing with something entirely different to the standard grief cycle.'

He falls silent, lost in his memories, and I wonder if perhaps he is going over that session in his mind, trying to pinpoint where he could have acted differently I know how he feels; I've done the same thing myself countless times.

'It was something Gemma said in that third session,' he continues after a while. 'We were talking one occasion when she had destroyed her bedroom and she said to me that she didn't even remember touching anything in the room. It was as if she went into a blind rage and things just flew around of their own accord.'

He holds up a hand before I can speak. 'I know what you're thinking,' he says. 'And in truth you'd be right. I only ever had Gemma's word about what had happened to her. Which is why we started the tests.'

My eyebrows rise of their own accord as Benson goes on to describe the various methods he used to test Gemma's supernatural abilities. When they all proved fruitless, he turned up the pressure, chipping away at the girl until she was close to a nervous breakdown. Eventually she set fire to the family kitchen in the course of conducting her own experiments. She wanted to prove to Benson that she was special – at least that was what she told the police officer.

'And she did that with her mind?' I ask incredulously.

'No.' Benson shakes his head. 'The fire investigator found an exploded lighter and accelerant in the kitchen. Gemma had nearly set fire to the whole house and those in it trying to prove herself to me. She was sent here instead of prison and I gave up medicine in disgrace.'

'Wait, so you brought me here to tell me that you never found any proof of the supernatural at all? But your website—'

'Hasn't been updated since I found out the truth. And I brought you here to show you what happens when you mess with the minds of children. I brought you here to stop you turning into me.'

83

Ellie

Mary squeezes Ellie's hand gently as she leads her out into the garden.

'What are we doing?' Ellie asks. Mary has been acting strange ever since school, like she's nervous and excited all rolled into one. Now she smiles. 'Don't be scared,' she says, giving Ellie a small pat on the shoulder. 'It's just like I said, we're going to do some experiments. We're going to help you control your power so you can use it properly.'

Use it properly? What does Mary think she's been trying to do? But her anger is growing every day, and the way people have treated her here is to blame. All the hateful thoughts she has, and the nightmares. They come to her every night now, Ms Gilbert, and Imogen's baby, and they scream and scream. She hears the baby most of all – it is crying and crying and nothing she can do will make it stop. In her nightmares she sees Naomi falling into the road, Billy's face rising up in front of her, his mouth no longer glued shut but sewn with thick black stitches through each of his lips. He tries to mumble something at her but he can't, and as he struggles to speak, the stitches begin to burst, thick red blood oozing from the holes they leave behind.

'Have you told anyone about this?'

Mary shakes her head, her face suddenly a shade paler, and in her eyes Ellie sees fear. Good. She should be a bit afraid. She doesn't have any idea what she's dealing with. Ellie hasn't told her about the latest visions; she thinks she'll keep those to herself a little longer.

Ellie nods. 'What do you want me to do?'

'Okay,' Mary says, pointing to the low wall that runs between the grass and the patio. 'See those Coke cans over there? I set them up earlier. We need to go a little bit closer.' She puts a hand on Ellie's shoulder and guides her closer to the wall. Ellie sees immediately what is going on. 'Okay,' Mary says, 'that's right. Now I want you to knock one of them off.'

'And how do you expect me to do that?'

Mary sighs impatiently. 'How am I supposed to know? You're the one that does these things, you're the one with the power. Maybe just think about it falling off or something.'

Think about it falling off. Oh for goodness' sake.

She squeezes her eyes shut, does a bit of light mumbling for effect. She wonders about waving her hands in the air but that would be going too far. After a minute she opens her eyes and they both look expectantly at the cans on the wall. Not one of them has moved. What a surprise.

'I don't think it works like that, Mary. I don't think I can just think about things and make them happen.'

'But how do you do it then?'

'I've already told you,' Ellie says, trying to remain calm. 'When someone upsets me, I just think bad things about them, and then something happens.'

'Well can't you think bad things about the cans?' Mary snaps. Ellie holds back a smirk.

'Well . . . it's not as if the cans have ever done anything to me . . .'

321

'For goodness' sake, Ellie!' Mary explodes in frustration, making Ellie's eyes widen in surprise.

'Look, I'm sorry.' Mary takes a step back and rubs her face with one hand. 'I didn't mean to snap at you. I just thought that maybe you'd have a bit more of an idea of how it works.' She looks truly apologetic. 'Why don't we try something else?'

Ellie shrugs, irritated by Mary's loss of control. They all show their true colours eventually, friends, teachers, parents.

'What if you imagine that those cans are people?' Mary suggests. 'Imagine they are the people who have upset you in the past. Imagine that can is Naomi Harper and she's saying all those mean things to you.' She lowers her voice. 'Imagine she's whispering to you, "You're a freak, Ellie Atkinson, nobody likes you, you've got no friends, your mum and dad are probably glad they—"'

She lets out a scream. One of the cans has flown clear off the wall, as though someone has shot a pellet gun at it.

'Whoa.' She looks stunned. 'How did you do that?'

Ellie pretends not to know what is going on here. It's best that way for now. She raises an eyebrow. 'Pretty cool, huh?'

'Pretty cool?' Mary repeats, dumbfounded. 'Ellie, that was more than pretty cool. If you can learn to control this, if you can figure out how you did it, just imagine . . . they will never be able to hurt you again.'

The words run through her mind like a silk scarf through her fingers. *Never be able to hurt you again* . . . Mary doesn't have a clue how right she is.

'Do you want to try again?' Mary asks. 'Or are you too tired? Is it tiring? How does it feel?'

Ellie shakes her head, tries to look young and vulnerable. That's what Mary expects, after all. 'No, I'm not tired, I feel fine. Maybe a bit funny. I'm not sure whether that's just because I'm nervous and scared. My tummy feels a bit sick.'

'Can I get you anything?' Mary asks immediately.

'No thank you, I'm fine. What else did you have in mind?'

'Well, if you're sure . . .'

'I am,' Ellie says, acting eager to please. *Don't overdo it, Ellie.* 'I'm fine, Mary, I promise.'

'Okay then.' Mary grabs her hand and pulls her excitedly over to the tree, the one Ellie was sitting under on the night of Ms Gilbert's death. She's avoided this tree ever since; when she's around it, all she can hear is the screaming.

Mary must have noticed that her face has paled. 'You sure you're okay, El?' She reaches out a hand and strokes her face. 'You don't look very well.'

Ellie shakes her head in irritation. 'I said I'm fine, didn't I?' She nods towards the tree. 'What do you want me to do over there?'

Mary points towards a twig dangling from a piece of string on the lowest branch of the tree. 'I set that one up earlier too,' she explains. 'I just wondered if maybe you can make it spin or something. There's no wind, so we'll know it's you if it moves.'

Ellie nods, and Mary claps her hands and goes to stand by the trunk of the tree. 'Okay, go!'

Ellie stares at the twig, widens her eyes a bit and tries to look as though she's concentrating hard. The twig remains motionless.

'This is no good,' she sighs. 'I don't know why it happens. I don't know how to control it.'

'When it happened over there,' Mary gestures towards the can at the foot of the wall, 'you looked so angry you might explode. So maybe that's it. Maybe you just have to get really furious. It was when I mentioned your parents . . .'

She stops talking, obviously uncertain as to whether mention Ellie's parents for fear of upsetting her. But that's exactly what Ellie needs; for these things to happen, she has to get really, truly mad. Just picturing the faces of children who have upset her isn't enough. It has to be anger.

'I hate you,' she mutters at the stick. She tries again, picturing everyone who has called her names, laughed at her. 'I hate you, I wish you were all dead, I wish you could feel pain, real pain, I wish you knew what it feels like to be laughed at and hated and ignored . . .'

Mary gasps. At first Ellie thinks she is gasping at the words that have come from the mouth of sweet, strange little Ellie Atkinson. And then she looks at the twig and sees that it is spinning, spinning uncontrollably. She lets her legs go weak and falls to the floor, her knee grinding against the jagged stones and her arm bending behind her back. Mary dashes over to her and kneels by her side.

'Are you okay, Ellie? Are you all right?'

'They will never be able to hurt me again,' she mutters. 'That's what you said, isn't it, Mary? Never be able to hurt me again.'

And then everything goes black.

84

Imogen

I knock on the door, glancing furtively from side to side as I do. I'm sure that from deep inside the house I hear voices, and the car is on the drive. They must be in.

I shouldn't be here, I know that. But I can't think of any other way to stop Ellie before she hurts someone else. After my disastrous meeting with Dr Benson, I feel more alone than ever. I didn't realise just how much I'd got my hopes up that he might be able to help me. The irony doesn't escape me that Hannah Gilbert came to me once, just like this, pleading for my help, and I turned her away. Now I'm about to do the same to Sarah.

When no one comes to the door, I knock again, a little louder this time. I pray that Ellie won't be the one to answer; that I won't have to face her. The thought of seeing those cold, dark eyes terrifies me.

Just as I'm about to bang again, harder this time, the door opens half an inch. 'What do you want?' Sarah Jefferson stands behind the door, using it as a shield against me.

'I'm not here to cause a scene,' I promise. 'I just want to talk to you, in private, please.'

'Now is not a good time.' She goes to close the door and

325

I block it with my foot. 'Please, Sarah, just for a few minutes. I won't stay long, I promise, and if you ask me to leave, I'll go straight away.'

From behind the door, she sighs. 'All right,' she says. 'Just a couple of minutes though; it really isn't a good time. Let me take the chain off.'

I remove my foot and the door closes and opens again. Sarah looks exhausted. I wonder whether things are getting worse.

'You look terrible,' I comment as she ushers me in.

'Thanks.' She gives a humourless laugh. 'I could say the same about you.'

She directs me through to the empty kitchen.

'Where's Ellie?' I ask quietly.

'She's in the garden with Mary,' Sarah says, inclining her head towards the back window. 'What's this about? I thought you were told to stay away from Ellie.'

'I was, and I will,' I promise. 'It's just . . . I want to talk to you about what you said, in the coffee shop.'

Sarah shakes her head. 'You need to forget about that,' she says quickly. 'I wasn't thinking straight. I was angry and scared; I was just being stupid.'

'You seemed pretty convinced at the time,' I remind her. 'You didn't seem confused.'

Sarah looks pained. 'Look, please, just don't tell anyone about what I said; just forget it. I can't afford for . . .' She stops as though she might have said too much.

'For what?' I ask. 'What can't you afford?'

Sarah looks through the kitchen door out into the hallway, as though she is expecting someone to appear at any moment. Then she glances behind her at the two girls in the garden. 'I just can't afford for anyone to think there have been problems. That I might've done or said anything against Ellie.'

'You're still scared of her?'

Sarah shakes her head. 'No, it's not that. It's just that . . . Ellie is fine as long as . . . well, as long as she's fine. As long as we don't upset her, as long as we don't make her angry. And the situation has changed somewhat . . .'

'You heard what happened to me?' I venture, feeling rotten for using my baby like this.

Sarah nods. 'Yes, I did, and I'm very sorry. But you can't think that Ellie . . .?'

'It's like you said,' I say. 'Everything is fine as long as we don't make her angry. You must've heard what she said to me as we parted that day?'

She shakes her head. 'No, I didn't hear anything. By the time Ellie opened the door, you'd already stopped talking. What did she say?'

I swallow. Even though the words have been running through my head for over a week now, they are still difficult to say out loud. But if I want to convince Sarah Jefferson that Ellie is dangerous, she needs to know the truth. All of it. 'She told me that I didn't deserve my baby. That it would be better off dead.'

Sarah gasps. 'But how did she know? Did you tell her? You can't honestly think . . .'

I say nothing.

'That's crazy!' Sarah says. 'How would she be able to . . .?'

'How could she do any of the things that she has been accused of doing? You know there's something different about her, Sarah. That's why you came to me that day.'

'No,' Sarah says. 'I mean yes, I did think she had some-thing to do with what happened to Billy. And there have been other things . . . But not like you're talking about. There's no way she could have . . .' Her words trail off, as though she can't even say it. *Killed your baby.*

'But what if she did?' I glance away, look through the window at the two girls playing with tin cans outside. 'I

327

know it sounds crazy, Sarah, but there's this man, Dr Benson . . . I went to see him . . . he specialises in this sort of thing. In psychokinesis.' I choose not to tell Sarah the warning Benson gave me at the end of our conversation, or that he is no longer a doctor.

Sarah gasps. 'You're crazy,'

'And was Hannah Gilbert crazy too? Because she thought exactly the same. She came to see me before she died, and I told her much the same as you've told me. I never saw her again. She was murdered.'

Sarah takes a couple of steps backwards, a horrified look on her face. 'You're not suggesting . . .?'

'Ellie called me on the night of Hannah's death,' I say. 'She was talking about hearing screaming, in her mind. What if it wasn't in her mind? What if she heard screaming because there *was* screaming? Hannah Gilbert's screaming.'

Sarah walks towards the kitchen door and opens it wider. 'You need to leave.'

I don't move. 'That's what I did too,' I say. 'I got mad at Hannah, told her to go. Told her she was crazy. I—' My words are interrupted by the sound of a baby's cry from the next room. My eyes widen. 'What was that? You have a baby here already?'

Sarah walks quickly through into the hallway. 'It's just a visitation; she hasn't moved in yet. That's what I mean when I say things have changed. Mark and I, we've wanted a baby since the beginning. It's why we got into fostering, and now I can't have anything, anything I've said or done, taken the wrong way.'

'But that—'

'You really have to leave,' Sarah says, pushing my arm. 'If Ellie hears you, she'll get upset, and I've got to see to Lily.'

'But this changes everything,' I say. 'Can't you see? It's

not just you in danger any more; you have a baby in the house.'

'None of this is any of your concern,' Sarah says firmly. 'You don't think I'm going to let anything happen to Lily, do you? And do you really think that Ellie, that girl you spent so long defending, would hurt a defenceless six-month-old baby?'

An feeling of intense dread washes over me. What am I supposed to do now? If I was able to walk away before, if I was able to let Sarah Jefferson control the situation by herself, I certainly can't now. Not now there's an innocent baby involved. I'm going to have to stop Ellie myself.

85

Imogen

'You know you sound like a fucking idiot, right?' Pammy takes a big lick around her ice cream and grimaces. 'Brain freeze. Don't worry, you should be fine; you need to have a brain to get that.'

I groan. 'Please, Pam, don't. You are literally the only person I can talk to about this. I feel like the woman in one of those shitty horror films we used to watch in your bedroom, desperately trying to convince her friends she isn't crazy before the evil spirit tears them apart limb from limb.'

Pammy shudders. 'Okay, well I don't want my limbs torn off, so thanks for that imagery.'

'Can you please just assume what I've told you is right? Just for the sake of one conversation? Then you can go back to looking at me as though I've grown a second head.'

Pammy points her cone at me. 'You're mixing your metaphors. You just threatened me with loss of limbs; now you're growing new ones. Make your mind up.'

I scowl. 'This isn't funny. This isn't even close to funny.'

When I called Pammy to ask her to talk, I was fairly sure she wasn't expecting what I've just told her. I started at the beginning, my very first day here, when Naomi Harper fell into the road for no apparent reason; my first sighting of Ellie Atkinson, looking scared and confused. Was Ellie aware then of the power she wielded? Or was that an accident, the start of something she couldn't control? According to the school and Sarah Jefferson, there had been incidents before then. How far back does Ellie's reign of terror spread? Her dead parents? Further?

Pammy said nothing, except to order an ice cream from the van that pulled up alongside the park we'd wandered to. She listened silently right up until I'd finished with the loss of my baby, at which point she delivered her cutting verdict. That I was a fucking idiot.

'I'm not laughing, seriously, Im. You sound like you're losing the plot. Meeting with bloody parapsychologists, talking about an eleven-year-old girl with psychic powers going around killing her teachers and wreaking bloody revenge on her peers. You're worrying me. You're worrying me because I think you're serious and that you actually believe you lost your baby because you fell out with some kid. I think you need therapy, hon; you're suffering, and I would be an awful friend if I just went along with this to humour you.'

I sigh, staring out over the park, watching a mother tapping on her phone with one hand whilst impatiently pushing a toddler in a swing with the other. It was a bad idea to come here – it had never been the plan to head to a place where children gathered; we just kind of gravitated here, the way we had when we were fifteen.

'You could be right. It makes perfect sense that you are. I felt exactly the same when I first started working with her. I was furious that people were treating her with fear and suspicion; I thought Hannah Gilbert was a mad bitch who had an unfair grudge against someone too young to have earned it. I defended Ellie, but the whole time I knew something was off, something didn't feel right. Then—'

'Then something bad happened to you and you're too full of grief to see straight,' Pammy says, but her voice isn't unkind. 'You needed someone to blame, so rather than accepting that what happened was an awful but totally natural event, you've taken your anger and frustration and directed it towards a vulnerable messed-up child. You need help, Imogen. And I say that to you as a friend because I've known you since you were a vulnerable messed-up child yourself.'

'And if I'm right? Like I know I am?'

'Like you were with that boy back in your old job? Because you were so convinced you were right then and it cost you your job. What if the same happens here? Can you put yourself through that a second time?'

'That's not fair,' I argue. 'That was a totally different situation.'

'Was it? Can you honestly sit there and tell me that what happened with that little boy, and how involved you've got with this girl, they're not part of the same thing? It's all about you trying to save the lost child you were twenty years ago, and if you can't see that, I'm not sure how you ever got that psychology degree.'

'Maybe it was, before,' I admit. 'But can't you see that it's not about me saving anyone any more? I'm not trying to save Ellie; I'm trying to figure out a way to stop her.'

'Save her, stop her.' Pammy shrugs. 'It's all the same. It's all about you trying to prove you aren't invisible nobody Imogen Tandy any more. Otherwise why wouldn't you just walk away from all this? Ask to be transferred to a different school, forget you ever heard of the Jeffersons and Ellie Atkinson. Let the police find out what happened to Hannah Gilbert and concentrate on saving your marriage.'

THE FOSTER CHILD

'You make it sound so simple,' I murmur.

'That's because it is simple, Immy. You can't always save the world. Sometimes you just have to settle for saving yourself.'

86

Ellie

The car journey home is spent in silence. Mary hasn't said a word, and Ellie isn't sure whether Sarah and Mark are upset with her or scared that if they say something they might provoke an angry outburst from their daughter. It has finally happened – they are bringing the baby home, and for good this time.

They have been home for about an hour now, and the baby starts to scream as soon as they carry the car seat into the house, as though somehow she knows that these are unfamiliar surroundings. That this is not where she is supposed to be. Ellie knows exactly how she feels. Sarah and Mark are downstairs, trying everything they can to soothe the screaming child, and Mary and Ellie are upstairs in Mary's room. Mary is restless, stalking up and down, and Ellie feels as though her head might burst if the screaming doesn't stop. She closes her eyes, tries to calm the anxiety that is building inside her. The last time she felt this tightly wound someone died. She has to do something; she has to learn to control this before she kills someone else.

87

Imogen

The bench is cold and uncomfortable, and every time the wind whips up around me, I feel as though I am being stabbed with tiny pins of ice, but even that is better than being at home. It's my second week off work following the miscarriage; I wanted to go back in after the first few days – it was torture sitting around the house not knowing what to say to my husband of five years – but HR gently suggested that I take at least two weeks to come to terms with what had happened and make sure I was fully recovered.

I look out over the dark river, and the sense of being lifted from my life and transported back twenty years is upon me. This exact bench, precariously perched on the riverbank, placed here at a time when the banks were wider and it was set back from the dark, still water, was where I would escape to whenever my real life became too much to bear. I found it aged nine. My mother never asked where I disappeared to for hours after school; I wasn't sure she even noticed what time it was when I slipped quietly into the cold, silent house and straight up to my room. Now, despite how desperate my childhood was, the river feels safe and familiar. And with everything that is going on in my life, I need to feel safe.

I can tell that Dan wants to forgive me – he's always hated to keep arguments running for long – but I also know that his prolonged display of anger and disappointment means that I've really messed up this time. Looking back to only a short week ago, I genuinely have no idea why I was so reluctant to tell him about the baby. Now, it is all I can think about: how much I want to hold our child in my arms, how much I want to smell its soft skin and have it look up at me with eyes filled with love and adoration. What difference would it make to this tiny life that my own mother cared so little? That the house was never clean enough to invite friends round – not that I had any, with my second-hand uniform always so grubby and faintly smelling of body odour. I don't believe that our biology shapes who we are. We are nurture, not nature.

I'm going to have to tell Dan everything if our marriage is going to survive. Everything about my childhood in Gaunt, about the people who looked the other way when my mother and I entered a shop or walked down the street. About the duvet that was donated by one of my teachers, a young woman called Miss Rogers, who used to bring me sandwiches and packets of crisps because she knew that I wouldn't eat much beyond school lunch.

One time we were doing a school project about our dream house, and while the other children drew water slides from their bedroom windows and ice-cream machines in their kitchens, I drew the softest, thickest mattress and duvet I could imagine, walls filled with bookshelves and – the biggest indulgence I could think of – a TV in my bedroom. Miss Rogers looked at my picture and her eyes glistened. At seven years old, I thought it was because it wasn't as good as the other kids' drawings, not as imaginative or grand. Some years on, I realised that she was unable to contain her sadness that my dream house was what most people would think of as a normal everyday household.

THE FOSTER CHILD

I squeeze my eyes shut, resetting the images and memories in my mind. That isn't what I came here to dwell on. I've escaped the suffocating silence at home and taken refuge on the cold bench because I want to think about what the hell I'm going to do about Ellie Atkinson. No matter that I know I should stay away from the girl – and after what happened to me, who could blame me if I did? – I also know that I have a duty of care to the child the Jeffersons are about to take in. How could I live with myself if I heard on the grapevine in a few weeks' time that something had happened to the baby? That would be horrific.

I need to talk to someone, someone with influence who might be able to have Ellie moved somewhere she can't harm anyone else. But where? If she went to another family, there's no guarantee they wouldn't already have children, or eventually take in others. And even if they didn't, how am I going to protect the children Ellie goes to school with, her teachers? My mind flashes to an image of Hannah Gilbert standing in the doorway. *You had better hope you live to regret not listening to me . . .*

Knowledge didn't help Hannah. She'd suspected – if not outright known – what Ellie was, and she still died alone in that block of abandoned flats. Verdict: misadventure.

But what if new evidence comes to light about her murder? My mind leafs through the possibilities. What if they find something at the scene that links Ellie to the death? Risky: I'd have to get into the Jeffersons' house again, steal something of hers and take it there, all with a risk of being caught. Is there any way I can lure her to the flats, make sure she leaves her fingerprints there? Getting her back on side will be easy – I just have to apologise and promise never to let her down again. But if she realises what I'm trying to do . . . maybe she already does. She knows things.

What extent do her powers run to? Is anyone safe, even if she is in prison? Even if she confesses all and . . .

'Yes!' I hiss under my breath. If I can get her to confess, all I have to do is make sure I capture it on tape.

I shiver. Listen to yourself, I think. You're going crazy. I pull Dan's huge coat tighter around me. The river is so calm and still, the silence so complete, that the cough from behind me makes my heart jump into my throat.

The man stands a few yards from the bench. He is well protected against the early-morning chill by a navy-blue padded jacket so thick that it is impossible to tell his size, and the black scarf he wears along with the black beanie hat on his head means that he is devoid of most of his defining features. All I can see of him is his mouth, nose and eyes.

'Sorry, I didn't mean to startle you.' He holds up a hand. 'I'll leave you to it.'

I realise that this is one of those times when I should probably say nothing and let him go, but I find myself saying instead, 'No, you don't have to. You're welcome to join me.' There is something in his voice, something in his whole demeanour that suggests this man isn't a threat. He seems as broken inside as I feel.

He looks like he's considering my invitation. Clearly he expected to be alone in what I suppose is probably as special a place to him as it is to me.

'I won't talk to you if you don't want me to,' I add.

The man gives a half-smile, half-grimace and joins me on the bench, sitting as far towards the other end as it's possible to get. I try a smile. 'It's nice here, isn't it?'

He doesn't look at me, instead stares out across the water as though it holds all the answers to his unspoken questions.

'Sorry,' I mutter, mortified that I have broken my promise instantly.

For five minutes we sit gazing out across the river in silence. Eventually he speaks.

'I used to come here a lot,' he says. 'I stopped for a while. Maybe I thought I didn't need it. It feels a bit like church; people only come to places like this when they're missing something. Can a place be good when all it takes in is negative energy?'

'I think it's like a tree,' I reply. The man turns his face to me, his eyes frowning. 'I mean, trees take in carbon dioxide, which is bad for us, and they turn it into oxygen, which is vital for us to live. It's like they take our poison away in order for us to keep living. And we don't even notice it happening. I think this place is like that. It takes in our negativity so we can leave it behind here, so we can go back to real life unburdened. Or that's what I used to tell myself when I was a kid.'

He considers this for a minute. 'Sounds like you were a smart kid.'

I give a rueful smile. 'I was. Sometimes I wonder how I ended up so dumb.'

'That happens to the best of us,' he laughs, but he doesn't sound amused. 'I didn't realise you lived here when you were a child. I thought you were new in town.'

Now it's my turn to look puzzled.

'You're the Place2Be worker, aren't you? I'm Evan Hawker.' He waits a beat for the realisation to sink in. 'Yes, *that* Evan Hawker.'

88

Sarah has been exhausted for days. Her head feels like it is about to cave in on itself and her eyes sting. Spots are starting to break out as if she was sixteen again, and her hair is perpetually scraped back into a lank greasy ponytail. She doesn't remember it being this difficult with Mary, but then that was fifteen years ago and time has a magnificent way of rose-tinting your memories until all you can remember is your beautiful gurgling, cooing baby. Sleepless nights and trapped wind are erased as easily as holding down the delete button.

Now the kids are back from school and there is no chance of popping upstairs for a quick nap. Lily is sleeping in her baby bouncer in the front room, while Sarah is in the kitchen wondering about the quickest way of getting caffeine directly into her bloodstream. Mary is in the back garden tidying up some tin cans that she and Ellie have been messing with, picking them up and inspecting them as though they hold the meaning of life. She really can't figure that girl out – she took so well to Ellie, protecting her as though she were her real sister, so why has she gone so frosty since Lily arrived? Sarah has already assured her that Ellie won't be leaving any earlier because of Lily's appearance, and Mary hasn't had to give up her room or make any other sacrifices. And okay, Sarah might have intimated that they wouldn't be doing this again, not after how much bother they've had with Ellie, but even she seemed to have calmed down slightly since that incident in the woods. Sarah feels bad about making out it was all nothing when Imogen's boss called the house, but she really can't have people thinking that any of the children in her care are in danger. And Ellie wasn't hurt, was she? It was all just kids mucking around, a prank that went too far.

She scans the garden for signs of Ellie, but she's not out there. Probably in her room, reading or something. Such a strange one, the way she looks at you as though she can hear your thoughts. She won't be sorry when the girl is found a permanent home, that's for sure. She goes to take her mobile out of her pocket to have a quick flick through Facebook when she realises she's left it in the front room. Shit, it's probably on loud, and if Mark calls, it's going to wake Lily. She moves quickly with the stealth only a woman with a sleeping baby possesses. It's not until she reaches the door to the front room that she hears the voice. It is low, but it is unmistakably Ellie's voice.

'He isn't here any more,' she is saying. 'He died. My parents weren't doing their job properly, they didn't bother to save either of us. He was only little and he couldn't have reached the door handle to his room – it was their job to get him out.'

Sarah knows she is tired and overemotional, but she feels tears well up. Ellie might be a strange girl, but she is still young enough to believe that her parents should have been able to keep their children safe. She doesn't understand that the fumes would have overwhelmed them before they even woke up – that if she hadn't managed to get to the window, she herself wouldn't be here.

'That's the thing with adults, they're all so distracted most of the time. They don't have any idea of where the real dangers are. And if they don't see them, how can they protect you from them?' Ellie's voice hardens. 'They can't. Sarah can't protect you all the time. No one can. You are all on your own . . .'

As Sarah stands with her shaking hand on the handle, the door opens from the inside and Ellie stands in the doorway. She doesn't jump or look in any way startled or guilty.

'Hi, Sarah.' She gives a small wave and walks past her into the hall. Sarah's breath catches in her throat and she can't even speak. Because Ellie's words didn't sound like the innocent chattering of a child. In fact, Sarah will swear to the police later that week that they sounded like a threat.

89

Imogen

I'm shocked into silence. Here, sitting on the bench next to me, gazing out across the river, is a man that many people think is capable of murder. And I invited him to pull up a chair, sharpen his machete. In my defence, he doesn't look capable of murder right now. He looks a mess. Close up, I can see that his face is shaded with rough stubble – not the freshly trimmed designer kind, but the kind that suggests a man who has more on his mind than self-care. His face is lined with grief and there are dark circles under his eyes that suggest more than one sleepless night.

'Is it stupid of me to ask how you're coping?' I ask quietly. I don't know what else to say. Suddenly I realise why I've heard so little from the people around me since I lost my baby. Why Dan finds it hard to look me in the eye. Because what do you say to someone whose life is tainted with loss? To whom giving advice and platitudes would sound hollow and insincere. Someone who wants nothing more than to turn back time and do something, anything, differently.

Evan gives a snort. 'Would it be stupid of me to ask the same?'

So here we are, two people united by the worst possible

scenario. If I could have chosen anything other than grief to have in common with Evan Hawker . . .

'Do you think it gets any less shitty?' I ask in reply. He shakes his head.

'Nope.' His foot scuffs at the dirt beneath us and he doesn't look at me. 'This is it now; these things, they define the rest of your life. I will always be the man responsible for my lover's death.'

Responsible. Does he mean that Hannah would still be alive if they hadn't been having an affair? Or does he mean it in a more literal sense?

'You shouldn't feel responsible,' I say after a pause. 'It was an accident.'

He looks at me then, his eyes clouded with grief. 'Do you really believe that? Do you believe she fell down those stairs?'

'Presumably that means you don't?'

'No. We'd been in that place plenty of times before she went there that night. Hannah knew her way around; she'd never so much as stumbled before. And even if it was an accident, why was she there in the first place?'

'Maybe . . . maybe she was meeting someone else?' I suggest tentatively.

Evan gives a rueful smile. 'That's not possible. I realise how hypocritical this sounds, given both of our marital situations, but Hannah and I were in love. She wouldn't have cheated on me.'

It's the same thing Florence Maxwell said – two of the people who seemed to know Hannah best.

'So what do you think she was doing there?'

Evan shrugs. 'She thought she was meeting me.'

I picture Hannah Gilbert getting ready for a late-night tryst with an illicit lover, applying make-up and slipping into her best underwear, all the while heading towards disappointment and death.

'Florence told me about the notes in the tree.'

'Stupid.' Evan lets out a breath. 'Stupid and arrogant of us to believe that no one would suspect. We knew there was a chance they would be found – kids leave no stone unturned when looking for places to hide their cigarettes – but Hannah said that even if someone stumbled across them, they would have no idea they were ours. Even after the note she found . . .'

'What note?'

'Someone put a note in the tree that said, "I know what you're doing" on a Post-it in the shape of an apple. Hannah said she knew who it was; she'd seen the Post-its in one of her student's bags. She said she'd take care of it.'

'She thought it was Ellie, didn't she?'

Evan nods. 'Ironic, really, that Ellie is the only person who *couldn't* have killed Hannah.'

'Why not? Because she's young and sweet-looking?'

Evan laughs. 'Imogen, please. I'm a maths teacher – do you think I'm fooled by young and sweet-looking? No, Ellie Atkinson couldn't have been to blame because she was with me when Hannah died.'

I feel as though the wind has been knocked from me.

'With you?' I repeat stupidly. 'What do you mean?'

'I live in the next street down from the Jeffersons' house. Ellie showed up at about ten to ten that evening, looking confused and lost. I heard a noise outside, and she was just standing in the garden, staring at the house. When I went outside to find out what was going on, she looked as though she'd just woken up and discovered she'd been sleepwalking or something. She couldn't remember how she'd got to my house or why, but she thought she'd had something important to tell me. I took her in, my wife made her a hot drink and then I walked her back home. She begged me not to ring the bell and she went in through the side gate. I waited about ten minutes to make sure she didn't come back out. I thought about it all night, how I should have just rung the bell and made sure she got in properly. Then all the stuff with Hannah happened and I pretty much forgot about it until the police asked what I'd done that night.'

'Was there anything strange about her?'

Evan snorts. 'Other than her practically sleepwalking to a teacher's house in the middle of the night?'

'I mean did she look angry?'

'No, just confused.'

'But her sister told me that Ellie had been with her all night. Why would she do that? Why would she lie?'

Evan shrugs. 'Maybe Ellie didn't tell Mary where she'd been. Perhaps Mary thought Ellie did have something to do with what happened to Hannah. She probably thought that by lying for her, she was protecting her.'

'Mm,' I murmur. What was Ellie trying to tell Evan that night? Was she trying to save Hannah's life, or was she responsible for her death? Is she a monster or a victim?

90

Imogen

In a place like Gaunt, the title 'doctor's surgery' is a dramatic overstatement. Two GPs work from what can only be described as an oversized hut, and if it's seen better days, then I certainly can't remember them. The doctors' rooms are sparsely decorated, and if you stare at the skirting boards as I am now, you can see that some of them haven't even been completely glossed. Despite the fact that he hasn't completely forgiven me for not telling him about the existence of our baby, my husband is clutching my hand as though it's a life raft and he is drowning. I'm not sure who's more nervous, although from his colourless face and fixed neutral expression, I would say it's Dan.

We're here to find out the results of the tests I underwent in hospital, tests that will determine the reason our baby didn't survive past ten weeks. I've already been warned that it's not unusual; a lot of women miscarry at that stage without ever knowing they were pregnant. It probably happens to people without them even realising, with women putting stomach cramps and heavy bleeding down to a bad period. The hospital were reluctant to even do the tests; I felt like the consultant was constantly trying to bite back the words

347

'one of those things', and had Dan not insisted, I probably wouldn't have pushed the situation. Not least because I don't need a scan to tell me why my baby didn't survive; I know the reason and it's not one you can argue with health professionals over. I just hope Dan isn't too devastated when the doctor tells us that there is no logical reason for our baby's death.

'As you probably realise, we called you in because we have the results of your scans.' The doctor is a young, fairly attractive man with thick wavy dark hair, wearing jeans and a light pink pinstripe shirt. I realise with a guilty jolt that I would feel much more comfortable discussing my intimate parts if he was old and grey, with wire-rimmed glasses.

'Yes, we're obviously hoping it's not bad news,' Dan replies.

The doctor frowns slightly. 'Well, it's not entirely positive, I'm afraid. Usually in circumstances like this there are very few indications of why the unfortunate loss of the foetus occurs. However, in your case, Mrs Reid,' he looks at me with what I'm sure is supposed to be sympathy, 'the scans show that you are suffering from a condition called endometriosis. This is when cells similar to those that line the womb are found outside the womb. Your scans show a number of these cells around the uterus and ovaries, and this is the most likely cause of your miscarriage.'

My mind blanks. I was so certain that the scans would show up nothing at all that it never really crossed my mind how I would feel if there was something actually wrong with me.

'Is there anything that can be done?' Dan's voice cracks and I know what he's thinking. That we will never have a family. Will he still want to be married to me if I can't give him a child? I was so caught up in wondering if I wanted children that I never stopped to think about the fact that it might not be a possibility.

'There might not be any need,' Dr Richardson says. 'As you haven't noticed the symptoms, it's difficult to tell how long the condition has been present—'

'So it could be recent?' I interject.

The doctor shakes his head. 'From the amount of tissue we detected, it's certainly not recent, although it's impossible to tell you when it began. As far as treatment is concerned, if there aren't any symptoms that affect your day-to-day life—'

'Surely losing our child is classed as affecting our day-to-day life?' Dan cuts in angrily. 'You're not going to tell us that budget cuts are so bad that my wife has to be in daily agony before you'll treat her?'

I don't know whether his outburst is indignation on my behalf or fear that his perfect family life is slipping from his grasp. The doctor looks embarrassed.

'I'm sorry, Mr Reid, I certainly didn't mean to suggest that the loss of a child doesn't have an effect on your lives. What I was going to say is that sometimes treatment for this condition can be more invasive than the actual condition itself. Three out of ten cases of endometriosis will get better by themselves, but there is no known cure. How to best treat it depends on a lot of factors, your fertility, Mrs Reid, being one of them. We can prescribe hormone treatment for the pain; however, that can prevent pregnancy due to the oestrogen blockers involved. What I'd recommend is that you continue to try to conceive naturally for at least twelve months, and after that we can look at your fertility levels and discuss the treatments available to you.'

I nod, but Dan look incensed.

'You want us to wait and see?' His face is reddening and his jaw is tight. I put out the hand that he isn't squeezing tightly enough to break my fingers and touch his arm.

'The doctor knows what he's talking about, Dan,' I say quietly.

He shoots me a look that in ordinary circumstances he would never use on me. A look that says, *Don't make me say something I'll regret.*

'And does the doctor know what it's like to lose a child you didn't even know was alive?' Dan's voice is tight and trembling. I realise with horror that he's trying not to cry.

'I don't,' Dr Richardson replies. 'And I won't pretend I do. All I can say is that Mrs Reid has conceived once under these circumstances and it's entirely possibly she can do so again. Recent events suggest that your wife is not infertile, and the last thing I want to do right now is start recommending treatments that might change that. Were she in constant pain, or experiencing heavy bleeding, I would be making different suggestions. It's very early days and her body has been through a lot. To attempt any kind of surgery this soon would not be good for her.'

Dan drops his eyes to the floor and it's his turn to look embarrassed. 'Of course,' he mutters. 'I apologise. I only want the best for Immy too.'

'No apology necessary,' the doctor says kindly. 'I really do want to help you both, and there are many, many things we can try. Twelve months seems like a long time, but it's perfectly normal for couples without these complications to take that long to get pregnant. And if anything changes, if you start to experience pain or heavy bleeding, please come straight back and we'll re-evaluate. In the meantime,' he peels off a leaflet from a stack on his desk, 'here are some websites that might help you understand what is happening. If you have any questions, don't hesitate to ask.'

We thank him, and leave in silence. I know I should be grateful to have some kind of explanation for what happened, but all I can think of is how abysmally wrong I was. There is no way that Ellie can be responsible for a condition I've had since long before we even met. Humiliation burns inside me like an inferno. I actually told Pammy, and Sarah bloody Jefferson, that Ellie caused the death of my child. I'm no better than any of the people who only a few days ago I was shouting abuse at, telling them they should be ashamed of themselves. *I* should be ashamed of myself. I am.

And if Ellie isn't responsible for the loss of my baby, then all my anger towards the girl, all my fear and mistrust, has been completely misplaced. Which leaves me with one question about everything that has happened since I arrived here – just what the hell is going on in Gaunt?

91

Imogen

The Harpers' house is bigger and grander than the one Ellie and the Jeffersons live in. They were obviously tempted by the rural location; the house is off the beaten track down a long winding lane, and I almost missed the turning completely. My heart pounds in my chest just thinking of the reception I am bound to receive from Madeline Harper – after my one meeting with the woman, I have little faith that I'll be invited in for hot chocolate. Still, I need answers, and as long as she doesn't call the police the moment she sees me on the door-step, I might get some here.

Standing on the threshold, I take a deep breath and ring the doorbell. After a few minutes I hear the clicking of keys in the lock and the door swings open.

'Yes?'

Madeline Harper would be attractive if it wasn't for the fact that she looks as though she is chewing a wasp. I know all about women like this – resting bitch faces, Pammy calls them. Women who can't help looking miserable even when their feelings are neutral.

'My name is Imogen Reid; we met briefly on the high street when your daughter fell in front of our car.'

A brief look of recognition crosses Madeline's face. 'Naomi told me you were working at her school,' she says. So far so good – no mobile phone in hand waiting to call the police.

'Yes, I've been working with Ellie Atkinson. I wondered if I might have a word with Naomi if she's in?'

'Whatever that girl has said, she's lying. Did you know she attacked Naomi at school? The school says there is no proof it was her, but Naomi says it was and that's good enough for me. She needs locking up.'

'That's exactly why I'm here,' I explain quickly. 'There have been a few incidents at the school that I believe Ellie may have been involved in. I wanted to see what Naomi knew about them – about Ellie's involvement.'

I know that the slightest mention that Naomi's own hands might be less than clean will be met with the slamming of the door. Madeline looks as though she's trying to decide whether I pose any kind of threat to her precious daughter. Before she can tell me to fuck off, however, there is a voice from the hallway behind her.

'Let her in, Mum, I'll speak to her.'

Madeline looks unsure, then glances back at her daughter, who nods. She opens the door wider and sighs.

'I don't want any trouble,' she warns as I walk past her into the hallway. 'I know you've been defending that girl all over the school, and if I hear you upsetting my Naomi . . .' She doesn't finish her sentence but I get the point. I nod, and she motions me through to the kitchen.

Naomi looks nothing like the attractive, confident girl I saw that day in town with Ellie. Her long hair is gone, replaced by a pixie crop that looks completely out of place on her head. She sits down, fingering the remains of her hair self-consciously. I sit opposite her without being invited.

'What do you want to know?' she asks without preamble.

I clear my throat, trying not to sound as nervous as I feel.

'I know that you and Ellie haven't always seen eye to eye. I'm not here to cast blame or point the finger; what I'd like to know is how it started.'

'She pushed Naomi in front of your car,' Madeline points out before her daughter can speak. 'Naomi was too trauma-tised to tell the police officer—'

'Mum,' Naomi interrupts. 'Could you leave us alone, please? I'd like to talk to Imogen on my own.'

If possible, Madeline looks even more like she's trodden in something disgusting, but she gives a tight nod. 'I'll be in the drawing room if you need me.' She turns to walk away, shooting a warning look at me as she leaves.

'Ellie didn't push me in front of your car. I genuinely did trip,' Naomi says quietly. 'I was kind of confused at the time – she was muttering something and she looked so weird, I thought she was casting a spell on me. I started backing up to get away from her and I slipped.'

Finally. I knew that day what I'd seen. 'What made you think she was casting a spell on you? That's a pretty extreme assumption to make just because she was muttering some-thing.'

'Well that's what witches do, isn't it? They cast spells. The funny thing is, I'd started to think I'd been wrong about her, that she was pretty cool, until that thing in the lunch hall.'

'And you're sure it was Ellie who attacked you?'

Naomi nods. 'It must have been. After all, whoever it was came out of nowhere. No one saw them, not even me. It must have been Ellie – only a witch could do something like that.'

'Okay.' I don't point out that the room was dark, the children were hysterical, screaming and jumping up from their seats at the sudden descent into darkness. It could have been anyone who attacked her. 'And what made you think Ellie was a witch?' I ask gently. 'Because she survived the fire that killed her family?'

'No,' Naomi replies, looking at me as if I'm stupid. 'I didn't *think* she was a witch, I knew it. Someone told me.'

Curse Hannah Gilbert, I think. She was the start of this whole thing. My face reddens at how easily I myself believed Ellie was dangerous after the loss of my baby.

'Whatever your teacher told you, Naomi, I'm afraid she was mistaken. Ms Gilbert—'

'It wasn't Ms Gilbert.' Naomi looks confused. 'Teachers aren't allowed to say stuff like that about kids. It was Ellie's sister who told me. It was Mary.'

92

Ellie

'You know the plan?' Mary hisses at Ellie as they stand at the school gates. Ellie looks around to double-check for teachers and nods.

'I just don't see how I'm not going to get into trouble for this . . .'

'You haven't got into trouble for anything you've done before, have you?' Mary waves a hand. 'You killed someone, for God's sake, Ellie. If you didn't get in trouble for that, you won't for anything. You're untouchable.'

93

Imogen

As I leave the house, my mind is reeling with the information I've been given. *It was Mary*. Mary, Ellie's only friend and confidante, started the rumour that Ellie was a witch, the rumour that caused all Ellie's problems at school. Why would she do that?

I pull open my car door just as the phone in my handbag begins to ring.

'Hello?'

'Imogen? Is that you?' The voice on the other end of the phone is breathless, frantic and instantly recognisable.

'Sarah, calm down,' I instruct. 'What is it?'

'It's Ellie.' I hear Sarah Jefferson's voice tremble. 'She left school at lunchtime. I don't know where she is.'

I sigh. Repeat after me, I tell myself. Not your circus, not your monkeys.

'I'm not Ellie's case worker any more, Sarah. I was removed. Her truancy isn't really my remit any longer.'

'You don't understand.' Sarah's voice is urgent now. 'It's not Ellie I'm worried about. It's Lily.'

My hand automatically flies to my stomach before I remember that the baby is no longer there.

'What about Lily, Sarah?'

Sarah lets out a noise somewhere between a sob and a wail. 'She's missing. Ellie has taken the baby.'

94

Imogen

As I drive towards the Jeffersons', praying that the local police have better things to do tonight than sit at the side of the road with speed cameras, my mind is racing. Why would Mary tell the kids at school that Ellie was a witch? She's the only person who's stuck up for her, who's insisted that Ellie is innocent and that the adults are idiots. Has she been playing me all along?

I think of all the places Ellie could have taken the baby. Gaunt suddenly feels so big, and I am just one person. Sarah Jefferson has already called the police; I know they will attend in force for a missing baby. I don't have to take this on my shoulders. So why do I feel like it is all my fault?

Sarah has been looking out for me, and she opens the door as I walk up the path, her mobile phone in one hand and the landline in the other.

'Mark's out searching for them,' she tells me. 'I've got to stay here for the police.'

'Sarah, how exactly do you know Ellie has the baby?'

'My neighbour saw her go, over an hour ago. Lily was napping, so I just lay down on the sofa and closed my eyes for a minute; next thing I knew, it was an hour and a half later and Lily was gone. When I ran outside, June from next door said she'd seen Ellie taking her out for a walk – she thought I'd said it was okay.'

'She can't have gone far on foot,' I say, pulling Sarah in to hug her close. I can't imagine what she is feeling right now. I hold her at arm's length. 'We'll find her. Why don't you pull up a map of the area on Google before the police get here? We'll mark out how far she might have got in an hour; it'll give them a search radius.'

I know the police will already have thought of that – they will have mobilised officers to start the search before they even get here – but Sarah needs to be kept busy, to feel as though she is doing something productive.

'Can I take a look in Ellie's room?' I ask. Sarah is already sitting down at the PC to start her task.

'Of course, anything you think will help,' she replies.

But when I get to the top of the stairs, it's not Ellie's room I head for, it's Mary's. What Naomi told me is still weighing heavily on my mind. Mary lied for Ellie, but was it to give herself an alibi for the night Hannah Gilbert was pushed down those stairs?

I open the door to Mary's room. It is a typical teenager's haven, although Mary doesn't favour bright pink walls and boy-band posters. She is more dark purples and rap stars. Her desk is strewn with stationery, as it was the first time I was in here.

I'm rummaging through piles of papers, not knowing what I'm looking for, when I see them. Apple-shaped Post-its. I've seen these in here before, the first time I was in Mary's room – how could I have forgotten that? With a jolt, I remember my conversation with Evan on the riverbank and I realise: Mary sent Hannah the note about her affair with Evan. Was she also the one to send her the last note she would ever receive?

I'm checking out the rest of the room when my phone beeps a message. It's Facebook Messenger, and the profile picture is Emily Murray.

I can't really go into the reasons I left Place2Be, it was personal and nothing to do with my cases. As far as working with Ellie Atkinson goes, u should be careful. That girl scares me.

I tap out a reply – *Why? What did Ellie do to you?* – then shove the phone back into my pocket and open the wardrobe door. In the bottom is a plastic bag full of rubbish: tins and twigs. I pull one of the tins from the bag; around the neck is tied a thin line of near-invisible fishing line. The twig is tied to a piece of thick rope, but there is fishing line attached to that too. I don't have time to work out if it means anything and shove it all back into the bottom of the wardrobe. I've been up here long enough; I don't want Sarah to find me rummaging through Mary's room.

As I turn to leave, I notice a notebook lying on Mary's desk, a piece of paper folded and shoved inside the cover. Pulling it out by the corner, I unfold it, revealing various half-finished drawings of a young girl scratched out in pencil. Underneath the last one is scrawled *Smelly Ellie smells of piss.*

My phone beeps in my pocket and I pull it out. It's Emily again. But before I can read the message, I hear a voice.

'What are you doing in my room?'

95

Ellie

Ellie pushes the baby through and climbs in after her. It's as easy as Mary said it would be; there is even somewhere to put the baby down – a pouffe, her mum used to call it. She lights the candle Mary has given her and places it upright in an empty dirt-encrusted glass on the counter top. Picking up the baby and carrying it towards the stairwell, she doesn't notice the flame catch the edge of the pile of newspapers and begin to crawl upwards.

96

Imogen

'I was . . .' I'm lost for words. I've been caught, there's no point in lying. 'I was looking for ideas where Ellie might be.'

'And you thought you'd find them in my room?'

'I found this.' I hold out the pictures. 'Why would you have these?'

'I found them in Naomi's bag.'

'You're lying.' I point at the apple-shaped sticky notes. 'Those are the Post-its that Hannah Gilbert was threatened with.'

'It wasn't a threat,' Mary snaps, and her face colours as she realised what she's said. 'Ellie wrote them. She told me what they said.'

'Bullshit,' I shoot back. 'They were in your handwriting. The police already have them.'

It's a bold lie, but she's only fifteen and it works.

'So what?' She sets her jaw defiantly. 'It hardly proves anything.'

'They've also got the note you sent her pretending to be Mr Hawker and telling her to go to the flats that night.'

'Ha! You screwed up there, Imogen. I took that note back, there's no way the police could have it.'

'And there's no way you could have taken it back if you weren't in the flat when Hannah died,' I reply, bile rising in my throat at the idea. This girl is evil. Not Ellie; her foster sister, Mary.

Tears well up in Mary's eyes, but I'm having none of it. Not from a girl who has all but admitted murder.

'Where's Ellie?' I demand in a voice so confident I surprise myself.

Mary's eyes glint. 'How should I know?'

'The police will be here any minute to talk to your mother about where Ellie might have taken Lily. I suggest you start thinking.'

Mary turns to walk out of the room, but I catch her arm. 'I don't think so.'

'I'll refuse to say anything,' Mary threatens. 'If you don't let me go, I'll keep my mouth shut and you'll never find her in time.'

Shit. I believe she would do just that, and either one or both of the missing children are in danger.

'Take me to them,' I demand. 'Take me to them and I won't tell the police what I know about Hannah Gilbert.'

Mary seems to consider this, then nods.

'Fine,' she agrees. 'Let's go.'

364

97

Imogen

'It didn't start out how you think,' Mary tells me.

We are in my car, having fled the house without saying a word to Sarah, who is still in the kitchen on the PC. At the top of the road we pass a police car turning in. Mary barely glances at it.

'I never planned for it to go this far. If you want to look for someone to blame, blame the adults.' She glares.

'Oh, I do,' I reply darkly. 'Me included. But what I want to know is how exactly you came up with the idea to convince an entire town that an eleven-year-old girl was capable of witchcraft.'

The little bitch actually looks as though she is proud of herself.

'I just wanted to cause a bit of trouble, make Mum and Dad see what the endless stream of broken children was doing to our family.' She shrugs. 'Some of the things I even tried to pin on Billy at first, but Mum got it into her head that Ellie was doing them because she was so quiet and weird. She was kind of afraid of Ellie, I think, because of how strange she was. Then when I sent those notes to Ms Gilbert and stuck the Post-its in Ellie's bag – that's when it really all began. Gilbert turned up at our house, ranting to Mum about Ellie knowing things she shouldn't, something about her threatening Gilbert about an exam. Which is bloody ridiculous when you think about it. I mean, I knew all about her and Mr Hawker, and I'm not frigging psychic. People think because we wear school uniform we must be stupid, but we're teenagers, we're not blind.'

'How did Ellie know I was pregnant?'

'I told her. You were puking everywhere when you came to our house that day, and I saw folic acid pills in your handbag. Mum takes them constantly, even though she knows she's barren.'

The callous words send a shudder through me. I remember that first day, how I hadn't even realised that Mary was paying attention to me, how I thought I was assessing her. I only even had those tablets in my bag to keep Dan happy.

'Anyway,' she continues, preening like a peacock now. 'Some of the stuff Gilbert said made Mum all weird. She was pretty convincing, about Ellie being strange and different, maybe even dangerous. I guessed she was just trying to lay the tracks for if Ellie squealed on her and Hawker, but it gave me an idea. If Mum and Dad thought the foster kids were dangerous, maybe they'd think it was more trouble than it was worth to have more.'

'So that was when you started making it look as though Ellie was doing these things on purpose? Like she had some kind of power over people?'

Mary laughs. 'Yeah, though I never thought it would work.' She motions left. 'Turn here. The spiders – that really was a good touch. I knew Gilbert had a phobia – I saw her freaking out in the lunch hall one day – so I convinced Ellie that it would be a good idea to do her project on a different kind of pet; told her it would make her stand out as having tried a bit harder. And that's all she wanted, poor Ellie.' Mary smirks, and I have never wanted to strike someone more. 'To try her best to fit in.'

'So you planned from the start to put the spiders in Hannah's desk?'

'Mm-hm. I started off by catching them myself, right back when Ellie began the project. Figured I had a couple of weeks. But the little bastards kept escaping – either that or they were eating each other. I only had about ten at a time and I knew that wouldn't be enough. Then I went on Reddit and found a bloke who actually sold them. There are some right nutters around these days. I used Mum's PayPal – she's too busy to even notice the money going missing. I never asked him how he got them to stop eating each other.' She looks pensive. 'Wish I had. I ordered fifty, then added some more in the day before. There were about seventy when I tipped them into the drawer. Some of them were already dead, but that didn't matter too much. Still freaked Gilbert out. According to the kids in the class, there were thousands.' She cackles. 'And obviously she thought it was Ellie.'

'And what about what happened to Tom Harris? That was you too?'

Mary huffs impatiently. 'It was all me. Don't you get it? But it wasn't me who accused Ellie. Never once did I try to pin the blame on her. That was the absolute beauty of the whole thing. That I never had to make it look like she was responsible. People just automatically assumed she was. Even when there was no way it could have been her! I mean, she was sitting in a room full of witnesses when those lights went out. Wicked bit of luck that they'd left the curtains closed – I never could have reached them myself.' She looks pensive. 'I didn't think I'd hit her that hard though, that was weird. Oh . . .' She clicks her fingers as though she's just remembered something. 'I lied about trying to frame Ellie, totally forgot. I dropped the scissors in her bag, the ones I'd used to cut that Naomi's hair. And this, this is the best bit. She got rid of them. See, it wasn't just the adults who believed Ellie could make things happen – I made her believe it herself. We even did an experiment, that bag of cans and stuff in my room. A few pieces of fishing wire attached to some cans and even a smart kid like Ellie thinks she's got the power to knock things over with her mind. I mean, as a psychologist you must find that pretty fascinating, right?'

I literally can't believe what I'm hearing. She's a fifteen-year-old girl, barely old enough to understand the consequences of what she's done, the damage she's caused, and yet here she is talking about the psychology of manipulation and mass hysteria. It's as though the part of her brain that deals with empathy has been taken over by the part that wants to try out her experiments on live subjects. I wonder whether, for the first time in my life, I am engaged in conversation with a real psychopath.

'And what about Hannah Gilbert?' I ask quietly, ignoring Mary's question. Because the answer is yes, I do find it fascinating, and sickening. Fascinating that so many grown adults could be manipulated by such a young girl. And sickening that I was one of them.

Mary's eyes widen. 'I didn't mean for her to fall. Okay, so I was the one who got her there; I just wanted to freak her out a bit, make her think that Ellie was running around in the block of flats without being seen. I set up a recording of Ellie whispering Hannah's name, played it in three different places from my old iPod and my phone. It was just a bit of fun. I put the radio on, messed with her a bit. Then she started freaking out, like her mind was totally playing tricks on her. I didn't really expect that. Afterwards I realised that she had an overactive imagination – I mean, she was practically the one who came up with the whole Ellie-as-evil-devil-child thing. So I probably should have expected it.' She shrugs, as though her teacher's death is nothing more than a mild inconvenience.

'But you didn't push her?'

'No! What kind of person do you think I am? She went all weird, started running around like a lunatic even when I was nowhere near her. Tripped down the stairs and still carried on trying to run away. Nuttier than a squirrel's poo, as my dad would say.'

I feel a wave of nausea overcome me. The pounding at the front of my head has intensified – it's stopping me thinking clearly and all I want to do is close my eyes and go to sleep. Not that I think I'll ever be able to sleep again.

'So what now?' I ask, my voice a weary sigh. 'What happens now, Mary? What's your plan?'

She shrugs, and for a minute she looks every inch the fifteen-year-old girl she is. 'I dunno. You were lying about keeping this to yourself, weren't you? I can't just promise it won't happen again and we can forget about it and move on with our lives.'

'No, you're right about that,' I agree.

'Will I go to prison?' Her face is shadowed with fear, and for a fraction of a second I actually feel sorry for her. Has she got any idea of how wrong what she has done really is? Or has she convinced herself, as she tried to convince me, that it is everyone else's fault?

'I don't know what will happen to you,' I answer truthfully. Aside from Hannah's death, which Mary swears was an accident, all the other things that have happened have been relatively minor. What she did to Naomi could possibly be classed as grievous bodily harm – but it's only her word against mine, and any good solicitor would warn her not to say a thing. The truth is, she will probably get away with all the pain she's caused. I put a hand to my head to try and stop the pain. 'I'll take you home and speak to your mother about all of this. Then we'll decide what to do.'

'And what about Ellie?' Mary's tone has changed to one of innocent bystander, and I feel my heart plummet.

'What about her, Mary?'

'What's going to happen to her? If she hurts the baby?'

I fight to push down my fear. 'You just said Ellie's got nothing to do with what's been happening. Why would she hurt the baby?'

Mary smiles, a smile that freezes the blood in my veins. 'Because I asked her to.'

98

Imogen

'Where is she, Mary? Do you even know?' Listening to her confession, I have almost forgotten where we are going, and why. Now the need to find Ellie and the baby smashes through me.

'She's at the flats. The ones where Gilbert died.'

99

Imogen

The first thing I see when I pull up at the abandoned flats where Hannah Gilbert lost her life is the flames.

'Call the fire brigade,' I shout at Mary, who is still sitting in the passenger seat, frozen in fear. 'Do it now, or Ellie will die!'

I bolt across the grass, but I can't seem to move fast enough. It's like one of those dreams where I'm trying to run away from the bad guy but my legs just freeze. Still I keep running towards the place that I am certain is going to claim another life.

The fire is tearing through the block of flats with the unbridled fury of a monstrous beast. The heat is almost unbearable, and black smoke claws at my throat and lungs, while the flames roar around me, pounding in my ears. If I carry on, surely I'm going to die. People don't run into burning buildings and survive – they run away from them if they want to live. But the thought of leaving Ellie alone, frightened and abandoned, is worse than the thought of dying in here. Maybe this is what I came back to Gaunt to do. To die here next to poor sad Ellie Atkinson.

Upstairs I fall to my knees and crawl along the hallway.

The smoke is less dense down here, but still my lungs burn with the effort, and more than once I have to stop, to rest my head against the wall. When I come to the flat Mary had described on the way here, the one where Hannah and Evan Hawker would meet to conduct their illicit affair, I grasp the door handle, praying that it is the right one, and push with all my might. I fall sprawling into the hallway beyond and scrabble to kick the door closed behind me. There is less smoke in here; I can see the entire open-plan flat. It is empty.

'Ellie?' My voice comes out as no more than a croak. I crawl into the bedroom: empty. And then I see it, the only place big enough for a child to hide. Using the last of my strength, I throw myself towards the wardrobe, grasp the handle and pull it open. The little girl sits huddled in the bottom, looking smaller than ever, as though she has shrunk into the wardrobe itself. Her eyes are squeezed tightly closed and tears run down her cheeks. I try to lift her, but she is like a dead weight in my arms, and we both collapse against the wardrobe floor, where we lie half in and half out.

'Ellie?' I shake the girl's arms but get no response. She is completely catatonic. 'Ellie, listen to me, we have to get out of here. Where is the baby? Where's Lily?'

At my words, she opens her eyes slowly, as though realising for the first time that I'm there. 'We can't get out of here,' she says in a strange voice. 'This is where we die. Just like them. Just like my family.'

'No, Ellie,' I say urgently. 'I don't want to die here. I'm not ready to die, and neither are you. This is not what your parents would have wanted. We have to find Lily and get out.'

She looks so closely into my eyes, so deep inside me that I feel as though she is reading my very soul. 'I'm sorry,' she whispers at last. 'I'm sorry, I caused all this, it was me.'

'It wasn't you, Ellie, none of it was you.'

She shakes her head despondently. 'It was; all along it was me.'

'Do you know that?' I ask. 'Did you actually do those things? Did you actually start this fire? Or do you just feel as though you did? Just because you had those thoughts sometimes doesn't mean you made anything happen. You don't have the power to do that Ellie. You're just a little girl.'

'What about your baby?' Ellie whispers. 'You think I did that.'

'No I don't. It wasn't your fault.'

'You're just saying that to get me to come with you. To save Lily.'

'I promise you, Ellie, I'm not.' My voice is pleading. 'I always believed in you. I always believed you weren't capable of doing those things. I just lost my way for a while, and I'm sorry.'

Ellie looks around the room, as though she is just coming to her senses. 'If that's true, if what you're saying is the truth and I didn't cause all this, then who did?'

I don't have time to explain, and I don't think Ellie will believe me if I try. 'That doesn't matter right now; we'll talk about it later. What we've got to do now is get that baby out of here. We need to survive, to make sure we tell everyone that you're not to blame. To make sure everyone knows. If you save the baby, you'll be a hero.'

Ellie shakes her head. 'I don't care what they think, it doesn't matter. All I care is what *you* think. You're the only one who believed in me, and if you stop believing in me, then there's no point any more. There is no one else on my side.'

'I'm on your side, Ellie,' I promise. I don't want to explain about Mary here and now – the news of her manipulation will only upset Ellie further. This whole building is going to burn down if we don't get out, and I still have no idea where the baby is. 'Why do you think I came here? Why do you think I came into a burning building for you? I wouldn't do that if I believed you were evil.'

'It's too late,' Ellie whispers. 'It's too late for all of us.'

I shake my head in frustration, and my heart sinks as Ellie blurs in front of my eyes. The smoke is thickening.

I have to make a choice. The only way I can save the baby is if Ellie tells me where she is; if she doesn't, then all three of us are going to die. With a strength I didn't even know I possessed, I scoop up the eleven-year-old girl and drag her across the room, shielding her eyes and nose from the thick smoke with my free arm.

'What are you doing?' Ellie croaks and coughs up a lungful of smoke. 'I can't breathe. Where are you taking me?'

'We are getting out of here,' I say determinedly.

'No!' It's supposed to be a shout but it's barely a loud whisper. 'Lily. She's on the balcony. I didn't want the smoke to get her.'

The balcony. Why the hell didn't I think of that? These flats all have what is grandly labelled a balcony but is little more than a glorified ledge – I used to see the inhabitants of the flats sitting out there in their dressing gowns having a cigarette when I was on my way to school. I drag Ellie towards the large double doors, which are hidden by a thick rotting curtain.

The baby is in the far corner of the tiny balcony. I practically throw Ellie through the doors and greedily gulp in fresh air. When my legs allow me to stand again, I pluck Lily from the cushion on which Ellie has placed her and hug her close to my chest. The sound of sirens wails through the night and I sink to the floor again, my knees giving way in relief. We are going to be saved. If we just stay here, they will get to us.

Ellie, who has been standing frozen in the centre of the

balcony, sways at the sound of the sirens and her face morphs into an expression of abject terror. Taking a couple of unsteady steps backwards, she flattens herself against the rotting guard-rail. The rail gives an almighty screech and folds like a paper concertina, sending the girl plunging downwards, followed by my despairing screams.

100

PL: Interview with Mary Jefferson. Ten fifty-four a.m. Present are Detective Inspector Petra Leigh, Detective Inspector Carl Younis, Maxine Erskine from legal aid, Tony Vine from social services and Mary Jefferson.

PL: Mary, do you know why you're here today?

PL: For the benefit of the tape Mary has shrugged. So it hasn't been explained to you why you have been bought here?

MJ: You want to ask me about what happened to Ms Gilbert.

PL: Okay, good. So can you tell us where you were the night Ms Gilbert died?

CY: Again, Mary is shrugging. You see, Mary, we've spoken to Imogen Reid, and she's told us that you admitted to luring your teacher to the block of flats where she died, and that you were there it happened. Is that true?

MJ: *Inaudible*

377

PL: Could you speak up for the tape?

MJ: I said yeah.

CY: Thank you. Can you tell us why you left Ms Gilbert the note telling her to go to the flats that night?

MJ: It was just a trick.

CY: And what was the point of the trick? To embarrass her? Inconvenience her? Blackmail her?

MJ: I just wanted to scare her. Freak her out a bit.

PL: So you didn't go there to tell Ms Gilbert that you knew about her affair with your maths teacher, Mr Hawker? For the benefit of the tape Mary is shaking her head.

MJ: No, I wasn't even going to show my face. I wanted her to think it was Ellie who'd set her up.

PL: That's Ellie Atkinson, your foster sister? For the—

MJ: Yes, my foster sister. For the benefit of the tape. Ms Gilbert already hated her, I was just trying to get her in a bit of trouble.

CY: Why did you want to get Ellie in trouble, Mary?

MJ: Because I wanted to get rid of her. I wanted them to stop taking in any more kids.

PL: You wanted to get rid of her. Is that why you did those other things? The things at school?

ME: If you are asking Mary to admit to something she may later be charged with you need to be more specific with the question.

PL: Is that why you attacked Naomi Harper in the lunch hall?

MJ: I don't know what happened then.

PL: What do you mean, you don't know what happened? You did attack Naomi, didn't you. Imogen Reid stated—

MJ: I know what Imogen stated. I did whack Naomi, and I chopped a chunk out of her hair but there is no way I hit her hard enough to put her in hospital. And I only cut off a chunk, not half her head.

PL: Are you suggesting someone else hurt Naomi at the exact same time as you?

MJ: I'm not suggesting anything. I'm just saying I didn't hit her that hard. I'm not Anthony Joshua.

CY: And the night Ms Gilbert died, Mary, did you kill her but not that much?

ME: Detective. Mary that was the detective being facetious and you don't have to answer that.

CY: Sorry Mary, Mrs Erskine is right. So can you answer me this; did you push Ms Gilbert down the stairs?

MJ: No.

PL: You sound pretty certain of that. Are you sure you didn't bang into her by accident?

MJ: No, I didn't touch her.

PL: Or that the pair of you didn't argue when she caught you in the flats? Perhaps you threatened to tell her husband about her affair and you fought? Maybe you were just defending yourself?

ME: I'm fairly certain that Mary made it clear she didn't make physical contact with Hannah Gilbert.

PL: Of course. Did you see Hannah fall, Mary?

MJ: Kind of.

PL: What do you mean by kind of?

MJ: I'd made some noises, footsteps and stuff. I put the radio on in the flat and she went and turned it off but she must not have done it right because it came straight back on. Next minute she was freaking out as though she was being chased. Then I heard her fall.

PL: But you were nowhere near her when she fell?

MJ: No! I swear. She just went a bit mental. I didn't even think I'd been that scary.

PL: And what about Imogen Reid? She claims she was pushed into the canal on—

MJ: I didn't push Imogen into the canal. I wasn't even there. We're not supposed to go there because people get robbed.

CY: So are you saying Imogen fell into the canal?

THE FOSTER CHILD

ME: You don't have to answer that, Mary. She's just told you she wasn't there, and therefore can't speculate what happened to Imogen Reid.

PL: So you honestly expect us to believe that you had nothing to do with Hannah Gilbert falling down the stairs, despite being there when she fell and admitting you lured her there in the first place, and you aren't responsible for Naomi Harper's injuries despite having . . . 'whacked her'?

MJ: Yeah I do. I don't know what happened to Gilbert or Naomi, I'm telling you—

CY: Mary, sit down please.

MJ: But I'm telling you and you won't listen, that wasn't me! I wasn't trying to hurt them, it was just . . . I was just . . . I didn't push her, that's all. I don't know what happened. I don't know.

TV: I think that's enough for now. Clearly Mary is distressed and she's answered your questions. We need to take a break.

MJ: But I didn't do it! You need to make them understand! It was . . . I just didn't kill anyone, all right?

PL: Interview terminated at eleven twenty-three.

Epilogue

Six months later

The young girl sits with her back to us at the bottom of the long sloping garden. She is sitting in an electric wheelchair, a large sketch pad resting precariously on her knees, and she seems to be focusing all her attention on whatever it is she's drawing,

'How's she getting on?' I ask, turning away from the kitchen window and taking a sip of my coffee. Pammy smiles.

'She's doing great. The doctors have said she'll be walking again fine in no time. She's a fighter. She doesn't even use the chair half the time now. Don't me get wrong, she's too clever by half and can be a stroppy teenager already, but so far she's not turned anyone into a frog or cursed us to live for all eternity as a tea set. Sooo . . .' she shrugs, 'so far so good.'

I let out a laugh, and it feels good. 'Very funny.'

'Oh, and don't ask me how, but she can get that log fire roaring in minutes. Takes me a good hour to get a spark.'

'All right, stop it.' I cross to where my friend is sitting at the kitchen table and join her. 'I'm so glad you and Richard took her in, Pam. I was worried that after what happened, people round here would want her out for good.' I still have nightmares where I see Ellie plunging to the ground, but instead of landing on the balcony below as she did that night, in my nightmares she keeps falling, and falling, and falling . . .

'People here aren't that bad,' Pammy says, her quiet voice pulling me back into the kitchen. 'Yes, it can be a bit *League of Gentlemen* if you aren't from around here – and yes, before you say it, I remember full well that you grew up around here, thanks, but all those years in between, well, you've forgotten that this can be a good place too. That for all their idiosyncrasies—'

'Oh, that's what you call accusing a child of witchcraft?'

Pammy ignores me, and to her credit doesn't mention those few crazy days when I took leave of my senses. 'For all their idiosyncrasies, people here really do stick together when it comes to it. Look what happened when Mary went postal. You should stick around a bit longer. Sell your mum's place, buy somewhere else, start again.'

'I'm not so sure, Pam. We've been here almost a year and literally all we have are bad memories. The baby, the fire . . .'

At least work is going well. When I went back after the fire, there were two huge bouquets of flowers waiting for me, and Lucy took me out to lunch, where she told me all about Emily's affair with Edward – the real reason she left in a hurry. It seems all you need to be accepted into the inner circle is a near-death experience.

'You can't just keep running every time something goes wrong. And she'll miss you.' Pammy inclines her head to where Ellie is still deeply engrossed in her task. 'You were the only one who believed in her. You saved her life. Isn't that a good memory?'

'I shouldn't have had to. I should have seen sooner what Mary was up to. When the chips were down, I treated Ellie exactly the same as everyone else did. I was ready to crucify her too, although thank goodness she doesn't know that. I'm not proud of the person I've been since I got here. I owe Dan, and our baby, a better person than that.'

Pammy shrieks. 'You're . . .?'

I shake my head. 'No, not yet. But we're trying. The doctors say it might never happen again, so we have to prepare ourselves for that. I suppose one good thing has come out of what happened, though: me and Dan have never been stronger. I finally told him everything, about my mother, and what life was like here for me. I'm not sure he understands why that makes me so afraid of having children – in his eyes, I just have first-hand experience of how *not* to do it – but at least now if I freak out he knows why.'

'I did try and tell you to be honest with the poor bloke. And while we're on the subject of babies, and honesty . . .' She picks up the two empty coffee cups and takes them around to the sink so her back is to me. I realise what she's getting at and gasp.

'You're not? But that's wonderful!'

Pammy spins around, a huge smile lighting up her pretty features. 'I am. Eight weeks. You're the first person I've told, apart from Richard,' she adds, seeing the frown cross my face. 'We have our first scan in three and a half weeks. I'm shitting myself. Actually, I'm literally shitting myself – does pregnancy make you poo more?'

I laugh, but a heavy feeling settles in my stomach. 'What about Ellie? I know the fostering was only supposed to be temporary, but I'd so hoped . . .'

'We're going to start the adoption process as soon as possible,' Pammy says. She looks over her shoulder at where Ellie has stopped drawing and is gazing out across the fields at the back of the garden. 'If she wants us to, that is. I thought she'd want to leave Gaunt altogether, but she seems to like it here, and we love her. We have an appointment with social services next week, though Ellie doesn't know yet. We want to get a feel for whether they think it will be possible, how long it might take before we should speak to her.'

'Pammy, that's wonderful.' I envelop my friend in a hug. Although I'm genuinely pleased for her, I can't help that tiny nugget of jealousy – no, sadness at my own situation – blooming in my stomach. The doctors warned me and Dan just how difficult it will be for me to carry a baby to full term; we are in for a tough time. And I know Ellie expected me to request to be the one to look after her following the fire, but despite knowing that she isn't to blame for the things that have happened since we arrived in Gaunt, I can't help but associate her with heartbreak and death. I know it's not fair, but every time I look at her, it all comes flooding back. I couldn't have been happier when Pammy offered to go through the various classes and security checks to make sure Ellie has a safe, calm environment to live in.

'Thanks. I felt bad about telling you because . . . you know . . .'

'Don't be ridiculous,' I say. 'It's fantastic news. And Ellie will be over the moon. She'll have a family of her own again.'

'I hope so,' Pammy says, gazing out at her new daughter-to-be. 'We just want her to be happy here.'

Ellie sits with her sketchbook balanced on her knees, the picture nearly finished. She's certain this one is her best yet; it's a bit of a shame that she can't show anyone. The lilac and pink of the moth as it takes flight against the cornflower blue of the sky really works, and the bright orange and red of the flames that envelop its wings, the ash from the burning moth trailing in the air behind it, the insect not yet realising that it is seconds from death . . . She's really caught it all this time.

Everyone thought she would want to move away after the fire, start again somewhere else. Imogen, the social workers, they were all ready to ship her off somewhere completely new, until she asked if perhaps they wouldn't mind finding her a foster family closer to where she was now. They don't realise how much work she's put in, how much things have changed since she arrived. She doesn't want to start over again somewhere else.

And then there's Pammy and Richard. They have been so kind to her, taking her in when Imogen refused, treating her like a real daughter. Ellie looks at the lighter in her hand, pushes her thumb against the flint.

Flick, flame. Flick, flame. Flick, flame.

And now Pammy's gone and got pregnant. They think she doesn't know about the baby, about how excited they are to have a real child of their own. Ellie wonders how long it will be before they send her packing, like the Jeffersons planned to do. But they aren't taking in any babies now, are they? The police think Mary pushed Hannah down the stairs and that Ellie was just an innocent victim. It has all worked out better than she could have planned. And now she's going to be replaced by a baby, just like with her mum and dad, just like the Jeffersons.

She removes her thumb from the flint and the flame continues to spring from the lighter by itself.

Flick, flame. Flick, flame. Flame, flame, flame.

She can't let that happen again.

Acknowledgements

There are a million people who bring a book to life, and it's at this stage I'm crippled with the overwhelming fear that I'll forget to thank one of them. So please be assured that if you helped in any way – however small you think it might be – with this book, I am forever grateful.

There are some people that I must thank individually. As always, my amazing agent Laetitia Rutherford. How you put up with me at certain stages I have no idea, I can only assume you have my breakdowns scheduled into your calendar by now. To Megan and all at Watson, Little: you rock.

To everyone in the Headline family, but in particular my editor, Kate Stephenson. Also Millie, Jo, Ella and Siobhan – it is a pleasure to work with such wonderful women.

For those at my day job I can only imagine I have been an absolute nightmare, so a deep thank you to all at Shropshire Fire and Rescue Service. I know you will be furious at me for the liberties I have taken with the effects of fire. (Now you know why I left before release date!) I have been lucky enough to have had two amazing managers, Maxine and Yvonne, and I shall miss my SFRS family immensely. Also to Pammy for the loan of her name and her colourful language.

Thank you to Mr Maxwell and his wife Florence for their generosity at the charity auction, and also to Nicky Black for hers. That my books can help raise money for such worthy causes makes me happier than anything that has happened to me on my publishing journey.

To all my friends, family and the hilarious bunch of cock-blankets on the crime scene. You all keep me sane. Ish. And thank you most of all to my mum and dad, to whom this book is dedicated. You are the most wonderful people and I am so lucky to have you to lean on.

Ash. You have put up with more from writer me than I would imagine possible. A writer is a hellish creature to live with, and you do an admirable job of not using any of the various means of killing a wife and destroying the evidence that I have so unwittingly taught you. You and the boys are my world, and if it were time it would be forever. To Connor and Finlay, I promise to buy you all the sweets when this is done.

And of course, my most important thank you goes to you, wonderful buyer of books. To the bloggers who support authors constantly with no reparation, to the casual summer reader and the voracious devourer, to the audio-book addict and the first time dabbler. Without you my books would be no more than mutterings into the abyss. I hope you enjoy this one.

THRILLINGLY GOOD BOOKS
FROM CRIMINALLY
GOOD WRITERS

CRIME FILES BRINGS YOU THE LATEST RELEASES FROM
TOP CRIME AND THRILLER AUTHORS.

SIGN UP ONLINE FOR OUR MONTHLY NEWSLETTER AND BE THE FIRST
TO KNOW ABOUT OUR COMPETITIONS, NEW BOOKS AND MORE.